P9-AOQ-461

THINGS
WE
NEVER
GOT
OVER

Center Point
Large Print

**This Large Print Book carries the
Seal of Approval of N.A.V.H.**

THINGS WE NEVER GOT OVER

LUCY SCORE

CENTER POINT LARGE PRINT
THORNDIKE, MAINE

This Center Point Large Print edition
is published in the year 2023 by arrangement with
Sourcebooks.

Copyright © 2022 by Lucy Score.

All rights reserved.

The characters and events portrayed in this book are
fictitious or are used fictitiously. Any similarity to
real persons, living or dead, is purely coincidental
and not intended by the author.

The text of this Large Print edition is unabridged.
In other aspects, this book may vary
from the original edition.
Printed in the United States of America
on permanent paper sourced using
environmentally responsible foresting methods.
Set in 16-point Times New Roman type.

ISBN: 978-1-63808-713-7

The Library of Congress has cataloged this record
under Library of Congress Control Number: 2023930231

To Josie, Jen, and Claire, the bravest hearts.

1

Worst. Day. Ever.

Naomi

I wasn't sure what to expect when I walked into Café Rev, but it sure as hell wasn't a picture of myself behind the register under the cheery headline "Do Not Serve." A yellow frowny face magnet held the photo in place.

First of all, I'd never set foot in Knockemout, Virginia, let alone done anything to warrant a punishment as egregious as withholding caffeine. Second, just what did a person have to do in this dusty little town to have a mug shot hanging in the local café?

Ha. Mug shot. Because I was in a café. Gosh, I was funny when I was too tired to blink.

Anyway, third, it was an incredibly unflattering picture. I looked like I'd had a long-term threesome with a tanning bed and cheap eyeliner.

Right about then, reality penetrated my exhausted, dazed, bobby-pinned-to-within-an-inch-of-its-life head.

Once again, Tina had managed to make my life just a little bit worse. And considering what had gone down in the last twenty-four hours, that was saying something.

"Can I help . . ." The man on the other side of the

counter, the one who could give me my precious latte, took a step back and held up hands the size of dinner plates. "I don't want any trouble."

He was a burly guy with smooth, dark skin and a shaved, nicely shaped head. His neatly trimmed beard was snow white, and I spotted a couple of tattoos peeking out of the neck and sleeves of his coveralls. The name Justice was stitched on his curious uniform.

I tried my most winning smile, but thanks to an overnight road trip spent crying through fake eyelashes, it felt more like a grimace.

"That's not me," I said, pointing a finger with a wasted French-tip manicure at the photo. "I'm Naomi. Naomi Witt."

The man peered at me with suspicion before producing a pair of spectacles from the front pocket of his coveralls and slipping them on.

He blinked, then gave me a head-to-toe scan. I saw the realization begin to hit.

"Twins," I explained.

"Well, shit," he murmured, stroking one of those big hands through his beard.

Justice still looked a little skeptical. I couldn't exactly blame him. After all, how many people actually had an evil twin?

"That's Tina. My sister. I'm supposed to meet her here." Though why my estranged twin asked me to meet her in an establishment where she clearly wasn't welcome was another question I was too tired to ask.

Justice was still staring at me, and I realized his gaze was lingering on my hair. Reflexively, I patted my head, and a wilted daisy fluttered to the floor. *Whoops.* I probably should have looked in the mirror at the motel before I set foot in public looking like a disheveled, unhinged stranger on her way home from a role-playing festival.

"Here," I said, reaching into the pocket of my yoga shorts and thrusting my driver's license at the man. "See? I'm Naomi, and I would really, really like a gigantic latte."

Justice took my ID and studied it, then my face again. Finally, his stoic expression cracked, and he broke into a wide grin. "I'll be damned. It's nice to meet you, Naomi."

"It's really nice to meet you too, Justice. Especially if you're going to make me that afore-mentioned caffeine."

"I'll make you a latte that'll make your hair stand on end," he promised.

A man who knew how to meet my immediate needs and did it with a smile? I couldn't help but fall just a little bit in love with him right then and there.

While Justice got to work, I admired the café. It was decked out in what looked like manly garage style. Corrugated metal on the walls, shiny red shelves, stained concrete floor. All the drinks had names like Red Line Latte and Checkered Flag Cappuccino. It was downright charming.

There were a handful of early-morning coffee

drinkers seated at the small round tables scattered throughout the place. Every single person was looking at me like they were *really* not happy to see me.

"How do you feel about maple and bacon flavors, darlin'?" Justice called from the gleaming espresso machine.

"I feel great about them. Especially if they come in a cup the size of a bucket," I assured him.

His laugh echoed through the place and seemed to relax the rest of the patrons, who went back to ignoring me.

The front door opened, and I turned, expecting to see Tina.

But the man who stormed inside was definitely *not* my sister. He looked to be in more dire need of caffeine than I was.

Hot would be a decent way to describe him. Hot as hell would be even more accurate. He was tall enough that I could wear my highest pair of heels and still have to tilt my head up to make out with him—my official categorization of male height. His hair was in the dirty blond range and was cut short on the sides and swept back on top, which suggested he had good taste and reasonable grooming skills.

Both of those criteria landed high on my List of Reasons to be Attracted to a Man. The beard was a brand-new addition to the list. I'd never kissed a man with a beard, and I had a sudden, irrational interest in experiencing that at some point.

Then I got to his eyes. They were a cool blue gray that made me think of gunmetal and glaciers.

He strode right on up to me and stepped into my personal space like he had a standing invitation. When he crossed tattooed forearms across a broad chest, I made a squeaky sound in the back of my throat.

Wow.

"Thought I made myself real clear," he growled.

"Uh. Huh?"

I was confused. The man was glaring at me like I was the most hated character on a reality TV show, yet I still wanted to see what he looked like naked. I hadn't exhibited such poor sexual judgment since I was in college.

I blamed my exhaustion and emotional scarring.

Behind the counter, Justice stopped mid–latte creation and waved both hands in the air. "Hold on now," he began.

"It's okay, Justice," I assured him. "You just keep making that coffee, and I'll take care of this . . . *gentleman.*"

Chairs pushed back from tables all around us, and I watched as every last customer beelined for the door, some with their mugs still in hand. None of them made any eye contact with me on their way out.

"Knox, it's not what you think," Justice tried again.

"I'm not playing any games today. Get the fuck out," the Viking ordered. The blond god of sexy fury was rapidly plummeting lower on my sexy checklist.

I pointed at my chest. "Me?"

"I've had enough of your games. You got five seconds to walk out this door and never come back," he said, stepping in even closer until the tips of his boots brushed my exposed toes in their flip-flops.

Damn. Up close, he looked like he'd just stormed off a marauding Viking vessel . . . or the set of a cologne commercial. One of those weird artsy ones that didn't make any sense and had names like Ignorant Beast.

"Look, *sir*. I'm in the midst of a personal crisis, and all I'm trying to do is get a cup of coffee."

"I fucking told you, Tina. You are not to come in here and harass Justice or his customers again, or I'll personally escort your ass out of town."

"Knox—"

The bad-tempered, sexy man-beast held up his finger in Justice's direction. "One second, bud. Looks like I gotta take out the trash."

"The *trash?*" I gasped. I thought Virginians were supposed to be friendly. Instead, I'd been in town barely half an hour and was now being rudely accosted by a Viking with the manners of a caveman.

"Darlin', your coffee's up," Justice said, sliding a very large to-go cup onto the wooden counter.

My eyes darted toward the steamy, caffeinated goodness.

"You even think about picking up that cup, and

we're gonna have a problem," the Viking said, his voice low and dangerous.

But Leif Erikson didn't know who he was messing with today.

Every woman had her line. Mine, which was admittedly drawn too far back, had just been crossed.

"You take one step toward that beautiful latte that my friend Justice made especially for me, and I will make you regret the moment you met me."

I was a nice person. According to my parents, I was a good girl. And according to that online quiz I took two weeks ago, I was a people pleaser. I wasn't great at doling out threats.

The man's eyes narrowed, and I refused to notice the sexy crinkles at the corners.

"I already regret it, and so does this whole damn town. Just because you change your hair doesn't mean I'm gonna forget about the trouble you've caused here. Now get your ass out the door, and don't come back."

"He thinks you're Tina," Justice cut in.

I didn't care if this ass thought I was a serial-killing cannibal. He was standing between me and my caffeine.

The blond beast turned his head toward Justice. "What the hell are you saying?"

Before my nice friend with the coffee could explain, I drilled my finger into the Viking's chest. It didn't go very far, thanks to the obscene layer of muscle under the skin. But I made sure to lead with the nail.

"Now *you* listen to *me,*" I began. "I don't care if you think I'm my sister or that weasel who jacked up the price of antimalarial drugs. I am a *human being* having a really bad day after the worst one of her life. I do *not* have it in me to stuff down these emotions today. So you'd better get out of my way and leave me alone, Viking."

He looked downright bemused for a hot second.

I took that to mean it was coffee time. Side-stepping him, I picked up the cup, took a delicate sniff, and then shoved my face into the steaming hot life force.

I drank deeply, willing the caffeine to perform its miracles as flavors exploded on my tongue. I was pretty sure the inappropriate moan I heard came from my own mouth, but I was too tired to care. When I finally lowered the cup and swiped the back of my hand over my mouth, the Viking was still standing there, staring at me.

Turning my back on him, I flashed my hero Justice a smile and slid my emergency coffee twenty-dollar bill across the counter. "You, sir, are an artist. What do I owe you for the best latte I've ever had in my life?"

"Considering the morning you're having, darlin', it's on the house," he said, handing my license and cash back to me.

"You, my friend, are a true gentleman. *Unlike some others.*" I cast a glare over my shoulder to where the Viking was standing, legs braced, arms crossed. Taking another dive into my drink, I

14

tucked the twenty into the tip jar. "Thank you for being nice to me on the worst day of my life."

"Thought that day was yesterday," the scowling behemoth butted in.

My sigh was weary as I slowly turned to face him. "That was before I met you. So I can officially say that as bad as yesterday was, today beat it out by a slim margin." Once again, I turned back to Justice. "I'm sorry this jerk scared away all your customers. But I'll be back for another one of these real soon."

"Looking forward to it, Naomi," he said with a wink.

I turned to leave and smacked right into a mile of grumpy man chest.

"Naomi?" he said.

"Go away." It felt almost good to be rude for once in my life. To take a stand.

"Your name's Naomi," the Viking stated.

I was too busy trying to incinerate him with a glare of righteous anger to respond.

"Not Tina?" he pressed.

"They're twins, man," Justice said, the smile evident in his voice.

"Fuck me." The Viking shoved a hand through his hair.

"I worry about your friend's vision," I said to Justice, pointing at the mug shot of Tina.

Tina had gone bleached blond at some point in the past decade-plus, making our otherwise subtle differences even more obvious.

"I left my contacts at home," he said.

"Next to your manners?" I quipped. The caffeine was hitting my bloodstream, making me unusually feisty.

He didn't respond with anything other than a heated glare.

I sighed. "Get out of my way, Leif Erikson."

"The name is Knox. And why are you here?"

What the hell kind of name is that? Is it a hard Knox life? Does he tell a lot of Knox Knox jokes? Is it short for something? Knoxwell? Knoxathan?

"That's none of your business, *Knox*. Nothing I do or don't do is your business. In fact, my existence is none of your business. Now, kindly get out of my way."

I felt like screaming as loud as I could for as long as I could. But I'd tried that a couple of times in the car on the long drive here, and it hadn't helped.

Thankfully, the beautiful oaf heaved an annoyed sigh and did the decent, life-preserving thing by getting out of my way. I swept out of the café and into the summer swelter with as much dignity as I could muster.

If Tina wanted to meet up with me, she could find me at the motel. I didn't need to wait around and be accosted by strangers with the personalities of cacti.

I'd head back to my dingy room, take every last pin out of my hair, and shower until the hot water ran out. Then I'd figure out what to do next.

It was a solid plan. It was only missing one thing. My car.

Oh no. My car *and* my purse.

The bike rack in front of the coffee shop was still there. The laundromat with its bright posters in the window was still across the street next to the mechanic's garage.

But my car was not where I'd left it.

The parking spot I'd squeezed into in front of the pet shop was empty.

I looked up and down the block. But there was no sign of my trusty, dusty Volvo.

"You lost?"

I closed my eyes and clenched my jaw. "Go. Away."

"Now what's your problem?"

I turned around and found Knox watching me intently, holding a to-go coffee cup.

"What's my problem?" I repeated.

I wanted to kick him in the shins and steal his coffee.

"Nothin' wrong with my hearing, sweetheart. No need to yell."

"My *problem* is while I wasted five minutes of my life getting to know you, my car was towed."

"You sure?"

"No. I never have any idea where I park my car. I just leave them everywhere and buy new ones when I can't find them."

He shot me a look.

I rolled my eyes. "Obviously, I'm being sarcastic."

17

I reached for my phone only to remember I no longer had a phone.

"Who pissed in your Cheerios?"

"Whoever taught you to express concern for a person did it wrong." Without another word, I stalked off in what I hoped was the direction of the local police station.

I didn't make it to the next storefront before a big, hard hand locked around my upper arm.

It was the sleep deprivation, the emotional rawness, I told myself. Those were the only reasons I felt the jittery *zing* of awareness at his grip.

"Stop," he ordered, sounding surly.

"Hands. Off." I flailed my arm awkwardly, but his grip only tightened.

"Then stop walking away from me."

I paused my evasive flailing. "I'll stop walking away if you stop being an asshole."

His nostrils flared as he stared up at the sky, and I thought I heard him counting.

"Are you seriously counting to ten?" *I* was the one who was wronged. *I* was the one with a reason to pray to the heavens for patience.

He got all the way to ten and still looked annoyed. "If I stop being an asshole, will you stay and talk for a minute?"

I took another sip of coffee and thought about it. "Maybe."

"I'm letting go," he warned.

"Great," I prompted.

We both looked down at his hand on my arm.

Slowly he loosened his grip and released me, but not before his fingertips trailed over the sensitive skin inside my arm.

Goose bumps broke out, and I hoped he wouldn't notice. Especially because, in my body, goose bumps and pointy nipple reactions were closely related.

"You cold?" His gaze was most definitely not on my arm or shoulders but my chest.

Damn it. "Yes," I lied.

"It's eighty-four degrees, and you're drinking hot coffee."

"If you're finished mansplaining internal temperature, I'd like to go find my car," I said, crossing my free arm over my traitorous boobs. "Perhaps you could point me in the direction of the nearest impound lot or police station?"

He stared at me for a long beat, then shook his head. "Come on then."

"Excuse me?"

"I'll give you a ride."

"Ha!" I choked out a laugh. He was delusional if he thought I'd willingly get in a car with him.

I was still shaking my head when he spoke again. "Let's go, Daisy. I don't have all day."

2

A Reluctant Hero

Knox

T he woman was staring at me like I'd just suggested she French-kiss a rattlesnake.

My day wasn't even supposed to be started yet, and it had already gone to shit. I blamed her. And her asshole sister, Tina.

I also threw some blame in Agatha's direction for good measure, since she'd been the one to text me that Tina had just walked her "trouble-making ass" into the café.

Now here I was, at what counted as the ass crack of dawn, playing town bouncer like an idiot and fighting with a woman I'd never met.

Naomi blinked at me like she was coming out of a fog. "You're kidding me, right?"

Agatha needed to get her fucking eyes checked if she mistook the pissed-off brunette for her bleached-blond, baked-tan, tattooed pain-in-the-ass sister.

The differences between them were pretty fucking obvious, even without my contacts. Tina's face was the color and texture of an old-ass leather couch. She had a hard mouth bracketed by deep frown lines from smoking two packs a day and feeling like the world owed her something.

Naomi, on the other hand, was cut from a different cloth. A classier one. She was tall like her sister. But instead of the crispy fried look, she went in the Disney princess direction with thick hair the color of roasted chestnuts. It and the flowers in it were trying to escape some kind of elaborate updo. Her face was softer, skin paler. Full pink lips. Eyes that made me think of forest floors and open fields.

Where Tina dressed like a biker babe who'd gone through a wood chipper, Naomi wore high-end athletic shorts and a matching tank over a toned body that promised more than a handful of nice surprises.

She looked like the kind of woman who'd take one look at me and hightail it to the safety of the first golf shirt–wearing board member she could find.

Lucky for her, I didn't do drama. Or high maintenance. I didn't do doe-eyed princesses in need of saving. I didn't waste time with women who required more than a good time and a handful of orgasms.

But since I'd already stuck my nose into the situation, called her trash, and yelled at her, the least I could do was bring the situation to a fast conclusion. Then I was heading back to bed.

"No. I'm not fucking kidding you," I stated.

"I'm not going anywhere with you."

"You don't have a car," I pointed out.

"Thank you, Captain Obvious. I am aware I don't have a car."

"Let me get this straight. You're a stranger in a new town. Your car disappears. And you're turning down the offer of a ride because . . ."

"Because you stormed into a café and screamed at me! Then you chased me down and you're *still* yelling. I get in a car with you, and I'm more likely to get chopped into pieces and scattered about in a desert than end up at my destination."

"No deserts here. Some mountains though."

Her expression suggested she didn't find me helpful or amusing.

I exhaled through my teeth. "Look, I'm tired. I got an alert that Tina was causing trouble at the café again, and that's what I thought I was walking into."

She took a long hit of coffee while looking up and down the street like she was debating escape.

"Don't even think about it," I told her. "You'd spill your coffee."

When those pretty hazel eyes went wide, I knew I'd hit the mark.

"Fine. But only because this is the best latte I've had in my entire life. And is that your idea of an apology? Because just like the way you ask people if something's wrong, it sucks."

"It was an explanation. Take it or leave it." I didn't waste time doing things that didn't matter. Like making small talk or apologizing.

A bike roared up the street with Rob Zombie blaring from the speakers despite the fact that it was barely seven a.m. The guy eyed us and revved his engine. Wraith was knocking on seventy years old, but he still managed to nail an astronomical amount of tail with the whole tattooed silver fox thing he had going on.

Intrigued, Naomi watched him with her mouth open.

Today was not the day Little Miss Daisies in Her Hair would take a walk on the wild side.

I gave Wraith the fuck-off nod, snatched Naomi's precious coffee out of her hand, and headed down the sidewalk.

"Hey!"

She gave chase like I'd known she would. I could have taken her by the hand, but I wasn't exactly a fan of the reaction I'd had when I touched her. It felt complicated. "Should have stayed in fucking bed," I muttered.

"What is wrong with you?" Naomi demanded, jogging to catch up. She reached for her cup, but I held it just out of reach and kept walking.

"If you don't want to end up hog-tied over the back of Wraith's bike, then I suggest you get in my truck."

The disheveled flower child muttered some uncomplimentary-sounding things about my personality and anatomy.

"Look, if you can stop bein' a pain in my ass for five whole minutes, I'll take you to the station.

23

You can get your damn car, and then you can get out of my life."

"Has anyone ever told you you have the personality of a pissed-off porcupine?"

I ignored her and kept walking.

"How do I know you aren't going to try to hog-tie me yourself?" she demanded.

I came to a stop and gave her a lazy once-over. "Baby, you're not my type."

She rolled her eyes so hard it was a miracle they didn't pop out and fall to the sidewalk. "Excuse me while I go cry myself a river."

I stepped off the curb and opened the passenger door of my pickup. "Get in."

"Your chivalry sucks," she complained.

"Chivalry?"

"It means—"

"Jesus. I know what it means."

And I knew what it meant that she'd use it in conversation. She had fucking flowers in her hair. The woman was a romantic. Another strike against her in my book. Romantics were the hardest women to shake loose. The sticky ones. The ones who pretended they could handle the whole "no strings" deal. Meanwhile, they plotted to become "the one," trying to con men into meeting their parents and secretly looking at wedding dresses.

When she didn't get in by herself, I reached past her and put her coffee into the cup holder.

"I am really not happy with you right now," she said.

The space between our bodies was charged with the kind of energy I usually felt just before a good bar fight. Dangerous, adrenalizing. I didn't much care for it.

"Get in the damn truck."

Considering it a small miracle when she actually obeyed, I slammed the door on her scowl.

"Everything all right there, Knox?" Bud Nickelbee called from the doorway of his hardware store. He was dressed in his usual uniform of bib overalls and a Led Zeppelin T-shirt. The ponytail he'd had for thirty years hung down his back, thin and gray, making him look like a heavier, less funny George Carlin.

"All good," I assured him.

His gaze skated toward Naomi through the windshield. "Call me if you need help with the body."

I climbed in behind the wheel and fired up the engine.

"A witness saw me get in this truck, so I'd think long and hard about murdering me at this point," she said, pointing to Bud, who was still watching us.

Obviously she hadn't heard his comment.

"I'm not murdering you," I snapped. *Yet.*

She was already buckled in, her long legs crossed. A flip-flop dangled from her toes as she jiggled her foot. Both her knees were bruised, and I noticed a raw scrape on her right forearm. I told myself I didn't want to know and threw the truck into reverse. I'd dump her at the station—

25

hopefully it was early enough to avoid who I wanted to avoid—and make sure she got her damn car. If I was lucky, I could still grab another hour of shut-eye before I had to officially start my day.

"You know," she began, "if one of us should be mad at the other, it's me. I don't even know you, and here you are yelling in my face, getting between me and my coffee, and then practically abducting me. You have no reason to be upset."

"You have no idea, sweetheart. I've got plenty of reasons to be pissed, and a lot of them involve your waste-of-space sister."

"Tina may not be the nicest of people, but that doesn't give you the right to be such an ass. She's still family," Naomi sniffed.

"I wouldn't apply the label 'people' to your sister." Tina was a monster of the first degree. She stole. She lied. She picked fights. Drank too much. Showered too little. And had no regard for anyone else. All because she thought the world owed her.

"Listen, whoever the hell you are. The only people who can talk about her like that are me, our parents, and the Andersontown High graduating class of 2003. And maybe also the Andersontown Fire Department. But that's because they earned the right. You haven't, and I don't need you taking your problems with my sister out on me."

"Whatever," I said through gritted teeth.

We drove the rest of the way in silence. The Knockemout Police Department sat back a few blocks from Main Street and shared a new building

26

with the town's public library. Just seeing it made the muscle under my eye twitch.

In the parking lot was a pickup truck, a cruiser, and a Harley Fat Boy. There was no sign of the chief's SUV. Thank Christ for small miracles.

"Come on. Let's get this over with."

"There's no need for you to come in," Naomi sniffed. She was eyeing her empty coffee with puppy-dog eyes.

On a growl, I shoved my own mostly untouched coffee at her. "I'm getting you to the desk, making sure they've got your car, and then never seeing you again."

"Fine. But I'm not saying thank you."

I didn't bother replying because I was too busy storming toward the front door and ignoring the big gold letters above it.

"The Knox Morgan Municipal Building."

I pretended I didn't hear her and let the glass door swing closed behind me.

"Is there more than one Knox in this town?" she asked, wrenching the door open and following me inside.

"No," I said, hoping that would put an end to questions I didn't want to fucking answer. The building was relatively new with a shit ton of glass, wide hallways, and that fresh paint smell.

"So it's your name on the building?" she pressed, jogging again to keep up with me.

"Guess so." I yanked open another door on the right and gestured for her to go inside.

Knockemout's cop shop looked more like one of those coworking hangouts that urban hipsters liked than an actual police station. It also annoyed the boys and girls in blue, who had taken pride in their moldy, crumbling bunker with its flickering fluorescent lights and carpet stained from decades of criminals.

Their annoyance at the bright paint and slick new office furniture was the only thing I didn't hate about it.

The Knockemout PD did their best to rediscover their roots, piling precious towers of case folders on top of adjustable-height bamboo desks and brewing too cheap, too strong coffee 24/7. There was a box of stale donuts open on the counter and powdered sugar fingerprints everywhere. But so far, nothing had taken the shine off the newness of the fucking Knox Morgan Building.

Sergeant Grave Hopper was behind his desk stirring half a pound of sugar into his coffee. A reformed motorcycle club member, he now spent his weeknights coaching his daughter's softball team and his weekends mowing lawns. His and his mother-in-law's. But once a year, he'd pack up his wife on the back of his bike, and off they'd go to relive their glory days on the open road.

He spotted me and my guest and nearly upended the entire mug all over himself.

"What's goin' on, Knox?" Grave asked, now openly staring at Naomi.

It was no secret around town that I had as little to

do with the PD as possible. It also wasn't exactly news that Tina was the kind of trouble that I didn't tolerate.

"This is Naomi. Tina's twin," I explained. "She just got into town and says her car was towed. You got it out back?"

Knockemout PD usually had more important things to worry about than parking and let its citizens park wherever the hell they wanted, when they wanted, as long as it wasn't directly on the sidewalk.

"Imma come back to that whole twin sister thing," Grave warned, pointing his coffee stirrer at us. "But first, it's just me in so far today, and I ain't towed shit."

Fuck. I shoved a hand through my hair.

"If you didn't, do you have any idea who else would have?" Naomi asked hopefully.

Sure. I swooped in to save the day and drive her down here, but grizzled Grave was the one who got the smile and sweet words.

Grave, the bastard, was hanging on her every word, smiling at her like she was a seven-layer chocolate cake.

"Well now, Tin—I mean Naomi," Grave began. "Way I see it, there's two things that coulda happened: (A) You forgot where you parked. But a gal like you in a town this small, that don't seem likely."

"No, it doesn't," she agreed amicably without calling him Captain Obvious.

"Or (B) someone stole your car."

I kissed my hour of sleep goodbye.

"I parked right in front of the pet shop because it was close to the café where I was supposed to meet my sister."

Grave slid me a look, and I nodded. Best to just get this part over with, like ripping off a damn bandage.

"So Tina knew you were coming into town, knew where you'd be?" he clarified.

Naomi wasn't picking up what he was putting down. She nodded, all wide-eyed and hopeful. "Yes. She called me last night. Said she was in some kind of trouble and needed me to meet her at Café Rev at seven this morning."

"Well now, sweetheart," Grave hemmed. "I don't want to cast aspersions, of course. But is it possible—"

"Your asshole sister stole your car," I interjected.

Naomi's hazel eyes sliced to me. She didn't look sweet or hopeful now. No. She looked like she wanted to commit a misdemeanor. Maybe even a felony.

"I'm afraid Knox here is right," Grave said. "Your sister's been causing trouble since she got into town a year ago. This probably ain't the first car she's helped herself to."

Naomi's nostrils flared delicately. She brought my coffee to her mouth, drank it down in a few determined gulps, then tossed the empty cup into the waste basket by the desk. "Thank you for your help. If you see a blue Volvo with a Nice Matters bumper sticker, please let me know."

Christ.

"Don't suppose you've got one of those apps on your phone that'll tell you where your car is, do ya?" Grave asked.

She reached for her pocket, then stopped and squeezed her eyes shut for a beat. "I did."

"But you don't no more?"

"I don't have a phone. Mine, uh, broke last night."

"That's all right. I can put a call out so officers will be on the lookout if you give me the license plate," Grave said, helpfully shoving a piece of paper and pen in her direction.

She took them and started to write in neat, swoopy cursive.

"You could leave your contact info too, where you're staying and such, so me or Nash can update you."

The name set my teeth on edge.

"Happy to," Naomi said, sounding anything but.

"Uh. You got maybe a husband or boyfriend whose contact info you can add?"

I glared at him.

Naomi shook her head. "No."

"Maybe a girlfriend or wife?" he tried again.

"I'm single," she said, sounding just unsure enough that my curiosity piqued.

"Imagine that. So's our chief," Grave said, as

innocent as a six-foot-tall biker with a rap sheet could sound.

"Can we get back to the part where you tell Naomi you'll be in touch if you find her car, which we all know you won't," I snapped.

"Well, not with that attitude, we won't," she chided.

This was the last fucking time I was riding to the rescue of anyone. It wasn't my job. Wasn't my responsibility. And now it was costing me sleep.

"How long are you in town?" he asked as Naomi scrawled her information on the paper.

"Only as long as it takes to find and murder my sister," she said, capping the pen and sliding the paper back. "Thank you so much for your help, Sergeant."

"My pleasure."

She turned to look up at me. Our gazes held for a beat. "Knox."

"Naomi."

With that, she swept right on out of the station.

"How can two sisters look that much alike and have nothing else in common?" Grave wondered.

"I don't want to know," I said honestly and headed outside after her.

I found her pacing and muttering to herself in front of the wheelchair ramp.

"What's your plan?" I asked in resignation.

She looked at me and her lips puckered. "Plan?" she repeated, her voice cracking.

My fight-or-flight instincts kicked in. I fucking

hated tears. Especially tears of the female persuasion. A crying woman made me feel like I was being ripped to shreds from the inside out, a weapon I'd never make public knowledge.

"Do not cry," I ordered.

Her eyes were damp. "Cry? I'm not going to cry."

She was a shit liar.

"Don't fucking cry. It's just a car, and she's just a piece of shit. Neither's worth crying over."

She blinked rapidly, and I couldn't tell if she was going to cry or yell at me again. But she surprised me by doing neither. She straightened her shoulders and nodded. "You're right. It's just a car. I can get replacement credit cards, a new purse, and another stash of honey mustard dipping sauces."

"Tell me where you need to go, and I'll drop you. You can get a rental and be on your way." I jerked my thumb toward my truck.

She looked up and down the street again, probably hoping for some suit-and-tie-wearing hero to appear. When none did, she sighed. "I got a room at the motel."

There was only one motel in town. A single-story, one-star shithole that didn't warrant an official name. I was impressed she'd actually checked in.

We walked back to my truck in silence. Her shoulder brushed my arm, making my skin feel like it was heating up. I opened her door again for her. Not because I was a gentleman but because some perverse part of me liked being close.

I waited until she'd belted in before shutting the door and rounding the truck. "Honey mustard dipping sauces?"

She glanced at me as I slid in behind the wheel. "You hear about that guy who drove through a guardrail in the winter a few years back?"

It sounded vaguely familiar.

"He ate nothing but ketchup packets for three days."

"You plan on driving through a guardrail?"

"No. But I like to be prepared. And I don't like ketchup."

3

A Pint-Size Criminal

Naomi

W hat room are you in?" Knox asked. I realized
we were already back at the motel.

"Why?" I asked with suspicion.

He exhaled slowly as if I were on his last nerve.
"So I can drop you at your door."

Oh. "Nine."

"You leave your door open?" he asked a second
later, his mouth tight.

"Yeah. That's the way it's done on Long Island,"
I deadpanned. "It's how we show our neighbors we
trust them."

He gave me another one of those long, frowny
looks.

"No. Of course I didn't leave it open. I closed
and locked it."

He pointed toward number nine.

My door was ajar.

"Oh."

He put the truck in park where it sat in the
middle of the lot with more force than necessary.
"Stay here."

I blinked as he climbed out and stalked toward
my room.

35

My weary eyes were drawn to the view of those worn jeans clinging to a spectacular butt as he stalked toward my door. Hypnotized for a few of his long strides, it took me a hot minute to remember exactly what I'd left in that room and how very much I didn't want Knox, of all people, to see it.

"Wait!" I jumped out of the truck and ran after him, but he didn't stop, didn't even slow down.

I turned on the speed in a last-ditch effort and jumped in front of him. He walked right into the hand I held up.

"Get your ass out of my way, Naomi," he ordered.

When I didn't comply, he brought a hand to my stomach and walked me backward until I was standing in front of Room 8.

I didn't know what it said about me that I really liked his hand there. "You don't have to go in there," I insisted. "I'm sure it's just housekeeping."

"This place look like it has housekeeping?"

He had a point. The motel looked like it should give out tetanus shots instead of mini bottles of shampoo.

"Stay," he said again, then stalked back to my open door.

"Shit," I whispered when he shoved it open. I lasted all of two seconds before following him inside.

The room had been unappealing, to say the least, when I'd checked in less than an hour ago.

36

The orange-and-brown wallpaper was peeling in long strips. The carpet was a dark green that felt like it was made out of the scrubby side of a dish sponge. The bathroom fixtures were Pepto-Bismol pink, and the shower was missing several tiles.

But it was the only option within twenty miles, and I'd figured I could rough it for a night or two. Besides, I'd thought at the time, how bad could it be?

Apparently pretty freaking bad. Between the time I'd checked in, stowed my suitcase, plugged in my laptop, and left to meet Tina, someone had broken in and ransacked the room.

My suitcase was upended on the floor, some of its contents strewn all over the carpet.

The dresser drawers were pulled out, closet doors left open.

My laptop was missing. So was the zippered pouch of cash I'd hidden in my suitcase.

"Sucker" was scrawled across the bathroom vanity mirror in my favorite lipstick. Ironically, the thing I didn't want my grumpy Viking to see, the thing that was worth more than whatever else had been stolen, was still there in a crumpled heap in the corner.

Worst of all, the perpetrator was sitting on the bed, dirty sneakers tangled in a clump of sheets. She was watching a natural disaster movie. I wasn't good at guessing ages, but I put her solidly in the child/preteen category.

"Hey, Way," Knox said grimly.

The girl's blue eyes flitted away from the screen to land on him before returning to the TV. "Hey, Knox."

It was a small town. Of course the town grump and the child felon knew each other.

"Okay, look," I said, sidestepping Knox to stand in front of the thing in the corner that I really didn't want to explain. "I don't know if child labor laws are different in Virginia, but I asked for an extra pillow, not to be robbed by a pint-size criminal."

The girl spared me a glance.

"Where's your mom?" Knox asked, ignoring me.

Another shrug. "Gone," she said. "Who's your friend?"

"That'd be your aunt Naomi."

She didn't look impressed. I, on the other hand, probably looked like I'd just been shot out of a cannon toward a brick wall.

"Aunt?" I repeated, shaking my head in hopes that it would fix my hearing. Another wilted flower petal fell out of what was left of my updo and flitted to the floor.

"Thought you were dead," the girl said, studying me with vague interest. "Nice hair."

"Aunt?" I said again.

Knox turned to me. "Waylay is Tina's kid," Knox explained slowly.

"Tina?" I parroted on a croak.

"Looks like your sister helped herself to your stuff," he observed.

"Said most of it was shit," the girl said.

I blinked rapidly. Not only had my sister stolen my car, she'd also broken into my hotel room, ransacked it, and left behind the niece I didn't know existed.

"She okay?" Waylay asked, not taking her eyes off the tornado that returned to the screen.

"She" was probably me. And I was most definitely not okay.

I grabbed a pillow off the bed. "Will you two please excuse me?" I squeaked.

Without waiting for an answer, I hauled ass out the door into the hot Virginia sunshine. Birds were chirping. Two motorcycles drove by, their engines a deafening roar. Across the street, an older couple climbed out of a pickup truck and headed into the diner for breakfast.

How could things have the audacity to look so normal when my entire life had just imploded?

I held the pillow to my face and let loose the scream that had been building.

Thoughts flew through my brain like a turbocharged spin cycle. Warner was right. People didn't change. My sister was still a terrible human being, and I was still naïve enough to fall for her lies. My car was gone along with my purse and my laptop. Not to mention the money I'd brought for Tina. As of last night, I had no job. I wasn't on my way to Paris, which had been the plan a mere twenty-four hours ago. My family and friends thought I'd lost my damn mind. My favorite lipstick had been ruined on a bathroom mirror. And I had a niece whose entire childhood I'd missed out on.

I sucked in another breath and let out one final scream for good measure before lowering the pillow.

"Okay. You can figure this out. You can fix this."

"About done with your pep talk?"

I whirled around and found Knox leaning against the doorframe, tattooed arms crossed over his broad chest.

"Yep," I said, squaring my shoulders. "How old is she?"

"Eleven."

Nodding, I shoved the pillow at him and marched back into the room.

"So, Waylay," I began.

There was a family resemblance in the upturned nose, the dimple in the chin. She had the same colt-like legs her mother and I had at that age.

"So, Aunt Naomi."

"Did your mom say when she'd be back?"

"Nope."

"Where do you and your mom live, honey?" I asked.

Maybe Tina was there now, going through her haul, figuring out what was worth keeping and what she wanted to ruin just for the fun of it.

"Over in Hillside Acres," she answered, looking around me to get a better view of the tornado tossing up cows on the screen.

"Need a minute," Knox announced and nodded toward the door.

I had all the damn time in the world apparently. All the time and not a single clue what to do. No next step. No to-do list quantifying and organizing my world into nice, neat line items. Just a crisis on top of a hot mess on top of a dumpster fire.

"Sure," I said, sounding only mildly hysterical.

He waited until I passed him before stepping out after me. When I stopped, he kept walking toward the faded soda machine outside the front office.

"You seriously want me to buy you a soda right now?" I asked, flummoxed.

"No. I'm trying to get out of earshot of the kid who doesn't realize she's been abandoned," he snapped.

I followed him. "Maybe Tina's coming back," I said.

He stopped and turned to face me. "Way says Tina didn't tell her anything. Just that she had something to take care of and she'd be gone a long time."

A long time? What the hell was a long time in Tina time? A weekend? A week? A month?

"Oh my God. My parents." This was going to devastate them. As if what I'd done yesterday wasn't upsetting enough. I'd managed to assure them last night on a highway in Pennsylvania that I was fine and definitely not going through some kind of midlife crisis. And I'd made them promise not to change their plans for me. They'd left for their three-week Mediterranean cruise

41

this morning. The first big, international vacation they'd ever taken together.

I didn't want my problems or Tina's disaster ruining it.

"What do you intend to do with that kid in there?" Knox nodded toward the open door.

"What do you mean?"

"Naomi, when the cops find out Tina's gone and left Waylay behind, it's straight into foster care."

I shook my head. "I'm her closest living relative who isn't a criminal. I'm responsible for her." Just like all Tina's other messes until we'd turned eighteen.

He gave me a long, hard look. "Just like that?"

"She's family." Besides, it wasn't like I had a whole lot going on at the moment. I was basically adrift. For the first time in my entire life, I didn't have a plan.

And that scared the crap out of me.

"Family," he snorted as if my reasoning wasn't sound.

"Listen. Thank you, Knox, for all the shouting and the rides and the coffee. But as you can see, I've got a situation to handle. So it's probably best for you to go on back to whatever cave you crawled out of this morning."

"I'm not goin' anywhere."

We were back to glaring at each other, the silence charged. This time, he broke first.

"Quit stallin', Daisy. What are you gonna do?"

"Daisy?"

He reached up and plucked a flower petal out of my hair with two fingers.

I batted his hand away and took a step back so I could think. "Okay. First I need to . . ." Definitely not call my parents. And I didn't really want to get the police involved—again—if I didn't have to. What if Tina showed up in an hour? Maybe the first thing I needed to do was get more coffee.

"Call the damn cops and report the break-in and the child abandonment," Knox said.

"She's my *sister*. Besides, what if she shows up in an hour?"

"She stole your car and abandoned her kid. That doesn't earn a fucking pass."

The tattooed, grouchy bear of a man was right. I really didn't like that about him.

"Argh! Fine. Okay. Let me think. Can I borrow your phone?"

He stood there staring at me, unmoving.

"For Pete's sake. I'm not going to steal it. I just need to make a quick call."

On a long-suffering sigh, he reached into his pocket and pulled out his phone.

"Thank you," I said pointedly, then stomped back into my motel room. Waylay was still watching her movie, now with her hands stacked behind her head.

I dug through my suitcase to find a notebook and went back outside.

"You keep a notebook of phone numbers with you?"

Knox was peering over my shoulder.

I shushed him and dialed.

"The hell do you want?"

My sister's voice always managed to make me cringe inwardly.

"An explanation for starters," I snapped. "Where are you?"

"Where are you?" she mimicked me in a high-pitched Muppet voice that I'd always hated.

I heard a prolonged exhale.

"Are you *smoking* in my car?"

"Looks like it's my car now."

"You know what? Forget the car. We have bigger things to discuss. You have a *daughter!* A daughter you abandoned in a motel room."

"Got shit to do. Can't have a kid holding me back for the next while. Got something big in the works. Why ya think I named her Waylay? Figured she could hang out with her aunt Goody Two-Shoes till I get back."

I was so mad I could only sputter.

Knox snatched the phone from my ear. "You listen and you listen good, Tina. You've got exactly thirty minutes to get back here, or I'm callin' the damn cops."

I watched as his face got harder, his jaw tighter, showing off little hollows under his cheekbones. His eyes went so cold I shivered.

"As always, you're a real fuckin' idiot," he said. "Just remember, next time you get picked up by the cops, you'll have warrants. That means your

44

stupid ass will be sittin' behind bars, and I don't see anyone rushin' to bail you out." He paused for a moment and then said, "Yeah. Fuck you too."

He swore again and lowered his phone.

"How exactly do you and my sister know each other?" I wondered out loud.

"Tina's been a pain in everyone's ass since she blew into town a year ago. Always lookin' for an easy buck. Tried a couple of slip-and-fall schemes on some of the local businesses, including your pal Justice. Every time she gets a little money in her pocket, she's rip-roarin' drunk and wreaking havoc all over town. Petty shit. Vandalism."

Yeah, that sounded like my sister.

"What did she say?" I asked, not really wanting the answer.

"Said she doesn't give a shit if we call the cops. She's not comin' back."

"Did she say that?" I'd always wanted kids, but not like this. Not jumping in one step shy of puberty when the formative years were already gone.

"Said she'd be back when she felt like it," he said, thumbing through his phone.

Some things never changed. My sister had always made her own rules. As an infant, she'd slept all day and stayed up all night. As a toddler, she was kicked out of three day cares for biting. And once we hit school age, well, it was a whole new ballgame of rebellion.

"What are you doing?" I asked Knox as he brought the phone back up to his ear.

"Last thing I want to," he drawled.

"Buying tickets to the ballet?" I hypothesized.

He didn't answer, just strode into the parking lot with rigid shoulders. I couldn't hear exactly what he was saying, but there were a lot of *fuck you*s and *kiss my ass*es.

I added "phone etiquette" to the growing list of things Knox Morgan was bad at.

He returned looking even angrier. Ignoring me, he produced a wallet and fished out a few bills, then fed them into the soda machine.

"What do you want?" he muttered.

"Uh. Water, please."

He punched the buttons harder than I thought necessary. And a bottle of water and two Yellow Lightnings fell out onto the ground.

"Here." He shoved the water at me and headed back to the room.

"Uh, thanks?" I called after him.

I debated for about thirty seconds whether I should just start walking until I found a new reality that was less terrible, but it was just a mental exercise. There was no way I could walk away. I had a new responsibility. And with that responsibility would come some sense of purpose. Probably.

I returned to my room and found Knox examining the lock on the door. "No finesse," he complained.

"Told her she should've picked it," Waylay said, cracking open her soda.

"It's barely eight in the morning, and you gave

her a soda," I hissed at Knox as I resumed my sentry stance in front of the mound in the corner.

He looked at me, then beyond me. Nervously I spread my arms and tried to block his view.

"That some kind of tablecloth?" he asked, peering past me.

"Wedding dress," Waylay announced. "Mom said it was ugly as hell."

"Yeah, well, Tina wouldn't know good taste if it hit her over the head with a Birkin bag," I said, feeling defensive.

"Does that dress mean I have an uncle out there somewhere?" she asked, nodding at the pile of lace and underskirt that had once made me feel like a fairy princess but now only made me feel like a fool.

"No," I said firmly.

Knox's eyebrows raised fractionally. "You just decided to take a wedding dress on a road trip?"

"I really don't see how this is any of your business," I told him.

"Hair's done up like she was going someplace fancy," Waylay mused, eyeing me.

"Sure looks that way, Way," Knox agreed, crossing his arms over his chest and looking amused.

I did not like the two of them ganging up against me.

"Let's worry less about my hair and a dress than what we're going to do next," I suggested. "Waylay, did your mom say anything about where she was going?"

The girl's eyes zeroed back on the screen. Her slim shoulders shrugged. "Dunno. Just said I was your problem now."

I didn't know what to say to that. Thankfully, I didn't have to answer, because a brisk knock had all three of us looking at the open door.

The man standing in it made me suck in a little breath. Knockemout sure grew them hot. He was dressed in a spotless dark-blue uniform with a very shiny badge. There was a nice layer of stubble accentuating a strong jaw. His shoulders and chest were broad, hips and waist tapered. His hair was close to blond. There was something familiar about his eyes.

"Knox," he said.

"Nash." His tone was as cold as his eyes.

"Hey, Way," the newcomer said.

Waylay gave the man a head nod. "Chief."

His eyes came to me.

"You called the police?" I squeaked at Knox. My sister was a terrible person, and I was definitely going to let her know that. But calling the police felt so *final*.

4

"You're not staying here."

Naomi

"Y ou must be Naomi," the cop said.

I might have been mid–panic attack, but I kind of liked the way he said my name in a friendly drawl.

Knox apparently did *not* like it, because he was suddenly placing his muscled bulk directly in front of me, feet planted wide, arms crossed.

"I am," I said, peering around Knox. The oaf didn't budge when I nudged him in the back.

The man looked back to Knox, and whatever he saw there had him grinning.

"I'm chief of police around here, but you can call me Nash. It's real nice to meet you, Naomi. Sorry it's under these circumstances. Mind if I ask you a few questions?"

"Um, okay," I said, suddenly wishing I would have taken a moment to wash my face and fix my hair. I probably looked like a deranged, zombie bridesmaid.

"Why don't we have ourselves a chat out in the parking lot," Nash said with a jerk of his head.

Waylay's attention was back on the movie as she sipped lime-green sugar.

"Sure." I followed him out and was surprised

49

when Knox joined us. He headed right over to Nash's SUV, which read Knockemout Police down the side, and leaned belligerently against the hood.

"You're not necessary for this part," Nash told him.

Knox bared his teeth. "You want me to leave, gonna have to make me."

"I'm sorry. He's been like this all morning," I explained to Nash.

"Honey, he's been like this his entire life," the chief countered.

It didn't hit me until they turned identical glares on each other. "You're brothers, aren't you?"

"No shit," Knox grumbled.

"Sure are," Nash said, turning his full wattage grin on me. "I'm the good one."

"Just do your fucking job," Knox said.

"Oh, now you want me to do my job. You can see how I'd be confused since—"

"Gentlemen," I cut in. This was going nowhere fast. I didn't have the energy to defuse the tension between the brothers, and we had more important concerns. "I don't mean to overstep. But can we get to the part about my sister?" I suggested.

"I think that's a fine idea, Naomi," Nash said, winking as he pulled out a notebook.

Knox growled.

"Let's get your statement, and then we'll figure out what needs to happen next."

A man with a plan and a smile. He was certainly more pleasant than his brother.

"You're saying I can just take possession of a human being?" I clarified a few minutes later. I really needed more coffee. My cognitive abilities were fading fast.

"Well, I wouldn't advise referring to it as 'taking possession.' But in Virginia, kinship care is a way for kids to stay with a family member as guardian when they can't be with their own parents."

I might have been imagining it, but I thought I saw a guarded look pass between the brothers.

"So I would become Waylay's guardian?"

Things were moving so fast. One second, I was getting ready to walk down the aisle. The next, I was suddenly in charge of deciding the future of an eleven-year-old stranger.

Nash swept a hand through his thick hair. "Temporarily. You're obviously a stable, healthy adult."

"What happens if I don't?" I hedged.

"Juvenile and Domestic Relations will place Waylay in a foster home. If you've got no problems staying in town for a few weeks while we figure things out, the law's got no issue with Waylay staying with you. If things work out, you can even make it permanent."

"Okay." I nervously wiped my hands on the back of my shorts. "What things are we going to be figuring out?" I asked.

"Mainly what your sister is up to and what that means for guardianship."

I'm in big trouble. I need money, Naomi.

I bit my lip. "She called me last night. Said she needed help and wanted me to bring cash. Do you think she's in actual danger?"

"How about this? You focus on Waylay and let me worry about your sister," Nash advised.

I appreciated the theory, but in my experience, the only way to make sure a mess was cleaned to my satisfaction was to do the cleaning myself.

"Did you bring cash?" Knox asked, his eyes on me.

I looked down at my feet, feeling stupid and embarrassed. I knew better. "I did."

"She get it?"

I focused on Nash's face since it was friendlier. "I thought I was being smart. I had half of it in the car and left the other half in my suitcase."

Nash looked sympathetic. Knox, on the other hand, grumbled something under his breath.

"Well, I guess I'd better get back in there and introduce myself properly to my niece," I said. "Please keep me posted."

"You're not staying here."

This proclamation came from Knox.

I threw my hands up. "If my presence bothers you that much, why don't you take an extended vacation?"

If looks could boil blood, mine would have turned to magma.

"You're *not* staying here," he repeated. This time, he pointed to the flimsy door with the busted lock.

Oh. That.

"I'm sure I can come up with a solution," I said brightly. "Chief—"

"Call me Nash," he insisted again.

Knox looked like he wanted to shove his brother's head through the already damaged door.

"Nash," I said, turning up the charm. "Do you know where Waylay and I could stay for a few nights?"

Knox pulled out his phone and glowered at the screen as his thumbs moved aggressively over it.

"I could give you two a ride to Tina's place. It's not exactly homey, but she's a lot less likely to break in and bust up her own stuff," he offered.

Knox stowed his phone in his pocket. His gaze fastened on me, and there was something smug about his expression that made me irrationally irritated.

"That is so nice of you. I can't tell you how much I appreciate your help," I told Nash. "I'm sure Knox has much better things to do than spend any more time in my vicinity."

"My pleasure," Nash insisted.

"I'll just pack up what's left of my things and tell Waylay where we're going," I decided and started back to the room.

My relief at finally being free of the bad-tempered, tattooed Knox was interrupted by a thunderous rumble.

A motorcycle with a man the size of a bear prior

to hibernation rocketed down the street at a speed that was definitely not the legal speed limit.

"God damn that Harvey," Nash muttered.

"Guess you better go get 'em," Knox said, still looking smug.

Nash jabbed a finger in his brother's direction. "You and me are gonna talk later," he promised, looking none too happy.

"Better hurry and uphold that law," Knox said.

Nash turned back to me. "Naomi, sorry to leave you in the lurch. I'll be in touch."

Knox wiggled his fingers antagonistically as his brother hustled back to his SUV and took up pursuit with lights flashing.

Once again, I was left alone with Knox. "You didn't have something to do with my nice, polite ride disappearing, did you?"

"Now why would I do that?"

"Well, it sure as hell isn't to spend more quality time with me."

"Come on, Daisy," he said. "Let's pack your shit. I'll take you and Way to Tina's."

"I'd prefer if you kept your hands off my shit," I said haughtily. The effect was ruined by my unladylike yawn. I was running on fumes and only hoped I could hold on long enough to get away from the Viking before I crashed.

5

A Vat of Lighter Fluid and a Nap

Naomi

Hillside Acres looked more like a festive camp-ground than a trailer park.

Kids played on a small, well-kept playground on a patch of grass that hadn't quite submitted to the long Virginia summer. The mobile homes had picket fences and vegetable gardens. Creative color schemes and cozy patios added to the curb appeal.

And then there was Tina's place.

It was a single-wide trailer in the back corner of the park. The beige box sloped hard to the right, looking like it was missing part of its foundation on that end. Weeds that had fought their way through the gravel hit me at the knee.

The trailer across the road had a cute screened-in porch with string lights and hanging plants. Tina's had makeshift cinder block steps leading to a rusty front door that hung slightly ajar.

Knox was glaring again. But for once, it wasn't at me. It was at the notice posted on the door. EVICTION.

"Stay here," he ordered without looking at me or Waylay.

I was too tired to be annoyed as he macho man–stepped inside.

Waylay rolled her eyes. "She's long gone. She busted in here before the motel."

On reflex, I reached for her and put my hands on her shoulders. She jumped back, looking at me like I'd just tried to give her a wedgie.

Note to self: Don't rush the physical affection.

"Uh, where have you two been staying?"

Waylay shrugged. "I stayed at my friend's house the last two nights. Her parents don't mind an extra kid for dinner. Dunno where she stayed."

The only time "responsible" could be applied to Tina was when she was impersonating me over the years. Even still, I found myself horrified at my sister's approach to parenting.

"It's clear," Knox called from inside.

"Told ya." Waylay bounded up the steps, and I followed.

The trailer was worse on the inside than it was outside.

The carpet had worn through in front of the door, leaving long, gnarled strings that stretched out in all directions. A recliner faced a cheap wooden console with the dusty outline of a TV stand. A small, pink beanbag sat directly in front of it.

"She took the TV. But I grabbed the remote while she wasn't looking," Waylay said proudly.

"Nice job, kid," Knox said, giving her hair a ruffle.

Swallowing hard, I left them in the living room and poked my head into the dingy kitchen.

The contents of the cabinets had been emptied into an overflowing garbage can in the middle of the green linoleum. Boxes of cereal, cans of soup, long since defrosted pizza snacks. There wasn't a vegetable in sight.

There was a bedroom on each end. The one with the double bed had an ashtray on either side. Instead of curtains, thin bedsheets were tacked directly to the wall to block out the sun. The closet and dresser were mostly empty. Everything had either ended up on the floor or been hauled out the door. On instinct, I peeked under the bed and found two empty bourbon bottles.

Some things never changed.

"She's coming back, you know," Waylay said, poking her head inside.

"I know," I agreed. What the girl didn't know was that sometimes it was years between visits.

"My room's on the other end if you wanna see it," she said.

"I'd like that if you don't mind."

I closed the door on Tina's depressing bedroom and followed my niece through the living room. Exhaustion and overwhelm made my eyeballs feel hot and dry. "Where's Knox?" I asked.

"Talkin' to Mr. Gibbons outside. He's the landlord. Mom owes a shit ton of back rent," she said, leading the way to the flimsy fake wood door off the living room. A hand-lettered sign said *KEEP OUT* in glitter and four shades of pink marker.

I decided to save the lecture on swearing for later when I wasn't mostly asleep on my feet.

Waylay's room was small but tidy. There was a twin bed under a pretty pink quilt. A sagging bookshelf held a few books but was mostly dedicated to hair accessories organized in colorful bins.

Was it possible Waylay Witt was a girlie girl?

She flopped down on her bed. "So? What are we doing?"

"Well," I said brightly, "I like your room. As for the rest of the place, I think we can make it work. A little scrubbing, some organization . . ." *A vat of lighter fluid and a box of matches.*

Knox prowled into the room like a pissed-off lion at the zoo. He took up too much space and most of the oxygen. "Get your shit, Way."

"Uh. All of it?" she asked.

His nod was brisk. "All of it. Naomi."

He turned and marched out of the room. I could feel the trailer shudder under his feet.

"Think that means you're supposed to follow him," Waylay said.

"Right. Okay. Just hang tight. I'll be back in a second."

I found him outside, hands on hips and staring at the gravel.

"Is there a problem?"

"You two aren't fucking staying here."

Suddenly too tired to function, I collapsed against the trailer's aluminum siding. "Look, Knox, my bones are tired. I've been up for a

58

million hours straight. I'm in a strange place in a stranger situation. And there's a little girl in there who needs someone. Unfortunately for her, that someone is me. You made up for the asshole routine with the chauffeur routine. You can just stop with the macho inconvenienced thing. I didn't ask you for help, so you're free to go. I need to start cleaning this mess up."

Literally and figuratively.

"About done?" he asked.

I was too tired to be infuriated. "Yeah. About."

"Good. Then get your ass in the truck. You're not staying here."

"Are you serious right now?"

"You two aren't staying in a motel with cardboard doors or a health violation of a trailer that's been broken into. Besides . . ." He paused his tirade to rip the eviction notice off the door. "This place ain't Tina's anymore. Legally, you can't crash here. Morally, I can't let you try. Got it?"

It was the longest speech he'd made in my presence, and I honestly didn't have the energy for a reply.

But he wasn't looking for one.

"So you're going to get your ass in the truck."

"And then what, Knox?" I pushed away from the trailer and threw my hands up. "What's next? Do you know? Because I haven't got a clue, and that scares the hell out of me."

"I know a place you can stay. Safer than the motel. Cleaner than this fuckin' mess."

"Knox, I've got no wallet. No checkbook. No phone or laptop. As of yesterday, I've got no job to go back to. How am I supposed to pay for . . ." I couldn't even finish the sentence. Exhaustion and despair overwhelmed me.

He swore and shoved a hand through his hair. "You're asleep on your feet."

"So?" I said sullenly.

He stared at me hard for a long beat. "Daisy, just get in the truck."

"I need to help Waylay pack," I argued. "And I need to go through the trash in there in case there's any important paperwork. Insurance, birth certificate, school records."

He stepped forward, and I moved back. He kept advancing on me until my back met his pickup. He opened the passenger door. "Gibbons will let you know if he finds anything important."

"But shouldn't I talk to him?"

"Already did. This ain't his first rodeo, and he's not a bad guy. He keeps important shit tenants leave behind and knows what to keep a lookout for. He'll call me if he finds something. Now. Get. In. The. Truck."

I climbed up on the seat and tried to think of other things that I needed to do.

"Way," Knox barked.

"Geez. Keep your pants on!" Waylay appeared in the doorway wearing a backpack and holding two garbage bags.

My heart shivered. Her life, all her treasured

possessions, fit into two trash bags. And not even the good kind with drawstrings.

Knox took the bags from her and put them in the bed of his pickup. "Let's go."

It was a quiet ride, and apparently if I wasn't making conversation or fighting with Knox, I didn't have the energy to remain conscious. I woke abruptly when the truck jostled. We were on a dirt road that snaked its way through woods. The trees created a canopy above us. I had no idea if I'd just dozed off or if we'd been driving for an hour.

Remembering my predicament, I whipped around and relaxed when I saw Waylay in the back seat, sitting next to the white, fluffy mound that was my wedding dress.

Turning back to Knox, I yawned. "Great. You're taking us out to the middle of nowhere to murder us, aren't you?"

Waylay snickered behind me.

Knox stayed stubbornly silent as we bumped along the dirt drive.

"Whoa." Waylay's exclamation had me focusing on the view through the windshield.

A wide creek meandered alongside the road before curling back into the woods. Just ahead, the trees thinned, and I spotted the "whoa." It was a large log home with a wide front porch that wrapped around one side of the first floor.

Knox continued down the drive past the house.

"Bummer," Waylay muttered under her breath when we drove on.

Around the next bend, I spied a small cabin with dark siding tucked into a copse of trees. "That's my place," Knox said. "And that's yours."

Just beyond it was a storybook-looking cottage. Pine trees towered over it, offering shade from the summer sun. Its white board-and-batten exterior was charming, the small front porch with cheery blue planks inviting.

I loved it.

Knox turned into the short gravel drive and turned off the engine.

"Let's go," he said, climbing out.

"I guess we're here," I whispered to Waylay.

We both exited the truck.

It was cooler here than in town. Quieter too. The rumble of motorcycles and traffic was replaced with the buzz of bees and the far-off drone of an airplane. A dog barked nearby. I could hear the creek as it burbled its way through whispering trees somewhere behind the cottage. The warm breeze carried the scent of flowers and earth and summer sunshine.

It was perfect. Too perfect for a runaway bride with no wallet.

"Uh. Knox?"

He ignored me and carried Waylay's bags and my suitcase to the front porch.

"We're stayin' here?" Waylay asked as she pressed her face to the front window to peer inside.

"It's dusty and probably stale as hell," Knox said as he propped open the screen door and pulled out his keys. "Hasn't been used in a while. You'll probably need to open the windows. Air it out."

Why he had a key to a cottage that looked like it lived on the pages of my favorite fairy tale was on my list of questions. Just above that were questions concerning rent and security deposits.

"Knox?" I tried again.

But he'd gotten the door open, and suddenly I was standing on the wide wood plank floor of a cozy living room with a tiny stone fireplace. There was an old rolltop desk crammed into an alcove between the stairs to the second floor and the coat closet. Windows brought the outdoors inside.

"Seriously. We get to stay here?" Waylay asked, her skepticism mirroring my own.

Knox dropped our bags at the foot of the tiny staircase. "Yeah."

She stared at him for a beat, then shrugged. "Guess I'll go check out the upstairs."

"Wait! Take off your shoes," I told her, not wanting to track any dirt inside.

Waylay glanced down at her filthy sneakers. There was a hole in the toe of the left one and a pink heart charm clipped to the laces of the right. With an extravagant eye roll, she toed them off and carried them upstairs.

Knox's mouth pulled up in the corner as we watched her go, pretending she wasn't the least bit excited or curious.

"Damn it, Viking!" The idea of spending a few weeks in a postcard-perfect cottage far away from the mess I'd left behind was intoxicating. I could organize the hell out of the shambles of my life while I sat on the back porch and watched the creek flow by. If I could afford it.

"Now what's your problem?" he asked, stepping into the dollhouse-size kitchen and staring out the window over the sink.

"You mean, 'What's wrong, Naomi?' Well, I'll tell you, Knox. Now Waylay's excited about this place, and I don't even know if I can afford it. She's going to be disappointed on top of abandoned. What if we end up back at the motel tonight?"

"You're not goin' back to the motel."

"What's the rent?" I asked, biting my lip.

He turned away from the view and leaned against the counter, looking annoyed. "Dunno."

"You have a key to this place and you don't know?"

"Rent depends," Knox said, reaching out to sweep a layer of dust off the top of the old marshmallow-white fridge.

"On what?"

He shook his head. "On who."

"Fine. Who?"

"Liza J. Your new landlord."

My new landlord?

"And does this Liza J even know that we're here?" I wasn't conscious of gravitating toward

64

him until my toes brushed the tips of his boots. Those blue-gray eyes were on me, making me feel like I was under a magnifying glass.

"If she doesn't, she will soon. She's rough around the edges but she's got a soft spot," he said, gaze boring into me. I was too tired to do anything but glare back at him.

"I picked our rooms," Waylay shouted from upstairs, breaking our staring contest.

"We good?" he asked quietly.

"No! We're not good. I don't even know where we are or how to get back to town. Do you have Uber here? Are there bears?"

His lips quirked, and I felt my face flush. He was studying me in a way that people didn't do in polite company.

"Dinner," he said.

"Huh?" was my erudite reply. I knew he wasn't trying to ask me out. Not after we'd spent an entire morning hating each other.

"Seven. At the big house down the road. That's Liza J's. She'll want to meet you."

"If she doesn't know she's my landlord, she's certainly not expecting us for dinner," I pointed out.

"Dinner. Seven. She'll be expecting you by then."

I was *not* comfortable with this kind of invitation. "What am I supposed to bring? Where's the closest store? Does she like wine?" Hostess gifts were not just respectful. In this case, they would set the tone of a good first impression.

His lips quirked as if my angst amused him. "Go take a nap, Naomi. Then go to dinner at Liza J's." He turned and headed for the door.

"Wait!"

I hurried after him, catching him on the porch.

"What do I say to Waylay?"

I didn't know where the question or the panicky note in my voice had come from. I wasn't a panicker. I performed miracles under pressure.

"What do you mean what do you say?"

"What do I tell her about her mom and me and why we're here?"

"Tell her the truth."

"I'm not sure what that is."

He started down the porch steps, and again, panic clawed at my throat. The only man I knew in this town was abandoning me with a child I didn't know, no transportation, and only the crap my sister hadn't stolen from me.

"Knox!"

He stopped again and swore. "Christ, Naomi. Tell her her mom left her with you, and you're looking forward to getting to know her. Don't make it more complicated than it has to be."

"What if she asks when Tina's coming back? What if she doesn't want to stay with me? Oh God. How do I make her listen to me?"

He stepped back up onto the porch and into my space, then did something I never saw coming.

He grinned. Full-on, panty-melting, 100-wattage grinned.

I felt woozy and hot and like I didn't know how any of my joints worked anymore.

"Wow," I whispered.

"Wow what?" he asked.

"Uh, you smiled. And it was just seriously wow. I had no idea you could look like that. I mean, you already look like"—I waved my hand awkwardly in front of him—"you know. But then you add the smile, and you look almost human."

His smile was gone, and the familiar annoyance was back. "Jesus, Daisy. Get some sleep. You're babbling like an idiot."

I didn't wait to watch him drive away. Instead I went back inside and closed the door. "Now what the hell am I going to do?"

Sleep deserted me abruptly, leaving behind a groggy, panicked confusion.

I was facedown on a bare mattress, a scrub brush still clutched in one hand. The room slowly came into focus as my eyes and brain returned to the land of the living.

Warner. Grr.

Tina. Ugh.

Car. Damn it.

Waylay. Holy crap.

Cottage. Adorable.

Knox. Grumpy, sexy, horrible, yet helpful.

The timeline of the last twenty-four hours intact, I pried myself off the mattress and sat up.

The room was small but cute, just like the rest

of the place. Paneled walls painted a bright white, antique brass bed. There was a tall dresser opposite the bed and a skinny table painted peacock blue tucked under the window that overlooked the meandering creek.

I heard someone humming downstairs and remembered.

Waylay.

"Damn it," I muttered, jumping off the bed. My first day on the job as a guardian, and I'd left my new charge unattended for who knew how long. She could have been abducted by her mother or mauled by a bear while I indulged in an afternoon nap.

I sucked, I decided as I raced down the stairs.

"Geez. Don't break your neck or anything."

Waylay sat at the kitchen table, swinging a bare foot while she chowed down on what appeared to be a peanut butter and jelly sandwich with thick white bread and enough jelly to cause instant cavities.

"Coffee," I croaked at her.

"Man, you look like a zombie."

"Zombie needs coffee."

"Soda in the fridge."

Soda would have to do. I stumbled my way to the refrigerator and opened it. I was halfway through the can of Pepsi before I realized there was food inside.

"Where food from?" I rasped. I was not an easy waker from naps. In the morning, I could bound out of bed with the energy of a sugared-up kinder-

68

garten class. But post-nap Naomi wasn't pretty. Or coherent.

Waylay gave me a long look. "Are you trying to ask me where the food came from?"

I held up a finger and downed the rest of the soda.

"Yeah," I wheezed finally as the cold caffeine and sugar burned my throat. "That." I paused to burp indelicately. "Excuse me."

Waylay smirked. "Chief Nash had a delivery lady drop off a bag of groceries while you were drooling all over your bed."

My eyeballs felt gritty as I blinked. The chief of police had seen to delivering food that I'd been too unconscious to provide for my niece. I was not going to get a gold star in guardianship today.

"Crap," I muttered.

"It's not crap," Waylay argued around a huge bite of PB&J. "There's some candy and some chips."

I needed to claw my way back up the scale toward responsible adult and needed to do it fast.

"We need a list," I decided, scrubbing my hands over my eyes. "We need to figure out how far we are from civilization, how to get there, what supplies we need for the next day or two."

Coffee. I definitely needed coffee.

"It's, like, half a mile to town," Waylay said. She had a smear of jelly on her chin, and besides her "my aunt is a lunatic" expression, she looked adorably childlike. "Why are your arms and knees all scraped up?"

I glanced down at the abrasions on my skin. "I climbed out of a church basement window."

"Cool. So we're going into town?"

"Yes. I just need to take a kitchen inventory," I decided, finding my trusty notebook and pen.

Coffee.

Food.

Transportation?

Job?

New purpose in life?

"We can take the bikes," Waylay piped up.

"Bikes?" I repeated.

"Yeah. Liza J dropped them off. Said we have to come to dinner tonight too."

"You met our landlord?" I squeaked. "Who else stopped by? The mayor? Exactly how long have I been asleep?"

Her eyes went wide and serious. "Aunt Naomi, you've been asleep for two whole days."

"What?"

She smirked. "Just messin' with you. You were out for an hour."

"Hilarious. Just for that, I'm buying brussels sprouts and carrots."

She wrinkled her nose. "Gross."

"Serves you right, smarty-pants. Now, make me a sandwich while I tackle this inventory."

"Fine. But only if you think about brushing your hair and washing your face before we go out in public. I don't want to be seen with Aunt Zombie."

6

Asparagus and a Showdown

Naomi

At this minute, I was supposed to be jet-lagged and wandering the streets of Paris on my honeymoon. Instead I was clinging to the handlebars of an ancient ten-speed bike, trying not to tip over.

It had been years since my ass had met a bike seat. Every bump and rut on the gravel road jarred both my teeth and my lady parts. The one and only time I'd talked Warner into trying one of those tandem bikes at the beach, we'd ended up headfirst in a shrub outside the kite store.

Warner had not been pleased.

There were a lot of things that hadn't pleased Warner Dennison III. Things I should have paid more attention to.

The thicket of woods passed in a buzzing blur as we rode through swirls of gnats and the thick southern humidity. Beads of sweat trickled down my spine.

"Are you comin' or what?" Waylay called from what seemed like a mile ahead. She was riding a rusty boy's bike with her arms dangling at her sides.

"What's your middle name?" I yelled back.

"Regina."

"Waylay Regina Witt, you put both hands on your handlebars this instant!"

"Oh, come on. You're not one of those fun-hatin' aunts, are you?"

I pedaled harder until I caught up. "I am *lots* of fun," I huffed, partially because I was offended but mostly because I was out of breath.

Sure, maybe I wasn't a ride-with-no-hands, sneak-out-of-a-sleepover-to-go-kiss-boys, or call-in-sick-to-go-to-a-concert fun kind of gal, but I didn't *hate* fun. There was usually just too much that needed doing before I could get to the fun.

"Town's this way," Waylay said, gesturing to the left with a flick of her chin. It was such a Tina gesture that it took away what remaining breath I had.

We abandoned gravel for smooth asphalt, and within minutes, I spotted the outskirts of Knock-emout up ahead.

For a second, I lost myself in the historic familiarity of a bike ride. The sun on my face and arms, the warm air as it brushed over my skin, the call and response of a billion insects in the throes of summer. I'd been an eleven-year-old on a bike once. Heading out for adventure into the morning swelter and not returning home until I got hungry or the fireflies came out.

There were sprawling horse farms on the outskirts of town with slick fences and emerald-green pastures. I could almost smell the wealth and privilege. It reminded me of Warner's parents' country club.

Four bikers in worn denim and leather roared past us on motorcycles, the engine rumble a vibration in my bones, as they escaped the confines of town.

Horse people and bikers. It was a unique combination.

The farms disappeared and were replaced by tidy homes on tidy lots that got closer and closer together until we were on the main street. Traffic was light, so I was able to pay more attention to the downtown area than I had this morning. There was a farm supply store and a gift shop next to the mechanic. Opposite was a hardware store and the pet store where my Volvo had been stolen.

"Grocery store's this way," Waylay called from ahead of me as she took another left turn much faster than I felt prudent.

"Slow down!" Great. Half a day in my care and my niece was going to end up knocking out her front teeth by riding face-first into a stop sign.

Waylay ignored me. She zipped down the block and into the parking lot.

I added *bike helmets* to my mental shopping list and followed her.

After parking our bikes on the rack by the front door, I pulled out the envelope I'd—thankfully—hidden in a box of tampons. Minutes before I was supposed to walk down the aisle, my mother had handed me a card full of cash.

It was supposed to be our wedding present. Spending money for the honeymoon. Now it was the only money I had access to until I could replace my stolen credit and debit cards.

I shuddered to think how much money I'd stupidly shelled out of my own savings for the wedding that never happened.

"Guess you can't buy too many brussels sprouts since we're on bikes," Waylay observed smugly.

"Guess again, smarty-pants," I said, pointing at the sign in the window.

Home Delivery Available.

"Aww, man," she groaned.

"Now we can get a truckload of vegetables," I said cheerily.

"No."

"What do you mean, no?" I demanded, waggling stalks of asparagus at Waylay.

"No to asparagus," Waylay said. "It's green."

"You don't eat green foods?"

"Not unless it comes in candy form."

I wrinkled my nose. "You have to eat some vegetables. What about fruits?"

"I like pie," she said, poking suspiciously at a bin of mangos as if she'd never seen them before.

"What do you usually eat for dinner with . . . with your mom?" I had no idea whether Tina was a touchy subject or if she routinely left Waylay to fend for herself. I felt like I was blindfolded and being forced to shuffle out onto a frozen lake. The ice would break under my feet sooner or later; I just didn't know where or when.

Her shoulders hiked up toward her ears. "Dunno. Whatever was in the fridge."

"Leftovers?" I asked hopefully.

"I make Easy Mac and frozen pizzas. Sometimes nuggets," Waylay said, growing bored with the mangos and moving on to frown at a display of green leaf lettuces. "Can we get Pop-Tarts?"

I was getting a headache. I needed more sleep and coffee, not necessarily in that order. "Maybe. But first we have to agree on a few healthy foods."

A man in a Grover's Groceries apron turned the corner into produce. His polite smile vanished when he caught sight of us. Eyes narrowed, lip curled, he looked as if he'd just spotted us drop-kicking a plastic, light-up Baby Jesus in an outdoor nativity scene.

"Hello," I said, adding an extra punch of warmth to my smile.

He gave a harrumph in our direction and stalked off.

I glanced at Waylay, but either she hadn't noticed the eye daggers or she was immune.

So much for southern hospitality. Though we were in northern Virginia. Maybe they didn't do the southern hospitality thing here. Or maybe the man had just found out that his cat had a month to live. You never knew what people were going through behind the scenes.

Waylay and I worked our way around the store,

and I noticed a similar reaction from a few other employees and patrons. When the woman behind the deli counter threw the pound of sliced turkey breast at me, I'd had enough.

I made sure Waylay was busy leaning over an open freezer of chicken nuggets. "Excuse me, I'm new here. Am I breaking some kind of store etiquette that results in hurled deli meats?"

"Ha. You ain't fooling me, Tina Witt. Now, you gonna pay for that turkey or try to stuff it in your bra like last time?"

And there was my answer.

"I'm Naomi Witt, Tina's sister and Waylay's aunt. I can assure you I've never stuffed deli meat in my bra."

"Bullshit." She said it cupping a hand to her mouth like she was using a bullhorn. "You and that kid of yours are no-good, shoplifting pains in the ass."

My conflict resolution skills were limited to people pleasing. Usually I would squeak out a terrified apology and then feel compelled to buy the offended party some kind of small, thoughtful gift. But today I was tired.

"Okay. You know what? I don't think you're supposed to talk to patrons like that," I said. I was going for firm and confident, but it came out tinged with hysteria. "And you know what else? Today I've been yelled at, robbed—twice—and turned into an inexperienced insta parent, and that was before lunch. I've slept about an hour in the last two days. And you don't see *me* hurling deli meat around. All I ask from you is that you treat me and my niece with a modicum of respect as a paying customer. I don't know you. I've never been here before. I'm sorry for whatever my sister did with her breasts and your meat. But I'd really like this turkey sliced thinner!"

I pushed the package back over the top of the cooler at her.

Her eyes were wide in that not-sure-how-to-handle-this-unhinged-customer way.

"You're not shittin' me? You're not Tina?"

"I am not shitting you." Damn it. I should have gone for the coffee first.

"Aunt Naomi, I found the Pop-Tarts," Waylay said, appearing with an armload of sugary breakfast treats.

"Great," I said.

"So," I said, sliding a strawberry kiwi smoothie in front of Waylay and taking the seat across from her. Justice, the man of my dreams, had made my afternoon latte in a mug the size of a soup bowl.

"So what?" Waylay asked sullenly. Her sneakered foot was kicking the pedestal leg of the table.

I wished I hadn't run over my phone at the rest stop so I could search for "ways to break the ice with kids."

"Uh, what have you been doing this summer?"

She looked me in the eyes for a long beat, then said, "What's it to you?"

People with kids made it look easy to talk to them. I stuck my face in my bowl o' latte and slurped, praying for inspiration.

"Thought you two ladies could use a little snack," Justice said, sliding a plate of cookies onto the table. "Fresh out of the oven."

Waylay's blue eyes went wide as she took in the plate and then looked up into Justice's face with suspicion.

"Thank you, Justice. That's so sweet of you," I said. I gave my niece a nudge.

"Yeah. Thanks," Waylay said. She didn't reach for a cookie but sat there staring at the plate.

This was an example I felt confident setting. I snatched up a peanut butter cookie and, between guzzles of my coffee, took a bite. "Ohmygod," I managed. "Justice, I know we just met, but I'd be honored if you marry me."

"She's already got the wedding dress," Waylay said.

He laughed and flashed the gold band on his left hand. "It devastates me to say I'm already spoken for."

"The good ones always are." I sighed.

Waylay's fingers furtively moved closer to the plate.

"My favorite is the chocolate chocolate chip," Justice said, pointing at the biggest cookie on the plate. With a wink, he was gone.

She waited until he was behind the counter before snatching the cookie off the plate.

"Mmm. So good," I mumbled, my mouth full of cookie goodness.

She rolled her eyes. "You're so weird."

"Shut up and eat your cookie." Her eyes narrowed, and I grinned. "Kidding. So what's your favorite color?"

We were on question ten of my half-assed getting to know you icebreaker when the door to the café flew open, and a woman strolled inside in ripped tights, a short denim skirt, and a Lenny Kravitz T-shirt. She had wild dark hair worn in a high ponytail, several earrings, and a lotus flower tattooed on her forearm. I couldn't tell if she was in her thirties or her forties.

"There you are," she said, grinning around a lollipop in her mouth when she spotted us.

The friendly greeting made me immediately suspicious. Everyone thought I was Tina, which meant if someone was happy to see me, they were probably a terrible person.

The woman grabbed a chair, spun it around backward, and flopped down at our table. "Ooh! Those look good." She helped herself to a cookie with red frosting, trading her lollipop for the baked good. "So, Naomi," she began.

"Uh, do we know you?"

Our uninvited guest slapped herself in the forehead. "Whoops. Manners! I'm already several steps ahead in our relationship. You'll just have to catch up. I'm Sherry Fiasco."

"Sherry Fiasco?"

She shrugged. "I know. Sounds made up. But it's not. Justice, I'll take a double espresso to go," she called.

My future husband raised a hand without turning around from the order he was working on. "You got it, Fi."

"So, as I was saying. In my head, we're already friends. Which is why I have a job for you," she said, biting the cookie in half. "Hey, Way."

Waylay studied Sherry over her smoothie. "Hey."

"So what do you say?" Sherry asked, shimmying her shoulders.

"Huh?"

"Aunt Naomi's kind of a planner," Waylay explained. "She wrote three lists so far today."

"Ah. A look-before-you-leap type," Sherry said, nodding sagely. "Okay. I'm a business manager, which puts me in charge of several small businesses in the area. One of them is down a server and desperately needs someone who can deliver beer and be generally charming."

"A waitress?" I'd spent the last five years of my life cooped up in an office answering emails, pushing papers, and settling human resource issues via carefully worded emails.

Being on my feet and around people all day sounded like it might be fun.

"It's honest work. The tips are great. The uniforms are cute. And the rest of the staff is a hoot. Mostly," Sherry said.

"I'd need to arrange child care," I hedged.

"For who?" Waylay demanded, her forehead scrunched up.

"For you," I said, ruffling her hair.

She looked appalled and dodged my hand. "I don't need a babysitter."

"Just because you're used to doing something one way doesn't mean it's the right way," I told her. "You've spent a lot of time looking out for yourself, but that's my job now. I'm not about to leave you alone while I go to work."

"That's stupid. I'm not a baby."

"No, you're not," I agreed. "But adult supervision is a necessity."

Waylay muttered something that sounded suspiciously like "bullshit." I decided to pick my battles and pretend I hadn't heard.

"If that's your only reservation, I can easily find someone to hang out with Way here while you rake in the tip money."

I chewed on my lower lip. I wasn't a fan of having to decide things on the spot. There were pros and cons to weigh. Research to do. Routes to calculate. Schedules to firm up.

"I wouldn't feel comfortable leaving Waylay with a stranger," I explained.

"Of course not," Sherry chirped. "I'll arrange a meeting, and you can decide then."

"Uh . . ."

Justice whistled from the counter. "Order's up, Fi."

"Thanks, big guy," she said, jumping up from

her chair. "Well, I'll see you two ladies later. First shift's tomorrow night. Be there at five."

"Wait!"

She cocked her head.

"Where is this job?"

"Honky Tonk," she said as if it were the most obvious thing in the world. "Bye!"

I watched Sherry Fiasco strut out of the café with the confidence of a woman who knew exactly where she was going and what she was doing.

Even when my five-year plan was intact, I hadn't had that kind of confidence.

"What just happened?" I whispered.

"You got a job and then turned me into a dumb baby." Waylay's face was stony.

"I didn't call you a dumb baby, and I didn't officially accept," I pointed out.

But I needed income, and the sooner the better. My checking account balance wasn't exactly going to support us indefinitely. Especially not with rent and security deposits and utilities to worry about. Not to mention the fact that I had no vehicle, no phone, and no computer.

I picked up another cookie and took a bite. "It won't be so bad," I promised Waylay.

"Yeah, right," she scoffed and went back to kicking the table.

7

A Punch in the Face

Knox

W here you think you're going?" I asked lazily from my lawn chair parked in the middle of the lane.

The SUV's bumper had stopped a generous foot from my knees, a cloud of dust rising up behind.

My brother slid out from behind the wheel and rounded the vehicle.

"Shoulda known I'd find you here," Nash said, his jaw tight as he pulled a slip of paper from his uniform pocket. He crumpled it and threw it at me. It hit me square in the chest. "Harvey said to pass this along to you since it was your fault he was speeding through town this morning."

It was a speeding ticket written in my brother's scrawl.

"I have no idea what Harvey's jabbering about," I lied and pocketed the citation.

"I see you're still an irresponsible asshole," Nash said as if there'd been a chance I'd changed in the past few years.

"I see you're still a law-abiding dickhead with a stick up his ass."

Waylon, my lazy basset hound, wandered his stumpy legs off the porch to greet his uncle.

Traitor.

If he thought he'd get more attention or more people food somewhere else, Waylon wasn't weighed down by loyalty and didn't hesitate to wander.

I pointed toward the cabin with my beer bottle. "I live here. Remember? Didn't look like you were slowin' down to pay me a visit."

Nash hadn't set foot in my place in more than three years. I'd done him the same courtesy.

He hunkered down to give Waylon some love. "Got an update for Naomi," he said.

"And?"

"And the fuck what? It doesn't involve you. You don't need to stand sentry like some ugly gargoyle."

Waylon, sensing he wasn't the focal point, meandered up to me and nosed at my hand. I gave him a thump on his side and the dog biscuit I'd stashed in the chair's cup holder. He took it and pranced back to the porch, white-tipped tail a blur of happy.

I raised the beer to my mouth. "Saw her first," I reminded Nash.

The flash of anger I saw in his eyes was gratifying. "Oh, fuck you, man. You pissed her off first."

I shrugged carelessly. "Same thing. Might as well just wander that law-abiding ass of yours back to Liza J's. I'll bring Naomi and Waylay to you."

"Can't stop me from doing my damn job, Knox."

I got out of my chair.

Nash's eyes narrowed.

"Give you one free shot," I offered, then drained the rest of my beer.

"One for one?" my brother clarified. He always did pay too much attention to the rules.

"Yep."

He placed his watch on the hood of the SUV and rolled up his sleeves. I put my beer in the cup holder and stretched my arms overhead.

"Never used to need to warm up before," Nash observed, adopting a boxer's stance.

I loosened up my neck and shoulders. "Fuck off. We're over forty. Shit hurts."

This was overdue. Fists were how we'd settled countless arguments for decades. Fight and move on. Until the thing punching each other in the face couldn't settle.

"What's the matter?" I taunted. "Having second—"

Nash's stupid fist plowing into my face cut off the rest of my sentence. It was a bell ringer. Right in the fucking nose.

Shit, that hurt.

"Goddammit," I hissed, prodding my face for deformities.

My brother bobbed and weaved in front of me, looking a little too fucking proud of himself.

I tasted blood as it trickled onto my upper lip.

"I got shit to do. I don't have time for conversation and kicking your—"

I let my fist fly, catching him in that goddamn mouth he was always running. The mouth he'd used to lay on the charm with Naomi. His head snapped back.

"Ow! Fuck!" He swiped his arm over his mouth, smearing his own blood up his sleeve. Another bead dripped onto the shirt of his uniform. It made me feel perversely accomplished. Messing up Nash was always gratifying.

"We really gonna do this?" he asked, looking up as his tongue darted out to taste the blood at the corner of his lip.

"Don't have to. You know how to stop it."

"She hates your guts. You don't even like her," he pointed out.

I used the hem of my T-shirt to stem the flow of blood from my nose. "Not the point."

Nash narrowed his eyes. "The point is you always wanna call the shots. Some brother."

"You're the idiot who doesn't know how to say thank you," I shot back.

He shook his head, looking like he was going to back down. But I knew better. I knew him better. We both wanted this. "Get out of my way, Knox."

"You're not gettin' past me today."

"I'd be happy to run you down with my truck. Say you were drunk and passed out in the middle of the lane and I didn't see you."

"Your ass would be behind bars before they even got mine to the morgue," I predicted. "Something happens to either one of us 'round here, everyone knows the first place to look is the other one."

"And what does that say about our happy fucking family?" Nash spat.

We were circling each other now, hands up, eyes locked. Fighting a man you grew up tumbling with was like fighting yourself. You knew all the moves even before they were coming.

"I'll ask you again, Knox. Why are you in my way?"

I shrugged. Mostly to annoy him, but partly because I didn't really know why I'd planted my ass between my brother and Naomi "Doe Eyes" Witt. She wasn't my type. He wasn't my problem. Yet here I was. The whole introspection thing was another one of those time wasters that I didn't bother with. I wanted to do something, I did it.

"You just want to put your hands on something fine and mess it up, don't you?" Nash asked. "You can't take care of a woman like that. She's got class. She's smart."

"She's needy as fuck. Right up your alley," I shot back.

"Then get out of my way."

Tired of the conversation, I threw a jab to his jaw. He returned it with a shot to my ribs.

I don't know how long we traded blows in the middle of the dirt lane, kicking up dust and hurling insults at each other. Somewhere in the midst of him calling me a fucking asshole and me putting him in a headlock so I could punch him in the forehead, I recognized my brother for the first time in a long-ass time.

"What in the holy hell are you doing? You can't assault an officer of the law!"

Naomi floated into my line of sight, looking exactly like the high-class woman I didn't want, exactly the type my brother did. Her hair was down now and daisy-free, draped over one shoulder, thick and sleek. Her eyes had lost the better part of the exhausted shadows. She was wearing one of those long sundresses that skimmed the tops of her feet and made men wonder what treasures lay beneath.

She was carrying a bouquet of flowers, and for a second, I wanted to know who the hell had given them to her so I could kick their ass.

Next to her was Waylay in shorts and a pink T-shirt, holding a plate covered in plastic wrap. She was grinning at us.

Nash used the distraction to throw an elbow to my gut. The wind went out of me, and I bent to catch my breath.

"Face's bleedin', Chief," Waylay cheerfully observed. "Got it all over that nice clean shirt of yours."

I grinned. The kid might have belonged to Tina, but she was funny as hell. And she was in my corner.

Waylon abandoned his perch on the porch and ambled back into the road to greet the newcomers.

"Thanks, Waylay," Nash said, swiping at his

bloody mouth again. "I was just coming to see you two."

While Waylay squished my dog's droopy jowls between her hands, Naomi peered around my brother at me.

"What is wrong with you?" she hissed. "You can't just start a fight with a cop!"

I slowly straightened, rubbing a hand over my sternum. "Doesn't count as a cop. He's my brother."

Waylon shoved his nose under the hem of Naomi's dress and stepped on her foot. He was a needy bastard.

"Well, hello," Naomi crooned, crouching down to pet him.

"His name's Waylon," Nash told her.

"Waylon and Waylay," she mused. "That won't get confusing."

My nose burned. My face fucking hurt. My knuckles were bleeding. But looking at her petting my needy-ass dog with an arm full of flowers made everything else start to fade away.

Fuck me.

I knew what attraction felt like. Knew what to do with it too. But not with a woman like this. One who didn't know it was smart to be afraid of me. One with a wedding dress and no ring. One with an eleven-year-old. This was the kind of situation that had me heading for the hills. But I couldn't stop looking at her.

"You're an idiot."

Nash grinned, then winced.

"And you," Naomi said as she turned on him. "I can't imagine you take that badge very seriously if you're fighting in the street with your own brother."

"He started it," Nash and I both said at the same time.

"Then we'll leave you to it," she said primly, putting a hand on Waylay's shoulder. "Let's go."

"Heading to Liza J's?" Nash asked.

"We are. We were invited for dinner," Naomi said.

Waylay raised the plate she was holding. "Brought cookies."

"I'll walk with you," Nash said. "We can talk on the way."

"Sounds good to me," I said, moving my chair out of the road.

"You're not invited," he said.

"Oh yes, I am. Seven sharp."

My brother looked like he was going to haul off and hit me again, which suited me just fine. Tarnishing his "aww, shucks" hero vibe would only further my cause. But just as I was about to goad him into it, Naomi stepped between us. Waylon followed her and sat on her feet.

The woman couldn't read signs. She was a danger to herself, trying to get between two bucks itching for a fight.

"Did you find my car?" she asked Nash.

"Did you find my mom?" Waylay asked.

90

"Maybe we should talk in private," he suggested. "Knox, be a good neighbor and take Waylay up to the house while I have a few words with Naomi."

"No way," Waylay said, crossing her arms.

"Fuck no," I agreed.

Our stare down lasted until Naomi rolled her eyes. "Fine. Let's just get this over with. Please tell me what you found."

My brother suddenly looked uncomfortable, and my interest piqued.

"Guess I'll just get right to it," Nash said. "I didn't find your car yet. But I did find something interesting when I ran the plates. It was reported stolen."

"No, shit, Sherlock. Naomi did that this morning," I reminded him.

Nash ignored me and continued. "It was reported stolen yesterday by one Warner Dennison III of Long Island, New York."

Naomi looked like she wanted the earth to swallow her up.

"You stole a car?" Waylay asked her aunt, looking impressed. I had to admit that I hadn't seen that one coming either.

"It's my car, but my ex-fiancé bought it. His name was on the title with mine."

She looked like the kind of woman a man would buy cars for, I decided.

"Don't you mean ex-husband?" Waylay piped up.

"Ex-fiancé," Naomi corrected. "We're no longer together. And we didn't get married."

" 'Cause she left him at the altar," the girl added knowledgeably. "Yesterday."

"Waylay, I told you that in confidence," Naomi hissed. Her cheeks turned a bright shade of scarlet.

"You're the one being interrogated for grand theft auto."

"No one is being interrogated," Nash insisted. "I'll talk to the office in charge and clear up any misunderstanding."

"Thank you," Naomi said. Her eyes were filling with what looked suspiciously like tears.

Fuck.

"I don't know about you all, but I could sure use a drink. Let's head up to the big house and solve this over alcohol," I suggested.

I didn't imagine the flicker of relief that flashed over her pretty face.

I spent the short walk to Liza J's wondering when the hell I'd turned into a sundress guy. The women I dated wore jeans and leather and rocker T-shirts. They didn't have prep school vocabularies or dresses that floated around their ankles like some summer fantasy.

I liked my women the way I liked my relationships—fast, dirty, and casual.

Naomi Witt was none of those, and I needed to remember that.

"You're seriously going to dinner like that?" Naomi asked me as Waylon wandered off the drive to lift his leg on a dogwood.

Behind us, Waylay peppered Nash with questions about crime in Knockemout.

"Liza J's seen worse," I said, biting into a cookie.

"Where did you get that cookie?" she demanded.

"Waylay," I said.

Naomi looked like she was going to slap it out of my hand, so I shoved the rest of it into my mouth.

"Those are for this mysterious Liza J I'm supposed to be making a good impression on," she complained. "This isn't a great way for me to meet a new potential landlord. 'Hi, I'm Naomi. I'm squatting in your cottage, and these guys were fighting in your driveway. Please give me affordable rent.'"

I snorted, then winced when my nose started to throb again. "Relax. Liza J would be worried if Nash and I didn't show up bleeding and pissed off at each other," I assured her.

"Why are you pissed off at each other?"

"Baby, you haven't got the time," I drawled.

We reached the steps of the big house, and Naomi hesitated, looking up at the rough-hewn timber, the cedar shakes. Behind overgrown azaleas and boxwoods, the porch stretched nearly fifty feet along the front.

I tried to see it from her eyes. New in town, running from a wedding, no place to stay, thrown into a guardianship she hadn't seen coming. To her, everything hinged on this meal.

"Don't chickenshit out now," I advised. "Liza J hates cowards."

Those pretty hazel eyes narrowed to slits. "Thanks for the advice," she said caustically.

"Nice place," Waylay said, joining us at the foot of the steps.

I thought about the trailer. The chaos outside that little bedroom with the KEEP OUT sign on the door. She'd done her best to keep the chaos and unpredictability out of her little world. I could respect that.

"Used to be a lodge. Let's go. I need that drink," I said, climbing the three short steps and reaching for the doorknob.

"Don't we need to knock or ring the bell?" Naomi hissed, grabbing my arm.

And there it was again. That electricity charging my blood, waking up my body like it had been exposed to some kind of threat, some kind of danger.

We both looked down at her hand, and she quickly dropped it.

"Not necessary around here," Nash assured her, unaware that my blood was on fire and Naomi was blushing again.

"Liza J," I bellowed.

The response was a fevered fit of barking.

"Oh my," Naomi whispered, putting herself between Waylay and the fur circus.

Waylon shoved himself between my leg and the doorframe just as two dogs raced into the foyer. Randy the beagle had earned his name by humping everything in sight for the first year of his life. Kitty was a one-eyed, fifty-pound pit bull who thought she was a lapdog. Both kept Liza J entertained in her solitude.

It was cooler inside. Darker too. The blinds stayed closed these days. Liza J said it was so no one could snoop on her business. But I knew the truth, and I didn't blame her for it.

"Quit your hollerin'," a voice said from the direction of the kitchen. "What's the matter with you? Your mama raise you in a barn?"

"No, but our grandma did," Nash called back.

Elizabeth Jane Persimmon, all five feet one inch of her, clomped out to greet us. She wore her hair cut short around her face as she had for as long as I could remember. Never missed a trim. Her rubber gardening clogs squeaked on the floor. She was in her typical uniform of cargo pants and a blue T-shirt. She wore the same thing nearly every day. If it was hot, she wore the pants with the zippered legs. If it was cold, she added a sweatshirt in the same color as the tee.

"Shoulda drowned you in the creek when I had the chance," she said, stopping in front of us and crossing her arms expectantly.

"Liza J." Nash dutifully pressed a kiss to her cheek.

I repeated the greeting.

She nodded her satisfaction. Warm and fuzzy time was over. "So what the hell kind of mess did you bring me?" Her gaze slid to Naomi and Waylay, who were being skeptically sniffed by the dogs.

Kitty broke first and headbutted Naomi in the legs in a bid for affection. Waylon, not to be left out, muscled his way in, knocking her off-balance. I reached out, but Nash got there first and steadied her.

"Put the disaster dogs out. Let 'em run off the devil for a bit," Liza J ordered.

Nash let go of Naomi and opened the front door. Three streaks of fur took off.

"Liza J, this is Naomi and her niece, Waylay," said. "They'll be staying at the cottage."

"They will, will they?"

She didn't like being told what to do any mo than I did. Neither one of us ever understood why Nash had gone all law and order. "Unless of course you want to throw them out on the street," I added.

"I remembered where I know you from," my grandmother announced, peering at Waylay through her bifocals. "Been buggin' me since I dropped off the bikes. You fixed my iPad at the library."

"You did?" Naomi asked the girl.

Waylay shrugged, looking embarrassed. "I go in there sometimes. And sometimes old folks have me fix stuff."

"And you look like that one's trouble-making mother." Liza J pointed at Naomi.

"That would be my sister," she said, smiling weakly.

"Twins," I interjected.

Naomi held out the bouquet. "We brought you

flowers and cookies to thank you for inviting us to dinner."

"Flowers, cookies, and two bleeding men," Liza J observed. "Might as well come on back. Dinner's about done."

"About done" in Liza J's house meant she hadn't started it yet.

We trooped into the kitchen, where all the fixings for sloppy joes and salad awaited.

"Meat," I called.

"Salad," Nash conceded.

"Not before you both clean yourselves up," Liza J said, pointing to the kitchen sink.

Nash did as he was told and turned on the water. I headed to the fridge and cracked open a beer first.

"Got some treats from the bakery today," Liza J said. She looked at Waylay, who was eyeing the salad ingredients with suspicion. "Why don't you put 'em on a plate with whatever cookies my grandsons didn't eat and maybe taste a couple to make sure they're fit for eatin'."

"Cool," Waylay said, making a beeline for the bakery box on the counter.

I peered over the kid's shoulder and helped myself to a lemon cookie. My favorite.

"I'll get the wine," Liza J said. "You look like you know your way around a wine opener."

She was addressing Naomi, who looked like she couldn't decide if it was a compliment or a judgment.

"Go on," I told her when Liza J headed out of the room.

She took a step closer, and I caught the scent of lavender. "Do not under any circumstances start another fight in front of my niece," she hissed.

"Can't promise anything."

If eyes could shoot actual fire, I would have had a need to regrow my eyebrows.

"Chief, I trust you can keep the order for a few minutes," she said.

Nash flashed her one of his stupid charming grins. "You can count on me."

"Kiss ass," I coughed into my fist.

Waylay snickered.

"I'll be right back," Naomi promised Waylay. "Chief Morgan is in charge."

The kid looked confused. I guessed no one had ever bothered to tell her they were leaving, let alone when they'd be back.

Naomi straightened her shoulders and followed my grandmother out of the room, that damn dress floating around her like she was some kind of fairy-tale princess about to face a dragon.

8

The Mysterious Liza J

Naomi

Unsure how I felt leaving Waylay in a room with two grown men who had been grappling in the road mere minutes earlier, I reluctantly followed Liza J into a dark dining room.

The wallpaper was a deep green in a pattern I couldn't quite make out. The furniture was heavy and rustic. The wide plank table stretched on for nearly twelve feet and was buried under boxes and stacks of papers. Instead of chafing dishes or family photos, the walnut buffet was stacked high with bottles of wine and liquor. Bar glasses were crammed into a nearby hutch so full the doors didn't close.

I itched to dig into the mess.

The only light in the room came from the far wall where an arched opening led into what looked like a sun porch with floor-to-ceiling glass that needed a good scrubbing.

"You have a beautiful home," I ventured, gently shifting a half-dozen china plates stacked precariously on the corner of the table. From what I'd seen so far, the house had buckets of potential. It was just buried under dusty drapes and piles of stuff.

Liza J straightened from the buffet, a bottle of wine in each hand. She was short and soft on the outside, like anyone's favorite grandma. But Liza J greeted her grandsons with chores and gruffness.

I was curious what it said about the Morgans that family relationships didn't make it into introductions. If anyone had a right to avoid claiming their family in this town, it was me.

"Used to run it as a small lodge," she began, setting the bottles on top of the buffet. "Don't anymore. Guess you'll be wanting to stay for a while."

Okay, not big on small talk. Got it.

I nodded. "It's a lovely cottage. But I understand if it's an inconvenience. I'm sure I could come up with an alternative soon." That wasn't exactly a truth so much as a hope. The woman before me was my best chance of creating a little stability in the short term for my niece.

Liza J swiped a cloth napkin over the dust on the wine label. "Don't bother. It was just sittin' there, goin' unused."

Her accent ventured a little farther south than the mid-Atlantic tone of northern Virginia.

I prayed that there was a dash of southern hospitality mixed in there somewhere.

"That's very kind of you. If you don't mind, I'd like to discuss the rent and security deposit."

She shoved the first bottle at me. "Opener's in the drawer."

I opened the top drawer of the buffet and found

a tangle of napkin rings, coasters, candlesticks, matches, and finally a corkscrew.

I went to work on the cork. "As I was saying, money's a little bit tight."

"That's what happens when you got yourself a sister who steals from you and a new mouth to feed," Liza J said, arms crossed.

Knox or Nash had a very big mouth.

I said nothing and popped the cork free.

"Guessin' you'll need work too," she predicted. "Unless you work from home or something."

"I recently left my job," I said carefully.

And my home. And my fiancé. And everything else in that life.

"How recently?"

People in Knockemout were not shy about sticking their noses into other people's business.

"Yesterday."

"Heard my grandson drove you out here with a wedding dress flying like a flag out the window. You a runaway bride?" She set two glasses next to the open bottle and nodded.

I poured. "I guess I am." After a full year of planning, of choosing everything from the cocktail hour appetizers to the color of the table runner on the charcuterie table, it was all over. Wasted. All that time. All that effort. All that planning. All that money.

She picked up a glass and held it aloft. "Good. Heed my words. Don't ever let a man you don't like make decisions for you."

It was odd advice coming from a stranger who I was trying to impress. But considering the day I'd had, I raised my glass to hers.

"You'll do okay here. Knockemout will take care of you and that little girl," she predicted.

"Well then. About the cottage," I pressed. "I have some savings I can access." Technically it was my retirement account, and I'd have to borrow against it.

"You and the girl can stay rent-free," Liza J decided.

My mouth opened wider than the fish mounted on the wall above us.

"You'll pay the utilities on the cottage," she continued. "The rest you can trade by helping around this place. I'm not the neatest housekeeper, and I need some help getting things cleaned up."

My squeals were internal. Liza J was my fairy godmother in gardening clogs.

"That's very generous of you," I began, attempting to process what was happening. But after the past twenty-four hours, my brain was on hiatus.

"You'll still need a paycheck," she continued, unaware of my mental predicament.

I still needed a lot of things. Bike helmets. A car. Some therapy appointments . . . "Oh, I had a job offer today. Someone named Sherry Fiasco said I could take a shift at a place called the Honky Tonk tomorrow night. But I need to find someone to watch Waylay."

We heard the scrabble of paws, and in seconds,

Waylon trotted into the room and looked at us expectantly.

"Way*lay,* not Way*lon,*" Liza J said to the dog.

He sniffed around, making sure we weren't dropping food on the floor, and then headed back into the kitchen.

"You didn't by chance mention to Knox about that job offer, did you?" Liza J asked.

"We don't have that kind of relationship. We just met," I said diplomatically. I didn't want to come out and tell my new landlord that I thought her grandson was a brutish oaf with the manners of a pillaging Norseman.

She studied me through her glasses, and the corner of her mouth turned up. "Oh, I can tell. Word of advice, maybe don't tell him about the new job. He might have opinions, and if he does, he'd definitely share them."

If Knox Morgan thought I was interested in his opinions on my life, I could add narcissistic tendencies to his long list of flaws.

"My business is my business," I said primly. "Besides, I don't think I'm going to be able to find someone I'm comfortable leaving Waylay with in such a short time."

"Already did. Though the girl probably don't need it. Probably been making her own dinners since she was six. She can stay with me. Hell, maybe she can make me dinner. Bring her by on your way to work tomorrow."

Keep an entire human being alive and safe went

into the major imposition column on my internal spreadsheet of things to avoid at all costs. Asking my fairy godmother landlord to please babysit my niece until who knew when while I worked a late shift in a bar rose to the top of that list, edging out helping me move and chauffeuring me to or from surgery.

Major impositions were only put on responsible family members and close friends. Liza J was neither of those.

"Oh, but I don't know what time I'll get off," I hedged. "It could be very late."

She shrugged. "Makes no difference to me. I'll keep her here with me and the dogs, then bring her back to the cottage after dinner. Don't mind waiting around there. Always liked that place."

She headed toward the doorway, leaving me with my feet glued to the rug and my mouth still gaping. "I'll pay you," I called after her, finally rediscovering the ability to move and speak.

"We'll discuss it," Liza J said over her shoulder. "I know you think you're getting the good end of the deal, but you got no idea what a mess you're getting involved in."

We found everyone, including the dogs, alive and unharmed in the kitchen in an oddly homey scene. Waylay was perched at the island, judging every ingredient Nash added to the salad as she added mixed seasoning and condiments in a bowl. Knox was drinking a beer and stabbing at the meat in the pan while reading out ingredients to Waylay.

There appeared to be no new bloodshed. Both men had cleaned up their wounds, leaving behind only bloodstains and bruises. Nash looked like a hero who had taken a few hits for a damsel in distress. Knox, on the other hand, looked like a villain who'd gone a few rounds with the good guy and come out victorious.

It was *definitely* my recent mistake with the good guy—on paper at least—that had me over-correcting and finding Knox and his villainous attitude attractive. At least that was what I told myself when Knox's gaze landed on me and I felt like hot bacon grease had just been poured directly into my spinal column.

I ignored him and his sexy standing-at-the-stove-ness, choosing to focus on the rest of the room instead.

Liza J's kitchen had an astronomical amount of counter space that had my fantasies shifting gears and thinking about the Christmas cookie baking potential. The refrigerator was ancient, the stove practically an antique. The countertops were battered butcher block. The cupboards were painted a lovely loden green. And judging from the contents visible inside the glass-fronted ones, they were all close to overflowing.

I'd start the cleanout in here, I decided. The kitchen was the heart of the home, after all. Though Liza J didn't seem like she was the sentimental type. More like the frozen-in-time type. It happened. Life threw someone an unexpected curve, and things like household maintenance went right out the window. Sometimes permanently.

When it was ready, we took the food and wine into the sunroom, where a smaller table looked out over the backyard. The view was all woods and creek, dappled in gold as the sun sank lower in the summer sky.

When I moved to take a seat next to Waylay, Liza J shook her head. "Uh-uh. These two sit next to each other, they'll be wrestling on the floor before cookies."

"I'm sure they can behave themselves for one meal," I insisted.

She snorted. "No, they can't."

"No, we can't," Knox said at the same time.

"Of course we can," Nash insisted.

Liza J jerked her head at Waylay, who scampered to the opposite side of the table with her plate. The dogs filed in and trotted up to claim their sentry positions around the table. Two of them had judged Waylay to be the one most likely to drop food and stationed themselves next to her.

Waylon plopped down behind Liza J at the head of the table.

Both men moved to take the chair next to mine, Knox winning it by throwing an elbow that nearly had Nash dropping his plate.

"See?" their grandmother said with a triumphant jab of her fork.

I took my seat and tried to ignore my acute aware-ness of Knox as he sat down. The task became downright impossible when his denim-clad thigh brushed against my arm as he sat down. I yanked my arm back and nearly put my plate in my lap.

"Why are you so jumpy?" Waylay asked.

"I'm not jumpy," I insisted, bobbling my wineglass when I reached for it.

"So what were you fightin' over this time?" Liza J asked her grandsons, magnanimously changing the subject.

"Nothin'," Knox and Nash said in unison. The glare that passed between them made me think they didn't like being on the same page about anything.

"Aunt Naomi broke 'em up," Waylay reported, studying a slice of tomato with suspicion.

"Eat your salad," I told her.

"Who was winnin'?" Liza J asked.

"Me," the brothers announced together.

The pronouncement was followed by another chilly silence.

"Rough and tumble as they come, these two," Liza J reminisced. " 'Course, they used to make up after a fight and be back to bein' thick as thieves in no time. Guess y'all outgrew that part."

"He started it," Nash complained.

Knox snorted. "Just 'cause you're the good one doesn't mean you're always innocent."

I understood the dynamics of the good sibling versus the bad one all too well.

"You two with Lucy thrown in the mix?" Liza J shook her head. "Whole town knew trouble was coming when you three got together."

"Lucy?" I asked before I could help myself.

"Lucian Rollins," Nash said as he used his bun to scoop up the ground beef that escaped to his plate. "An old friend."

Knox grunted. His elbow brushed mine, and I felt my skin catch fire again. I withdrew as far as I dared without ending up in Liza J's lap.

"What's Lucy up to these days?" she asked. "Last I heard he was some bigwig mogul in a suit."

"That's about the truth," Nash said.

"Kid was a hustler," Liza J explained. "Always knew he was meant for bigger and better things than a trailer and hand-me-downs."

Waylay's gaze slid to Liza J.

"Lots of people come from humble beginnings," I said.

Knox looked at me and shook his head in what might have been amusement.

"What?"

"Nothing. Eat your dinner."

"What?" I demanded again.

He shrugged. "Chivalry. Humble beginnings. You talk like you read the dictionary for fun."

"I'm so glad you find humor in my vocabulary. It just makes my day."

"Don't mind Knox," Nash cut in. "He's intimidated by women with brains."

"You want my fist up your nose again?" Knox offered gamely.

I kicked him under the table. It was purely on reflex.

"Ow! Fuck," he muttered, leaning down to rub his shin.

All eyes came to me, and I realized what I'd done. "Great," I said, throwing down my fork in mortification. "A few minutes here and there with you, and it's contagious. Next thing you know, I'll be putting strangers in headlocks on the street."

"I'd pay to see that," Waylay mused.

"Me too," Knox and Nash said together.

The corner of Liza J's mouth lifted. "I think you'll fit in just fine around here," she predicted. "Even if you do talk like a dictionary."

"I take it that means you're lettin' them stay," Knox prodded.

"I am," Liza J confirmed.

I didn't miss the quick flash of relief that played over Waylay's face before her mask returned.

One less thing to worry about. A nice, safe place to stay.

"You boys know our Naomi here's a runaway bride?"

"She left some guy standing in a church and stole his car!" Waylay announced with pride.

I picked up the bottle of wine and topped off Liza J's glass and then my own. "You know, where I'm from, we mind our own business."

"Better not be expecting that in a place like Knockemout," Liza J advised.

"What did he do?" Nash asked. But he wasn't asking me; he was asking Waylay.

She shrugged. "Dunno. She won't say. But I bet

it was something bad. 'Cause that was a real nice dress she ran out in. It would take something pretty damn bad to make me run away instead of showing it off to everyone."

I felt the heat of Knox's gaze on me and shriveled like a raisin. Waylon must have sensed my desperation because he lay down on my feet under the table. "How about we talk about something else. Anything else. Religion? Politics? Bloodthirsty sports rivalries?"

"Sure nice havin' you boys at the table at the same time," Liza J said. "This mean I don't have to do Thanksgiving in two shifts this year?"

"We'll see," Nash said, eyeing his brother.

I could feel the tension between them.

Not wanting to have dinner end in a wrestling match, I desperately changed the subject. "You know, I didn't actually steal the car."

"That's what Knox said when Mrs. Wheelan down at the Pop 'N Stop caught him with a pocket full of candy," Nash said.

"Not all of us were born with Dudley Do-Right shoved up our ass."

"For God's sake, Knox. Language." I elbowed him in the arm and pointed at Waylay.

She flashed him a toothy grin. "I don't mind."

"Well, *I* do."

Fireflies winked in and out of existence in the dusk as Knox and Waylay pitched pebbles into the creek. All three dogs took turns dashing into the creek, then turning around to shake themselves dry on the bank.

Waylay's giggle and Knox's low murmur echoing off the water made me feel like maybe today wasn't the worst day ever.

I had a belly full of sloppy joes and a cozy house to return to.

"Doin' okay?" Nash came up next to me on the grass. He had a nice, calming presence. I didn't feel the exasperation around him that I did with Knox.

"I think so." I turned to look at him. "Thank you. For everything. It's been a stressful day. You and Liza and I guess even your brother made it better for Waylay and me."

"Way's a good kid," he said. "She's smart. Independent. A lot of us in town know that."

I thought about the scene in the grocery store. "I hope you're right. And I hope I can do right by her until we get things figured out."

"That reminds me. I brought this for you," he said, handing over a brochure that it was too dark to read. "It's about kinship custody arrangements."

"Oh. Thanks."

"Basically, you're looking at an application process with a few legal hoops to jump through. If all that goes well, you'll have six months to decide if you want to make it permanent."

Permanent? The word sent me reeling.

I stared unseeing as Waylay and Knox took turns throwing a soggy tennis ball for the dogs.

"I asked around about Tina," Nash continued. "Rumor has it she got herself a new man a few weeks back, and there were whispers about some big score."

A new man and a big score were both painfully on-brand for my sister. "Do you really think she might not come back?"

Nash edged into my line of sight and dipped down until I looked him in the eye. "That's the thing, Naomi. She does come back, she's in a lot of trouble. No court's gonna be thrilled with the idea of letting her retain custody."

"And if it's not me, it's foster care," I said, filling in the unspoken blanks.

"That's the long and the short of it," he said. "I know it's a big decision, and I'm not askin' you to make it right this second. Get to know her. Get to know the town. Think on it. I've got a friend who does casework. She can help you get started with the application process."

He was asking me to put the next six months of my life on hold for a little girl I'd just met. Yep. It was safe to say my bruised and battered life plan had officially disintegrated.

I blew out a sigh and decided tomorrow was as good a day as any for panicking over the future.

"Waylay! It's time to go," I called.

Waylon galloped to me, ears flying. He spit the tennis ball out at my feet.

"Not you, buddy," I said, leaning down to pet him.

"Do we have to?" Waylay whined, dragging her feet as if they were encased in concrete.

I shared similar sentiments.

Knox put his hand on the top of her head and guided her in my direction. "Get used to it, kid. Sometimes we all gotta do things we don't want to."

9

Backyard Urination and Dewey Decimal

Naomi

I found the cottage's back porch to be a lovely little spot for organizing my daily to-do list by priority as I waited for the pot of coffee to brew. I'd slept. Like a coma patient. And when my eyelids popped open at 6:15 on the dot, I'd tiptoed across the hall to Waylay's room and peeked in to make sure my niece was still there.

She was. Tucked between fresh sheets in a white four-poster bed.

I stared down at my list and tapped the end of a blue highlighter against the page. I needed to contact my parents and let them know I was alive and not having some kind of breakdown. But I wasn't sure how much else to tell them.

Hey, guys, you remember your other daughter? The one who gave you migraines for twenty years before she vanished from our lives? Yeah, well, she has a daughter who has no idea you exist.

They'd disembark from their cruise ship in a hot minute and be on the first plane headed in our direction. Waylay had just been abandoned by her own mother and was now under the roof of an aunt she'd never met. Introducing grandparents into the

114

mix might not be the best idea this soon out of the gate.

Plus, it was my parents' first vacation together in ten years. They deserved three weeks of peace and quiet.

The choice was only *partially* weighted in favor of the fact that I wouldn't have to come up with a diplomatic way to explain that they had missed out on the first eleven years of their only grandchild's life. Yet.

I didn't like doing things until I knew the exact right way to do them. So I would wait until I knew Waylay a little better and my parents were back from their anniversary cruise, well rested and ready for crazy news.

Satisfied, I collected my notebook and highlighters and was just about ready to stand when I heard the distant squeak of a screen door.

Next door, Waylon trotted down the back stairs into the yard, where he promptly lifted his leg on a dead spot he clearly enjoyed using as a toilet. I smiled, and then the muscles of my face froze when another movement caught my eye.

Knox "the Viking" Morgan strolled off the deck in nothing but a pair of black boxer briefs. He was *all* man. Muscles, chest hair, tattoos. He stretched one arm lazily overhead and scratched the back of his neck, creating a picture of sleepy testosterone. It took me a full ten seconds of open-mouthed ogling to realize the man, like his dog, was peeing.

My highlighters flying made a rapid-fire racket

as they hit the wooden planks beneath me. Time froze as Knox turned in my direction. He was facing me with one hand on his . . . Nope.

Nope. Nope. Nope.

I left my highlighters where they were and fled for the safety of the cottage, all the while congratulating myself for not trying to get a better look at Knox Jr.

"Why's your face so red? You get sunburnt?"

I let out a shriek and crashed back against the screen door, nearly falling out onto the porch.

Waylay was standing on a chair trying to reach the Pop-Tarts I'd hidden above the fridge.

"You're so jumpy," she accused.

Carefully, I closed the door, leaving all thoughts of urinating men in the outside world. "Put the Pop-Tarts down. We're having eggs for breakfast."

"Aww, man."

I ignored her disdain and placed the house's only skillet on the stove. "How do you feel about going to the library today?"

The Knockemout Public Library was a sanctuary of cool and quiet in the Virginia summer swelter. It was a light, bright space with white oak shelves and farm-style work tables. Pairs of overstuffed armchairs were clustered by the tall windows.

Just inside the door was a large community bulletin board. Everything from piano lessons to yard sale announcements and charity bike rides dotted the corkboard in evenly spaced increments.

Beneath it sat a gray-washed table displaying several genres of books from steamy romance to autobiographies to poetry.

Glossy green plants in blue and yellow pots added life on shelves and sunny, flat surfaces. There was a colorful kids section with bright wallpaper and a rainbow of floor cushions. Quiet instrumental music murmured from hidden speakers. It felt more like a high-end spa than a public library. I approved.

Behind the long, low circulation desk was a woman who caught the eye. Tan skin. Red lipstick. Long, sleek blond hair streaked with a warm purply pink. The frames of her glasses were blue, and a tiny stud winked in her nose.

The only thing that screamed "librarian" about her was the large stack of hardbacks she carried.

"Hey, Way," she called. "You got a line already upstairs."

"Thanks, Sloane."

"You have a line for what?" I asked.

"Nothing," my niece mumbled.

"Tech support," the attractive and surprisingly loud librarian announced. "We get a lot of older folks who don't have access to their own eleven-year-olds to fix their phones and Kindles and tablets."

I recalled Liza J's comment at dinner the night before.

Which made me recall Knox and his penis this morning.

Whoops.

"The computers are over there near the coffee bar and the restrooms, Aunt Naomi. I'll be on the second floor if you need anything."

"Coffee bar?" I parroted, trying not to think of my nearly naked next-door neighbor.

But my charge was already striding purposefully past the book stacks toward an open staircase in the back.

The librarian tossed me a curious look as she shelved a Stephen King novel. "You're not Tina," she said.

"How'd you know?"

"I've never seen Tina so much as drop Waylay off here, let alone willingly cross the threshold."

"Tina's my sister," I explained.

"I gathered that from the whole you-look-almost-exactly-alike thing. How long have you been in town? I can't believe there hasn't been a trail of hot gossip blazed to my doorstep."

"I got in yesterday."

"Ah. My day off. I knew I shouldn't have buried myself in my fourth rewatch of *Ted Lasso*," she complained to no one. "Anyway, I'm Sloane." She juggled novels in order to hold out a hand.

I shook it tentatively, not wanting to dislodge the twenty pounds of literature she still held. "Naomi."

"Welcome to Knockemout, Naomi. Your niece is a godsend."

It was nice hearing good things about the Witt family around here for a change.

"Thank you. We're, uh, just getting to know each other, but she seems smart and independent."

Annnnd hopefully not too damaged.

"Wanna see her in action?" Sloane offered.

"I want it even more than a visit to your coffee bar."

Sloane's ruby-red lips curved. "Follow me."

I followed Sloane up the open staircase to the second floor, which housed even more book stacks, more seating, more plants, and a few private rooms off to one side.

In the back was another long, low desk under a hanging sign that said Community. Waylay sat on a stool behind the desk, frowning at an electronic device. The device's owner, an elderly Black man in a crisp button-down and trousers, leaned on the counter.

"That's Hinkel McCord. He's 101 years old and reads two books a week. He keeps messing with the settings on his e-reader," Sloane explained.

"I swear it's the damn great-grandkids. Those sticky-fingered little punks see an electronic device, and they go after it like kids went after sticks and candy in my day," Hinkel complained.

"She started coming in here a couple times a week after she and your sister moved here. One afternoon, some virus software update was giving the entire system shit, and Waylay got tired of listening to me yell at the computer. She popped behind the desk and voilà." Sloane wiggled her fingers in the air. "Fixed the whole damn thing in less than five minutes. So I asked her if she minded helping out a few other folks. I pay her in snacks and letting her check out double the number of books everyone else is allowed. She's a great kid."

I suddenly just wanted to sit down and cry. Apparently my face telegraphed just that.

"Uh-oh. You okay?" Sloane asked, looking concerned.

I nodded, willing away the damp from my eyes. "I'm just so happy," I managed to choke out.

"Oh boy. How about a nice box of tissues and an espresso?" she suggested, guiding me away from a group of senior citizens settled around a table. "Belinda, I have the latest Kennedy Ryan novel you were asking for."

A woman with a puff of white hair and a large crucifix nearly buried in her impressive cleavage clapped her hands. "Sloane, you are my favorite human being."

"That's what they all say," she said with a wink.

"Did you say espresso?" I whimpered.

Sloane nodded. "We have really good coffee here," she promised.

"Will you marry me?"

She grinned, and her nose stud sparkled. "I'm mostly into men these days. There was that one time in college."

She guided me into an annex with four computers and a U-shaped counter. There was a sink, a dishwasher, and a small refrigerator with a sign that said *FREE WATER*. Coffee mugs hung from cute hooks.

Sloane headed directly for the coffee maker and got to work. "You look like at least a double," she observed.

"I wouldn't say no to a triple."

"I knew I liked you. Have a seat."

I planted myself at one of the computers and tried to compose myself. "I've never seen a library like this," I said, desperate to make small talk that wouldn't render me an emotional lump of feelings.

Sloane flashed a smile at me. "That's what I like to hear. When I was a kid, the local library was my sanctuary. It wasn't until I got older that I realized that it still wasn't accessible to everyone. So I went to school for library science and public administration, and here we are." She set a cup in front of me and returned to the machine. "It's all about community. We've got free classes on everything from sex education and budgeting to meditation and meal prepping. We don't have a huge homeless population here, but we've got locker rooms and a small laundry facility in the basement. I'm working on free after-school programs to help families who can't swing the cost of day care. And of course there's the books."

Her face went soft and dreamy.

"Wow." I picked up my coffee, sipped, then said wow again.

A soft chime sounded over the music.

"That's the bat signal. Gotta go," she said. "Enjoy your coffee, and good luck with your feelings."

• • •

Naomi Witt checking account balance: Overdrawn. Suspected fraud.

Dear Mom and Dad,
I'm alive, safe, and completely sane. I swear. I'm so sorry I left like that. I know it was uncharacteristic. Things just weren't working out with Warner and . . . I'll explain some other time when you're not sailing off to paradise.

In the meantime, have a wonderful time and I forbid you from worrying about me. I stopped in a charming little town in Virginia and am enjoying the volume the humidity gives my hair.

Soak up some sun and send me proof of life pictures every day.

Love,
Naomi

P.S. I almost forgot. There was a teensy accident with my phone and unfortunately it didn't survive. Email is the best way to communicate for now! Love you lots! Don't worry about me!

Dear Stef,
I know. I'm sorry. I'm sorry. I'm sorry. Please don't hate me! We need to talk soon. But not on my phone since I ran over it at a rest stop in Pennsylvania.

Funny story. You'd think me running out on the wedding was the big news. (You looked great, by the way.) But the bigger whammy is my sister called me out of the blue, robbed me, and left me with a niece I didn't know existed.

Her name is Waylay. She's an eleven-year-old tech genius and underneath the bored facade might be a girly girl. I need reassurances that I'm not adding to her trauma.

I'm trying to be the cool yet responsible aunt in this place called Knockemout, where the men are unreasonably attractive and the coffee is excellent.

I'll be in touch as soon as I get my bearings. There was an incident with my car and my checking account. Oh and my laptop.

I'm still sorry. Please don't hate me.

Kisses,
N

Tina,
This is the last email address I have for you. Where the hell are you? How could you leave Waylay? Where's my freaking car? Get your ass back here. Are you in trouble?

Naomi

KINSHIP GUARDIAN TO-DO LIST

- Complete guardianship application, plus background check

- Participate in three face-to-face interviews with applicant
- Provide three character references (experience with children and caretaking)
- Home study
- Dispositional hearing with family court

10

Haircuts and Pains in the Ass

Knox

I was in a shit mood after a shit night's sleep.

Both of which I blamed on Naomi "Flowers in her Fucking Hair" Witt. After spending half the night tossing and turning, I'd woken up for Waylon's first a.m. bathroom break with a raging hard-on thanks to a dream featuring my new next-door neighbor's smart mouth sliding down my cock, the kind of noises that men fantasize about coming out of her throat.

It was the second night of sleep she'd ruined for me, and if I didn't get my head out of my ass, it wouldn't be the last.

Beside me in the passenger seat, Waylon expressed his own exhaustion with a loud yawn.

"You and me both, bud," I said, pulling into a parking space and staring at the storefront.

The color scheme—navy with maroon trim—shouldn't have worked. It had sounded stupid when Jeremiah suggested it. But somehow it classed up the brick and made Whiskey Clipper stand out on the block.

It was wedged between a tattoo parlor that changed hands more often than poker chips and

125

the neon-orange awning of Dino's Pizza and Subs. They didn't open until eleven, but I could already smell the garlic and pizza sauce.

Until a few years ago, the barbershop had been a crumbling institution in Knockemout. With a little vision from my partner, Jeremiah, and a lot of capital from me, we'd managed to drag Whiskey Clipper into the twenty-first century and turn it into a small-town gold mine. Now a trendy salon, the shop didn't just serve old men born and raised here. It attracted a clientele that was willing to brave the NOVA traffic from as far away as downtown DC for the service and the vibe.

On a yawn of my own, I helped my dog out of the truck, and we headed for the front door.

The inside was as eye-catching as the outside. The bones of the space were exposed brick, tin ceiling, and stained concrete. We'd added leather and wood and denim. Next to the industrial-looking reception desk was a bar with glass shelves housing nearly a dozen whiskey bottles. We also served coffee and wine. The walls were decorated with framed black-and-white prints, most highlighting Knockemout's storied history.

Beyond the leather couches in the reception area, there were four hair stations with large round mirrors. Along the back wall were the restroom, the shampoo sinks, and the dryers.

"Mornin', boss. You're here early." Stasia, short for Anastasia, had Browder Klein's head in one of the sinks.

I grunted and went straight for the coffeepot next to the whiskey. Waylon climbed up on the couch next to a woman enjoying a coffee and Baileys.

Stasia's teenage son, Ricky, swiveled back and forth rhythmically in the reception chair. Between booking appointments and cashing out clients, he played a stupid-looking game on his phone.

Jeremiah, my business partner and longtime friend, looked up from the temple fade he was doing on a client in a suit and $400 shoes.

"You look like shit," he observed.

Jeremiah wore his thick, dark hair rebelliously long but kept his face clean-shaven. He had a sleeve tattoo and a Rolex. He got a manicure every two weeks and spent his days off tinkering with the dirt bikes he occasionally raced. He dated both men and women—a fact that his parents were fine with but which his Lebanese grandmother still prayed over every Sunday at mass.

"Thanks, asshole. Nice to see you too."

"Sit," he said, pointing with the clippers at the empty station next to him.

"I don't have time for your judgmental grooming." I had shit to do. Paperwork to be inconvenienced by. Women to not think about.

"And I don't have time for you to bring down our vibe looking like you couldn't even be bothered to run a comb and some balm through that beard."

Defensively, I stroked a hand over my beard. "No one cares what I look like."

"We care," the woman with the Baileys and coffee called.

"Amen, Louise," Stasia called back, shooting me one of her mom looks.

Browder got to his feet and clapped a hand on my back. "You look tired. Got some bags under those eyes. Woman trouble?"

"Heard you went a few rounds with Not Tina," Stasia said innocently as she ushered Browder to her chair. The one thing Stasia and Jeremiah loved more than good hair was good gossip.

Not Tina. Great.

"Name's Naomi."

"Oooooooh" came the obnoxious chorus.

"I hate you guys."

"No, you don't," Jeremiah assured me with a grin as he finished the fade.

"Fuck off."

"Don't forget, you've got a cut at two and a staff meeting at three," Stasia called after me.

I swore under my breath and headed to my lair. I handled the business end, so my client roster was smaller than Jeremiah's or Stasia's. I'd have thought that by now, most of my clients would have been scared off by my excessive scowling and lack of small talk. But it turned out some people liked having an asshole cut their hair.

"Going to my office," I said and heard the thud of Waylon's body hitting the floor and the *tip-tap* of his nails on the floor following me.

I'd already owned Honky Tonk when this

building went up for sale. I bought it out from under some shiny-loafered developer out of Baltimore who wanted to put in a chain sports bar and a fucking Pilates studio.

Now the building was home to my bar, the barbershop, and three killer apartments on the second floor. One of which was rented by my jackass brother.

I headed past the restroom and the tiny staff kitchen to the door marked Employees Only. Inside was a supply room lined with shelving units and all the shit required to run a successful salon. On the back wall was an unmarked door.

Waylon caught up to me as I fished out my keys. He was the only one allowed in my inner sanctum. I wasn't one of those "my door is always open" bosses. If I needed to meet with staff, I used my business manager's office or the break room.

I headed into the narrow hallway that connected the salon to the bar and punched the code into the keypad on my office door.

Waylon bolted inside the second it opened.

The space was small and utilitarian, with brick walls and exposed ducting in the ceiling. There was a couch, a small fridge, and a desk that held a state-of-the-art computer with two monitors the size of scoreboards.

Over a dozen framed photos on the walls depicted a haphazard collage of my life. There was Waylon as a puppy, tripping over his long ears. Me and Nash. Shirtless, gap-toothed kids on mountain bikes in one. Men on the backs of motorcycles, adventure stretching out before us on the ribbon of open road, in another.

We two became three with the addition of Lucian Rollins. There, on the wall no one else saw, was a photographic time line of us growing up as brothers—bloody noses, long days in the creek, then graduating to cars and girls and football. Bonfires and Friday night football games. Graduations. Vacations. Ribbon cuttings.

Jesus, we were getting old. Time marched on. And for the first time, I felt a niggle of guilt that Nash and I no longer had each other's backs.

But it was just another example of how relationships didn't last forever.

My gaze lingered on one of the smaller frames. The color was duller than the rest. My parents bundled up in a tent. Mom grinning at the camera, pregnant with one of us. Dad looking at her like he'd waited his whole life for her. Both excited for the adventure of a lifetime together.

It wasn't there for nostalgia. It served as a reminder that no matter how good things were in the moment, they were bound to get worse until that once bright, shiny future was unrecognizable.

Waylon deflated on a sigh, pancaking onto his bed.

"You and me both," I told him.

I dropped into the chair behind the desk and fired up my computer, ready to rule my empire.

Social media ad campaigns for Whiskey Clipper

130

and Honky Tonk topped my list of things to do today. I'd been avoiding them long enough because they annoyed me. Growth disguised as change was, unfortunately, a necessary evil.

Perversely, I shuffled the ads to the bottom of my stack and tackled the schedule at Honky Tonk for the next two weeks. There was a hole. I rubbed the back of my neck and dialed Fi.

"What's up, boss?" she asked. Someone grunted obscenely next to her.

"Where are you?"

"Family jujitsu. I just threw Roger over my shoulder, and he's looking for his kidneys."

Fi's family was a shaken cocktail of weird, but they all seemed to like life better that way.

"My condolences to Roger's kidneys. Why is there a hole in the server schedule?"

"Chrissie quit last week. Remember?"

I vaguely remembered a server with a face and hair scurrying out of my way every time I stepped out of my office.

"Why'd she quit?"

"You scared the shit out of her. Called her a tray-dropping gold digger and told her to give up on marrying rich because even rich guys want their beers cold."

It rang a bell. Vaguely.

I grunted. "So who's replacing her?"

"I already hired a new girl. She starts tonight."

"Does she have experience, or is this another Crystal?"

"Chrissie," Fi corrected. "And unless you want to start doing your own hiring, I suggest you gracefully back down and tell me I've been doing a kick-ass job and you trust my instincts."

I yanked the phone away from my ear when Fi let out an ear-splitting "Hi-ya!"

"You've been doing a kick-ass job, and I trust your instincts," I muttered.

"That's a good boy. Now, if you'll excuse me, I have to put my son on his ass in front of his crush."

"Try not to splatter too much blood. It's a bitch to clean up."

Waylon let out a snore from the floor. I penciled in "New Girl" on the empty shifts and jumped into some vendor payments and other bullshit paperwork.

Both Whiskey Clipper and Honky Tonk were showing consistent growth, and two of the three apartments were rented for additional income. I was pleased with the numbers. It meant that I'd managed to do the impossible and turn dumb luck into an actual solid future. Between the businesses and my investments, I'd taken a windfall and built on it.

It was a good feeling even after a sleepless night. With nothing left to do, I reluctantly called up Facebook. Advertising was one kind of evil, but advertising that required you to have a social media presence that opened you up to millions of pain-in-the-ass strangers? That was straight-up bullshit.

I bet Naomi was on Facebook. She probably liked it too.

My fingers casually typed Naomi Witt into the search bar before the sane, rational part of me could hit the brakes.

"Huh."

Waylon lifted his head quizzically.

"Just checking on our neighbor. Making sure she's not into Amway sales or running a long con as a pretend twin," I told him.

Satisfied that I would save him from whatever threats social media held, Waylon fell back to sleep with a rumbling snore.

The woman obviously had never heard of privacy settings. There was a lot of her to get to know on social media. Pictures from work, vacations, family holidays. All without Tina, I noted. She ran 5Ks for good causes and raised funds for neighbor's vet bills. And she lived in a nice-looking house at least twice the size of the cottage.

She went to high school and college reunions and looked damn good doing it.

Throwback pictures proved my theory that she'd been a cheerleader. And someone on the yearbook committee had been a fan, since it seemed like her entire senior year had been dedicated to her. I blinked at the handful of pictures of Naomi and Tina. The twin thing was undeniable. So was the fact that, beneath the surface, they were very different women.

I was already invested. There was no pulling me

out of the online stalking rabbit hole. Especially not when the only other things I had to do were boring.

So I dug further.

Tina Witt fell off the digital plane of existence after high school graduation. She didn't smile in her cap and gown. Certainly not next to young, fresh Naomi with her honor cords.

She'd already had an arrest record by then. Yet there was Naomi, an arm around her sister's waist, beaming wide enough for the two of them. I was willing to bet money that she'd done what she could to be the good one. To be the low-maintenance kid. The one who didn't cause their parents sleepless nights.

I wondered how much living she'd missed out on wasting all that time being good.

I followed the Tina line a little deeper, discovering a trail on Pennsylvania District Magistrate court cases and then again in New Jersey and Maryland. DUIs, possession, skipping out on rent. She'd done time about twelve years ago. Not much, but enough to have made a point. Enough to have her becoming a mother less than a year later and steering clear of the cops.

I went back to Naomi's Facebook and stopped on a family picture from her teenage years. Tina scowling, with her arms crossed next to her sister as their parents beamed behind them. I didn't know what went on behind closed doors, but I did know that sometimes a bad seed was just a bad seed. No matter what field it was planted in, no matter how it was tended, some just came up rotten.

A glance at the clock reminded me I only had a little time before my two o'clock. Which meant I should get back to the ad campaigns.

But unlike Naomi, I didn't like worrying about what I "should" do. I typed her name into a search engine and had immediate regrets.

Warner Dennison III and Naomi Witt announce their engagement.

This Dennison guy looked like the kind of asshole who hung out on golf courses and always had a story to top everyone else's. Sure, he was vice president of whatever, but it was at a company with his last name on it. I doubted he'd earned his fancy title. Judging from her face this morning, this Warner suit had never taken a piss in the great outdoors.

Naomi looked heart-stoppingly gorgeous, not to mention happy, in the formal photo. Which for some stupid reason annoyed me. What did I care if she was into men who ironed their pants? My next-door neighbor was no longer any of my damn business. I'd found her and Waylay a place to stay. Anything that happened from here on out was her own problem.

I closed out of the window on my screen. Naomi Witt no longer existed to me. I felt good about that.

My phone buzzed on the desk, and Waylon's head popped up.

"Yeah?" I answered.

"Vernon's here. Want me to get him started?" Jeremiah offered.

"Get him a whiskey. I'm on my way out."

"Will do."

"There he is!" Vernon Quigg called when I returned to the shop. The retired marine was six feet tall, seventy years old, and the proud owner of an impeccable walrus mustache.

I was the only person allowed near the 'stache with scissors. It was both an honor and an annoyance, seeing as how the man loved nothing more than fresh gossip.

"Afternoon, Vernon," I said, clipping the cape around his neck.

"Heard about you and Not Tina throwin' down in Café Rev yesterday," he said gleefully. "Sounds like those twins are carbon copies of each other."

"I heard that she's the complete opposite of her sister," Stasia said, plopping down in the empty chair next to my station.

I reached for my comb and gritted my teeth.

"I heard there's a warrant out for Tina, and Not Tina helped her escape," said Doris Bacon, owner of Bacon Stables, a farm with a reputation for turning out champion horseflesh.

Fuck me.

11

The Boss from Hell

Naomi

I accepted the leather and denim apron Sherry "Fi" Fiasco handed me and tied it around my waist.

"Shirt looks good," Sherry said, giving my Honky Tonk V-neck an approving nod.

"Thanks," I said and tugged nervously at the hem. The shirt was tight and showed more cleavage than I was used to accentuating. But per my research at the library, ladies with their "girls" showing tended to make higher tips.

Honky Tonk felt like a country bar that had a brief but satisfying affair with a glitzy speakeasy. I liked the "fancy cowboy" vibe.

"This here's Maxine, and she'll be training you on the POS," Fi said, plucking the lollipop out of her mouth. "It's also how you clock in and out and order your own meals. Here's your PIN." She handed over a sticky note with 6969 scrawled across it in Sharpie.

Nice.

"Hi," I said to Maxine. She had dark skin dusted with glitter over her enviable cheekbones and modest cleavage. Her hair was cut short and left to curl tightly in tiny magenta coils.

"Call me Max," she insisted. "You ever sling drinks before?"

I shook my head. "I worked in HR until two days ago."

I gave her points for not rolling her eyes at me. I wouldn't want to train me either.

"But I learn fast," I assured her.

"Well, you're gonna have to since we're short-handed tonight. So unless you suck, I'll be pushing you out of the nest early."

"I'll do my best not to suck," I promised.

"You do that. We'll start with the drinks for my eight-top. We've got two drafts of Bud," Maxine began, fingers flying over the screen. Her glittery nails hypnotized me with their speed.

I was nervous but highly motivated. My bank had told me it would take up to a week for me to receive my replacement debit and credit cards. And Waylay had already polished off the entire box of Pop-Tarts. If I wanted to keep my niece in groceries, I was going to have to be the best damn server this town had ever seen.

"Then you hit Send, and the printer at the bar spits out the order. Same for food, only it goes straight to the kitchen," Max explained.

"Got it."

"Great. Here's the next one. Your turn."

I only fumbled twice and earned a "good enough" nod from my trainer.

"Let's get those tips flowing. I hope your feet are prepared," Maxine said with a quick grin.

I blew out a breath and followed her into the crowd.

My feet hurt. I was hours behind on my water intake. And I was really tired of explaining that I wasn't Tina. Especially since that seemed to have earned me the nickname Not Tina.

Silver the bartender said something that I missed as I wearily unloaded glasses at the service bar.

"What?" I yelled over the music.

"Hangin' in there?" she repeated louder this time.

"I think so." Max had given me two tables of "understanding regulars" to handle on my own, and so far, no one besides me was wearing beer or complaining about how long it took to get their brisket nachos, so I felt like I was doing an adequate job.

I felt like I'd walked ten miles just going between the bar and the tables.

Most of the patrons seemed like regulars. They knew each other's names and drink orders and razzed each other over sports rivalries.

The kitchen staff was nice enough. And while Silver wasn't exactly friendly, she was a pro pulling pints with both hands while taking a to-go order over the phone.

I admired her efficiency.

I'd just dropped off a fresh round of drinks when I realized I'd spent the last few hours not thinking about . . . well, anything. I hadn't had time to worry about Waylay at Liza J's or about the four emails from Warner I hadn't opened. And the small roll of cash in my apron made me forget all about my thieving sister and my overdrawn accounts.

I also hadn't given my hot, grumpy, urinating neighbor a passing thought.

That was when I lost my focus and walked smack into a solid wall of chest under a black T-shirt.

"Pardon me," I said, slapping a hand to the muscley obstacle to stay upright.

"What the fuck are you doing?"

Not. Again.

"Are you kidding me?" I squeaked, looking up to find Knox scowling at me.

"What are you doing here, Naomi?"

"I'm checking Santa's naughty list. What does it look like I'm doing? I'm working. Now get out of my way, or I'll hit you with my tray, and I've had a *lot* of espresso today. I could get you on the floor in three or four whacks."

He didn't respond verbally. Probably because he was too busy taking me by the arm and dragging me out into the hallway. He stormed past the restrooms and the kitchen door and opened the next door with a well-placed boot.

"Evenin', Knox," Fi said without looking up from her monitors.

"What the fuck is this?" he snapped.

Sherry spared him a glance. "This?" she repeated blandly.

He pulled me farther into the room. "This," he said again.

"This is Naomi. A human person who is halfway into her first shift," Sherry said, going back to her monitors.

"Don't want her working here, Fi."

I'd had enough of the pissed-off-at-the-world-in-general-and-me-in-particular routine. I yanked my arm free and whacked him in the chest with my tray.

Sherry looked up again, her mouth falling open.

"I don't care if you don't want me working here, Viking. Fi hired me. I'm here. Now, unless you have a reason for detaining me at a job I desperately need, you blond Oscar the Grouch, I suggest you take up your hiring concerns with this establishment's management."

"I *am* this establishment's management," he snarled.

Great. *Of course* he was management. I'd hit my new boss with a tray.

"I wouldn't have taken this job if I'd known you managed this place," I bit out.

"Now you know. Get out."

"Knox," Sherry sighed wearily. "We needed a replacement for the server you scared off with all your scowling and Oscar the Grouching."

He pointed a threatening finger in her direction. "I'm not letting you make that a thing. Call what's her name and get her to unquit."

Sherry leaned back and crossed her arms. "If you can tell me her name, I'll call her up right now."

Knox muttered a curse.

"That's what I thought," she said smugly. "Now, who makes the hiring decisions around here?"

"I don't give a shit if it's the damn pope," he growled. "She's not working here. *I* don't want her around."

Deciding I had nothing to lose, I hit him again with the tray. "Listen, Viking, I don't know what your problem is with me. Whatever narcissistic, delusional roller coaster you're on, I'm *not* here to ruin your life. I'm trying to earn back some of the money my sister stole from me, and until the bank unfreezes my account, I'm not letting you or anyone else stand in the way of Waylay's Pop-Tarts."

"Unless you want to take her tables for her, boss, I'm siding with Naomi," Sherry said.

Knox's eyes glowed with icy fire. "Fuck. Fine. One shift. You make one mistake, get one complaint, and your ass is gone."

"Your magnanimity won't be forgotten. I've got tables waiting."

"One mistake," he called after me.

I flipped him off over my shoulder and stormed into the hall.

"Get rid of her, Fi. I'm not working with some uppity, needy pain in the ass." His words carried to me outside the door. My cheeks flamed.

An uppity, needy pain in the ass. So that was what the gorgeous, bad-tempered Knox Morgan saw when he looked at me.

142

• • •

I kept it together, pushing all thoughts of my stupid boss out of my mind and putting my full attention into getting the right drinks to the right people, busing tables for turnover, and being helpful wherever I could.

I squeezed in the shortest dinner break in the history of dinner breaks, sneaking a pit stop at the bathroom and a few bites of a spectacularly good grilled chicken salad from Milford in the kitchen. Then I made a beeline for the bar, where Silver was pouring a stream of liquor into a cocktail shaker with one hand and opening a beer bottle with the other.

Her hair was buzzed short, leaving nothing to distract from the dramatic smoky eye makeup and tiny eyebrow ring. The sleeves of her black blazer were rolled up, and she wore a striped tie loose over a Honky Tonk tank. She was androgynously attractive in a way that made me feel like an eighth grader with a crush on the cool girl.

"Silver, do you mind if I use the phone to check in with my babysitter?" I asked over the thump of the music.

She jerked her head toward the phone between the two tap systems, and I took that as approval.

I checked my watch and dialed the cottage's number. Liza J answered on the third ring.

"We ordered pizza stead of eatin' that mound of veggies you left us," she said over the blare of the TV on her end.

"Are those gunshots?" I asked, plugging my ear with a finger so I could hear her over the musical stylings of country singer Mickey Guyton on my end.

"Can you believe she's never seen *The Usual Suspects*?" Liza J scoffed.

"Liza!"

"Relax. We're just shooting real guns in the house, not watching R-rated movies."

"Liza!"

"You're right. Your aunt really is wound tighter than a necktie on Friday," Liza J said, presumably to my big-mouthed niece. "Everything's fine. Way helped me in the garden. We ate pizza, and now we're watching a PG-13, edited-for-TV action movie. Sylvester Stallone just called someone a poop head."

I sighed. "Thank you so much for this. I really appreciate it."

"Kinda nice to have company for once. When's your next shift?"

I bit my lip. "I'm not sure. This might be a one and done. My new boss doesn't seem to like me."

She laughed softly. "Give him time."

I realized my babysitting fairy godmother had predicted this and wondered what she knew that I didn't.

"This ain't social hour. Get your ass off the phone, Daisy."

I gritted my teeth at Knox's interruption. "Your grandson says hi."

Liza J chuckled. "Tell him to kiss my ass and to pick up a rotisserie chicken for me tomorrow. I'll see ya when ya get home," she said.

"Thanks again. I owe you. Bye."

I turned and found Knox looming over me like a sexy turkey vulture. "Your grandmother says kiss her ass and bring her a rotisserie chicken."

"Why are you on the phone with *my* grandma on *your* first and last bar shift?"

"Because she's watching my eleven-year-old niece so I can earn money for groceries and back-to-school clothes, you uncharitable oaf!"

"Figures," he muttered.

"Lay off, Knox," Silver said as she shook two cocktail shakers at once. "You know being a dick costs you in turnover."

"I *want* this one to turn over," he insisted. "Why don't you hide in the kitchen and text like everyone else?"

"Because I don't have a cell phone," I reminded him.

"Who in the fuck doesn't have a cell phone?"

"Someone who lost hers in a tragic rest stop accident," I shot back. "I'd love to continue this stimulating conversation, but I need to help Max turn over some tables."

"You tell him, Not Tina," Hinkel McCord crowed from his barstool.

Knox looked like he was going to pick him up and hurl him through the door. I took a cleansing breath and did what I did best—stuffed all my feelings into a little box with a tight lid. "Is there something you need before I go back to work?"

His eyes narrowed at my polite tone. We stared each other down until we were interrupted.

"There she is," a familiar voice boomed over the din.

"Justice!" My café-owning future husband had his arm around a beautiful woman.

"I brought the wife so she could meet my fiancée," Justice joked.

"Wait'll Muriel hears about this," Hinkel cackled, whipping out his phone.

"I'm Tallulah St. John," Justice's wife said, leaning over the bar to offer her hand. "Hubs told me all about your first day in town." She was tall with a cascade of long braids down her back. She was wearing a St. John Garage T-shirt, jeans, and cowboy boots. "Sorry I missed your first time in the café. Heard it was quite a show."

"This one hasn't been half-bad either," Hinkel interjected.

"It's nice to meet you, Tallulah," I said. "I'm sorry for proposing to your husband, but the man makes coffee that angels sing about."

"Don't I know it," she agreed.

"Where's your section? We're here to patronize you," Justice said.

Knox rolled his eyes.

"Don't mind him," Silver said, elbowing the boss out of the way. "He's just pissy because Nay hasn't screwed up yet."

I wanted to kiss her for giving me a nickname other than Not Tina.

"He gave me one shift and no mistakes," I explained, not caring that he was standing behind me.

"Knox Morgan," Tallulah chided. "That's not how we welcome new Knockemouts. Where's your sense of community?"

"Go away, Tally," Knox grumbled, but there was no heat to it.

"Naomi, I'll have your darkest, strongest beer," Tallulah said. "And the hubs here will have a piña colada with whipped cream."

Justice rubbed his palms together in anticipation. "And we'll split an order of the pulled pork flatbread. Extra jalapeños."

"No sour cream," Tallulah interjected.

"You got it," I said with a wink. "Have a seat, and I'll bring your drinks right out."

"You gonna write that down?" Knox asked as the couple wove their way through the crowd.

I flipped my hair over my shoulder. "Nope."

He looked at his watch and smirked. "You won't even make it to the end of the shift at this rate."

"I'll be happy to prove you wrong."

"In that case, you just got yourself another table."

He pointed to a rowdy table in the corner where an older man with a potbelly and a cowboy hat appeared to be holding court.

"Don't do that to her on her first night, Knoxy," Max chided him.

"If she's so confident she can handle it, no use letting her wade around in the kiddie pool. Gotta throw her in the deep end."

"There's a difference between sink or swim when you introduce sharks," Silver argued.

12

A Ride Home

Knox

I had paperwork to do, but I was more interested in the impending crash and burn of my newest employee.

Naomi strutted her high-class ass right on up to the table like an idealistic kindergarten teacher on her first day. I hated Wylie Ogden for good reason, but I didn't mind using him to prove my point.

She didn't belong here. And if I had to prove that by dangling her in front of a wolf, then so be it.

Wylie's squinty little eyes zeroed in on her, and his tongue darted out between his lips. He knew the rules. Knew I wouldn't hesitate to toss his ass out of here if he so much as touched one of my employees. But that didn't stop him from being a creepy old man.

"What's your problem with Not Tina?" Silver asked, punching the button on the blender and pouring vodka into three rocks glasses.

I didn't reply. Answering questions only encouraged conversations.

I watched as Wylie lavished Naomi with his pervy brand of attention without feeling the least bit guilty.

She wasn't my type on any plane of existence. Hell, even in jeans and a Honky Tonk T-shirt, she still looked high-class and high-maintenance. She wouldn't settle for a few nights between the sheets.

She was the kind of woman with expectations. With long-term plans. With honey-do lists and *would you mind*s and *can you please*s.

Normally I could ignore an attraction to a woman who wasn't my type.

Maybe I needed a break? It had been a while since I'd taken a few days off, had some fun, gotten laid.

I did the math, winced.

It had been more than a while.

That was what I needed. A few days away. Maybe I'd hit the beach. Read a few fucking novels. Drink a few beers out of someone else's inventory. Find a good lay with no strings or expectations.

I ignored the knee-jerk "meh."

After hitting forty, I'd noticed an alarming ambivalence when it came to the hunt. Laziness most likely. The hunt, the narrowing of the field, the flirtation. What had once been entertaining started to seem like a lot of work for just a night or two.

But I'd work up the energy, work off the sexual frustration. Then I could come back here and *not* feel compelled to jerk off every time I saw Naomi Witt.

Matter settled, I poured myself a water from the soda gun and watched Naomi try to leave the table only to be stopped by Wylie. The fucker actually grabbed her by the wrist.

"Ooh, shit," Silver said under her breath as I came off the barstool.

"Goddammit," I muttered as I made my way across the bar.

"Now don't you dally, Naomi," Wylie was saying. "The boys and I sure like lookin' at your face."

"Among other things," one of his idiotic friends said, sending the table into spasms of laughter.

I'd expected her to be clawing her way free, but Naomi was smiling. "I knew you boys were going to be trouble," she teased lightly.

"There a problem?" I snapped.

Wylie's hand fell away from Naomi's wrist, and I didn't miss the fact that she immediately took a step back.

"Problem?" Wylie said. "I don't see no problem."

"Wylie and his friends were introducing themselves," Naomi said. "I'll be right back with your drinks."

With a parting glare in my direction, she sauntered back to the bar.

I stepped into Wylie's line of sight, ruining his view of her departing ass.

"You know the rules, Ogden."

"Boy, I was running this town when you were nothing but a spark in your daddy's eyes."

"Don't run shit now, do you?" I said. "But this place? This is mine. And if you wanna be able to drink here, you'll keep your goddamn hands to yourself."

"I don't appreciate the insinuations, boy."

"And I don't appreciate having to serve your crooked ass. Guess we're even."

I left him and his cronies and went in search of Naomi. I found her at the POS by the bar.

Chewing on her lower lip, she didn't bother glancing up from the screen where she carefully entered an order. From the Sex on the Beach and Flaming Orgasm, I guessed it was Wylie's table of morons.

"You hit me with a fucking tray for talkin' shit, but you let that sweaty asshole put his hand on you?"

"I don't have time to point out the fact that you told me if I upset one table, you were firing me, so you'll have to settle for this," she said, holding up her middle finger in my face.

Hinkel McCord and Tallulah burst out laughing.

"Y'all aren't gettin' dinner and a show," I warned before turning back to Naomi.

"Dammit. Where's the substitute button?" she muttered.

I reached around her and paged through the options to the right one. Having her caged between me and the screen was making my libido malfunction.

To be contrary, I didn't step back while she keyed in the rest of the order. When she was finished, Naomi turned to look at me. "You sent me over there on purpose, knowing what would happen. I didn't react the way you wanted me to. Get over it."

"I sent you over there so you'd be creeped out by Wylie, not so he could put his fucking hands on you. If he does it again, I wanna know."

She laughed. Right in my face. "Yeah. Sure, Viking. I'll come running."

"Drinks up, Nay," Silver called.

"Gotta go, *boss,*" Naomi said with the kind of fake, bright politeness she'd used on Wylie. It made me want to punch a hole in the wall.

Ten minutes later, I was still thinking about punching something when my brother strolled through the door. His gaze went directly to Naomi, who was delivering a second round of drinks to Justice and Tallulah.

About a second later, he'd clocked Wylie at the table. The two exchanged a long stare before Nash headed my way.

"Look what the cat dragged in," Sherry crowed. My soon-to-be-fired business manager had come out of the office to watch the Naomi show.

Nash dragged his eyes away from Naomi's ass and flashed her an easy grin. "How's it goin', Fi?" he asked.

"Never a dull moment. You here to see the new girl?" she asked slyly, shooting me a look.

"Thought I'd drop in and see how Naomi's first day is going," he said.

"You and half the fucking town," Max said as she breezed by with a tray of drinks.

"She's doing great," Sherry told him. "Despite some headbutting with management."

Nash glanced my way. "Doesn't surprise me."

"Hi, Nash," Naomi chirped as she passed us on her way to the bar.

He nodded. "Naomi."

Sherry elbowed me in the gut. "Somebody's got a crush," she sang.

I grunted. Two somebodies had a crush, and if I had anything to say about it, neither of us was going to get the girl.

"Pull up a stool, Chief," Silver said.

Nash took her up on the offer and sat at the corner closest to the server station.

"On call or off for the night?" Silver asked.

"Officially off."

"Beer it is," she said with a little salute.

"Don't you have payroll to approve?" Sherry asked innocently as I hovered behind my brother.

"Maybe I already did it," I hedged, watching as Naomi approached Wylie's table again.

"I get an alert when it's been submitted, smart-ass."

Tattletale technology. "I'll get to it. Don't you have businesses to manage?"

"Right now, I've got a man to manage. Quit being a dick to Naomi. She's good. The customers like her. The staff likes her. Your brother likes her. You're the only one with a problem."

"My place. I get to have a problem if I wanna have a problem." I sounded like a fucking toddler denied a cookie.

Sherry slapped a hand to my cheek and squeezed.

154

Hard. "Boss, you're a perpetual ass, but this isn't like you. You never paid attention to new hires before. Why start now?"

Naomi breezed by again, and it pissed me off that I watched her every step of the way.

"Come here often?" Naomi asked, giving my brother a full wattage smile as she trayed up another round of drinks.

"Thought I'd drop by and give you the good news."

"What good news?" she asked, looking hopeful.

"I cleared up your little grand theft auto misunderstanding."

You would have thought my brother had just whipped out a solid-gold ten-inch dick with the way Naomi flew into him and wrapped him in a hug. "Thank you, thank you, thank you!" she chanted.

"No manhandling the customers," I snarled.

She rolled her eyes at me and gave Nash a peck on the cheek that made me want to set my own brother on fire.

"Also figured I'd see if you wanted a lift home after your shift," he offered.

Fuck me.

She didn't have a car. She probably rode her goddamn bike here and planned to ride it home after closing. In the dark.

Over my dead fucking body.

"That is so sweet of you to offer," Naomi said.

"Not necessary," I said, butting into the conversation. "She's already got a ride. Sherry'll take her."

"Sorry, Knox. I'm off in ten," my business manager said smugly.

"Then so's she."

"I can't close out my tables and do my side work in ten minutes," Naomi argued. "Max is showing me how to close in case you don't fire me after tonight."

"Fine. Then *I'm* driving you home."

"I'm sure you have better things to do than to drive a needy pain in the ass home."

"Burn," Fi whispered gleefully.

"I'm driving you home. Law and order here lives right upstairs. You're out of his way. It'd be an inconvenience to him to haul your ass home."

I knew I'd pushed the right button when Naomi's smile faltered.

"I don't mind," Nash insisted.

But Naomi shook her head. "As much as it pains me to admit it, your brother is right. It'll be late, and I'm out of your way."

Nash opened his mouth, but I cut him off. "I'm driving her."

I could probably keep my mouth shut and my hands off her for the five-minute drive.

"In that case, you got a minute?" he asked Naomi.

"You can have her for ten minutes," Max said, pushing Naomi at my brother.

She laughed and held up a hand. "Actually, I have

tables I need to get to. Do you need something, Nash?"

He glanced my way. "DC cops found your car today," he said.

Her face lit up. "That's great news."

Nash winced and shook his head. "Sorry, honey. It's not. They found it at a chop shop in pieces."

Naomi's shoulders slumped. "What about Tina?"

"No sign of her."

She looked even more dejected, and I was just about to order her to quit worrying when Nash reached out and tipped her chin up. "Don't let this get you down, honey. You're in Knockemout. We take care of our own."

Once my handsy fucking brother and Wylie Ogden left, I locked myself in my office and focused on paperwork rather than watching Naomi bravely smile her way into the hearts of Knockemout.

Business was good, and I knew how important staff was to that bottom line. But Jesus. Working with Naomi day in and day out? How long would it take before she'd spout off something smart, and I'd pin her to a wall and kiss her just to shut her up?

I kept an eye on the security monitor while I worked my way through the list of stuff Fi needed me to do.

Payroll submitted. Liquor order finalized. Emails returned. And I'd finally gotten around to working on the ads. It was midnight, closing time, and I was beyond ready to call it a night.

"Come on, Waylon," I called.

The dog bounded out of his bed.

We found the bar empty of patrons.

"Decent night tonight," Silver called from the register where she was scanning the day's report.

"How decent?" I asked, doing my best to ignore Naomi and Max as they rolled utensils into napkins and laughed about something. Waylon charged over to them to demand affection.

"Good enough for shots," Silver said.

"Did someone say shots?" Max called.

I had a deal with the staff. Every time we beat the previous week's sales, the entire shift earned shots.

Silver slid the report across the bar to me, and I flipped to the bottom line. Damn. It had been a good night.

"Maybe new girl's our lucky charm," she said.

"Nothing about her is lucky," I insisted.

"You still owe us."

I sighed. "Fine. Line 'em up. Teremana." I glanced over my shoulder. "Let's go, ladies."

Naomi cocked her head, but Max jumped out of her seat. "I knew it was a good night. Fat tips too. Come on," she said, pulling Naomi to her feet.

I didn't miss the wince as Naomi stood. She obviously wasn't used to being on her feet for hours at a time. But I respected her for stubbornly trying to hide her discomfort on the way to the bar. Waylon followed on her heels like a lovesick idiot.

"Boss called tequila," Silver said, producing the bottle.

Max whistled and drummed the bar.

"Tequila?" Naomi repeated on a yawn.

"Tradition," Silver explained. "Gotta celebrate the wins."

"One more," I said before Silver started to pour.

Her eyebrows winged up as she produced another glass. "Boss man is in. This is a first."

Max looked surprised too.

"Wait. Don't we need salt or lemons or hot sauce or something?" Naomi asked.

Silver shook her head. "That's for shitty tequila."

Shots poured, we held our glasses aloft.

"You gotta make the toast," Max said to me when it became clear no one else was going to do it.

"Fuck. Fine. To a good night," I said.

"Lame," Silver said.

I rolled my eyes. "Shut up and drink."

"Cheers." We touched glass to glass and then to the wood of the bar. Naomi mimicked us, and I watched her as she knocked back her shot.

I expected her to start gasping and wheezing like a sorority sister during pledge week. But those hazel eyes went wide as she looked at her empty glass. "So apparently I've never had good tequila before."

"Welcome to Honky Tonk," Max said.

"Thanks. And now that my first shift is officially complete"—Naomi put her glass and apron on the bar and turned to me—"I quit."

She headed for the door.

"Nooooo!" Silver and Max called after her.

"You better do something," Silver said, pinning me with a glare. "She's good."

"And she's trying to support a kid, Knoxy. Have a heart," Max pointed out.

I swore under my breath. "Walk each other out," I ordered and then went after Naomi.

I found her in the parking lot next to an ancient ten-speed.

"You're not riding that thing home," I announced, grabbing the handlebars.

Naomi let out a long sigh. "You're lucky I'm too tired to pedal or fight. But I still quit."

"No, you don't." Handing her the apron, I hauled the bike over to my truck and put it in the bed.

She limped along after me, shoulders slumped.

"Jesus, you look like you got trampled by a herd of horses."

"I'm not used to being on my feet for hours at a time. Okay, Mr. Pushes Paper from a Comfy Desk Chair?"

I opened the passenger-side door and gestured for her to get in. She winced when she climbed up.

I waited until she was settled before shutting her door, then rounding the hood and sliding behind the wheel. "You're not quitting," I said just in case she hadn't heard me the first time.

"Oh, I'm definitely quitting. It's the only thing that got me through the shift. I plotted all night. I'd be the best damn server you ever saw, and then when you had your change of heart, I'd tell you I quit."

"You're unquitting."

She yawned. "You're just saying that so you can fire me."

"No, I'm not," I said grimly.

"You wanted me to quit," she reminded me. "I quit. You win. Yay you."

"Yeah, well, you didn't suck. And you need the money."

"Your benevolence is astounding."

I shook my head. Even exhausted, her vocabulary still hit high on the SAT scale.

She rested her head against the seat. "What are we waiting for?"

"Making sure the girls walk out together and get in their cars."

"That's nice of you," she said, yawning again.

"I'm not a complete asshole all the time."

"So just with me then?" Naomi asked. "I feel so lucky."

"Cards on the table?" I didn't feel like sugar-coating it. "You're not my type."

"Are you kidding me right now?" she said.

"Nope."

"You're not attracted to me, so that means you can't even be civil to me?"

The back door opened, and we watched Max and Silver exit with the last bag of trash. They marched it to the dumpster together and high-fived after heaving it in. Max waved, and Silver tossed me another salute on their way to their respective cars.

"I didn't say I wasn't attracted to you. I said you're not my type."

She groaned. "I'm definitely going to regret this, but I think you're going to have to break it down for me."

"Well, Daisy. It means my dick doesn't care that you're not my type. It's still standing up, trying to get your attention."

She was quiet for a long beat.

"You're too much work. Come with too many complications. And you wouldn't be satisfied with just a quick fuck."

"I believe Knox Morgan just said he couldn't satisfy me. If only I had a phone to immortalize that statement on social media."

"(A) You're getting a new phone immediately. It's irresponsible to go without one when you have a kid to think about."

"Oh, shut up. It's been a handful of days. Not months. I didn't know I was going to have a kid to think about," she said.

"(B) I could satisfy the hell out of you," I plowed on, pulling out of the parking lot. "But you'd just want more, and that doesn't suit me."

"Because I'm an 'uppity, needy pain in the ass,' " she said to the darkness out her window.

I didn't have a defense. I was an asshole. Plain and simple. And the sooner she realized that, the farther she'd stay from me. Metaphorically speaking.

162

Naomi let out a weary sigh. "You're lucky I'm too tired to slap you, jump out of this vehicle, and crawl home," she said finally.

I turned onto the dirt lane that led to home. "You can slap me tomorrow."

"Probably just make you want me more."

"You're a pain in my ass."

"You're just mad because now you have to find a new spot to pee in your yard."

13

History Lessons

Naomi

Waylay and I had survived nearly an entire week together. It felt like a monumental accomplishment as our lives continued to hang in limbo. There had been no contact from the court system or Child Protective Services yet.

But I'd ground up zucchini and green beans into last night's meatloaf to sneak past Waylay Witt's discerning nose just in case anyone was watching.

I'd worked two more bar shifts, and the tips were starting to add up. Another financial boon was the arrival of my new credit and debit cards in the mail. I hadn't gotten all Tina's charges erased from my credit card statement, but having access to my meager savings had helped immensely.

I'd had the foresight to pay the mortgage early this month in anticipation of being too deliriously happy on my honeymoon to worry about things like bills. That plus the fact that I no longer had a car payment or insurance to cover meant I could stretch a dollar surprisingly far.

To earn that free rent, I carved out a few hours to spend at Liza J's.

"Who's that?" Waylay asked, pointing at a framed

photo I'd found tucked into the back of one of the cabinets in the dining room.

I looked up from my dust rag and furniture polish to look. It was a picture of an older man looking proud enough to burst with his arm around a beaming redhead in a cap and gown.

Liza J, who had said repeatedly she didn't like cleaning but still insisted on following us from room to room, looked at the photo like she was seeing it for the first time. She took a slow, shaky breath. "That's, uh, my husband, Billy. And that's our daughter, Jayla."

Waylay opened her mouth to ask another question, but I interrupted, sensing Liza J didn't want to talk about more family members who hadn't been mentioned until now. There was a reason this big house had been closed up from the rest of the world. And I guessed the reason was in that picture.

"Have any plans this weekend, Liza?" I cut in, giving Waylay a little shake of my head.

She put the photo facedown on the table. "Plans? Ha!" she scoffed. "I do the same thing every damn day. Drag my ass out of bed and putter. All day, every day. Inside, outside."

"What are you puttering on this weekend?" Waylay asked.

I gave her a thumbs-up that Liza J couldn't see.

"Garden needs some attention. Don't suppose either of you like tomatoes? Got 'em comin' out of my ears."

"Waylay and I *love* tomatoes," I said as my niece mimed vomiting on the floor.

"I'll send you home with a bushel then," Liza J decided.

"I'll be damned. You got all the burnt crusty stuff off the stove top," Liza J observed two hours later. She was leaning over her range while I rested on the floor, my legs stretched out in front of me.

I was sweating, and my fingers were cramped from aggressive scrubbing. But the progress was undeniable. The mound of dishes was done and put away, and the range gleamed black on all surfaces. I'd taken all the papers, boxes, and bags off the island and tasked Liza J with sorting it all into keep and toss piles. The keep pile was four times the size of the toss pile, but it still counted as progress.

Waylay was making her own kind of progress. As soon as she'd fixed the errant e-reader that had eaten Liza J's download and a printer that had lost its Wi-Fi connection, Liza J had handed over an old Blackberry I'd found in the drawer next to the sink. If Waylay could coax it back to life, Liza J said I could have it. A free phone with a number none of my old contacts had? It was perfect.

"I'm starving," Waylay announced, throwing herself down dramatically on the now-visible counter. Randy the beagle barked as if to emphasize the direness of my niece's starvation. Kitty the pit bull was sound asleep in the middle of the floor, her tongue lolling out onto the floor.

"Then let's eat," Liza J said, clapping her hands.

On the word *eat,* both dogs and my niece snapped to attention.

" 'Course, I'm not cooking in here. Not with it looking showroom new," Liza J added. "We'll go to Dino's. My treat."

"Their pepperoni is the best," Waylay said, perking up.

"I could eat a whole pepperoni pie myself," Liza J agreed, hitching up her cargo shorts.

It was nice to see my niece getting comfortable with an adult, but I would have liked it better if I was the one she was sharing pepperoni preferences with.

I couldn't shake the feeling that I was failing a test in a class I'd forgotten to attend all semester.

I changed out of my cleaning clothes and into a sundress, then Liza J drove us into town in her old Buick that floated around corners like a Macy's Thanksgiving Day Parade float. She squeezed into a parking space in front of a storefront under an orange awning. The sign in the window said Dino's Pizza.

A few doors down was some kind of salon or barbershop, its brick facade painted a deep blue. An arrangement of whiskey bottles and cacti in clay pots created an eye-catching window display.

When we got out, a pair of bikers strolled out of the pizza shop, headed toward two Harleys. One of them shot me a wink and a grin.

"That ain't Tina," Liza J bellowed.

"I know," he called back. "How's it goin', Not Tina?"

Well, at least the fact that I wasn't Tina was starting to sink in. But I wasn't very fond of the Not Tina nickname. I waved awkwardly and pushed Waylay ahead of me toward the restaurant door, hoping that the Not Tina thing wouldn't catch on.

Liza J ignored the Please Wait to Be Seated sign and shoved herself into an empty booth.

Waylay marched after her while I hesitated, wanting permission.

"Be right with y'all," the guy behind the counter called.

Relieved, I slid into the booth next to Waylay.

"So what do you think of Knockemout so far?" Liza J asked me.

"Oh, uh, it's very charming," I said, perusing the salads on the menu. "How did the town get its name?"

"Don't know if there's an official answer. Just that this town has always settled its differences with a good old-fashioned fight. None of this dragging things out in court, getting hoity-toity lawyers involved. Somebody does you wrong, you ring their bell, and then you're square. Simple. Quick."

"That's not how everyone solves problems," I told Waylay sternly.

"I don't know. It's awful satisfying punching

someone in the face," my niece mused. "You ever try it?"

"Physical violence is never the answer," I insisted.

"Maybe she's right," Liza J said, addressing Waylay. "Look at my grandsons. Some things can't be solved with a couple of punches."

"Knox had Nash in a headlock," Waylay said.

"Where is our server?" I asked no one in particular.

"Sounds about right," Liza J agreed with Waylay.

"What are they fightin' about?" my niece asked.

"Those mule-headed boys are always fighting."

"I heard it was about a woman."

I jolted as the server leaned over the table to throw down napkins and straws.

"Now what woman would that be, Neecey?" Liza J said.

"I'm just repeatin' what I heard."

"Seein' as how everyone knows Knox hasn't dated a girl from this town since high school. Remember Jilly Aucker moved herself to Canton just to see if a change in zip code would push him over the edge?"

"Yeah. Then she met that lumberjack and had his four lumberjack babies," Neecey said.

I didn't want to be interested in that particular information, but I couldn't help myself.

"I'm just repeatin' what I heard. It's a damn shame neither of those boys have ever settled down." Neecey adjusted her glasses and cracked her gum. "If I were twenty years younger, I'd end their feud by selflessly offering to share myself with both of them."

"I'm sure your husband would have something to say about that," Liza J ventured.

"Vin's fallin' asleep on the sofa five nights out of seven every week for the past ten years. In my book, you snooze, you lose. You must be Not Tina," the server said. "Heard you and Knox got into screaming matches at the café and Honky Tonk, and then he apologized, but you broke a chair over his head, and he needed six stitches."

I was rendered speechless. Waylay, on the other hand, erupted into peals of laughter.

This town certainly loved its gossip. With rumors like that, it was no wonder I hadn't heard anything from the caseworker yet. They were probably working on a warrant for my arrest.

"This here's Naomi and her niece, Waylay," Liza J said, making the introductions.

"And I didn't break a chair over anyone's head, no matter how much they deserved it. I'm a very responsible adult," I told Neecey in hopes that she'd pass that rumor along.

"Huh. Bummer," she said.

"Can I have a dollar to play some music?" Waylay asked, pointing at the jukebox in the corner after we'd placed our orders.

Before I could say anything, Liza J shoved a crumpled five-dollar bill at her. "Play some country. I miss hearing it."

170

"Thanks!" Waylay snatched the bill out of Liza J's hand and headed for the jukebox.

"Why don't you listen to country anymore?" I asked.

That same look she'd had when Waylay asked her about the photo came back. Wistful and sad. "My daughter was the one who played it. Had it on the radio morning, noon, and night. Taught the boys to line dance practically before they could walk."

There was a lot of past tense in that sentence. Spontaneously, I reached out and squeezed her hand. Her focus came back to me, and she squeezed my hand back before pulling free.

"Speakin' of family, my grandson sure has shown some interest in you."

"Nash has been so helpful since I got to town," I said.

"Not Nash, you ninny. Knox."

"Knox?" I repeated, certain I'd heard her wrong.

"Big guy? Tattoos? Pissed off at the world?"

"He hasn't shown interest, Liza. He's shown disdain, disgust, and malice." He'd also shared an aggressive announcement that his body found my body attractive, but the rest of him found the rest of me revolting.

She hooted. "I bet you're the one."

"The one what?"

"The one who's gonna have him reconsidering this whole bachelor deal. Bet money you're the first girl he dates from this town in twenty-plus years. And by *dates,* I mean—"

I held the menu up over my face. "I understand what you mean, but you're very, *very* wrong."

"He's quite the catch," she insisted. "And not just cause of the lottery money."

I was 100 percent certain she was messing with me.

"Knox won the lottery?" I asked dryly.

"Eleven million. Couple of years back."

I blinked. "You're serious, aren't you?"

"As a heart attack. And he wasn't one of those buy-a-big-ass-mansion-and-a-fleet-of-foreign-cars winners. He's even richer now than when he got that big check," she said with pride.

The man's boots were older than Waylay.

He lived on his grandmother's property in a cabin.

I thought of Warner and his family, who definitely did not have $11 million but acted as if they were the crustiest of the upper crust.

"But he's just so . . . *grumpy*."

Liza J smirked. "Guess it just goes to show money can't buy happiness."

We were just digging into a large pepperoni and salad—well, technically I was the only one with salad on my plate—when the front door opened and in walked Sloane the librarian, followed by a young girl.

Today, Sloane wore a long tie-dye skirt that skimmed her ankles and a fitted T-shirt with cuffed sleeves. She wore her hair down, creating a long, golden curtain that moved like the material of her skirt. The girl behind her was a chubby-cheeked cherub. She had dark skin and assessing brown eyes, and she wore her hair in an adorable puff on top of her head.

"Hey, Sloane!" I greeted her with a wave.

The librarian's red lips curved in a smile, and she jerked her head at the girl who followed. "Well, if it isn't Liza, Naomi, and Waylay. Chloe, do you know Way?" Sloane asked.

The girl tapped a sparkly pink-nailed finger to her chin. "We had B lunch together last year, didn't we? You sat with Nina—the short one with black hair, not the tall one with bad breath. She's really nice, but she just doesn't do a good job with the brushing. I'm in Mrs. Felch's class this year, and I'm not happy about it 'cause everyone says she's a mean old lady. I heard she's even meaner 'cause she and her husband are talking about a divorce."

I noticed that Waylay was staring at Chloe with wary interest.

"Chloe!" Sloane sounded both amused and embarrassed.

"What? I'm only repeating what I heard from several very good sources. Whose class are you in?" she asked Waylay.

"Mrs. Felch," Waylay said.

"Sixth grade is gonna be awesome even if we do have mean old Mrs. Felch because we get to switch rooms and teachers for science, art, gym, and math. Plus we've got Nina and Beau and Willow in class with us," Chloe plowed on. "Do you know what you're wearing on the first day? I can't decide between an all-pink ensemble or a pink-and-white ensemble."

It was a lot of words to take in from such a small person.

"If you ever need to know anything about anyone, just ask my niece, Chloe," Sloane said, looking amused.

Chloe grinned, showing a dimple in one cheek. "I'm not allowed to visit Aunt Sloane at the library cause she says I talk too much. *I* don't think I talk too much. I just have a lot of information that needs to be disseminated to the public."

Waylay was staring at Chloe with half of her slice of pizza hanging out of her mouth. It had been a long time since I'd been in school and faced with a cool girl. But Chloe had *cool girl* written all over her.

"We should get our moms, or I guess your aunt and my mom or my aunt, to schedule a playdate. Are you into crafts or hiking? Maybe baking?"

"Uh," Waylay said.

"You can let me know at school," Chloe said.

"Thanks?" Waylay croaked.

It occurred to me that if people in the grocery store were giving her the evil eye, Waylay might not have a lot of friends at school. After all, it wasn't hard to imagine mothers not wanting their daughters to bring home Tina Witt's daughter.

Inspiration struck. "Hey, we're throwing a little

174

dinner party Sunday. Would you two like to come?"

"My day off, *and* I don't have to cook? Count me in," Sloane said. "What about you, Chlo?"

"I'll check my social calendar and get back to you. I have a birthday party and tennis lessons on Saturday, but I think I'm free Sunday."

"Great!" I said. Waylay shot me a look that made me think I sounded a little bit desperate.

"Perfect! Let's grab our to-go order before it gets cold," Sloane suggested, steering Chloe toward the counter.

"Damn, that kid can talk," Liza J observed. She looked at me. "So when were you gonna invite me to this dinner party?"

"Uh . . . now?"

We ate our pizza, I ate our salad, and Liza J picked up the bill like the patron saint of temporarily broke tenants. We hit the sidewalk and the Virginia heat. But Liza J headed in the opposite direction of the car. She tottered down to the building on the corner and knocked loudly on Whiskey Clipper's plate glass window.

Waylay joined her, and they both started waving.

"What are you two doing?" I asked, hurrying after them.

"Knox owns this place too and does some barbering," Liza J said with a hint of pride.

Wearing his usual uniform of worn jeans, a fitted T-shirt, and ancient motorcycle boots, Knox Morgan was standing behind one of the salon chairs, taking a straight razor to a customer's cheek. He had a leather apron-like organizer hung low on his hips with scissors and other tools tucked in the pouches.

I'd never had a barber fetish before. I didn't even know if that was a legitimate fetish. But watching those tattooed forearms, those dexterous hands work, I felt an annoying pulse of desire spark to life under the pizza I'd inhaled.

His gaze met mine, and for a second, it felt like the glass wasn't there. It felt like I was being dragged into his gravity against my will. It felt like it was just the two of us sharing some kind of secret.

I knew what I'd be thinking about and hating myself for when I lay down in bed tonight.

14

The Dinner Party

Knox

"B eer and catch a game? Beer and shoot the shit on the deck?" I asked Jeremiah as he and Waylon followed me up the steps to my cabin. Once every two weeks or so, I'd take an early night, and we'd get together outside work.

"I wanna find out what's got your beard so droopy. You were fine a couple of days ago. Your usual grumpy self. Now you're pouting."

"I don't pout. I ponder. In a manly way."

Jeremiah snickered behind me.

I unlocked the door and, despite my best efforts, glanced in the direction of the cottage.

There were cars parked in front of the cottage, music playing. Great. The woman was a socializer. Another reason to stay far the hell away from her.

Not that I had to, seeing as how she'd been avoiding me like *I* was the problem. The past week had been a struggle. An annoying one. Naomi Witt, I'd discovered, was a warm, friendly person. And when she wasn't feeling warm and friendly toward you, you definitely felt the cold. She refused to make eye contact with me. Her smiles and "Sure thing, boss" responses were perfunctory. Even when I drove her home and we were alone in the truck, the frostiness didn't thaw a degree.

Every time I thought I'd gotten a handle on it, she popped up. Either in her backyard or at my grandmother's. In my own bar. Hell, a few days ago, she'd floated up to the window at Whiskey Clipper like a goddamn vision.

She was driving me fucking nuts.

"See? That right there," Jeremiah said, pointing a finger in my face. "Pouting. What's going on with you, man?"

"Nothing." I noticed my brother's department vehicle parked at the cottage. "Fuck."

"There a reason you don't like seeing your brother's car parked at Not Tina's?"

"Is it the bisexual part of you that wants to talk about fucking feelings all the time?" I asked. "Or is it the 'I come from a big Lebanese family that knows everything about everybody' part that I can blame?"

"Why not both?" he said with a quick grin.

A particularly loud burst of laughter caught our attention, as did the scent of grilled meat.

Waylon's nose twitched. The white tip of his tail froze in the air.

"No," I said sternly.

I might as well have said, "Sure, bud. Go get yourself a hot dog." Because my dog took off like a streak.

"Looks like we're joining the party," Jeremiah observed.

178

"Fuck. I'm getting a beer first."

A minute later, cold beers in hand, we wandered around the back of the cottage to find half of Knockemout on Naomi's porch.

Sloane, the pretty librarian, was there with her niece, Chloe, who was wading knee-deep in the creek with Waylay and my grandmother's dogs. Liza J was sitting next to Tallulah while Justice manned the grill and my pain-in-the-ass brother flirted with Naomi.

She looked like summer.

Considering I'd had two sips of beer, I couldn't blame alcohol on my mental prose. My mouth went dry as my gaze started at her bare feet, then moved up the long, tan legs to where they disappeared under the flirty, lemon-yellow sundress.

"So *that's* the problem," Jeremiah said smugly. He was looking right at Naomi, and I didn't much care for it.

"I don't know what you're talking about," I said.

Waylon barreled his way up onto the porch and made a beeline for the grill.

"Waylon!" Naomi looked delighted to see my dog. She crouched down to greet him, and even from here, the peek of cleavage was enough to tie my balls in a knot.

"Waylon," I barked.

My jerk of a dog was too busy enjoying the affection of a beautiful woman to bother listening to me.

"Knox! Jer!" Tallulah called when she spotted us in the yard. "Join us."

Naomi looked up, and I saw the sunshine fade from her face when she spotted me. The ice walls went up.

"We don't want to impose," Jeremiah said, cagily eyeing the spread. There were deviled eggs, grilled vegetables, some kind of layered dip thing in a fancy dish, and four kinds of desserts. On the grill, Justice was turning chicken breasts and hot dogs.

"You're welcome to join us," Naomi said through a smile that was more gritted teeth than invitation. Her message was clear. She didn't want me here at her cozy little dinner party.

Well, I didn't want her in my head every time I closed my fucking eyes. So I considered the score equal.

"If you insist," Jeremiah said, shooting me a triumphant look.

"Nice flowers," I said. There was a blue vase overflowing with wild blooms in the center of the table.

"Nash brought them," Naomi said.

I wanted to smack the smug look of satisfaction right off my brother's face.

So he brought a girl flowers, and I could barely get her to say two words to me. He should know better than to challenge me like that.

I played dirty. Even when I didn't care about winning. I just wanted Nash to lose.

Between eating and shooting the shit with Naomi's eclectic guests, I watched her. She sat between

180

Waylay and Nash, who had all but pushed me out of the way like we were playing musical chairs. The conversation was lively, the mood upbeat.

Naomi laughed and talked and listened, all while keeping an eye on everyone's plates and glasses, offering second helpings and top-ups with the expertise of someone who spent their life looking out for others.

She was warm, attentive, funny. Except to me.

So maybe I'd been a bit of a dick. Personally, I didn't think that was enough of an infraction for me to be relegated to Ice Town.

I noticed every time Sloane or Chloe mentioned something about school starting, Naomi got pale and sometimes excused herself to go inside.

She talked to Jeremiah about hair and Whiskey Clipper. She talked about coffee and small business with Justice and Tallulah. And she had no problem smiling at any stupid thing that came out of my brother's mouth. But no matter how long I watched her, she never once glanced in my direction. I was the invisible dinner guest, and it was rubbing me the wrong way.

"Liza J was telling us stories of you and Nash growing up earlier," Justice said to me.

I could only imagine which stories my grand-mother had decided on. "Was it the rock fight in the creek or the zip line from the chimney?" I asked my brother.

"Both," Nash said, lips quirked.

"It was quite the childhood," I told Justice.

"Did your parents live with you?" Waylay asked. It was an innocent question coming from a kid who knew what it was like to not live with her parents.

I swallowed and looked for an escape.

"We lived with our parents until our mom passed," Nash told her.

"I'm so sorry to hear that." That came from Naomi, and this time she was looking right fucking at me.

I nodded stiffly.

"Naomi, did you pick up Waylay's school laptop yet?" Sloane asked. "My sister said Chloe's was a little buggy."

"Yeah, every time I open the internet, it restarts. How am I supposed to watch age-appropriate videos on YouTube with no internet?" Chloe chimed in.

"Or, I don't know, do school work?" Sloane teased.

"I could probably take a look at it," Waylay offered.

Chloe's brown eyes widened. "You're a STEM girl?"

"What's that?" Waylay asked with suspicion.

"Science, technology, engineering, and math," Sloane filled in.

"Yeah. Nerd stuff," Chloe added.

Sloane elbowed her niece.

"Ow! I don't mean nerd like *bad*. Nerds are good. Nerds are cool. Nerds are the ones who grow up to run companies and make bazillions of dollars," Chloe said. She looked at Waylay. "Nerds are definitely good."

The tops of Waylay's ears turned pink.

"My mom always said nerds were losers," she said quietly. She shot Naomi a look. "She said girls who liked dresses and doing their hair were . . . uh, bad."

I had the sudden urge to hunt down Tina and drop-kick her ass into the creek for not being the kind of mother her kid needed.

"Your mom got a lot of things mixed up, kiddo," Naomi said, running her hand over Waylay's hair. "She didn't understand that people could be more than one thing or like more than one thing. You can wear dresses and makeup and build rockets. You can dress in suits and play baseball. You can be a millionaire and work in your pajamas."

"Your mom doesn't like dresses and hair?" Chloe scoffed. "She's missing out. I had *two* wardrobe changes for my birthday last year, *and* I got a bow and arrow. You be you. Don't let someone who doesn't like fashion tell you anything."

"Listen to Chloe, who's about to lose a hot dog off her plate. Get down, Waylon," Liza J said.

My dog froze, midsneak.

"We can still see you even if you're not movin', dumbass," I reminded him.

Waylay giggled.

Pouting, Waylon slunk back under the table. Seconds later, I noticed Waylay tear off a piece of her hot dog and casually tuck it under the checkered cloth.

Naomi noticed it too but didn't tattle on either one of them.

"If you brought your laptop along, I could take a look," Waylay offered.

"Well, if you're doing a little after-dinner tech support," Tallulah said, pulling a huge iPad out of her work bag, "I just got this for the shop, and I'm having trouble transferring everything over from the old one."

"Ten dollars a job," I said, slapping the table.

Everyone's eyes came to me. Waylay's lips quirked.

"Waylay Witt doesn't work for free. You want the best? You gotta pay for it," I told them.

Her tiny smile was a smirk now, which morphed into a full-out grin when Tallulah yanked a ten-dollar bill out of her purse and handed it over. "First paying customer," Tallulah said proudly.

"Aunt Sloane!" Chloe hissed.

Sloane grinned and went for her purse. "Here's a twenty for your trouble. Miss Fashion here also dribbled honey on the space bar when she was making tea."

Waylay pocketed the bills and sat down to get to work.

This time, Naomi locked eyes with me. She didn't smile, didn't say "thank you" or "get me naked tonight." But there was still something there. Something I itched to unlock simmering in those hazel eyes.

And then it was gone.

"Excuse me," she said, pushing back from the table. "I'll be right back."

Nash watched her walk away, that bright yellow material sliding over tanned thighs.

I couldn't blame him. But I also couldn't let him have her.

When Jeremiah caught his attention with a question about football, I used it as an opportunity to follow Naomi inside. I found her bent over the rolltop desk next to the stairs in the living room.

"Whatcha doing?"

She jumped, shoulders hitching. Then she spun around, holding her hands behind her back. When she saw it was me, she rolled her eyes. "Is there something you need? A slap across the face? An excuse to leave?"

I closed the distance between us slowly. I didn't know why I was doing it. I just knew that watching her smile at my brother made my chest tight, that being frozen out was getting to me. And the closer I moved to her, the warmer I felt.

"Thought money was tight," I said when she tilted her head to look up at me.

"Oh, bite me, Viking."

"Just sayin', Daisy, your first night on the job, you gave me a sob story of losing your savings and supporting your niece. Now it looks like you're feeding half the county."

"It's a *potluck,* Knox. By the way, you're the only one who didn't bring anything to share. Besides, I wasn't doing it to socialize."

I liked the way she said my name when she was exasperated. Hell, I just liked my name on those lips.

"All right then. Why are you hosting half of Knockemout for a potluck?"

"If I tell you, do you promise to do us both a favor and go away?"

"Absolutely," I lied.

She bit her lip and peered over my shoulder. "Fine. It's because of Chloe."

"You're throwing a dinner party for an eleven-year-old?"

She rolled her eyes. "No! That adorable chatter-box is the most popular girl in Waylay's grade. They have the same teacher this year. I was just trying to give them a chance to spend some time together."

"You're matchmaking sixth graders?"

Naomi's jaw jutted out, and she crossed her arms over her chest. I didn't mind because it pressed her breasts up higher against the neckline of her dress.

"You wouldn't understand what it's like to walk through town and be judged by people just because of who you're related to," she hissed.

I took a step closer to her. "You're dead wrong about that."

"Okay. Fine. Whatever. I want Waylay to go to school with actual friends, not just rumors that she's Tina Witt's abandoned daughter."

It was probably a solid play. I'd had my brother and Lucian on the first day of school when we'd moved here. No one in school had the guts to say shit about one of us since we were protected by the pack.

"Then what's this?" I asked, grabbing the notebook she had clutched in one hand.

"Knox! Stop!"

"Emergency Back-to-School To-Do," I read. "Pick up laptop. Try to schedule meeting with teacher. Back-to-school clothes and supplies. Money." I let out a low whistle. "A lot of question marks after that one." She lunged for the notebook, but I held it out of her reach and flipped back a page. I found another to-do list and another one. "Sure do like lists," I observed.

Her handwriting started out nice and neat, but the farther down the list it got, I could practically feel the panic in her penmanship. The woman had a lot on her plate and not much to do it with if the glimpse of her bank balances scrawled at the bottom of a shopping list were any indicator.

This time, I allowed her to snatch the notebook back. She threw it on the desk behind her and picked up her wineglass.

"Stay out of my business, Knox," she said. Her cheeks were pink, and there wasn't a hint of frost in those gorgeous hazel eyes now. Every time she took a deep breath, her breasts grazed my chest and drove me just a little more insane.

"You don't have to do this alone, you know," I said.

She clapped her non-wine-holding hand to her

forehead in mock excitement. "Of *course!* I can just ask for handouts from strangers. Why didn't I think of that? That wouldn't make me look like I'm incapable of taking care of a child in the eyes of the law. Problem solved."

"There's nothin' wrong with accepting a little help now and then."

"I don't need help. I need *time,*" she insisted, her shoulders tensing, hand fisting at her side. "Sloane mentioned she might have a part-time position opening up at the library after school starts. I can save up and get a car. I can make this work. I just need time."

"You want extra shifts at Honky Tonk, say the word." I couldn't seem to stop wanting this woman's orbit to overlap with my own. It was a stupid, dangerous game I was playing.

"This from the man who called me an 'uppity, needy pain in the ass' and tried to fire me on the spot. Forgive me if I don't ever ask you for anything."

"Oh, come on, Naomi. I was pissed off."

She looked at me like she wanted to light me on fire. "And?" she said pointedly.

"And what? I said some shit because I was pissed off. You weren't supposed to hear it. Not my fault you were eavesdroppin' on a private conversation."

"You yelled two seconds after I walked out the door! You can't just do that! Words have power. They make people *feel* things."

"So stop feelin' things, and let's move on," I suggested.

"That might be the most ridiculous thing I've ever heard in my life."

"Doubt that. You grew up with Tina."

The ice in her had thawed and turned to molten lava. "I did grow up with Tina. I was nine when I overheard her telling my best friend they should play without me because I was too snobby to have any fun. I was fourteen when she kissed the boy she knew I liked and told me I was too needy for him or anyone to ever want me."

Fucking A. This was why I hated talking to people. Sooner or later, you always stuck your finger in a wound.

I ran my hand through my hair.

"Then along comes Knox Morgan, who doesn't want me around because, despite my defective personality of being uppity and needy, you still managed to be attracted to my body."

"Look, Daisy, it's nothing personal."

"Except it is *deeply* personal."

"Put a lot of thought into being pissed off about this, haven't you?" Maybe I wasn't the only one losing sleep.

"Go screw yourself, Knox!"

The brisk knock at the front door made Naomi jump. Wine sloshed over the rim of her glass.

"Am I interrupting?" The woman on the other side of the screen door was a few inches shy of Naomi and wore a rumpled gray suit. Her dark hair was pulled back in a tight bun.

"Umm," Naomi managed as she tried to blot

at the wine on her chest with her hands. "Uh."

"I'm Yolanda Suarez. With Child Protective Services."

Ah. Fuck me.

Naomi went rigor-mortis stiff next to me. I snatched the box of tissues off the top of the desk and handed it to her. "Here," I said.

When she just stared at the visitor without moving, I yanked a few tissues out and started to blot up the disaster.

It took about two dabs into her cleavage before she snapped out of it and slapped my hands away.

"Um, welcome. This isn't my wine," Naomi said, eyes wide. The visitor's gaze slid to the now-empty glass Naomi was holding. "I mean it *is*. I don't know why I said that. But I'm not drinking a lot of it. I'm responsible. And I hardly ever yell at men in my living room."

"Okaaaaaay. Is Chief Morgan here? He asked me to stop by," Mrs. Suarez asked coolly.

15

Knox Goes Shopping

Naomi

Two days later, I was still having mini heart attacks every time someone came to the door. Nash had invited Mrs. Suarez, Waylay's caseworker, to stop by so he could introduce us. He'd just had no idea that she'd show up when I was in the middle of unloading a lifetime of baggage on Knox Morgan.

The introduction had been brief and awkward. Mrs. Suarez handed over a paper copy of the guardianship application, and I could feel her classifying me as a screaming shrew with a taste for too much wine. On the bright side, Waylay had been mercifully polite and didn't mention how I was torturing her with vegetables in her meals.

I'd overanalyzed the informal meeting to the point where I was convinced I'd barely survived an interrogation and Yolanda Suarez hated me. My new mission wasn't just to be judged an "acceptable" kinship guardian—I was going to be the best kinship guardian northern Virginia had ever seen.

The very next day, I'd borrowed Liza J's Buick and marched into Knockemout's consignment shop. Pack Rats had coughed up $400 for my custom-made, barely worn wedding dress. Then I'd grabbed a coffee from Justice and gone straight home to finalize the back-to-school shopping list.

"Guess what we're doing today," I said to Waylay as we had our lunch of sandwiches and carrot sticks on the back porch.

The sun was shining, the creek burbling lazily as it flowed past the edge of the grass.

"Probably something boring," Waylay predicted as she tossed another carrot stick over her shoulder into the yard.

"Back-to-school shopping."

She looked at me with suspicion. "Is that a thing?"

"Of course it's a thing. You're a kid. Kids grow. They outgrow old stuff and need new stuff."

"You're taking me shopping. For clothes?" Waylay said slowly.

"And shoes. And school supplies. Your teacher hasn't answered my emails yet, so I got a copy of the supply list from Chloe's mom." I was babbling because I was nervous. Waylay and I had yet to connect, and I was willing to attempt to buy her affection.

"Do I get to pick the clothes?"

"You're the one wearing them. I might retain veto power in case you decide to go for a fur coat or velour tracksuits. But yeah. You get to pick."

"Huh. Okay," she said.

She wasn't exactly jumping up and down and

192

throwing her arms around me like she had in my imagination. But there was a twinkle of a smile happening at the corners of her mouth as she ate her turkey and provolone.

After lunch, I sent Waylay upstairs to get ready while I reviewed the mall research I'd printed at the library. I was only halfway through the store descriptions when there was a knock at the front door. Fearing it was another drop-in from Mrs. Suarez, I took a moment to run my fingers through my hair, check my teeth for lipstick, and close the lid on the rolltop desk so she couldn't judge my obsession with notebooks and planners.

Instead of Mrs. Suarez, I found the most annoying man in the world standing on the porch in jeans, a gray T-shirt, and aviators. His hair looked a little shorter on top. I guessed when you owned a barbershop, you could get a haircut whenever you wanted. It was annoying how attractive he was, all bearded and tattooed and aloof.

"Howdy, neighbor," he said.

"Who are you and what have you done with blond Oscar?" I asked.

"Let's go," he said, hooking his thumb toward his truck.

"What? Where? Why are you here?"

"Liza J said you needed a ride. I'm your ride."

I shook my head. "Oh, no. I'm not doing this with you today."

"Not playing games, Daisy. Get your ass in the truck."

"As charming as that invitation is, Viking, I'm taking Waylay back-to-school shopping. You don't strike me as a 'spend the day shopping with the girls' kind of neighbor."

"You're not wrong. But maybe I'm a 'drop the girls off at the mall and pick them up when they're done' kind of neighbor."

"No offense. But no. You're not that either."

"We can stand here arguing about it for the next hour, or you can get your ass in the truck." He sounded almost cheerful, and that made me suspicious.

"Why can't I just borrow Liza's car?" That had been the plan. I didn't like when things didn't go according to plan.

"Can't now. She needs it." He leaned around me and called into the house. "Waylay, get a move on! Bus is leaving."

I heard the thunder of feet upstairs as my niece forgot to play it cool.

I put a hand to his chest and pushed him back until we were both standing on the porch. "Listen, this trip is important. I'm trying to bond with Waylay, and she's never been back-to-school shopping before. So if you're going to do anything to ruin it, I'd rather take a Lyft to the mall. In fact, that's what I'm going to do."

He looked downright amused. "And how are you going to do that with a piece of shit phone that's too old to download apps?"

Damn it.

Waylay vaulted into the living room, landing with both feet before rearranging her expression into a look of boredom. "Hey," she said to Knox.

"Knox is going to drive us," I explained with zero enthusiasm.

"Cool. How much stuff are you planning to buy if you need a whole entire pickup truck?" Waylay wondered.

"Your aunt said she plans to buy out half the mall. Figured it was best to come prepared," Knox said.

I caught the little half smile on her face before she led the way down the porch steps and said, "Let's get this over with."

My suspicions were further heightened when we got in the truck, and I found a coffee for me and a smoothie for Waylay.

"What's your game?" I asked Knox when he slid behind the wheel.

He ignored me to frown over a text.

There was something about the way he hesitated that gave me a bad feeling. "Is Liza okay? Did something happen at Honky Tonk?"

"Relax, Daisy. Everybody and everything are fine."

He fired off a response and started the truck.

We headed east and joined the slog of northern Virginia traffic. I checked my tidy stack of cash again while Knox and Waylay made small talk. I tuned them out and tried to squash the anxiety. Yesterday at the library, I'd logged into my accounts to confirm some budget numbers. Money was tight. The bar shifts and free rent were helping, but my income wasn't enough to impress any judge in any court, especially not if I added a car payment into the mix.

I had three options: (1) Find a day job while Waylay was in school. (2) Borrow against my retirement savings. (3) Sell my house on Long Island.

Inwardly, I cringed. It had represented so much more to me than just three bedrooms and two baths. It was a gratifying step that was part of a larger plan. I'd landed a good job at Warner's family's investment firm, fallen for him, and bought a nice house to start a family.

If I sold it, I was officially saying goodbye to the dream. Then where would I go after my six months of temporary guardianship with Waylay were up?

By the time we got to the mall, I was marinating in the misery of regrets and failures.

"Thanks for the ride," I said to Knox, who was now on his phone carrying on a conversation that seemed to consist of monosyllabic questions and answers. I hopped out, still clutching my coffee.

Waylay climbed out of the back seat and slammed her door.

I expected him to accelerate away, leaving us in a cloud of fumes, but instead he got out and shoved his phone in his back pocket.

"What are you doing?"

"Are you shopping with us?" Waylay asked. She didn't sound horrified—she sounded excited.

Damn you, Knox Morgan.

"Got some things on my own shopping list. Figured you ladies could show me the ropes."

We entered the air-conditioned mall, and with a cursory glance in my direction, Waylay made a beeline for an accessories store.

As soon as she disappeared into the store, I grabbed Knox's tattooed arm. "What. Are. You. Doing?"

"Shopping."

"You don't shop. You don't go to malls."

He rolled back on his heels, looking amused. "That a fact?"

"You're the kind of guy who wears his clothes until they disintegrate, and then you either start wearing something some female relative got you for Christmas or you order the same exact thing you wore out online. You do *not* go to malls. You do *not* shop with girls."

Knox moved into my space. Those eyes, more gray than blue today, went serious. "You got a problem with me tagging along?"

"Yes! What are you doing here, Knox? I'm trying to bond with Waylay. Everything else I've tried so far hasn't put a crack in those walls. She's got a poker face at age eleven because of the amount of disappointment she's already faced. I want to see her smile. A real smile."

"Jesus, Naomi. I'm not here to fuck that up."

"Then *why* are you here?"

Waylay knocked on her side of the store window and held up two pairs of earrings to her unpierced lobes. I gave her a thumbs-up and mentally added "Pierce Waylay's ears" to the list.

"I got my reasons. Just like I got my reasons for not telling you."

"That's not an acceptable answer."

We were almost touching now, and my body was getting confused between the cold air-conditioning and the heat pumping off his spectacular body.

"Only answer you're getting for now."

"This is why you're single," I pointed out. "No woman in her right mind would put up with that."

"I'm single because I wanna be," he countered.

I was mid–eye roll when he decided to change the subject. "So you're trying to buy your way in with Way?"

"Yes, I am. Girls like presents."

"Do you like presents?" he asked.

I shook my head. "No, Knox. I don't. I freaking *love* presents."

It was true. I did.

Warner had half-assed his way through the past few years of Christmases and birthdays, making me feel materialistic when I'd shown any disappointment at the thoughtless gifts in the wrong sizes.

Knox cracked a half smile. "So where's the funding coming from for this spree? I know what you make at Honky Tonk."

I craned my neck to make sure Waylay was still inside. She was trying on a braided headband in pink and purple. It looked freaking adorable, and I itched to go in and drag her to the counter with it.

"Not that it's any of your business, but I sold my wedding dress."

"Things that bad?" he asked.

"Bad?"

"You just sold a wedding dress to pay for your niece's back-to-school shit. You don't have a phone. And you don't have a car."

"I have a phone," I said, digging out Liza J's old Blackberry and holding it up in his face.

"The letter E just fell off the keyboard."

Damn it. E was in a lot of words.

"I don't need your judgment, okay? Today, the priority is school stuff for Waylay. I'll figure out the rest. So you do your thing, and I'll shower my niece with stuff."

That half smile was back, and it was wreaking havoc with my nervous system. "Deal."

I headed toward the store, then stopped short to admire the window display. A wall of hot, hard chest crashed into me.

"Problem?" Knox asked. His beard tickled my ear.

I turned around to face him and gritted my teeth. "You're not going to leave us alone today, are you?"

"Nope," he said, walking me backward into the store with a hand spread across my stomach.

I thought for sure we'd lose him in the first tween store, but he'd stuck through all of them, including the shoes. He'd even voiced a few opinions when Waylay asked for them, and he'd made faces at her to keep her entertained while she got her ears pierced.

She was glowing. Her frosty "don't care" demeanor had started to thaw on the second pair of shoes and had melted into a puddle when I insisted she get the sundress with pink and yellow flowers. And that was before Knox had whipped out his credit card when she gasped audibly over a pair of hot pink sneakers with bedazzled flowers.

"Why do you keep feeling your forehead, Aunt Naomi?" Waylay asked.

"I'm trying to see if I have a fever, because I'm definitely hallucinating." The only alternative was I'd accidentally managed to fall into an alternate timeline in which Knox Morgan was a nice guy who liked to shop.

We ran into Waylay's friend Nina—with the nice breath and black hair—from school. I was happy to be introduced to her dads, Isaac and Gael, who seemed to accept it when Knox introduced himself only as our ride. Nina asked if Waylay could go to the arcade with them. I gladly said yes and was exchanging phone numbers with Isaac when Knox pulled a twenty-dollar bill out of his wallet.

"Go wild, Way," he said.

"Wow. Thanks!"

"Don't buy too much candy," I called after her. "We haven't had dinner yet!"

She waved over her shoulder, a gesture I assumed meant she had no intention of listening. I turned on Knox.

"Why are you still here? You've shadowed us to every store. You keep checking your phone like you're a teenager. And you haven't bought yourself anything. You're very confusing and annoying."

His face remained stony, and he didn't answer.

"Fine. I guess I'll just finish my shopping."

Since I was living out of a suitcase, I really did need new underwear. Ducking into Victoria's Secret wasn't exactly a ruse to get rid of him, but I figured there was no way on earth Knox Morgan would follow me inside.

I was shuffling through the sale bin when I felt a grumpy, looming presence. He was standing behind me, arms crossed over his chest. I rolled my eyes and decided to ignore him.

What I couldn't ignore was the fact that every time a woman entered the store, she stopped in her tracks and stared.

I couldn't blame them. He was unfairly gorgeous. Too bad about the whole terrible personality thing.

I'd narrowed it down to two pairs of normal ol' briefs but kept coming back to sigh over a silky pair with lace cutouts on the side and back when a sales associate appeared.

"Can I get a dressing room started for you?" she asked.

I thought about it. At least Knox couldn't follow me into the dressing room.

"She'll take these," he said, snatching the briefs out of my hand and pushing them at the saleswoman. My mouth fell open as he dug into the bin and yanked out three more pairs of the impractical, sexy as hell ones. Pink, purple, and red. Then he grabbed a pair of adorable boxer-style undies with red hearts all over them. "And these."

He shoved them all at the woman, who gave me a sly grin before marching over to the register.

"Knox, I'm not buying all those," I hissed at him.

"Shut it," he said and whipped out his credit card.

"If you think for one second that I'm allowing you to buy me underwear—"

He cut off my tirade by slinging an arm over my shoulder and covering my mouth with his hand. "Here," he said, sliding his card across the counter. I was squirming against him until he leaned down. "If this is what it takes to get out of this fucking store without passing out from a goddamn hard-on, I'm buying you the fucking underwear."

By my count, this was the second time he'd mentioned his man parts having a reaction to me. I wasn't a big enough liar to pretend I wasn't happy that he found himself in the same predicament as me: turned on by the physical, turned off by everything else.

I stopped squirming when he pulled me in front of him. With my back flush to his front, I could feel the irrefutable evidence of his claim. My body reacted entirely without my brain's input and went into five-alarm arousal. I worried that I was going to need to be carried out of the store.

"That was incredibly inappropriate," I said, crossing my arms over my chest as we left the store, his arm still around me.

"You wanted me to buy something. I bought something."

"Underwear. For me," I screeched.

"You look tired," he said smugly.

"Tired? I'm exhausted. We've walked fifty miles in a mall. I spent every dime and then some. I'm tired. I'm hungry. Most of all, I'm confused, Knox! You're so mean all the time, and then you show up today and buy me nice underwear?"

"Maybe you'll think of me when you wear them," he said, his gaze scanning ahead of us.

"You're the worst."

"You're welcome. We got one more stop," he said, taking my hand.

I was tired. Too tired to fight. Too tired to pay attention to what store he dragged me into.

"Mr. Morgan." A tall, skinny kid with a dark goatee waved at us. "We just finished up," he said.

We were in a cell phone store. I dug my heels in, but Knox merely pulled me forward to the counter.

"Good timing, Ben."

"Here she is," the kid said, sliding a brand-new phone toward me. "It's all set up and in the case. If you need any help downloading your old contacts from the cloud, we'll be happy to help you. Your new number is written inside the box."

Baffled, tired, hungry, a little furious, and a lot confused, I stared down at the phone, then up at Knox.

"Thanks," Knox said to Ben, then handed me the phone.

The case had sparkly daisies on it. "You got me a phone?"

"Let's go," he said. "I'm hungry."

I let him pull me out of the store, remembering at the door to give Ben a wave and a "thank you."

We were halfway to the arcade when my brain started connecting the dots. "You walked me all over this damn mall without complaining just to wear me out so I'd be too tired to fight you on the phone, didn't you?"

"Burgers, sushi, or pizza?" he asked.

"Burgers. Knox?"

He kept on walking.

"Knox!" I poked him in the shoulder to get his attention.

When he looked down at me, he wasn't smiling and he didn't look smug. "You needed a phone. I got you one. Don't make this into a thing."

"You call me needy. You yell at me for working at your bar and tell me the only part of me worth spending time with is my body. Then you show up on my shopping trip *uninvited* and buy me underwear and a really expensive phone."

"That about sums it up, minus the only part of you worth spending time with."

204

"Are you always this . . . this inconsistent? This confusing?"

He stopped walking and looked down at me. "No, Naomi. I'm not always this fucking inconsistent. And I blame you. I don't *want* to be into you. I don't *want* to spend an entire day wandering around a goddamn mall and fighting traffic for you. I sure as hell don't *want* to watch you try on underwear. But I also don't want you home alone when there's some guy back in Knockemout looking for you."

Uh-oh.

"Some guy? Who is it?"

"Dunno. Justice and Wraith are taking care of it. They'll call Nash in if they need to," he said grimly.

"What do you mean 'taking care of it'?" I had visions of bodies and tarps and duct tape.

"Don't worry about it."

I started laughing and kept right on going. I couldn't help it. I'd spent the last four years in a relationship where I took care of everything. Every dinner reservation. Every vacation. Every load of laundry. Every grocery run.

Here I was in town for less than two weeks, and the grumpy guy who mostly hated me had just taken care of me.

Maybe someday I'd find a guy who both liked me *and* was willing to share the burden of taking care. Or maybe I would just end up alone like Tina had always predicted.

"You having some kind of breakdown? 'Cause I sure as hell have better things to do than watch that."

"Oh, good," I said, smothering my hysteria. "Grumpy Knox is back. What does this guy look like?"

"According to Justice, he looks like some dude named Henry Golding."

"Henry Golding the hot actor or Henry Golding some local biker?" It was a very important distinction.

"I don't know any Henry Golding biker. But this guy showed up at the café asking for you. Justice said he about lost it when he saw your sister's mug shot behind the register."

I was never going to live this down.

"You know him?"

It was my turn to be evasive. "Can we get Waylay and go for those burgers?"

16

The Infamous Stef

Naomi

On the way home, I programmed Nina's dads' numbers into my shiny, new phone. They were not the first numbers in there. Knox had already programmed contacts for Liza J, Honky Tonk, Sherry, Waylay's school, and Café Rev.

There was even one for himself.

I didn't know what that said or meant. And frankly, I was too damn tired to worry about it. Especially when I had a bigger problem.

That bigger problem was sitting on the front steps of the cottage with a glass of wine.

"Stay in the truck," Knox growled.

But I was already halfway out. "It's fine. I know him."

Waylay, crammed in the back seat with all our purchases, rolled down her window and stuck her head out. "Who's that?"

"That's Stef," I said.

He put down the wine and opened his arms.

I ran into them. Stefan Liao was the world's perfect man. He was smart, funny, thoughtful, outrageously generous, and so pretty it hurt to look directly at him. The only son of a real estate–

developing father and an app-developing mother, he was born with an entrepreneurial spirit and exquisite taste in everything.

And somehow I'd gotten lucky enough to land him as a best friend.

He swept me up in his arms and twirled me around.

"I'm still incredibly pissed at you," he said with a grin.

"Thank you for loving me even when you're pissed," I said, wrapping my arms around his neck and breathing in his expensive cologne.

Just seeing him, hugging him, made me feel more grounded.

"You gonna introduce me to Blondie and the Beast?" Stef asked.

"Not done hugging yet," I insisted.

"Hurry it up. Beast looks like he wants to shoot me."

"He's more of a Viking than a beast."

Stef tilted my head back with his hands and planted a kiss on my forehead. "It's all gonna be fine. I promise."

Tears stung my eyes. I believed him. And the relief I felt from that was enough to release Niagara Falls of tears.

"Where do you want your shit?" Knox growled.

That was enough to dry up Niagara Falls. I spun around and found him standing only a foot away. "Seriously?"

"Got things to do, Daze. Don't have all night to

stand around watching you make out with Henry Golding."

"Henry Golding? Nice," Stef said.

"Waylay, come meet my friend," I called.

High from her shopping, arcade, and burger experience, Waylay forgot to look annoyed.

"Waylay Witt, Knox Morgan, this is Stefan Liao. Stef for short. Way for short. And Leif Erikson when he's being moody."

Stef grinned. Knox growled. Waylay admired Stef's shiny smartwatch.

"The pleasure is all mine. You look like your aunt," Stef said to Waylay.

"Really?" Waylay looked not too horrified by that statement, and I wondered if my shopping bribery had worked its magic. *Score.*

Knox, on the other hand, looked like he wanted to dismember Stef.

"What's your problem?" I mouthed at him.

He glared at me as if I was the one to blame for his sudden mood swing.

"Knox," Stef said, holding out a hand. "I can't thank you enough for looking out for my girl here."

Knox grunted and stared at the offered hand for a beat before shaking it.

The handshake went on longer than necessary.

"Why are their fingers turning white?" Waylay asked me.

"It's a man thing," I explained.

She looked skeptical. "Like pooping for forty-five minutes?"

"Yeah, something like that," I said.

The handshake was finally over, and both men were now locked in a staring contest. If I wasn't careful, the penises and rulers would be next.

"Knox very graciously took us shopping today," I explained to Stef.

"He bought me pink sneakers, and he bought Aunt Naomi underwear and a phone."

"Thank you for that information, Way. Why don't you go inside and not talk anymore?" I suggested, giving her a shove toward the house.

"That depends. Can I have the last ice cream sandwich?"

"It's yours as long as you stuff it in your mouth instead of talking."

"Pleasure doing business with you. See ya, Knox!"

He was already halfway back to his truck.

"Don't leave on my account," Stef called after him.

Knox didn't say anything, but I did hear some sort of growl coming from his general direction. "Hang on a second," I said to Stef. "He's got the better part of a mall in his back seat, and I don't want him to drive off with it."

I caught him just as he was opening his door.

"Knox. Wait!"

"What? I'm busy. I have shit to do."

"Can you give me one minute to get Waylay's department store out of your back seat?"

He muttered a few colorful expletives and

yanked open the back door. I looped as many bags as I could over my wrists before his frustration took over. He marched all the new stuff to the porch and set it in a pile next to Stef.

"You *did* get new underwear," Stef said, sneaking a peek into the Victoria's Secret bag.

Another low growl emanated from the vicinity of Knox's chest, and then he was storming back to his truck.

I rolled my eyes and ran after him.

"Knox?"

"Christ, woman," he said, rounding on me. "Now what?"

"Nothing. Just . . . Thank you for everything today. It meant the world to Waylay. And me."

When I turned to leave, his hand shot out and caught my wrist. "Future reference, Daze. My problem is always you."

I don't know why I did what I did next, but I did it. I raised on tiptoe and pressed a kiss to his cheek.

He was still standing there when Stef and I walked inside with a dozen shopping bags between us.

With Waylay asleep in a shopping-induced coma, I changed into pajamas and wondered why in the world I'd left my closet doors wide open, then decided it had probably been Waylay. I was surprised at the effect an additional human had on a household. Toothpaste tubes were squeezed haphazardly in the middle. Snacks disappeared.

And the TV remote was never where I left it.

I closed the closet doors firmly and returned downstairs.

The back door was open, and through the screen, I saw Stef on the porch. He'd turned my back porch into a citronella candle fantasy land.

"You can't tell my parents about any of this yet," I said without preamble as I stepped out onto the porch.

Stef looked up from the tray of fancy meats and cheeses he was organizing on the picnic table. "Why would you even say that? I'm always Team Naomi," he said.

"I know you talk to them."

"Just because your mom and I have a standing date at the spa every month doesn't mean I'd rat you out, Witty. Besides, I didn't tell them I was coming."

"I just haven't figured out how to tell them about Waylay. It took me an hour on the phone after I pulled a runaway bride before Mom agreed to still go on the trip. I know if I were to tell them what was going on, they'd be off the boat and on a plane in a second."

"That does sound like something your parents would do," he agreed, handing me a glass of wine. The man had brought an entire case with him. "Your beast wants to devour you like a dozen hot wings."

I flopped down on the lawn chair next to him. "How is that the first thing you say to me?"

"It's the most pressing."

"Not 'why did you leave Warner at the altar?' Or 'what the hell were you thinking answering your sister's call for help?'"

He propped his long legs on the railing. "You know I never liked Warner. I was ecstatic when you pulled the disappearing act. I only wish you would have let me in on it."

"I'm sorry," I said lamely.

"Stop saying you're sorry."

"I'm s—our?"

"You're the one who has to live your life. Don't apologize to other people for the decisions you make for yourself."

My voice of reason best friend. No judgments. No second-guessing. Just unconditional love and support . . . and the occasional truth bomb. He was one in a billion.

"You're right. As usual. But I still should have let you know I was pulling a runaway bride."

"You definitely should have. Although I did get great pleasure seeing Warner's mother break the news to him in front of the entire congregation. Watching them both trying not to freak out to keep their porcelain reputation intact was comedic. Besides, I took one of the groomsmen home."

"Which one?"

"Paul."

"Nice. He looked good in his tux," I mused.

"He looked better out of it."

"Hey-oh!"

"Speaking of hot sex. Back to the beast."

I choked on my wine. "There's no sex happening with the beast. He called me needy and uppity and a pain in his ass. He's rude. He's constantly yelling at me or complaining about me. Telling me I'm not his type. As if I wished I were his type," I scoffed.

"Why are you whispering?"

"Because he lives right there," I said, pointing my glass in the direction of Knox's cabin.

"Ooh. Grumpy next-door neighbor. That's one of my favorite tropes."

"The first time he met me, he called me trash."

"That bitch."

"Well, technically he thought I was Tina when he was yelling at me in front of an entire café full of strangers."

"That vision-impaired bitch."

"God, I love you." I sighed.

"Back at you, Witty. So to clarify, you're defi-nitely *not* sleeping with the hot, grumpy, tattooed neighbor who took you shopping for underwear and a phone?"

"I am five thousand percent definitely not sleeping with Knox. And he only went shopping with us because there were reports of a man in town looking for me."

"You're telling me he's a grumpy, *overprotective* hottie next door and you're not going to sleep with him? How wasteful."

"How about instead of talking about Knox, I tell

you *why* I burned rubber out of the church parking lot and ended up homeless in Knockemout?"

"Don't forget carless," he added.

I rolled my eyes. "And carless."

"I'll get the truffles I hid in your bedroom," Stef volunteered.

"I really wish you were straight," I said.

"If I could be straight for anyone, it would be you," he said, clinking his glass to mine.

"Where did these glasses come from?" I asked, frowning at the barware.

"These are my car wineglasses. I always carry a pair."

"Of course you do."

Dear Naomi,

Your father and I are having a wonderful time even though you haven't been updating us on what's going on in your life. Barcelona was beautiful, but it would have been even more beautiful if we knew our daughter wasn't spiraling into depression or some sort of midlife crisis.

Guilt-tripping over. You should have seen our tour guide, Paolo. Hubba hubba as the kids say. I attached a photo that I took. He's single if you want me to bring you back a souvenir.

Love,
Mom

17

Man-to-Man

Knox

It was too damn early for someone to be banging on my front door. They deserved what they got. I yanked on a pair of gym shorts and stumbled down the stairs, rubbing sleep out of my eyes.

"Someone better be dead," I muttered, nearly taking a header over Waylon, who put on the speed on the last three steps.

"What?" I said, yanking the door open.

The obnoxiously good-looking Stef—stupid, misleading name—peered at me over his expensive sunglasses.

"Good morning to you too," he said. He wore golf shorts and one of those patterned button-downs that only lean guys who spent hours a week at the gym could pull off.

My dog shoved half his body out onto the porch and gazed lovingly up at the intruder.

"Who's a good boy? Who's a handsome boy?" Stef said, squatting down to pet him.

Waylon basked in the attention.

I rubbed a hand over my face. "What do you want?"

Mr. Smooth held up two cups of coffee in a to-go tray. "Coffee talk."

I snatched one out of his hand and stomped away from the door into the kitchen. Waylon trotted after me, anticipating his breakfast.

I popped the lid off the coffee and guzzled while I scooped up a helping of kibble.

Dog fed, I shoved my head under the faucet and turned on the cold water, willing the shock to wake up my brain.

I came up for air and found a hand towel hovering in front of my face.

I took it without a thank-you and dried off.

"Why are you bringing me coffee at an inhuman hour?"

"To talk about Naomi, of course. I assumed you were quicker than this."

"I am when my sleep isn't interrupted."

So maybe it hadn't been the sleep I was pissed off about. Maybe it was the dream involving Naomi's cherry-painted lips that had just been getting warmed up when this asshole decided to be social.

"My apologies. I figured this talk couldn't wait," he said, pulling out a stool at the counter.

I crumpled up the towel and threw it in the sink. "Is this the part where you tell me to back off your girl?"

Stef laughed.

"Something funny?"

"You're one of those straights with baggage that complicates everything," he said, leaning on the counter.

"You have until I finish this coffee before I throw you out."

"Fine. I appreciate you looking out for Naomi. You hear a stranger is asking questions around town looking for her, and you got her and Waylay out, made sure they were safe. She's not used to someone taking care of her like that."

"Didn't do it because I want to get in her pants."

"No, even though you do, because you're not stupid. You did it because you wanted to protect her. So even though you've got this whole Oscar the Sexy Grouch thing going, you're already miles beyond Warner in my opinion."

I kept my face neutral, not willing to show any interest in this new topic.

"Warner used her. And I tried to warn her. Hell, I even warned him. But Naomi did what she's always done."

"Cleaned up everyone else's messes," I said.

Stef raised an eyebrow. "Well, well, well. Look who's been paying attention."

Waylon let out a hearty burp from the floor. He sat staring at his now empty dish as if expecting it to magically refill.

"What's your point?"

"She's spent her entire life trying to make up for her sister, who sucks, by the way. And it keeps biting her in the ass. Be the perfect student. Get the perfect job. Marry the perfect guy. Now she's signed up to take care of an eleven-year-old in a strange place and is hoping that if she can just be

218

good enough, she can stop her parents' hearts from breaking again."

I shoved a hand through my hair. "What does any of this have to do with me?"

Stef held up his hands and grinned. "Look, I get if you're in that whole 'I'm not interested' phase. The last thing Naomi needs right now is a hot and heavy relationship that's going to get messy because of your baggage. But if you keep looking out for her like you did yesterday, we won't have a problem."

"And if I don't?"

"If you use that accommodating nature of hers against her, then we're going to have a huge problem. I can be very creative when it comes to finding ways to make you regret being an asshole."

It was ballsy. I had to give it to him. Showing up to a stranger's house with coffee and then threatening him. It felt like something I might do, minus the coffee thing.

"What kind of creative problem is this Warner asshole having right now?"

Stef took a long sip of coffee. "Right now, I'm letting the humiliation of being left at the altar by the woman he told his friends was 'beneath his class' do its work. But if he comes near her again, I'll ruin him."

"What did he do?" I asked.

He blew out a breath and took another sip of coffee. "I didn't know specifics until last night, and I've been sworn to secrecy."

"Bad?"

Stef's jaw clenched. "Bad," he agreed.

I didn't like that this guy had Naomi's confidence. That he had access to her secrets, and I was on the outside, left guessing. But I could think of a few dozen things that fell under the category of bad. Any one of them would be worth breaking an asshole's jaw over.

"He better hope he's never dumb enough to step foot in town limits," I said, putting my cup down.

"Hate to break it to you," Stef said, looking up from the full-body scratch he was giving Waylon. "He's definitely that dumb. Besides, where else would he go when he realizes that Naomi's the one who solved every problem he ever had? He's already emailing her every day. It's only a matter of time before he figures out where she is."

"I'll be ready for him," I said grimly.

"Good. I'm still sticking around for a while. At least until I know she's okay. But I can't be next to her at all times. It helps to know there's someone else looking out for her."

"She wouldn't take him back, would she?" I surprised myself with the question.

Stef seemed to enjoy the fact that I'd asked the question. "No. But she's soft enough that she might try to help him clean himself up."

"Fuck."

"There's nothing our girl loves more than getting her hands on a disaster and making it shine." He gave me a long, even look, and I didn't much care for the connotation.

I wasn't a disaster. There was nothing wrong with me. I had my fucking life figured out.

"Fine. So what do we do in the meantime?"

"Money's tight for her. She spent most of her own savings on the wedding."

Fucking romantics. Never even considering that things could and would go horribly wrong.

"She's prickly about taking loans or handouts. Though she might have no choice once her parents catch wind of the situation."

"They blow into town pissed off at Evil Twin and then try to take care of down-on-her-luck Good Twin," I guessed.

He tossed me a salute. "That about sums it up."

I blew out a sigh. "She's got no car, no computer. She's picked up some bar shifts from me."

But it wasn't enough for a family of two to live off for long. And the best paying shifts were nights, which meant someone had to watch Waylay.

Single moms were the world's unsung fucking heroes.

Stef took his phone out of his back pocket, thumbs moving over the screen. "I'm going to apply some charming pressure and push her to put her house up for sale. She's only had it two years, but she had a decent down payment, and property values are going up in that neighborhood. There should be enough equity there to help her cash flow problem."

I searched my memory for something that was niggling in the back of my head. "Librarian said something about a part-time gig if a grant comes through. I could make sure that grant lands."

He looked at me over his screen. "Putting those lottery winnings to good use?"

So Mr. Smooth had looked me up. It wasn't exactly a secret. And I'd have done the same in his place.

"What exactly do *you* do?" I asked.

He shrugged, still typing. "A little of this, a little of that. I've got a guy who can deal with the house. As soon as she gives the okay, we'll have an offer within a week. Two tops," he predicted.

I drained the last of the coffee. "So she didn't live with this asshole?"

"Not officially. He was going to move in with her after the wedding. Reluctant bastard liked having his own place. Especially since Naomi cleaned it for him and took care of his meals and laundry. I hope that fucker is sitting in a pair of dirty underwear sobbing into a pot of Campbell's."

I stared at him a beat. "Who the fuck are you?"

"Me?" Stef laughed, stowing his phone back in his pocket. "I'm the best friend. Naomi is family."

"And you two never . . ."

He sat there smugly and waited for me to say it. "Never what?"

"Never . . . dated?"

"Not unless you count taking her to senior prom because Tina got caught with her mouth on Naomi's date's dick in the locker room at school."

Fucking Tina.

"Naomi's been my ride-or-die before ride-or-die was a thing. She has never once let me down, and she's forgiven me for the handful of occasions that I've let her down. She's the most amazing woman I know, and that's counting her mother, who's pretty fucking awesome too. I don't like it when people fuck with my family."

I could respect that.

"I'll take that grunt to mean we have an understanding. You'll watch out for her. You won't fuck with her. And together we'll make sure Warner Fucking Dipshit the Third never gets within a city block of her."

I nodded again. "Fine."

"Give me your phone," he said, holding out his hand.

"Why?"

"Oh, you want me to text Naomi when Warner shows up looking for her?"

I handed it over.

Stef held it up to my scowling face to unlock it. "Huh. Wonder if it would unlock if you were smiling."

"I don't know. Never tried."

He smirked. "I like you, Knox. You sure you're not interested in our girl?"

"Definitely not," I lied.

Stef studied me. "Hmm. You're either dumber than you look or you're a better liar than I thought."

"Are you done? I'd like to get back to not having you in my house."

18

Makeovers for Everyone

Naomi

S urprise!" Stef said as he pulled into a parking
space directly in front of Whiskey Clipper.

Uh-oh.

"What are we doing here?" I asked.

"Back-to-school hair," Stef said.

"Seriously?" Waylay asked, biting her lip. She
couldn't quite pull off the bored preteen vibe, and
I knew it was going to be a good idea, even if it
meant braving a run-in with Knox.

"Deadly, darling," Stef said, hopping out from
behind the wheel of his spiffy little Porsche SUV.
He opened the back door for her. "First day of
school is a fresh start for everyone. And from the
reviews, this is *the* place for hair."

I climbed out and joined them on the sidewalk.

Stef slung an arm around both of us. "First hair.
Then lunch. Then nails. Then fashion show for
first-day outfits."

I grinned. "Outfit*s?*"

"You're walking Way to the bus. You need something that says 'responsible yet hot aunt.'"

Waylay giggled. "Most moms just show up in
pajamas or in sweaty workout stuff."

"Exactly. We need to make a statement that the Witt women are fierce and fashionable."

I rolled my eyes.

Stef caught me and crossed his arms in impatience. "What have I always told you, Naomi? And you listen to this too, Way."

"When you look good, you feel good," I recited.

"Good girl. Now get your cute little asses in there."

The interior of Whiskey Clipper was cooler than any salon I'd ever set foot in. Instead of the muted pastels and spa music typical in most hair establishments, here it was brick walls and '70s rock. Black-and-white photos of Knockemout in the early part of the twentieth century hung in stylish gallery frames. One entire wall was dominated by a bar of decanters and bottles of whiskey. Exotic flower arrangements occupied the low, curved front desk and the whiskey bar.

The waiting area looked more like a VIP lounge with its leather couches and glass side tables. The concrete floor was covered with a faux cowhide rug.

It felt cool, a little steampunk-y. And a lot expensive.

I turned to my friend and lowered my voice. "Stef, I know you were being nice, but money—"

"Shut your stupid beautiful face, Witty. This is on me." He held up a hand when I opened my mouth to argue. "I didn't get you a wedding present."

"Why not?"

He looked at me dryly for a long beat.

"Right. Of course you predicted it."

"Look, you're getting your 'my fiancé likes my hair long' shit cut into something *you* love. And that adorable smart-ass niece of ours is getting a style that is going to be more interesting to those little fuckers in the sixth grade."

"You're impossible to argue with, you know that?"

"You might as well save your energy and quit trying."

"Hello, ladies and gentleman," Jeremiah called from a station with an ornate mirror and a scarlet cape draped over the chair. "Who's ready to change their lives today?"

Waylay sidled up to me. "Is he serious?"

Stef took her by the shoulders. "Listen, shorty. You've never experienced the miracle of the kind of haircut that is so good it parts the clouds and makes the angels sing. You're in for a treat today."

"What if I don't like it?" she whispered.

"If you don't like it, our next stop will be Target, and I'll buy you every hair accessory in existence until we find the perfect way to style your new hair."

"Your hair is yours. You get to decide what to do with it," I assured her.

"You get to decide how you show up in this world. No one else gets to dictate to you who you are," Stef said.

I knew he was saying it for Waylay's benefit,

but the truth resonated deep down inside me too. I'd lost myself while trying to convince someone else that I was what he wanted. I'd forgotten who I was because I'd let someone else take over the definition.

"Okay," Waylay said. "But if I hate it, I'm going to blame you guys."

"Let's do this," I said with conviction.

"There she is," Stef said, booping my nose and then Waylay's. "Now, let's get started." He made a beeline for Jeremiah.

"Your friend is weird," Waylay whispered.

"I know."

"I kinda like him."

"Yeah. Me too."

Maybe it was the second glass of champagne Jeremiah poured for me. Or maybe it was the fact that having a man's fingers massaging my scalp and playing with my hair was a long-forgotten delight. But whatever the reason, I felt relaxed for the first time in . . . I couldn't count backward that far.

It wasn't that I didn't have things to worry about. There were plenty of those looming. Like the guardianship. And money. And the fact that I still hadn't told my parents about their granddaughter.

But right now, I had a gorgeous man's hands rubbing delicious circles into my scalp, a glass full of bubbles, and a niece who couldn't stop giggling over whatever Stasia was saying to her while they worked on temporary lowlights.

Stef and Jeremiah were deep in conversation about hair textures and product. I wondered if I was imagining the hint of spark between the two. The lingering smiles, the long flirtatious glances.

It had been a while since Stef had been in anything resembling a relationship, and the gorgeous, talented Jeremiah was definitely his kind of catnip.

I heard the roar of a motorcycle out on the street. The engine revved once before cutting off abruptly. A few seconds later, the front door opened.

"Hey, boss," Stasia called out.

My bubble of bliss popped.

The responding grunt had my heart trying to flutter its way out of my chest like an anxiety-ridden butterfly trapped in a glass jar.

"Stay," Jeremiah said firmly, pressing a hand to my shoulder.

I couldn't see Knox. But I could feel his presence.

"Knox," Stef drawled.

"Stef."

I opened my eyes, wondering when the two of them had gotten on a grudging first-name basis.

"Hey, Way," Knox said, his voice a little softer.

"Hi," she chirped.

I heard the approach of his boots, and every muscle in my body went rigid. No woman looked good with wet hair in a salon chair. Not that I was going for alluring or anything. Although I was wearing the underwear he'd bought me.

"Naomi," he rasped.

What was it about my name from that mouth that made my nether regions feel like they were being electrocuted? In a super sexy, fun way.

"Knox," I managed to choke out.

"Your face is red," Jeremiah noted. "Is the water too hot?"

Stef snickered.

I swear to God I could hear a smugness in the steady clomp of boots as they slowly retreated to the back of the shop.

Way to be cool, me.

Stef let out a low whistle from the barber chair he was occupying. "Spaaaaarks," he sang quietly.

I raised my head out of the sink, sending a tidal wave of water over the lip of the bowl. "What is the matter with you?" I hissed. "Shut. Up."

He raised his palms in surrender. "Fine. Sorry."

As Jeremiah gently stuffed me back into the sink, I fumed. I didn't want or need sparks, and I certainly didn't want or need anyone else calling attention to them.

Jeremiah wrapped a towel around my sodden hair and led me back to his station. Waylay was in the chair behind me, discussing cut and style options with Stasia and Stef.

"So, how do we feel about getting rid of some dead weight?" Jeremiah asked, holding my gaze in the mirror. He hefted the bulk of my damp hair in one hand and held it above my shoulders.

"We feel really good about that," I decided.

• • •

I was mid-second-thought panic as Jeremiah aggressively snipped his way through my long hair when Knox returned with a cup of coffee and some kind of short leather apron over his worn jeans. With his tattoo-adorned arms, the ruthlessly trimmed beard, and those scarred motorcycle boots, he looked like the definition of a man.

Our eyes locked in the mirror, and my breath caught in my throat.

After a too-long beat, Knox whistled and hooked his thumb at the client in the waiting area. The man hefted his tall frame out of the chair and lumbered back.

"How's it going, Aunt Naomi?" Waylay called from behind me. "Still look like a wet mop?"

Kids were jerks.

"She's being transformed as we speak," Jeremiah promised, sliding his long fingers through my significantly shorter hair. I choked back a purr.

"How's your hair?" I asked my niece.

"Blue. I like it."

She said it with a mix of reverence and excitement that had me smiling. I gave up worrying about whether I was overcompensating and turning Waylay into an entitled brat and decided to just go with it.

"How blue? Like Smurfette blue?"

"Who's Smurfette?" Waylay asked.

"Who's Smurfette?" Stasia scoffed. I heard her rummaging through her pockets and then the telltale sound of the Smurf theme song coming from a phone. "That's Smurfette."

"Wish my hair was as long as hers," Waylay said wistfully.

"You cut it pretty short before you came in here. But it'll grow," Stasia told her with confidence.

Waylay was silent for a moment, and I craned my neck for a glimpse of her in the mirror. "I didn't cut it," she said, eyes meeting mine.

"What's that, sweetheart?" Stasia asked.

"I didn't cut it," Waylay said again. "My mom did. As a punishment. Couldn't ground me 'cause she was never around. So she chopped off my hair."

"That fucking b—ouch!"

I kicked Stef, then spun my chair around.

Waylay shrugged at the suddenly silent adults around her. "It wasn't a big deal."

That was what she'd told herself. I remembered the tidy bins of hair accessories in her old bedroom. Tina had taken something from her, something she'd taken pride in.

Stef and Stasia looked to me, and I searched for the right words to make this okay.

But someone beat me to it.

Knox dropped the razor on a metal tray with a clang and crossed to Waylay's chair. "You get that that was a dick move, right?"

"Knox, language," I hissed.

He ignored me. "What your mom did was born out of a place of unhappiness and meanness inside her. It had nothing to do with you. You didn't cause it or deserve it. She was just being an asshole, yeah?"

Waylay's eyes narrowed as if she were waiting for the punchline. "Yeah?" she said tentatively.

He nodded briskly. "Good. I don't know why your mom does the things she does. I don't really want to know. Something's broken inside her, and that makes her treat others like shit. Got it?"

Waylay nodded again.

"Your aunt Naomi over there isn't like that. She's not broken. She'll probably still fuck up now and then, but that's cause she's human, not broken. Which is why when you mess up—and you will, 'cause you're human too—there has to be a consequence. It won't be cutting your hair or not making you dinner. It'll be boring shit like chores and grounding and no TV. Got it?"

"I got it," she said quietly.

"From here on out, if anyone says they have a right to decide what to do with your body, kid, you kick 'em in the ass, then come find me," Knox told her.

Well, hell. The man's hotness had just escalated into underwear-melting territory.

"And me," Stef agreed.

Jeremiah gave her a level look. "Me too."

Waylay's lips quirked, and she was having a hard time keeping her smile under wraps. I, on the other hand, suddenly felt a little damp in the eye *and* underwear areas.

"Then when they're done kicking ass, you come find me," Stasia said.

"And me. But preferably me first, before anyone goes to jail," I added.

"Party pooper," Jeremiah teased.

"You got it, Way?" Knox pressed.

The tiniest of smiles played on her lips. "Yeah. I got it," she said.

"In that case, let's get back to giving you the best haircut in the world," Stasia said with extra cheer.

My phone buzzed in my lap, and I glanced at the screen.

Stef: Told you your sister was a gigantic waste of DNA.

I sighed and tossed him a glare, then typed.

Me: I'm first in line for face punching when she turns up.
Stef: Good girl. Also, I added a bikini wax to your mani-pedi.
Me: Mean! Why?
Stef: Growly Tattoo Guy deserves to get laid after that speech. Also, Jer is fifty shades of gorgeous.

"Agree on both counts," Jeremiah said from where he was reading over my shoulder.

Stef laughed while I turned six shades of scarlet.

"What are you agreeing to?" Knox demanded.

233

I clutched my phone to my chest and spun myself around to face the mirror. "Nothing. No one is agreeing to anything," I said sharply.

"Face is burning up, Daisy," Knox observed.

I considered crawling under my cape like a turtle and hiding there for the rest of my life. But then Jeremiah put his magic hands in my hair and did something lovely to my scalp, and I began to relax against my will.

Everyone went back to other conversations while I snuck surreptitious glances in Knox's direction.

Not only had the man just given a little girl a hero, he also appeared to be a competent barber. I'd never considered haircuts sexy until this moment as Knox, arm muscles flexing, trimmed and shaped his client's thick, dark hair.

Lots of mundane things were sexy when Knox Morgan was doing them.

"Ready for the razor?" he asked gruffly.

"You know it," the man mumbled from under the hot towel on his face.

I watched in fascination as Knox got to work with a straight razor and a sweet-smelling shaving cream on his friend's face.

It felt more relaxing than all those pressure-washing videos I'd binged while planning the wedding. Straight, clean lines leaving behind nothing but smooth shine.

"You really should think about it," Jeremiah whispered as he liberated a curling iron from a tool organizer.

"Think about what?"

He caught my eye in the mirror and tilted his head in Knox's direction.

"Hard pass."

"Self-care maintenance," he said.

"I beg your pardon?"

"Some women get manicures. Some get massages or go for therapy. Some hit the gym or their favorite bottle of Shiraz. But the best self-care maintenance, in my opinion, is regular, earth-shattering orgasms."

This time, I felt even the tips of my ears go pink.

"I just ran away from a groom and a wedding. I think my tank is topped off for a while," I whispered.

Jeremiah deftly worked his way through my hair with the barrel of the iron. "Suit yourself. But don't you dare waste this style."

With a flourish, he whipped the cape from me and pointed at my reflection.

"Holy sh—crap." I leaned in, shoving my fingers into the touchable chin-length bob. My dark brown hair now had russet highlights and curled in what I liked to call "sex waves."

Stef let out a wolf whistle. "Damn, Naomi."

I'd spent two years growing my hair out for the perfect wedding updo because Warner liked long hair. Two years planning a wedding that didn't happen. Two years wasted, when I could have looked like this. Confident. Stylish. Sexy as hell. Even my eyes looked brighter, my smile bigger.

Warner Dennison III was officially done taking things from me.

"What do you think, Aunt Naomi?" Waylay asked. She stepped in front of me. Her blond hair was cut short with a sweep of sleek bangs over one eye. A subtle blue teased through from the bottom layers.

"You look like you're sixteen," I groaned.

Waylay gave her hair an experimental toss. "I like it."

"I love it," I assured her.

"And with a sassy new cut, we'll be able to coax some length out of your hair if you want to grow it long again," Stasia told her.

Waylay tucked a strand behind her ear and looked at me. "Maybe short hair isn't so bad after all."

"Stasia, Jeremiah, you're miracle workers," Stef said, pulling cash out of his wallet and pressing it into their hands.

"Thank you," I said, offering first Stasia and then Jeremiah a hug. Knox's eyes met mine in the mirror over Jeremiah's shoulder. I released him and looked away. "Seriously. This was amazing."

"Where are we going now?" Waylay wanted to know, still staring at herself in the mirror with that tiny smile on her lips.

"Nails," Stef said. "Your aunt's hands look like talons."

I felt the weight of cool blue-gray eyes on me and looked up. Knox watched me with an unreadable expression. I couldn't tell if he was smoldering or pissed off. "See ya around, boss."

I carried the weight of his attention with me as I strutted for the door.

Dear Mom and Dad,

I hope you're having the best time on your cruise! I can't believe three weeks is almost up.

Things here are good. I have some news for you. Actually, it's really Tina's news. Okay. Here goes. Tina has a daughter. Which means you have a granddaughter. Her name is Waylay. She's eleven years old, and I'm watching her for Tina for a while.

She's really great.

Call me when you get home, and I'll tell you the whole story. Maybe Waylay and I can drive up for a weekend so you can meet her.

Love,
Naomi

19

High Stakes

Naomi

W ell, look who just strutted her fabulous ass in here," Fi called from the corner of Honky Tonk's bar, where she was keying the night's specials into the system.

I held out my arms and did a slow turn.

Who knew a haircut could make me feel ten years younger and a thousand times sassier? Not to mention the short denim skirt Stef had talked me into.

The man set the gold standard for being a best friend. While waiting for me to prance out of the dressing room in my new skirt, Stef had been on a conference call with his "people," arranging to have my stuff packed and my house on Long Island put on the market.

Tonight, he was staying with Waylay, and I wasn't sure who was more excited about their plans to binge-watch *Brooklyn Nine-Nine*.

"You like the hair, Fi?" I asked, giving my head a shake to make the curls bounce.

"Love it. My brother's a damn genius with hair. Speaking of Jer, is your Stef single, and if so, can we play matchmaker?"

"Why? Did Jeremiah say anything about Stef?" I demanded.

"He only casually mentioned that your friend was the hottest gay man to strut into Knockemout in a decade."

I squealed. "Stef asked me if Jeremiah was seeing anyone!"

"Oh, it's so on," Fi announced, pulling the lollipop out of her mouth. "By the way, I've got good news for you."

I grinned as I stowed my purse behind the bar. "Did Idris Elba come to his senses and offer to whisk you away to a private island?"

She grinned wickedly. "Not quite that good. But you've got a party in the private room starting at nine. High rollers."

I perked up. "High rollers?"

Fi jerked her head toward the hallway. "Poker game. Hush-hush. Half a dozen big spenders who feel like throwing away six figures on cards."

"Six figures?" I blinked. "Is this legal?" I whispered the question despite the fact that we were alone in the empty bar.

The lollipop returned to her mouth. "Weeeell, let's just say if Chief Morgan wanders his fine ass in here tonight, he doesn't get in that room."

I wasn't sure how I felt about it. As someone who was supposed to be looking good in the eyes of the court, I probably shouldn't be lying to law enforcement about anything.

But I'd cross that bridge when I had to tonight.

Feeling happy, I swung into the kitchen to get set up for the busy night.

The extent of my professional poker knowledge was entirely based on the snippets of games I'd seen on TV while changing channels. I was pretty sure the players on TV looked nothing like the ones crowded around the round table in Honky Tonk's secret back room.

Beneath his turquoise polo shirt, the British-accented Ian had muscles that looked like he bench-pressed cars all day. He had dark skin, short-cropped hair, and the kind of smile that made a woman's knees go weak. He was wearing a wedding ring with a whole lot of diamonds.

On Ian's right was Tanner. He had reddish-blond hair that looked like a woman's fingers had just left it. He wore the DC commuter uniform of expensive, fitted trousers, rolled-up shirtsleeves, and a loosened tie. No wedding ring, and he'd made certain I'd noticed with every top-shelf scotch I brought him. He fidgeted constantly and jumped every time the door opened.

On Tanner's right was a man the rest referred to as Grim, though I doubted his parents had actually named him that. He looked like he'd walked right off the pages of a silver fox motorcycle club romance novel. Tattoos crisscrossed every inch of visible skin. He kept his sunglasses and scowl firmly in place as he lounged in his chair, sticking to club sodas.

Next to Grim was Winona, the only woman at the table. She was tall, built, and Black, and she wore pink metallic eyeshadow that complemented the accents on her figure-hugging denim romper. Her hair was big and bold, just like her laugh, which she was sharing with the man next to her.

"Lucy, Lucy, Lucy," she said. "When are you gonna learn not to bluff me?"

Lucian was the kind of handsome that made women wonder if he'd made some pact with the devil. Dark hair. Dark, smoldering eyes. Dark suit. He gave off hints of power, wealth, and secrets like a cologne.

He'd arrived later than everyone else, shedding his jacket and rolling up his sleeves as if he had all the time in the world. He took his bourbon neat and didn't try to look down my shirt when I served it.

"Maybe when you stop distracting me with your wit and beauty," he teased.

"Please," Winona scoffed, elegantly stacking her winnings with long red fingernails.

I was in the middle of trying to figure out how much one chip was worth and topping off the pitcher of ice water in the corner when the door burst open.

Tanner and I both jumped.

Knox strode into the room, looking annoyingly sexy as always. "You son of a bitch," he said.

Everyone held their breath. Everyone, that is, except for Lucian, who continued to deal the next hand, unruffled by the interruption. "I was wondering how long it would take word to travel," he said blandly. He set the deck down and came to his feet.

For a second, I was sure they were going to launch themselves at each other like stags fighting for supremacy in a nature documentary . . . or, you know, actual nature.

Instead, Knox's scowl melted and was replaced with the kind of grin that made me feel as warm and gooey inside as a chocolate chip cookie fresh from the oven.

Note to self: Make chocolate chip cookies.

The two men shook hands and exchanged back slaps that would have put me in a chiropractor's office.

"What the hell are you doing here?" Knox asked, less aggressively this time.

"Currently losing to Winona and thinking about ordering another drink."

"I'll get it. Anyone else want another round?" I squeaked.

Knox's gaze fell on me. His grin vanished so quickly I wondered if he'd sprained a facial muscle. He took a leisurely, scowling tour of my appearance from hair to feet, disapproval snapping off him like electricity.

"Naomi, outside. Now," he growled.

"Seriously? What's your problem this time, Viking?"

"There a problem?" Grim asked, his voice low and dangerous.

"None of your concern." Knox's voice had dropped into subzero temperatures.

"Go ahead and bring everyone a round, Naomi," Ian suggested, his eyes on Knox.

I nodded and headed for the door.

Knox was on my heels.

He shut the door behind us and took me by the arm, steering me down the empty hallway away from the bar, past his secret lair office. He didn't stop until he'd opened the door at the far end of the hall, which opened into Whiskey Clipper's supply room.

"What the hell, Knox?"

"What the fuck are you doing in that room dressed like that?"

I gestured at my empty tray. "What does it look like? I'm serving drinks."

"This ain't tea time at some goddamn country club, sweetheart. And those people aren't on the PTA."

I pinched the bridge of my nose. "I'm going to need a pie chart or a Venn diagram or a database to catalog all the many ways I piss you off. Why are you mad that I'm doing my job?"

"You shouldn't be serving that party."

"Look, if you're not going to explain, then I don't think I'm responsible for listening. I have drinks to deliver."

"You can't just wander into dangerous situations like this."

I threw up my arms. "Oh, for Pete's sake. I didn't

wander. I showed up for my shift. Fi gave me the table because she knew they'd tip well."

He stepped close enough that his boots brushed the tips of my shoes. "I want you out of that room."

"Excuse me! You're the one who lets them play here, and you're the one who hired me to serve drinks. Ergo, you're the one with the problem."

He leaned in until we were almost touching. "Naomi, these aren't just weekend warriors on bikes or your typical Beltway roadkill. They can be dangerous if they want to be."

"Yeah? Well, so can I. And if you try to take me off that table, you're going to find out exactly how dangerous."

"Fuck me," he muttered under his breath.

"That's not happening," I scoffed.

He closed his eyes, and I knew the big dummy was counting to ten. I let him get to six before stepping around him.

My hand had just closed around the doorknob when he caught me, trapping me between the door and his body. His breath was hot on the back of my neck. I could feel my heartbeat in my head.

"Daze," he said.

Goose bumps prickled on my arms. Warner's only pet name for me had been "babe." And for a moment, I was paralyzed with a desire so intense I didn't recognize it as my own.

"What?" I whispered.

"They're not your kind of people. If that dickhead Tanner gets too much overpriced scotch

244

in him, he starts hittin' on anything with a rack and losing hands. That skirt you're barely wearing is already a distraction. He loses too much, he starts talkin' shit and startin' fights. Grim? He runs his own motorcycle club in DC. Mostly personal protection now, but he still dabbles in less legal ventures. Trouble follows him."

Knox was close enough to me that his chest brushed lightly against my back.

"Ian's made and lost more millions than anyone else at that table. He's got enough enemies out there that you don't wanna be standing next to him when one of them shows up. And Winona carries a grudge. She feels she's been done wrong, she'll burn down your world with a smile on her face."

"What about Lucian?"

For a moment, there was nothing but the sound of our breathing to cover the silence between us.

"Lucy is a whole other kind of dangerous," he said finally.

Carefully, I turned to face him, not quite managing to cover the flinch when my breasts brushed his chest. His nostrils flared, and my heart rate picked up.

"I've had no problems at that table. And I'm willing to bet if it were Fi or Silver or Max on that party, you wouldn't be having this conversation."

"They know how to handle trouble."

"And I don't?"

"Baby, you showed up in town in a fucking wedding dress with flowers in your hair. You scream into pillows when you get stressed out."

"That doesn't mean I can't handle myself!"

He put a hand on the door behind me and leaned into the last bit of my space. "You need a goddamn keeper."

"I'm not some helpless damsel in distress, Knox."

"Really? Where would you be if it wasn't me who found you in the café? Staying in Tina's shit-hole trailer with Way? No job. No car. No phone."

I was getting very close to whacking him over the head with my tray. "You caught me on a bad day."

"Bad day? Fuck me, Naomi. If I didn't drive your ass to the goddamn mall, you still wouldn't have a cell phone. Like it or not, you need someone watching out for you because you're too damn stubborn to do it yourself. You're too busy trying to take care of everyone else to bother with yourself."

His chest was pressing against mine, and I was having trouble focusing on the fury that rose in my throat. Hot, hard muscle against soft flesh. His proximity made me feel drunk.

"You're not kissing me," I insisted. In hindsight, the warning was a tad presumptuous, since he'd never kissed me before. But to be fair, he *really* looked like he wanted to kiss me.

"I'd rather wring your pretty little neck right now," he said, eyes narrowing on my mouth.

I licked my lips, preparing to definitely *not* kiss him.

The low rumble in his chest vibrated through my body as he dipped his head toward mine.

A new vibration interrupted us.

"Fuck," he hissed, yanking his phone out of his pocket. "What?" He listened, then let out a string of colorful curses. "Don't let him past the bar. I'll be out in a second."

"What's wrong?" I asked.

"See? That right there is your problem," he said, pointing a finger in my face as he yanked the door open.

"What?"

"You're suddenly too worried about me to watch your own ass while you're serving a table of criminals."

"Has anyone ever told you you're ridiculously dramatic?" I asked as he hauled me out. He was texting with his free hand.

"No one who didn't have a death wish. Let's go, Daze. This time, I'll let you make my problem yours."

20

A Winning Hand

Knox

My problem—besides the length of Naomi's skirt—was leaning against the bar in full uniform, making small talk with a handful of regulars.

I dragged Naomi with me into the alcove of the kitchen doors. "My brother doesn't get near that room. Got it?"

Her eyes widened. "Why are you telling me?"

"Because you're going to distract him and get him the hell out of here."

She dug in her heels and crossed her arms. "I don't recall the section on my job application that required me to lie to law enforcement."

"I'm not telling you to lie. I'm telling you to get those good girl eyes and that cleavage over there and flirt with him until he forgets all about busting that game."

"That doesn't sound any better than lying. It sounds like prostitution, and I'm pretty sure any family court judge would frown upon that during a custody hearing!"

I blew out a breath through my nostrils, then dug out my wallet. "Fine. I'll give you a hundred bucks."

"Deal."

I was still blinking when she snapped the bill out of my hand and headed in my brother's direction. It was an asshole move on my part, using her need for cash and putting her in a sketchy position. But I knew my brother, and Nash wouldn't do anything to hurt Naomi's chances at becoming Waylay's guardian. Hell, any idiot with one good eye could tell the woman was several classes above her sister.

"Fuck," I muttered to no one.

"Interesting."

I found Fi leaning against the wall, smugly enjoying one of the lollipops that served as a cigarette surrogate.

"What?"

Her eyebrows wiggled. "You never freaked when Max or me served that party."

"You and Max know how to handle yourselves," I argued.

"Looks like Naomi was handling herself just fine in there. Maybe the problem isn't her?"

"You wanna be my new problem, Fiasco?" I snarled.

She was not remotely intimidated. Which was exactly why a boss shouldn't be friends with their employees.

"I think Knox Morgan is Knox Morgan's biggest problem. But hey, what do I know?" she said with an annoying little shrug.

"Don't you have work to do?"

"And miss the show?" Fi nodded over my shoulder.

I turned and spied Naomi putting a flirtatious hand on my brother's arm.

When she laughed and tossed her hair, my brilliant plan didn't seem so brilliant.

"Goddammit."

I left Fi and maneuvered my way through the crowd, getting close enough to hear Nash say, "Let me guess. Illegal poker game in the back room, and you were sent to distract me."

Fuck me.

Naomi's eyes went wide, and I realized the woman had no poker face whatsoever.

"Uh, are you always this handsome and intelligent?" she asked.

"I am," Nash said with a stupid wink that made me want to punch him in his stupid face. "But it also helps that this town doesn't know how to keep its mouth shut. I'm not here for the game."

"Well, you're not here for my waitstaff, so what the hell are you doing here?" I said, interjecting myself into their cozy little conversation like a jealous idiot.

Nash shot me a smug look as if he knew exactly how annoying I found him. "Heard an old friend was in town."

"The rumors are true."

We all turned and found Lucian standing just outside our circle.

My brother grinned and shoved me out of the way. He welcomed Lucian with a hard hug and a slap on the back. "Good to have you back, brother."

"It's good to be back," Lucian agreed, returning the hug. "Especially since the waitstaff got even more interesting." He gave Naomi a wink.

Why the fuck the entire town suddenly decided winking at Naomi was a good idea was beyond me, and I was going to put a stop to it as soon as possible.

"Yeah, yeah. Everything's great," I said. "Don't you have drinks to serve?"

Naomi rolled her eyes. "I didn't get rid of your brother yet."

"You can keep the hundred if you go away," I said, needing to get her out from between my brother and my best friend.

"Deal. Lucian, I'll see you back in there with a fresh drink," she promised. "Nash, it was fun flirting with you."

"The pleasure was all mine, darlin'," my brother drawled, tossing her a little salute.

We all watched her sashay to the bar.

My head hurt from not yelling. My jaw was so tight I worried I'd crack a tooth. I didn't know what it was about that woman, but Naomi Witt had me tied up in fucking knots. I didn't like it one bit.

"What are you doing back in town?" Nash asked Lucian.

"You sound like a cop," Lucian complained.

"I *am* a cop."

Chief Nash rankled me.

The three of us had grown up raising hell and bending laws until they broke. Nash growing up to be a cop felt like some kind of betrayal. The straight and narrow was too confining for me. I didn't stray too far from the line these days, but I made sure to step into the gray every now and again for old time's sake.

Lucian was another story. Trouble didn't follow him. He had a tendency to make it wherever he went. If he was back in Knockemout, it sure as hell wasn't for a stroll down memory lane.

"A man can't feel nostalgic for his childhood?" Lucian mused, expertly avoiding the question.

"Your childhood sucked," Nash pointed out. "You haven't been back in years. Something brought you back, and it better not be trouble."

"Maybe I got tired of hearing how the Morgan brothers are too stubborn to remove their heads from their asses. Maybe I came back to help you bury the hatchet."

Naomi breezed by with a tray full of drinks and an easy smile for Lucian and Nash. The smile changed to a scowl when she looked at me.

"No one needs any help with any hatchet," I insisted, stepping in front of him to cut off his view of Naomi's curvy, retreating ass.

"That hatchet that you two have been wrestling over for two years is stupid. Get over it and move the fuck on," Lucian said.

"Don't use that Beltway bullshit tone with us," Nash said.

Lucian had built a political consulting firm that involved far too many shadows for Nash's liking. Our friend had a gift for putting the fear of God into his clients or the people who stood between his clients and what they wanted.

"That shit don't fly in Knockemout," I reminded him.

"You two have nothing to worry about. Let's have a drink for old time's sake," he suggested.

"Can't tonight," Nash said. "On duty."

"Then I guess you'd better get back to work," I told my brother.

"Guess I better. Try not to let any pissed-off poker players bust up the place tonight. I don't feel like handling the paperwork."

"Dinner. Tomorrow night. Your place," Lucian said, pointing upstairs.

"Works for me," I said.

"Fine," Nash agreed. "It is good to see you, Lucy."

Lucian gave him a half smile. "It's good to be seen." He turned to me. "I'll catch up with you when you're hovering over Naomi."

I flipped him off.

When he left, Nash turned to me. "You got a second?"

"Depends."

"It's about Tina."

Fuck.

"I'll walk you out."

The August night was still smotheringly humid when we went through the kitchen and walked out into the parking lot.

"What's the problem?" I asked when we got to Nash's SUV.

"Got a few more details on Tina. She and her new man were moving stolen goods. Nothing major. TVs and phones. Tablets. But rumor has it the boyfriend is connected to some bigger criminal enterprise."

"Who's the boyfriend?"

He shook his head. "Either no one knows his name or they're not sayin' it to me."

"Don't got much of anything, do you?"

"Just a gut feeling Tina didn't just decide to abandon her kid for fun. I think she's in deep with some shit." He looked up at the inky night sky. "Heard a couple of people saying they think they saw her over in Lawlerville."

Lawlerville was less than a half hour's drive. Which meant Tina probably wasn't planning on staying gone.

"Fuck," I muttered.

"Yeah."

I knew what Nash wanted from me. Any other circumstance, I would have made him ask. But since this involved Naomi and Waylay, I wasn't in the mood to fuck around.

"I'll ask around. See if any sources who avoid cops will feel chatty with me," I told him.

"Appreciate it."

Instead of going home like I'd planned, I pretended to check a few things off my list. I played barback for Silver while Max took her dinner break, then I answered the two dozen or so emails I'd been avoiding. I even ducked into the shop's supply room

254

and cut down cardboard boxes for the recycler.

The fourth time I caught myself heading in the direction of the poker game, I decided to remove myself from temptation and headed for the keg room. I hoped the chill and the physical labor of moving full kegs around would take the edge off my annoyance.

I had a whole list of reasons to be pissed off at the world, and most of them revolved around Naomi Witt. Every conversation with her ended in me having a headache and a hard-on.

Watching other men trip over their tongues when she was around only made it all worse. I didn't want her, but I wanted to claim her as mine just to keep every other asshole away from her.

I needed to get drunk and laid. I needed to forget she existed.

My hands were fucking frozen and my temper had cooled by the time I finished restacking the kegs. It was almost eleven. I figured I'd check in at the bar, then go the hell home.

When I hit the bar, Silver glanced up from the moonshine she was pouring.

"Mind checking in on the private party?" she asked.

"Why?"

She shrugged. "Been a while since I've seen Naomi."

My temper reignited like someone had thrown a gas can and a lighter on it.

I didn't exactly kick the door open, but it was a more dramatic entrance than I usually made.

Tanner, the skinny idiot who partied too hard to hold on to his money, fell out of his chair.

Naomi, however, didn't bother looking up. She was squeezed in between Winona and Grim, tongue poking out between her lips as she studied the cards in her hand. "Okay. Tell me again what beats a pair," she said.

Ian launched into a Texas Hold'em 101 lecture while Grim leaned over to look at her hand. "Raise 'em," he advised.

Tentatively, she picked up a blue chip and looked at him. He shook his head. She added two more chips and, on his nod, tossed them into the pile at the center of the table. "Raise," she announced, wiggling her ass in her seat.

I rounded the table and leaned in. "What the fuck are you doing, Naomi?"

She finally looked up at me, bemused. "Learning to play poker."

"Fold," Winona sighed. "Never trust a rookie's luck."

"I'll see you and raise you," Lucian decided, dropping a fistful of chips onto the table.

"Leave her alone, Morgan," Ian told me. "Our drinks are full, and she's never played."

I bared my teeth.

"Relax, Morgan," Winona said. "We all staked her some chips. It's just a friendly hand."

Lucian and Naomi were engaged in a stare down.

I leaned in again and whispered in her ear, "Do you know what those chips are worth?"

She shook her head, watching as the action returned to Ian, who folded. "They told me not to worry about it."

"That's twenty grand in the pot, Naomi."

I'd pushed the right button. She stopped staring at Lucian and looked at me as she started to come out of her chair.

Grim put a hand on her shoulder to hold her in place, and I fixed him with a cold glare.

"Fucking relax, Knox," he said. "Winona's right. It's a friendly hand. No loans. No interest. She's a quick learner."

"Twenty thousand *dollars?*" Naomi squeaked.

"I'll call," Tanner decided, throwing in his chips.

"Show 'em," Grim growled, shoving a matching stack of chips into the center of the table.

Tanner lay down a shitty two pair. Lucian took his time arranging his cards before revealing a nice little straight.

"Uh-oh," Winona hummed under her breath.

"Your turn, sweetheart," Grim said, his face unreadable.

Naomi dropped her cards faceup on the table.

"I believe this is a bigger straight than yours, Lucian," she said.

The table erupted in cheers. "You just won $22,000," Winona told her.

"Holy shit! Holy shit!" Naomi looked up at me, and the joy on her face was a sucker punch to my windpipe.

"Congratulations. Now get your ass up," I said, still capable of being an ass.

Lucian groaned. "Suckered in by those innocent eyes. Every damn time."

I didn't want him looking at her eyes or any other part of her. I pulled Naomi's chair out for her.

"Wait! Do I get a victory dance? How do I pay everyone back?"

"You definitely get a victory dance," Tanner said, lecherously patting his lap. Ian saved me the trouble and slapped him in the back of the head.

"Naomi. Now," I said, hooking my thumb toward the door.

"Hold your horses, Viking." She carefully counted out equal shares of the chips and started returning them to their original owners.

Grim shook his head and covered her hand with his tattooed one. "You won fair and square. You're keeping the winnings, and you can have my stake."

"Oh, but I couldn't," she began.

"I insist. And when I insist, people do what I tell them."

Naomi didn't see a scary biker sort of criminal making that proclamation. She saw a cuddly, tattooed fairy godfather. When she tossed her arms around his neck and gave him a noisy kiss on the cheek, I saw the man actually smile, a feat previously thought to be impossible.

"For that reaction, you'll keep mine as well," Lucian said. Naomi whooped and rounded the table and kissed him loudly on the cheek.

Ian and Winona did the same and laughed through Naomi's stranglehold hugs.

"Get that niece of yours something pretty," Winona told her.

Christ on a cracker, exactly how much of her autobiography had she shared with them?

"I'm, uh, just gonna hang on to mine," Tanner said, pulling back the chips he'd loaned her.

The rest of the table glared at him.

"Cheap ass," Winona said.

"Come on. It's been a rough week," he whined.

"In that case, here's a tip from me," Naomi said, handing over a $100 chip.

The woman was a sucker. And it looked like Tanner was officially in love.

"Ladies, gentlemen, what do you say we call it a night? I hear there's a band out front tonight. We could steal one or two of Knox's private bottles and reminisce about the good old days," Ian suggested.

"Only if Lucy promises me a dance," Winona said.

I waited until they'd cashed out and exited the room, leaving Naomi and me alone.

She looked up from the pile of cash they'd left in front of her. It was one hell of a tip. "Can we leave the lecture for tomorrow so I can just enjoy?"

"Fine," I said through gritted teeth. "But I'm driving you home tonight."

"Fine. But you're not allowed to yell at me on the drive."

"I can't make any promises."

21

A Family Emergency

Naomi

My feet were begging for a break, but the $20,000 in my apron gave me more than enough energy to face the final hour of my shift.

"Naomi!"

I spotted Sloane at a table in the corner with middle-aged biker babes and library board members Blaze and Agatha. Sloane had her hair pulled back in a perky ponytail and was wearing cutoffs and flip-flops. Blaze and Agatha were in their usual uniforms of denim and vegan leather.

"Hey!" I greeted them with a spring in my step. "Out on the town?"

"We're celebrating," Sloane explained. "The library just got a big, fat grant that I didn't even remember applying for! Not only does that mean we can start offering free community breakfasts *and* upgrade the second-floor computers, I can also officially offer you that part-time gig."

"Are you serious?" I asked, elation rising inside me.

"As serious as a nun in detention," Blaze said, slapping the table.

Sloane grinned. "It's yours if you want it."

"I want it!"

The librarian held out her hand. "Welcome to the Knockemout Public Library, Ms. Community Outreach Coordinator. You officially start next week. Come by this weekend, and we'll talk about your new duties."

I grabbed her hand and shook it. Then I hugged her. Then I hugged Blaze and Agatha. "Can I buy you beautiful, amazing ladies a round?" I asked, releasing a dazed-looking Agatha.

"A public librarian can't say no to free drinks. It's in the town charter," Sloane said.

"Neither can us literary supportive lesbians," Agatha added.

"My wife is right," Blaze agreed.

I floated through the crowd on the dance floor and plugged in the order for my new bosses. I was thinking about the car I could now afford and the desk I wanted to buy Waylay for her room when Lucian appeared.

"I believe you owe me a dance," he said, holding out his hand.

I laughed. "I guess it's the least I can do since you let me win."

"I never let anyone win," he assured me, taking my tray and setting it at a table of lady horse farmers who didn't seem to mind.

"That's very mercenary of you," I observed. The band shifted into a slow, twangy tune about lost love.

Lucian pulled me into his arms, and once again,

I found myself wondering why Knockemout had such a large population of impossibly sexy men. I was also wondering what Lucian's motive was for asking me to dance. He struck me as the type of man who never did anything without an ulterior motive.

"Knox and Nash," he began.

I congratulated myself on being so astute. "What about them?"

"They're my best friends. Their feud has run its course. I want to make sure it doesn't get stirred back up."

"What does that have to do with me?"

"Everything."

I guffawed right in the man's face. "You think *I'm* going to reignite some feud that I had nothing to do with in the first place?"

"You're a stunning woman, Naomi. More than that, you're interesting, funny, and kind. You're worth fighting for."

"Well, thank you for your kind but bizarre opinion. But you can rest easy knowing that Knox and I can barely stand being in the same room."

"That doesn't always mean what you think it means," he said.

"He's rude and mercurial, and he blames me for everything."

"Perhaps because you make him feel things he doesn't want to feel," Lucian pointed out.

"Like what? Murderous?"

"What about Nash?" he asked.

"Nash is the opposite of his brother. But I just got out of a long-term relationship. I'm in a new town trying to do what's best for my niece, who hasn't had the easiest life. There's no time left on the clock to explore things with any man," I said firmly.

"Good. Because I know you'd hate to unintentionally add fuel to the fire."

"What started their stupid fire in the first place?" I asked.

"Stubbornness. Idiocy. Ego," he said vaguely.

I knew better than to expect a straight answer from a man who was like a brother to the Morgans.

"Hey, Naomi! Can we add an order of—" Sloane cut off midsentence.

The petite blond was staring open-mouthed up at Lucian like she'd just been sucker punched. I felt Lucian's entire body go rigid.

My heart sank with the realization that I'd somehow betrayed my new friend.

"Hey," I said weakly. "Do you know—" My awkward introduction was unnecessary.

"Sloane," Lucian said.

While I shivered at the ice in his tone, Sloane had the opposite reaction. Her expression went mutinous, and an emerald fire snapped in her eyes.

"Is there an asshole convention in town I wasn't aware of?"

"Still charming as always," Lucian snapped back.

"Fuck off, Rollins." With that parting shot, Sloane spun around and marched toward the door.

Lucian still hadn't moved a muscle, but his gaze was glued to her retreating back. His hands, still on my hips, gripped me hard.

"You about ready to unhand my waitstaff, Lucy?" Knox growled behind me.

Startled, I yelped. There were too many pissed-off people in my vicinity. Lucian released me, gaze remaining on the door.

"Are you okay?" I asked him.

"He's fine," Knox said.

"I'm fine."

It was clearly a lie. The man looked as though he wanted to commit a cold-blooded murder. I wasn't sure who I should attempt to fix first.

"Dinner. Tomorrow," he said to Knox.

"Yeah. Dinner."

With that, he headed for the door.

"Is he okay?" I asked Knox.

"How the hell should I know?" he asked irritably.

The door opened just as Lucian got to it, and Wylie Ogden, creepy ex-police chief, stepped inside. The man flinched, then covered it—poorly—with a smirk when he saw Lucian in front of him. They stared at each other for a long moment before Wylie stepped sideways, giving him a wide berth.

"What in the hell was that?" I asked.

"Nothing," Knox lied.

Silver whistled from the bar and waved him over. Knox headed in her direction, swearing under his breath.

The guy was wound tighter than a mummy wrapped in Spanx.

"Did Sloane just leave?" Blaze demanded, arriving at my side with Agatha on her heels.

"Yeah. I was dancing with Lucian Rollins. She took one look at him and left. Did I do something wrong?"

Blaze blew out a breath. "That's not good."

Agatha shook her head. "Definitely not good. They hate each other."

"Who could possibly hate Sloane? Isn't she the nicest person in northern Virginia?"

Agatha shrugged. "There's some kind of sticky history between those two. They grew up next door to each other. Didn't run in the same crowds or anything. No one knows what happened, but they can't stand the sight of each other."

I'd been caught dancing with my new friend/boss's mortal enemy. Damn it.

I needed to make this right. At least ignorance was a plausible defense. I was already reaching for my phone when it started ringing.

It was Stef.

"Shoot. I have to take this," I told the bikers. "Hey, is everything okay?"

"Witty, I've got bad news."

My heart stopped and then stuttered to a start again. I knew that tone of voice. This wasn't "we're out of champagne and ice cream." This was "family emergency."

"What's wrong? Is Waylay okay?" I plugged my other ear with my finger to hear over the band.

"Way's fine," he said. "But Nash was shot tonight. They don't know if he's going to pull through. He's in surgery."

"Oh my God," I whispered.

"Some sergeant named Grave notified Liza J. He drove her to the hospital. He's sending someone to notify Knox."

Knox. I found him through the crowd behind the bar, half smiling at something a customer said. He looked up and locked eyes with me.

My face must have telegraphed something, because Knox vaulted over the bar and started pushing his way toward me through the crowd.

"I'm sorry, babe," Stef said. "I've got Way here at Liza's with all the dogs. We're fine. You do whatever you need to do."

Knox reached me and grabbed my arms. "What's wrong? Are you okay?"

"I have to go," I said into the phone and disconnected.

The front door opened, and I saw two officers in uniform looking grim. My breath hitched. "Knox," I whispered.

"Right here, baby. What happened?"

His eyes were bluer in this light, searingly blue and serious as he held on to me.

I shook my head. "It's not me. It's you."

"What's me?"

With a shaking finger, I pointed at the officers making their way to us.

"Knox, we need to talk," the taller one said.

• • •

I backed up the truck for the third time and pulled forward before finally being satisfied with my parking job. The hospital rose in front of me like a glowing beacon. An ambulance unloaded a patient on a gurney at the emergency department entrance. Its light painted the parking lot in red and white.

I puffed out a breath, hoping it would settle the anxiety that was burbling in my stomach like a bad chowder.

I could have gone home.

I should have. But when I'd finished my shift, I drove toward the man who had tossed me his keys and told me to drive myself home. He'd made me promise before he'd followed the deputies out the door into the night.

Yet here I was at two a.m., disobeying direct orders and sticking my nose where it didn't belong.

I should definitely go home. Yep. For sure, I decided, getting out of the truck and walking right on in through the front door.

Given the hour, there was no one sitting at the information desk. I followed the signs to the elevators and the surgical intensive care unit on the third floor.

It was eerily quiet on the floor. All signs of life were limited to the nurses' station.

I started toward it when I spotted Knox through the glass in the waiting room, the wide shoulders and impatient stance immediately recognizable. He paced the dimly lit room like a captive tiger.

He must have sensed me in the doorway, because he turned swiftly as if to face an enemy.

His jaw clenched, and it was only then that I saw the turmoil. Anger. Frustration. Fear.

"I brought you coffee," I said, lamely holding up the travel mug I'd prepared for him in Honky Tonk's kitchen.

"Thought I told you to go home," he growled.

"And I didn't listen. Let's just move past the part where either one of us pretends to be surprised."

"I don't want you here."

I flinched, not at his words but at the pain behind them.

I put the coffee down on an end table stacked with magazines that pretended they could distract visitors from the endless loop of fear. "Knox," I began, taking a step toward him.

"Stop," he said.

I didn't listen and slowly closed the distance between us. "I'm so sorry," I whispered.

"Just get the fuck out of here, Naomi. Just go. You can't be here." His voice was ragged, frustrated.

"I'll go," I promised. "I just wanted to make sure you were okay."

"I'm fine." The words came out bitterly.

I raised my hand to lay on his arm.

He flinched away from me. "Don't," he said harshly.

I said nothing but stood my ground. I felt like I could breathe in his anger like it was oxygen.

"Don't," he said again.

"I won't."

"If you touch me right now . . ." He shook his head. "I'm not in control, Naomi."

"Just tell me what you need."

His laugh was dry and bitter. "What I need is to find the motherfucking bastard who did this to my brother. What I need is to rewind the clock so I didn't waste the last however many years over some stupid fucking fight. What I *need* is for my brother to wake the fuck up."

His breath hitched, and I had no control over my own body. Because one second I was standing in front of him, and the next I was wrapping my arms around his waist, holding on and trying to absorb his pain.

His body was tight and vibrating as if he was seconds away from coming apart.

"Stop," he said on a broken whisper. "Please."

But I didn't. I held on tighter, pressing my face to his chest.

He swore under his breath, and then his arms were around me, crushing me to him. He buried his face in my hair and clung to me.

He was so warm, so solid, so alive. I held on to him for dear life and willed him to release some of what he'd kept bottled up.

"Why don't you ever fucking listen?" he grumbled, lips moving against my hair.

"Because sometimes people don't know how to ask for what they really need. You needed a hug."

"No, I didn't," he rasped. He was quiet for a long moment, and I listened to his heartbeat. "I needed you."

My own breath tripped in my throat. I tried to pull back to look up at him, but he held me where I was.

"Just shut up, Daisy," he advised.

"Okay."

His hand stroked down my back and then up again. Over and over until I melted into him. I wasn't sure which one of us was giving the comfort and which was receiving it now.

"He's out of surgery," Knox said finally, pulling back incrementally. His thumb traced my lower lip. "They won't let me see him till he wakes up."

"Will he want to see you?" I asked.

"I don't give a fuck what he wants. He's seeing me."

"What was the fight about?"

He sighed. When he reached up and tucked a strand of hair behind my ear, I swooned internally. "I don't really feel like talkin' about it, Daze."

"You have something better to do?"

"Yeah. Yelling at you to go the hell home and get some sleep. Waylay's first day of school is tomorrow. She doesn't need a zombie aunt pouring dish soap on her cereal."

"First of all, we're having eggs, fruit, and yogurt for breakfast," I began, then realized he was trying to distract me. "Was it about a woman?"

He looked at the ceiling.

"If you start counting to ten, I will kick you in the shin," I warned.

He sighed. "No. It wasn't about a woman."

"Besides love, what's worth losing a brother over?"

"Fucking romantics," he said.

"Maybe if you get it out instead of bottling it up, you'll feel better."

He studied me for another one of those long, pensive beats, and I was sure he was about to tell me to get my ass home.

"Fine."

I blinked in surprise. "Um. Okay. Wow. So this is happening. Maybe we should sit?" I suggested, eyeing up the empty vinyl chairs.

"Why does talking have to be a whole damn thing with women?" he grumbled as I led us to a pair of chairs.

"Because anything worth doing is worth doing right." I sat and patted the chair next to me.

He sat, stretching his long legs in front of him and staring blankly at the window. "I won the lottery," he said.

"I know that. Liza told me."

"Took home eleven million, and I thought it was the answer to everything. I bought the bar. A building or two. Invested in Jeremiah's plan for some fancy-ass salon. Paid off Liza J's mortgage. She'd been struggling since Pop died." He looked down at his hands as his palms rubbed against the thighs of his jeans. "It felt so fucking good to be able to solve problems."

I waited.

"Growing up, we didn't have much. And after we lost Mom, we didn't have anything. Liza J and Pop took us in and gave us a home, a family. But money was tight, and in this town, you've got some kids driving fucking BMWs to school on their sixteenth birthdays or spending their weekends competing on forty-thousand-dollar horses.

"Then there was me and Nash and Lucy. None of us grew up with anything, so maybe we took a few things that weren't ours. Maybe we weren't always on the straight and narrow, but we learned to be self-sufficient. Learned that sometimes you gotta take what you want instead of waiting for someone to give it to you."

I handed him his coffee, and he took a sip.

"Then Nash gets a bug up his ass and decides to become Dudley Fucking Do-Right."

Which must have felt like a rejection to Knox, I realized.

"I gave him money," Knox said. "Or tried to at least. The stubborn son of a bitch said he didn't want it. Who says no to that?"

"Apparently your brother."

"Yeah. Apparently." Restless, he shoved his fingers through his hair again. "We went back and forth about it for almost two years. Me trying to shove it down his throat, him rejecting it. We threw a few punches over it. Finally Liza J made him take it. And you know what my stupid little brother did with it?"

272

I set my teeth in my lower lip, because I knew.

"That son of a bitch donated it to the Knockemout PD to build a new goddamn police station. The Knox Morgan Fucking Municipal Building."

I waited for a few beats, hoping there was more to the story. But when he didn't continue, I slumped in my seat.

"Are you saying you and your brother have barely spoken in *years* because he put your *name* on a *building?*"

"I'm saying he refused money that could have set him up for the rest of his life and gave it to the cops instead. The cops who had hard-ons for three teenagers just raising a little hell. Fuck. Lucian spent a week in jail on some bullshit charges when we were seventeen. We had to learn to take care of things ourselves instead of running to a crooked chief and his dumb as fuck cronies. And Nash just up and hands over two fucking million bucks to them."

The picture was coming into focus. I cleared my throat. "Uh, are the same cops still with the department?"

Knox hitched his shoulders in a shrug. "No."

"Does Nash allow the officers under him to take advantage of their position?" I pressed.

He poked his tongue into the inside of his cheek. "No."

"Is it fair to say that Nash cleaned up the department and replaced bad cops with good cops?"

"Don't know how good Grave is, considering

he still likes to drag race on the weekends," Knox said stubbornly.

I put my hand on his arm and squeezed. "Knox."

"What?" he asked the carpet.

"Look at me."

When he did, I saw the frustration etched on his gorgeous face. I cupped his cheeks in my hands. His beard was coarse against my palms.

"I'm going to tell you something that you and your brother both need to know, and I need this to resonate in your soul," I said.

His eyes locked on mine. Well, more on my mouth than my eyes. But it was good enough.

"You're both idiots."

His gaze tore away from my lips, and his eyes narrowed. I squished his cheeks together before he could snarl at me.

"And if either of you wastes one more damn day on the fact that you two have both worked so hard and given so much to this town *in your own ways,* then the idiocy is terminal, and there's no cure."

I released his face and leaned back.

"If this is your way of cheering me up about my brother getting shot, you suck at it."

My smile spread slowly. "Take it from me, Viking. You and your brother have a chance to fix things and have an actual relationship. Some of us aren't that lucky. Some burnt bridges can't be rebuilt. Don't burn one over something as stupid as money."

"That only works if he wakes the fuck up," he reminded me.

I blew out a breath. "Yeah. I know."

We sat in silence. His knee and arm were warm and firm against mine.

"Mr. Morgan?" A nurse in blue scrubs stepped into the room. Knox and I both came to our feet. I wondered if he realized he'd taken my hand.

"Your brother is awake, and he's asking for you," she said.

I blew out a sigh of relief.

"How is he?" Knox asked.

"Groggy and he's looking at a long recovery, but the surgical team is happy."

The tension in his back and shoulders loosened.

I gave his hand a squeeze. "On that note, I think I'll head home to get Waylay's cereal and dish detergent ready."

He tightened his grip on my hand. "Can we have a minute?" he asked the nurse.

"Sure. I'll be right outside. I'll take you to him as soon as you're ready."

He waited until she stepped outside before drawing me in close.

"Thank you, Naomi," he whispered just before his lips met mine. Hot, hard, unyielding. His hand slid up to cup my jaw and neck, holding me in place as he kissed every thought out of my head, leaving me nothing but a riot of sensation.

He pulled back, eyes fierce. Then he pressed a kiss to my forehead and left the room.

22

One Hatchet, Two Bullets

Knox

Y ou look like shit," Nash rasped.

The lights were on low in the room. My brother was propped up in his hospital bed, chest bare to reveal bandages and gauze over his left shoulder.

Machines beeped, screens glowed.

He looked pale. Vulnerable.

My hands clenched into fists at my sides.

"I could say the same about you," I said, rounding the bed slowly to sink into the chair by the dark window.

"Looks worse than it is." His voice was barely a whisper.

I rested my elbows on my knees and tried to look relaxed. But inside, a rage simmered in my gut. Someone had tried to end Nash's life. You didn't mess with a Morgan and walk away from it.

"Some asshole tried to kill you tonight."

"You mad someone almost beat you to it?"

"They know who did it?" I asked.

The corner of his mouth lifted as if it were too much effort to smile. "Why? You gonna get him back?"

"You almost died, Nash. Grave said you came this close to bleeding out before the ambulance got there." The truth of it had bile rising in my throat.

"It's gonna take more than a couple of bullets and a wrestling match to end me," he assured me.

I ran my palms over my knees. Back and forth, trying to tamp down the anger. The need to break something.

"Naomi was here." Even as I said it, I didn't know why. Maybe just saying her name out loud made everything feel a little more bearable.

"Of course she was. She thinks I'm hot."

"I don't care how many bullet holes you've got in you. I'm moving on that," I told him.

Nash's sigh was closer to a wheeze. "About damn time. Quicker you screw it up, the quicker I can swoop in and be the good guy."

"Fuck off, dick."

"Hey, who's the one in the hospital bed, asshole? I'm a damn hero. Women can't resist a hero with bullet holes."

The hero in question winced when he shifted in the bed, his hand reaching for the tray, then falling back to the mattress.

I rose and poured the water bottle into the waiting cup. "Yeah, well, maybe you should stay in here out of my way for a couple of days. Give me a shot at fucking it all up."

I pushed the cup and straw to the edge of the tray and watched him reach for it with his good arm. Beads of sweat appeared on his forehead, and his hand shook as his fingers closed around the plastic.

I'd never seen him like this. I'd seen him every other way. Hungover, wrung out from the flu bug of 1996, exhausted after pouring his heart out in the homecoming football game his senior year. But I'd never seen him look weak.

Another nurse pulled back the curtain with an apologetic smile. "Just checking the fluids," he said.

Nash gave him a thumbs-up, and we lapsed into silence while the nurse busied himself with IVs. My brother was hooked to a half-dozen machines in the ICU. And I'd gone years with barely speaking to him.

"How's your pain?" the nurse asked.

"Fine. Practically nonexistent."

His answer was too quick. His mouth too tight. My brother had played the second half of that homecoming game with a broken wrist. Because he might be the nice brother, the good brother, but he didn't like showing weakness any more than I did.

"He's in it," I tattled to the nurse.

"Don't listen to him," Nash insisted. But he couldn't hide the grimace when he shifted on the mattress.

"A bullet just ripped its way through your torso, Chief. You don't have to be in pain to heal," the nurse said.

"Yeah. You do," Nash countered. "Pain is what tells you you're alive. You numb that, and how do you know you're still here?"

"She thinks we're both idiots," I said when the nurse left.

Nash gave a wheeze followed by a racking cough that looked like it was going to tear him apart before collapsing back on the bed. I watched the green spikes on his heart rate monitor slowly settle. "Who?" he said, finally.

"Naomi."

"Why would Naomi think I'm an idiot?" he asked wearily.

"Told her why things are the way they are."

"She wasn't impressed with your Robin Hood routine or my manly independence?"

"Not even a little. She may have made a few points."

"About what?"

"About how she thought it was over a woman. Not money."

Nash's head was slowly lolling to the side, his eyelids getting heavier. "So love is worth a family feud but a few million isn't?"

"That was the gist of it."

"Can't say she's wrong."

"Then why the fuck didn't you just suck it up and make it right?" I snapped.

Nash's smile was a ghost. His eyes were closed. "You're the big brother. And you were the one trying to make me beholden to you by shoving cash down my throat."

"The only reason I'm not kicking your ass right now is you're attached to too many machines."

He gave me a weak middle finger.

"Jesus," I grumbled. "I didn't want you to be beholden or whatever the fuck to me. We're family. We're brothers. One of us wins, we both win." It also meant if one of us lost, we both did. And that was what the last few years had been. A loss.

Fuck. I hated losing.

"Didn't want the money," he said, his words slurring. "Wanted to build things on my own."

"You could've put it away for retirement or some shit," I complained. The same old cocktail of feelings was trying to rise in me. Rejection. Failure. Righteous fury. "You deserved some good. After the shit we went through, then Liza J losing Pop. You deserved more than a cop salary from some shitty town."

"*Our* shitty town," he corrected. "Made it ours. You in your way. Me in mine."

Maybe he was right. But that didn't matter. What did matter was the fact that if he had taken the cash, he wouldn't be here in this hospital room. My little brother would be making a difference some other way. Without toeing the line. Without paying the price.

"Should have kept the money. If you had, you wouldn't be lying here like roadkill."

Nash shook his head slowly against the pillow. "I was always gonna be the good guy."

"Shut up and go to sleep," I told him.

"We went through some shit. But I always had my big brother. Always knew I could count on you. Didn't need your money on top of that."

Nash's shoulders sagged. Sleep took him under its spell, leaving me to sit in silent vigil.

The automatic doors opened, spilling me and a cloud of air-conditioning into the humidity of the breaking dawn. I'd stayed by Nash's bedside, letting my rage simmer. Knowing what came next.

I wanted to punch a hole through the building's facade. I wanted to bring a tidal wave of retribution down on the person responsible.

Idly, I picked up one of the smooth rocks from a flower bed and ran my fingers over it, wanting to send it flying. To break something on the outside instead of feeling all the cracks on the inside.

"I wouldn't do that if I were you."

I closed my fingers around the rock and squeezed.

"What are you doing here, Lucy?"

Lucian leaned against the limestone column just beyond the hospital entrance, the end of a cigarette glowing brighter as he sucked in a drag.

He only allowed himself one cigarette a day. I guess this counted.

"What do you think I'm doing?"

"Holding up the building? Hitting on sexy surgeons?"

He flicked ash to the ground, eyes locked on me. "How is he?"

I thought of the pain, the exhaustion. The side of my brother I'd never seen before. "Okay. Or at least he's gonna be."

"Who did it?" The cool, dispassionate tone didn't fool me.

We were down to business now. Lucian may not have been blood, but he was a Morgan in every way that counted. And he wanted justice as badly as I did.

"Cops don't know. Grave said the car was stolen. Nash hasn't given them a description of the suspect yet."

"Does he remember what happened?"

I shrugged and squinted up at the sky that was turning pink and purple as the sun worked its way off the horizon. "I don't know, man. He was pretty fucked up on anesthesia and whatever they put in his IV."

"I'll start digging," Lucian assured me.

"Let me know what you find. I'm not getting cut out of this."

"Of course not." He studied me for a beat. "You look like shit. You should get some sleep."

"People keep telling me that."

Lucian, on the other hand, looked like he'd just walked out of the board room in a slick suit sans tie.

"Maybe you should listen," he said.

"He almost died, Lucy. After I was an asshole to him, he almost bled out in a fucking ditch."

Lucian stubbed out his cigarette in the concrete ashtray. "We'll make it right."

I nodded. I knew we would. This wouldn't stand. And the man who'd put a bullet in my brother would pay.

"And you'll make the rest of it right too," he said, words clipped. "You both wasted enough fucking time. It's done now." Only Lucian Rollins could make a statement like that and will it into reality.

I thought of Naomi's proclamation. Maybe we had been idiots wasting time we thought we had. "It's done," I agreed.

"Good. I was tired of my childhood best friends acting like they were still children."

"Is that why you came back?"

His expression darkened. "One of the reasons."

"One of those other reasons have anything to do with a pretty little librarian who hates your guts?"

He sighed, absently patting his pockets.

"Already had your one," I reminded him.

"Fuck," he muttered. It was as flustered as he allowed himself to get.

I had the temper. Nash had the good nature. And Lucian had the self-control of a fucking monk.

"Whatever happened with you two anyway?" I asked, enjoying the distraction of his discomfort.

"Your brother is in an ICU bed," Lucian said. "That's the only reason I'm not knocking your teeth out right now."

As close as we'd all been, the one thing Lucian never shared was what made Sloane hate him. Up until last night, I'd thought the feeling was mutual. But I'd seen his face when he saw her, when she walked away. I didn't know much about feelings, but whatever was written all over his face didn't look like hate to me.

"You probably don't even remember how to throw a punch," I teased. "All those conference room negotiations. You just sic your lawyers on people instead of delivering a nice right cross to the face. Bet it's less satisfying."

"You can take the boy out of Knockemout but you can't take the Knockemout out of the boy," he said.

I hoped it was true. "Appreciate you bein' here."

He nodded. "I'll stay with him until Liza J comes back in."

"That'd be good," I said.

We stood in silence, legs braced as the sun rose, adding gold to the pink and purple. A new day had officially begun. A lot of things were gonna change, and I was keyed up to make it all happen.

"Get some sleep." Lucian dug into his pocket and tossed me his keys. "Take my car."

I caught them midair and hit the unlock button. A shiny Jaguar blinked its headlights at me from a primo parking spot.

"Always did have good taste."

"Some things never change."

But some things had to.

"I'll see you later, man."

He nodded. And then I surprised the hell out of us both by wrapping him in a hard one-armed hug.

"Missed you, brother."

23

Knox, Knox. Who's There?

Naomi

I was torn from a fitful sleep on the couch by pounding at the front door. Disoriented, I stumbled around the coffee table and tried to remember where I was.

The $20,000 in cash still tucked away in my apron.

Nash.

Knox.

Waylay's first day of school.

No wonder I'd fallen prey to a nap attack.

I opened the door and found a freshly showered Knox standing on the welcome mat. Waylon trotted inside, wagging his tail.

"Hey," I croaked.

A man of few words, Knox said nothing and stepped over the threshold. I rubbed the sleep from my eyes. He looked tense, like he was spoiling for a fight. Well, if he'd come here for a fight, he was going to be disappointed. I was too tired to deliver one.

"How's your brother?" I ventured.

He shoved a hand through his hair. "Long recovery ahead. But he'll be okay. Get Way off to school this morning?"

His brother had been shot, and the man remembered to ask about Waylay's first day. I didn't know how to reconcile that with the jerk who yelled at me in front of his own customers. If he could ever settle fully into the thoughtful grump and give up the pissed-off bad boy, he'd make some woman very lucky someday.

"Yeah," I yawned. "She slept at Liza's last night since I didn't get home until late. Liza, Stef, and I made her send-off breakfast there. Stef made chocolate chip pancakes even though I told him spikes in blood sugar make kids tired and unfocused at school."

I was tired and unfocused, not because of pancakes but because Knox's edginess made me nervous.

"Uh, speaking of Stef, I think he and Jeremiah might be into each other," I said, grasping for a topic that would warrant some kind of verbal reaction.

But Knox remained silent as he prowled the tiny living room, looking much too big to belong here. He was a man with a lot of feelings locked up tight. Part of me wanted to crack him open. The other part wanted to just go back to bed and forget everything for a few hours.

"Do you want some coffee? Maybe some alcohol?" I offered, following him as he moved toward the kitchen, his hands clenching into fists only to release again. Over and over again.

I didn't have any beer, and the hardest alcohol in the house was a cheap rosé I'd been planning to crack open with Sloane. But I could sacrifice it for the guy whose brother had just been shot.

He picked up the pretty yellow leaf on the counter. I'd found it in the lane that morning after walking Waylay to the bus. The temperatures still said summer, but the change to fall was inevitable.

Waylon hopped up on the couch in the living room.

"Make yourself at home," I told the dog. When I turned to face Knox, he was closing the distance between us.

"Naomi."

His voice was rough as it caressed the syllables of my name, and then his hands were on me, yanking me into him. His mouth found mine, and I was lost to sensation. Drowning in desire.

Neither of us wanted to want this. Maybe that was what made it feel so damn good. One hand slid into my hair while the other pressed my lower back until I was flush against him.

"Knox," I breathed. "This isn't what you want," I reminded him.

"It's what I need," he said before diving back into the kiss.

This wasn't the kiss from the waiting room. This was different, desperate.

I lost myself in it. Every thought tumbled out of my head until I was nothing but feeling. His mouth was hard and demanding, just like the man. I softened under him. Welcoming him.

He responded by tugging at my hair to angle

my head just the way he wanted as he slanted his mouth over mine. His tongue didn't twine or dance with mine—it battled mine into submission.

He stole my breath, my logic, every reason why this was a terrible idea. He took them all and made them disappear.

"That's what I need, baby. I need to feel you go soft under me. Need you to let me have you."

I couldn't tell if this was dirty talk or romantic prose. Whichever side of the line his words fell on, I loved it.

His fingers found the strap of my dress. My heartbeat skittered into high gear as he slid the fabric an inch down my shoulder, leaving my skin burning.

He needed this. Me. And I lived to be needed.

I reached for his shirt and slid my hands under the hem, finding the rigid muscle under warm skin.

For once in his life, Knox appeared to be feeling helpful and yanked the shirt over his head with one hand. God, all that skin and muscle and ink. I dragged my nails over his chest, and he growled into my mouth.

Yes, please.

With one deft swipe, he shoved the strap of my dress off my shoulder, then did the same to the other one.

"About time I find out what you've got on under these dresses," he murmured.

I sank my teeth into his lower lip and yanked hard on his belt.

I cursed myself for putting on my least sexy underwear this morning. But at least I hadn't bothered with a bra this morning. Between unsexy undies and unshackled boobs, I figured it all evened out.

He lost his jeans at about the same moment my dress slithered down my body and pooled at my ankles.

"Goddammit, baby. I fucking knew it."

His mouth was on my neck, nibbling and kissing its way south.

I shivered. "Knew what?"

"That you'd look like this. That you had a fuck-me body." He cupped one breast greedily.

He backed me into the fridge, and the cold metal had me yelping. "Knox!"

"I'd apologize, but you know I'm not the least bit sorry," he said as his tongue darted out to stroke my aching nipple.

I was no longer capable of forming words. I was no longer capable of drawing in a breath. All I could do was cup his erection through his boxer briefs and hang on for dear life. When his lips closed over my nipple and he started to suck, the back of my head hit the fridge. Those deep, decadent pulls echoed all over my body, and I had a feeling he knew it.

He didn't stop sucking as he shoved his free hand into my unsexy underwear.

We both moaned when his fingers found me.

"Knew it," he muttered again as his mouth moved

to my other breast. "Knew you'd be wet for me."

My moan turned into a cry when he parted my slit with two fingers. The man knew what he was doing. There was no fumbling. No wasted, awkward movements. Even driven by need, every touch was magic.

"Need to feel you from the inside," he said, brushing his beard over my sensitized nipple. When his fingers thrust into me, my knees buckled.

He was too much. Too skilled. Expert level. Professional ruiner of vaginas. And I didn't know if I could keep up. When he started moving those amazing fingers, I decided I didn't care.

His penis flexed in my grip. I clumsily shoved his briefs down, freeing his thick shaft, and gripped it hard.

Knox straightened on a groan and dropped his forehead to mine as we worked each other with eager hands.

"Need you in a bed," he growled as a drop of moisture leaked over my fingers.

I gripped him harder, stroked faster. "I sure hope you can get us to one, because I can't walk."

"Damn, baby. Slow the fuck down," he ordered through gritted teeth.

But I wasn't listening. I was too busy matching the pump of his fingers inside me.

I gasped when he pulled out of my throbbing core. "Mean!" I hissed against his neck.

But just when my body felt desolate over the loss, he tossed me over his shoulder.

"Knox!"

His only acknowledgment was a resounding slap on my behind.

"Which room?" he demanded, taking the stairs two at a time.

I was dizzy with lust and vertigo. "This one," I managed. In seconds, I found myself on my back in bed with the naked Knox ranging himself over me. "Oh my God. Is this really happening?"

Whoops. I hadn't actually meant to say that out loud.

"Do *not* come to your senses yet," he ordered.

"No sense here. Promise."

He was too busy looking pained to be amused. I couldn't blame him after I got my first good look at his erection. It was arousing, intimidating. A thick, purple-headed leader in the world of erect penises. I got a little dizzy when Knox fisted it.

I hoped to God he knew how to use it. Few things were more disappointing in this life than a well-endowed man who had no clue how to use his equipment.

Apparently it wasn't time to find out though, because Knox slid down my body, parting my legs and draping them over his shoulders.

When he pressed his face between my legs, my stomach muscles contracted so hard I worried I'd pulled something. *Oh. God.* His beard was abrasive between my thighs, and I freaking loved it.

His tongue. For being a man of few words, his tongue was pure magic.

He paired long, greedy strokes with short, shallow thrusts. In a matter of seconds, I was ready to come.

"Wait, wait, wait," I whimpered, gripping his hair.

He stopped immediately, earning serious points.

"What's wrong? You okay?" Concern warred with need in those steely blue-gray eyes.

"This is a one-time thing." I needed to say it aloud. To remind myself that this was the one and only time I was going to let Knox Morgan make me come.

"One time," he agreed, still watching me closely. "Final offer."

"Don't talk like a game show host when your face is between my legs."

"Don't ask me to have a conversation when you were just about to come on my goddamn tongue."

"Point taken," I said. My insides were actually pulsing with greedy desire. "One-time thing. Make it count."

"Then you better hang the fuck on."

It was a good thing I did as he told me, because a second or two after my hands wrapped around the brass headboard, he did something magical with his tongue at the same time that he crooked his fingers inside me, and my entire body imploded.

I closed so tight around his fingers I worried he was going to need an X-ray. Not worried enough to stop and check, of course. Because I was in the middle of the best orgasm of my life and I had priorities. If I had broken his fingers, he didn't seem to mind, because he just kept right on licking me through my bone-shattering release.

"Still coming. I can feel you," he said on a groan.

At least that was what I thought he said. My ears were ringing like I was in a church bell tower on Sunday morning.

"Gonna need a minute," I gasped, fighting to get oxygen into my lungs.

"Uh-uh. Making it count," he said from somewhere that sounded very far away. "Besides, I want to slide my cock in you while you're still coming."

" 'Kay."

I heard the distinct crinkle of the wrapper from either a Pop-Tart or a condom. It appeared to be the latter, because the wide crest of his erection was prodding at my very core.

He paused long enough to swipe his tongue over each of my breasts before rising up on his knees.

He looked like a vengeful warrior. Tattooed and muscled. His lids heavy, chest heaving. At least I wasn't the only one having a damn good time, I realized.

It was my last coherent thought before he thrust his hips and buried that long, thick weapon of mass destruction inside me.

Our eyes locked, and his face froze in agonized pleasure and triumph as he hit the very end of me.

I didn't realize I'd spasmed up into an ab curl

until he put one of those big hands on my chest and pressed me back down to the mattress.

"Relax, baby. Relax," he whispered.

I let out the breath that had been trapped in my lungs and sucked in another. He was so damn *big*. And he was right—I could feel the tiny little tremors working my muscles around him.

"You keep milking my dick like that, sweetheart, and this is gonna have to be a two-time thing."

"Mmph. Good. Yes."

He grinned down at me. "So this is what it takes for you to lose that fancy vocabulary of yours."

"Ugh. Are you gonna talk all day or are you going to move?" I grumbled. The need was already building in me again. I wondered if Knox's cock was some sort of magical wand that cast orgasm spells, rendering things like rally time and biological requirements nonexistent.

"Look at me, Naomi," he said.

I did as I was told.

"Goddammit, you're beautiful. And so fucking wet for me."

And he was rock-hard for me.

That was when he started to move. Slowly. Languidly. Sweat glistened on his skin. His jaw was set. But his hips pumped like a metronome as he glided in and out of me.

It felt like heaven. But I could tell he was holding himself back, and I wanted to give him everything he needed. Wanted him to take it.

"Don't be gentle," I groaned.

"Taking my time. Deal with it."

"Knox, if you get any more blood in that appendage, it's going to explode."

"You've got an opinion on everything. Even on how I fuck you."

"*Especially* on how you fuck me."

He kissed me probably just to shut me up, but I didn't care because when I hitched my hips higher, his thrusts came faster, went deeper. He was pushing me just past my comfort zone, making me take a little more than I was confident I could handle.

And damn if I didn't get off on it.

He was giving me what I needed without me having to spell it out for him and break it down. Without me having to ask. Without him saying, "maybe it's just easier if you do it yourself."

"Come back to me, Daisy."

I blinked, and Knox's face came back into focus, hovering over me and looking serious.

"You're right here when I'm inside you. Nowhere else. Got me?"

I nodded, embarrassed that I'd nearly gotten lost inside my head. He was right. How many times had I gotten so wrapped up in my plans and lists that I missed what was right in front of me? Or in this case, inside me.

To prove I was with him, I sank my nails into his shoulders and squeezed my muscles around his shaft as he drove deep.

"That's my girl," he groaned.

What we were doing felt so good. So *right*.

His chest hair tickled my puckered nipples as my heels dug into those perfect ass cheeks of his. Another orgasm was already starting to build.

It felt otherworldly good.

He felt it too. His thrusts were harder now, less controlled, and I wanted more.

"Can't decide how I want you," he confessed through gritted teeth. "Thought about too many ways."

"You have?" I breathed, trying to sound surprised, like I didn't have a regular fantasy of him banging me bent over the pool table at Honky Tonk.

He nipped at my bottom lip. "Up against a wall in my office. My hand over your mouth so no one can hear me making you come. You riding me in my truck. These perfect tits in my face so I can suck you while I fuck you. On your hands and knees looking over your shoulder while I work you from behind."

Okay, those were pretty good.

My breasts felt heavy, swollen. Every nerve ending in my body was lighting up. And those ab muscles I thought I'd torn with my first orgasm were tensing again.

"Fuck, baby. You just keep getting tighter."

I could feel every vein, every ridge, every inch of his arousal as he drove into me. Again and again, he rammed himself home. Euphoria filled my head like a fog.

His muscles were taut under my fingers. We were both shaking. I was going to come with him inside me and never be the same again. He forced a hand between us and cupped my breast, my greedy nipple pebbling against his palm.

"Take it all, baby."

And I did, opening as wide as I could and holding on for dear life as he drove me over the edge.

He didn't ease me into the orgasm—he detonated it. It shot through me like high voltage, making me tremble from head to toe. I buried my face in his neck and screamed.

"Ah, fuck. Fuck!"

I opened my eyes to find him powering into me, eyes half-closed. All vestiges of control snapped.

I felt his erection swell inside me as he grunted on the next thrust and the next. I was still coming when he jerked inside me, letting out a guttural shout of triumph. He buried himself deep and held there. Our bodies aligned, releases synchronizing. With every wrenching pulse of his erection, my muscles gripped him tighter.

"Naomi," he growled into my neck as we rode it out together. Hearts pounding as one.

24

Uninvited Guests

Naomi

A soft snore startled me from my incredibly steamy dream about Knox Morgan. When I heard the snore again, felt the warm, hard body against me, my eyelids flew open cartoon shade–style.

This wasn't a dream.

I'd accidentally had sex with my grumpy boss, infuriating neighbor, and flagrant backyard pee-er.

I waited for the stampede of regrets to charge through my brain like bison on a dusty prairie. But it seemed my body was too sated to allow for that. Knox had banged my brain *and* body into submission.

Carefully so as not to disturb my snoring bed partner, I rolled to face him. He was naked, the sheet tangled up in his legs, leaving most of his spectacular body on display. This was the first time I'd had the opportunity to study him up close without him knowing.

That thick, dark, dirty-blond hair was mussed from my hands. There was a small scar between his eyebrows and another one, longer, more jagged, near his hairline. His lashes were long enough to make me jealous. His lips, usually closed in that firm, disapproving line, were parted slightly.

He slept on his back, one tattooed arm under his head, the other around me. I hadn't pegged him for a cuddler. No one in their right mind would. But the hold he had on me said differently. His chest rose and fell with deep, even breaths. I studied his stomach muscles with fascination. Mine were sore from the unexpected ab workout orgasms delivered. His looked like they could withstand anything, tapering down to a taut V that disappeared beneath the sheet.

He looked so peaceful that even the perpetual line of annoyance between his eyebrows had smoothed.

I couldn't believe Knox Morgan was naked in my bed.

Oh, God.

Knox Morgan is naked.

In my bed.

And the sneaky son of a bitch had given me two of the most intense orgasms known to humankind. How in the hell was I supposed to look him in the eye now and *not* send my vagina into involuntary spasms?

Ah, there it is. My old friend, abject panic.

What was I doing in bed with a man I knew better than to sleep with mere weeks after running away from my own wedding?

I needed to get out of this bed, because if Knox woke up and gave me a sleepy-eyed stare, I'd throw caution to the wind and hop right back on that cock of his without another thought.

It took a few tries, but I managed to extricate myself from his surprisingly snuggly grip. Not wanting to wake him by rummaging through drawers, I grabbed the nightgown I'd set out for tonight and wiggled into it before tiptoeing out of the room.

"One-time thing," I chanted to myself as I made my way down the stairs.

It happened. It was over. Time to move on.

I tripped over a discarded boot on my way into the kitchen. "Ow! Damn it," I hissed.

Waylon lifted his head from the couch, let out a yawn, and stretched luxuriously.

"Hi," I said, feeling self-conscious that the dog might be judging me for sleeping with his human. But if the basset hound was feeling judgmental, it didn't last, because he rolled over and promptly went back to sleep.

I moved Knox's boots away from the foot of the stairs.

We'd left a trail of clothing on the first floor, something else I'd never done.

I'd pick it all up and fold it just as soon as I had a hit of coffee.

The late night, the worry over Nash and Waylay's first day, not to mention the mind-altering orgasms, had all rendered me nearly comatose.

I quickly started a pot of coffee, then rested my forehead on the counter while I waited for it to brew.

I thought about Waylay, trudging onto the big

yellow school bus in her purple dress and pink sneakers. Her new backpack full of supplies and snacks.

She hadn't been excited for her first day of sixth grade. I could only imagine how awful last year, her first in Knockemout, had been. Hopefully, between Nina, Chloe, and a new teacher, Waylay would get the second chance she so deserved. And if that didn't do the trick, I would find another solution. Waylay was a smart, funny, sweet kid, and I wouldn't let the world ignore that.

The coffee maker beeped its siren song of a finished pot. My fingers had just closed around the handle of the coffee carafe when there was a peppy knock at the front door.

Waylon's head popped back up from the couch.

Hastily, I poured a mug and took a scalding swallow before throwing open the door.

I choked on the mouthful of caffeine when I found my parents standing on the porch.

"There's our girl!" My mother, looking tan and happy, opened her arms.

At sixty-one, Amanda Witt still dressed to accentuate the curves that had caught my father's eye in college. She took pride in coloring her hair the same auburn it had been on their wedding day, though now she wore it in a daring pixie cut. She golfed, worked part-time as a school counselor, and breathed life into every room she entered.

"Mom?" I croaked, automatically leaning in for a hug.

"Lou, isn't this the *cutest* little cottage you've ever seen?" she said.

My father grunted. He had his hands stuffed into the pockets of his shorts and was nudging the porch railing with the toe of his sneakers. "Seems solid," he said.

Mom was impressed by pretty things. Dad preferred to appreciate sturdiness.

"How you doing, kiddo?" he asked.

I transferred my hug to him and laughed as my toes left the ground. While Mom was a few inches shorter than Tina and me, Dad was over six feet tall, a bear of a man who always made me feel like everything was going to be okay.

"What are you two doing here?" I asked as he carefully put me down.

"Sweetheart, you can't tell us we have a granddaughter and not expect us to drive straight here. Did we get you out of bed? That's a lovely nightgown," Mom noted.

Bed.

Nightgown.

Sex.

Knox.

Oh, God.

"Uh . . ."

"I told you we should have cut that cruise short, Lou," Mom said, slapping Dad in the shoulder. "She's obviously depressed. She's still in her pajamas."

"She's not depressed, Mandy," Dad insisted,

rapping his knuckles on the doorframe as he stepped inside. "What is this? Oak?"

"I don't know, Dad. Mom, I'm not depressed," I said, trying to figure out a way to get them out of the house before my naked guest woke up. "I just . . . uh . . . worked late last night, and there was a family emergency—"

Mom gasped. "Is something wrong with Waylay?"

"No, Mom. Sorry. Not our family. The family who owns this place and the bar I work at."

"I can't wait to see it. What's it called again? Hanky Pank?"

"Honky Tonk," I corrected her, spying my dress on the floor. "Did you see the living room?" It came out as an almost shout, and my parents exchanged a glance before pretending to be enthralled with the space I was waving at.

"Just look at that fireplace, Lou."

"Yes, look at the fireplace," I all but screeched.

Dad grunted.

As my parents admired the fireplace, I hooked the dress with my toes and swept it under the kitchen table.

"And you got a *dog!* My, you have been busy since the wedding." Waylon lifted his head, a jowl still stuck to the pillow. His tail thumped on the cushion, and my mom dissolved into a puddle of affection. "Who's a handsome boy? You are, sir. Yes, you are!"

"See, Mandy, she's not depressed. She's just busy," Dad insisted.

"Isn't the view of the woods great?" I said, the words sounding strangled as I pointed frantically at the windows.

When they turned to admire the woods through the glass, I grabbed Knox's jeans off the floor and threw them into the cabinet under the sink.

"Beeper, come meet your niece or nephew doggy!" My mother was using her "straight-A report card on the refrigerator" voice, which was definitely loud enough to wake the man upstairs in my bed.

"You guys brought Beeper?"

Beeper was my parents' latest rescue dog. She was a mix of breeds—I got them the DNA test for Christmas the previous year—that had been scrambled together and came out looking like a large, brown Brillo pad with feet. The Brillo pad appeared in the doorway and trotted inside.

Waylon sat up and gave an appreciative "woof."

"This is Waylon. He's not mine. He belongs to my, um, neighbor? Hey, do you guys want to get out of here and go for breakfast or lunch or just leave for any reason at all?"

Waylon hopped off the couch and booped noses with Beeper. Beeper let out a high-pitched yap, and the two of them began to zoom around the minuscule first floor.

"Daisy, baby, what the fuck are you doing down there?"

I watched in horror as bare feet attached to naked, muscular legs appeared on the stairs. Mom

304

and I froze to the spot as boxer briefs—thank God for penis-covering miracles—came into view.

Dad, moving quickly for a big guy, put himself between us and the approaching boxer briefs.

"State your business," Dad shouted at Knox's bare torso.

"Wow, wow, wow," Mom whispered.

She wasn't wrong. The man was freaking spectacular.

Waylon and Beeper chose that moment to take their zoomies up the stairs.

"Daze, you wanna explain what's goin' on?" Knox drawled as he sidestepped the canine catastrophe.

I ducked under Dad's arm and moved to stand between my parents and my boss . . . er, neighbor? One-time sex partner?

"Uh, okay. So . . . I really wish I would have had more coffee."

"Are those tattoos real? How many times a week do you go to the gym?" Mom asked, peering under Dad's armpit.

"What the hell is goin' on?" Dad rumbled.

"Oh, Lou. So old-fashioned," Mom said, giving him an affectionate pat on the backside before walking up to Knox and hugging him.

"Mom!"

Knox stood there woodenly, clearly in shock.

"Welcome to the family," she said, pressing a kiss to his cheek.

"Oh my God. I'm going to die of embarrassment," I decided.

Knox patted my mother awkwardly on the back. "Uh, thanks?"

She released him and then grabbed me by the shoulders. "We were so worried about you, sweetheart. It wasn't like you to just up and leave your own wedding like that. Not that we ever liked Warner that much anyway."

"Always thought he was a pretentious ass," Dad cut in.

"I thought maybe you were depressed," Mom continued. "But now it all makes sense! You fell in love with someone else and couldn't go through with a sham of a marriage. Isn't that wonderful, Lou?"

"I need coffee," Knox muttered and headed for the kitchen.

"Aren't you going to introduce us?" Dad demanded, still not looking very pleased.

"Naomi," Knox called from the coffeepot. "Pants?"

I winced. "Under the sink."

He gave me a long, unreadable look before bending to retrieve his jeans.

My mother gave me an incredibly inappropriate double thumbs-up as Knox turned his back on us and zipped the fly of his jeans.

Mom! I mouthed.

But she just continued flashing me the thumbs and a creepy smile of approval.

It reminded me of the time I'd taken her to see the Andersontown Community Theater's production of *The Full Monty*. My mom had an appreciation for the male form.

"Okay, I think we're getting a little ahead of ourselves. Mom, Dad, this is Knox. He's my neighbor and boss. We're not in love."

My mother's face fell, and Dad looked at the floor, hands on hips, his shoulders hunched. I'd seen that reaction before. Concern. Disappointment. Worry. But never for anything I'd done. It was always Tina bringing them trouble. I hated that this time it was me.

"Is this some one-night stand? Are you having some kind of midlife crisis, and this guy took advantage of you?" My father, who had won Best Hugger three years running at the Witt Family Reunion, looked as if he was about ready to start throwing punches.

"Dad! No one took advantage of anyone."

I shut up as Knox appeared at my side and handed me a fresh cup of coffee.

"How long are you two in town?" Knox asked my parents.

Dad glared at him.

"We haven't decided," Mom said to his tattoos. "We're very excited to meet our granddaughter. And we're a little concerned about *you know who*." She pointed at me as if I hadn't heard her stage whisper.

Knox looked at me and sighed. He put his free hand on the back of my neck and pulled me into his side. "Here's the situation. Your daughter blew into town trying to help her no-good sister, no offense."

307

"None taken," Mom assured him.

"I took one look at Naomi and fell hard and fast."

"Knox," I hissed. But he squeezed the back of my neck and continued.

"We're just seeing where this thing goes. Could be nothing, but we're enjoying it. You raised a smart, beautiful, stubborn woman."

Mom fluffed her hair. "She gets that from me."

"What is it you do for a living, Knock?" Dad demanded.

"Knox," I corrected. "He owns businesses and some property, Dad."

My father harrumphed. "Self-made man? Guess it's better than Mr. Nepotism." I assumed he was speaking of Warner, who got a job at the family company after college graduation.

"Got lucky a few years back and won the lottery. Invested most of it here in my hometown," Knox explained. "Thought I'd used up all my luck till Naomi here showed up."

Fake Romantic Knox was going to ruin all real romance for me if I wasn't careful.

"His name's on the police station," I said with forced brightness.

His grip on my neck tightened again. I reached behind him and pinched the skin just above the waistband of his jeans. He squeezed harder. I pinched harder.

"I need some Advil or something," Dad muttered, rubbing his forehead.

"You shouldn't have a headache, Lou. Our

daughter is *fine*. I was the one who was worried on the way down here, remember?" Mom said as if Knox and I weren't even in the room.

"Yeah? Well, now I'm the one who thinks there's something wrong with her."

"Let me get you something for your head," I offered, trying to extricate myself from Knox's grip. But he merely squeezed tighter and took a sip of his coffee.

"Don't be silly. I have all your father's favorite anti-inflammatories in my purse," Mom announced. She bustled over to where she'd planted her purse next to the front door. Dad shoved his hands in his pockets and wandered into the kitchen. I saw him frown at Knox's T-shirt where it lay crumpled on the stove top.

"Waylay is going to be so excited to meet you. Where are you two staying while you're here?" I asked, desperate to make small talk.

"There's a motel in town. We'll see if they have any rooms available," Dad said, opening cupboard doors and tapping the shelves.

After a three-week luxury Mediterranean cruise, I didn't think my parents would enjoy the moldy, dilapidated motel. I was already shaking my head when Knox spoke up.

"I think we can do better than that. We'll find room for you at Liza J's."

"Knox," I hissed. How was I going to pretend to be in a relationship with Knox with my parents staying practically next door?

He leaned in like he was going to nuzzle the side of my face and whispered, "Shut up." Then he brushed his lips over my temple, and my nipples went hard.

Mom waltzed by with a bottle of pills, beaming at me. I crossed my arms over my chest.

"I'm sure you'd want to stay as close to your daughter and granddaughter as possible," Knox said.

"Knox, can I see you outside?" I asked through clenched teeth.

"Do you see how they can't keep their hands off each other?" Mom trilled behind us.

"Yeah. You got any antacids in there?" Dad asked, looking ill.

I closed the door and dragged Knox onto the porch.

"So what are we supposed to do? Pretend to be in a relationship until my parents leave?"

"You're welcome. You fucking owe me, Daze. Do you have any idea what this is gonna do to my bachelor reputation?"

"I don't care about your reputation! I'm the one who has to pass a home study! Besides, I'm tired of owing you! Why do you keep riding to my rescue?"

He tucked a strand of hair behind my ear. "Maybe I like being the hero for once."

My knees threatened to buckle as the knee-jerk desire to swoon swept over me. His grin was downright sinful when he pulled me into him.

310

The contact with his body so soon after the best sex ever was frying my circuits. I didn't want to yell at him anymore. I wanted to kiss him.

"Or maybe," he whispered against my lips, "I just want to know what it feels like to have your smart mouth wrapped around my cock."

That was at least honest. And dirty. And I liked it.

He had one hand boldly cupping my rear end. The other held my hair at the base of my neck.

"Pardon the interruption."

Instinctively, I jumped back from Knox. Well, I tried to. He still had a pretty good grip on me. Which turned out to be a good thing, since I probably would have fallen right over the railing when I spotted caseworker Yolanda Suarez eyeing us from the foot of the steps.

"Mrs. Suarez, how lovely to see you again." I choked the words out.

25

A Family Fuss

Knox

E ven with the unwelcome intrusions of Naomi's parents followed by the disapproving case-worker who'd been missing a signature on a page, I was in a great fucking mood when I returned to the hospital.

Sure, the whole pretending to be in a relationship thing was probably—definitely—going to be a pain in the ass. But it would get Naomi out of a jam and piss my brother off.

I'd woken up that morning knowing that once wasn't going to be enough when it came to her. Now we could fool around for a few weeks, get each other out of our systems, and once her parents headed home, go back to our regular lives with itches scratched.

All in all, it wasn't a bad gig.

I stepped into Nash's room and found most of the Knockemout PD crowded inside.

"Let me know what you find from the office and the storage unit," Nash said from the bed. His color was a bit better.

"Sure glad you didn't kick the bucket, son," Grave said.

The rest of them nodded their agreement.

"Yeah, yeah. Now get the hell out of here and try to keep Knockemout from unraveling."

I nodded to each cop as they left, thinking about what Naomi had said about Nash cleaning up the department to better serve the town.

She was right. I guess we both wanted to do right by the town that had given us a place to call home.

"So how's Naomi?" Nash asked, sounding only a little irritated after the last officer walked out the door.

"Good," I said.

Morgan men didn't kiss and tell or fuck and tell. But I did allow the smallest of smirks.

"You fuck it up yet?"

"You're hilarious when you're pumped full of lead and drugs."

He sighed, and I could tell he was already sick of being cooped up in the hospital.

"What's with the staff meeting?" I asked.

"Couple of break-ins last night. An office and storage unit. Both owned by Rodney Gibbons. Office wasn't bad. Someone got the petty cash and rifled through the safe. Combination was on a sticky note next to the computer. Storage unit was trashed. No one saw anything at either place," he explained.

"How long they keeping you?" I asked.

Nash used his thumb to scratch between his eyebrows, a tell of frustration.

"Too fucking long. Said the soonest I can get out

313

is a couple of days. Then it's PT to see how much mobility I can get back."

If Nash didn't get back to 100 percent, he'd be handcuffed to a desk for the rest of his career, something even I knew he'd hate.

"Then don't fuck around," I advised. "Do what the docs say. Do your PT and get your shit together. No one wants you riding a desk."

"Yeah. Lucy is digging into it," he said, changing the subject. He didn't sound happy about it.

"Is he?" I hedged.

"You damn well know he is. It's police business. I don't need either of you amateurs out on the streets stirring shit up."

I was offended by the amateur remark. We'd been professional hell-raisers in our day. And though I might be a little rusty, I had a feeling our friend was even more dangerous now than he'd been at seventeen.

"Your boys get anything on the guy?" I asked.

Nash shook his head. "Stolen car. Wiped clean on the outskirts of Lawlerville. Locals found it about an hour ago."

"How clean?"

He shrugged, then winced. "Dunno yet. No prints on the wheel or door handles."

"Asshole's dumb enough to shoot a cop, he's dumb enough to leave prints somewhere," I predicted.

"Yeah," he agreed. He was moving his legs restlessly under the thin white blanket. "Heard Liza J has a few new guests."

314

I nodded. "Naomi's parents. Showed up this morning. Guess they're anxious to meet their granddaughter."

"Heard that too. Also heard that you made quite the impression coming downstairs in your birthday suit."

"Your grapevine needs some pruning. I was wearing underwear."

"Bet her dad loved that."

"He handled it."

"Wonder how you stack up against the ex-fiancé?" he mused.

"Her parents weren't fans of the ex," I said. Though I wasn't sure how I compared in Naomi's eyes. I peered down at Nash's untouched lunch tray. Broth and ginger ale. "How the hell are you supposed to survive on clear liquids?"

My brother made a face. "Something about not taxing the system. I'd kill for a burger and fries. The boys are too scared of the nurses to sneak in any contraband."

"I'll see what I can do," I promised. "Gotta head out. Some shit to take care of before the big family dinner tonight celebrating Way's first day and Naomi's parents coming to town."

"I hate you," Nash said. But there was no real heat to his words.

"Let this be a lesson to you, Little Brother. You gotta make your moves faster or else someone else'll make 'em for you."

I started for the door.

"Tell Way to let me know if anyone at school messes with her," Nash called.

"Will do."

"Tell Naomi she's welcome to swing by any time."

"Not happening."

Liza J's house no longer smelled like a mothball museum. It might have had something to do with someone opening the door to let four dogs in or out every five minutes.

Then again, it probably had more to do with the fact that rooms that hadn't been touched in fifteen years were getting Naomi's floor-to-ceiling treatment. Dusty drapes and the windows behind them opened wide.

The lights were on in the den, a room that hadn't been used since the house had welcomed paying guests. I spied Stef behind the desk on the phone, staring at the laptop in front of him.

There was music coming from the kitchen, and I could hear the sounds of people socializing in the backyard.

Maybe not all change was bad.

I knelt to give the pack of dogs their rubs. Naomi's parents' dog, Beeper, was standing on one of Waylon's ears.

"Fuck yeah!"

The exclamation came from the den. Stef closed his laptop triumphantly and stood behind the desk, arms overhead in a V.

The dogs, excited by his excitement, charged the doors and barreled into the room.

"Okay, no. Everyone out," Stef said. "These are very expensive Gucci loafers you're destroying with your doggy toenails."

"Good news?" I asked as he exited the den. The dogs took off toward the kitchen, moving as one clumsy organism of slobber and barks.

"Don't buddy up to me. I'm still mad at you," he said.

When Naomi and I brought her parents over to meet my grandmother, Stef had tried to cover the fact that he'd been in town for days.

No one would have bought his "what a coincidence, I just got here this morning" bullshit for long.

I just helped them get there by telling Amanda and Lou what a relief it was to have Stef under Liza J's roof for such a long visit.

"You'll get over it," I predicted.

"Just wait until you disappoint Mandy," he said. "It feels like kicking a litter of kittens."

I didn't really have anyone in my life to disappoint.

I followed him into the dining room, where my grandmother's buffet had been transformed into a high-end bar complete with cut lemons and limes, an ice bucket, and several bottles of decent liquor.

"What are you drinking?" he asked me.

"Bourbon or beer."

"It's too hot for straight, room-temperature liquor, and beer isn't celebratory enough. We're having G and Ts."

I could roll with that. "What are we celebrating?"

"Naomi's house," he said. "It went on the market two days ago, and she has three offers. Let's hope she thinks it's good news."

"Why the hell wouldn't she?"

Stef shot me a bland look, then started scooping ice into two highball glasses. "You know how some people have dream houses? Well, Naomi had the next-step house. She loved it. It was the perfect place to start a family. The right neighborhood. The right size. The right number of bathrooms. Giving up that house is like giving up on all her dreams."

"Plans change," I said as he cracked open a bottle of tonic water.

"I'll say, since she had no intention of getting in bed with you."

"Here we go," I muttered. "This is the part where you tell me I'm not good enough for her and I tell you to fuck off."

He poured a healthy slug of gin into each glass. "Let's skip to the bottom line. She's giving up everything to clean up Tina's mess. Again. As long as you're a pleasant distraction and not another mess to fix, I won't destroy your life."

"Gee, thanks. By the way, same goes if you hook up with Jer."

To Stef's credit, he didn't fumble the lime slices

or sprigs of rosemary he was adding to each glass when I mentioned my best friend.

"So that's what it feels like to have an obnoxious meddler sticking his nose where it doesn't belong," he said evenly.

"Yeah. Not great, is it?"

"Message received. Maybe a short-term palate cleanser is exactly what she needs to get Warner Fuckface the Third out of her head and start planning a life for herself and Way."

"I'll drink to that," I said, ignoring the way "palate cleanser" rubbed me the wrong way.

"Cheers. Let's go tell our girl that in fifteen days, her money troubles are officially over if she's willing to kiss her dreams goodbye."

We headed into the sunroom and out onto the deck. The humidity had broken just enough that it was almost comfortable outside. Oldies music poured from a speaker on the table.

Lou was manning the grill. The sizzle and scent of red meat made my mouth water. Amanda and my grandmother were sitting in Adirondack chairs, shading their eyes from the lowering sun.

The dogs, wet now, shook and sunned themselves in the grass.

But what caught and held my attention was Naomi. She was knee-deep in the creek, sunglasses on, that short, dark swing of hair pulled back in a clip. She was wearing a coral bikini that showed off every curve I'd enjoyed that morning.

Waylay, in a pink polka-dotted bathing suit,

doubled over and scooped two hands of cold creek water at her aunt.

Naomi's shriek and ensuing laughter as she attempted to exact revenge on the kid hit me someplace besides my cock. I felt a warmth in my chest that had nothing to do with the damn good gin and tonic in my hand.

Amanda adjusted her straw hat and sighed. "This is heaven," she said to my grandmother.

"You must have had a different Bible than the one I grew up on," Liza J quipped.

"I always dreamed of having a big family in a big house. All these generations and dogs all tangled up in each other's lives. I guess sometimes we're just not meant for certain things." She said it wistfully.

Stef cleared his throat. "Ladies, can I freshen up those Long Island iced teas?"

Liza J held up her empty glass. "I could do another round."

"I'm still working on mine, sweetie," Amanda told him.

"Have you decided to forgive me?" Stef asked.

"Well, you did sneak down here without a word," she said, lowering her sunglasses to give him what I identified as a mom look. "But you were just looking out for my girl. Anyone who does that is always all right in my book."

Stef dropped a kiss on top of her head. "Thanks, Mandy."

Naomi and Waylay were now in a full-fledged

splash battle. Arcs of water rose high, catching glints of the late afternoon sun.

"How much time left on those burgers, Lou?" Liza J called.

"Five minutes," he said.

"Knox," Amanda said, drawing my attention.

"Yes, ma'am?"

"Take a walk with me," she said.

Uh-oh.

Stef flashed a smug look at me and disappeared inside with Liza J's glass.

I followed Amanda to the end of the deck and down the stairs into the yard. It felt like only yesterday that it was Nash and me in the creek fooling around, scaring the fish. Pop manning the grill.

She slid her arm through mine as we walked.

"You've only known Naomi for a short time," she began.

I already didn't like where this was going.

"Sometimes you don't need a history to see the future," I said, sounding like a damn fortune cookie.

She squeezed my arm. "I meant, in her entire life, my daughter has never jumped into anything, especially bed with someone."

I didn't know what to say to that so I kept my mouth shut.

"She's a born caretaker. Always fussing over everyone else in the room. It's no surprise to me that she'd step up to keep Waylay even when the rest of her life is spiraling out of control. She gives until she's got nothing left."

This wasn't news to me. If Naomi wasn't slinging drinks to customers, she was doing everyone else's side work in the kitchen or cleaning out Liza J's mausoleum of a house.

"You brought her a cup of coffee doctored up just the way she likes it," she continued. "She also told me that you got her this place to stay and gave her a job. You drive her home. Stef mentioned you got her a cell phone when she didn't have one."

I was getting antsy. I wasn't known for my patience with conversations when I didn't know where they were going.

"She's a worrier but doesn't want anyone worrying about her," Amanda continued.

"I get that."

"You worrying about her, you taking care of her when you only just met, says a lot about your character. So does the fact that Naomi let you into her bed without the usual ninety-nine-point inspection."

I was equal parts uncomfortable and oddly pleased.

"All due respect, Amanda, I don't like talking about your daughter's sex life with you."

"That's because you're a man, sweetie," she said, patting my arm. "I just want you to know that I see how you're taking care of my girl. In all their time together, I never once saw Warner bring her a cup of coffee. Never once saw him do anything that benefited her unless it benefited him too. So thank you for that. Thank you for seeing my girl and wanting to be there for her."

"You're welcome." It seemed like the appropriate response.

"Out of curiosity, why do you call her Daisy?" she asked.

"She had flowers in her hair when I met her."

Amanda's smile broadened. "She left Warner and drove straight to you without even knowing it. Isn't that something?"

I didn't know if it was something or nothing. "Yeah. Something."

"Well, I like you, Knox. Lou will come around. Eventually. But I like you already."

"Dinner's ready," Liza J bellowed from the deck. "Get your behinds around the table."

"I'm starving," Amanda announced. "Why don't you get our girls out of the creek?"

"Uh . . . sure."

I stood there as Naomi's mother made a beeline for the house steps.

Naomi's laugh and another splash caught my attention.

I walked over to the edge of the creek and whistled. Waylay and Naomi paused their water fight, both laughing and dripping.

"Dinner's ready. Get your asses out of the water," I said.

"He's so bossy," Naomi said in a stage whisper. Waylay let out a girlish giggle.

I tossed a starfish towel over Waylay's wet head. "How was your first day, kid?"

"Fine," she said, peering quizzically out from under the towel.

The kid was a fucking rock. Abandoned by a no-good mother. Taken in by an aunt she didn't know. Then meeting her grandparents for the first time on the first day of school. And it was fine.

She turned and ran for the stairs and the promise of food.

"Go wash your hands, Way," Naomi called after her.

"Why? I just got out of the water!" Waylay yelled back.

"Then at least don't pet the dogs until after you eat! Fine. That's all she'd tell me too," Naomi said as I helped her up onto the bank.

"You worried?" I asked, unable to tear my gaze off her breasts.

"Of course I am. How am I going to fix any problems if I don't know they exist?"

"So talk to the teacher," I said, watching the outline of her nipples get more pronounced under the two triangles of fabric that stood between me and what I wanted.

"I think I will," she said. "How's Nash doing?"

Instead of answering, I clamped a hand over her wrist and hauled her over to the shady patio under the deck. Her skin was cold from the creek. Seeing her curves all wet like that was messing with my head.

I picked up the fluffy beach towel next to her neatly folded clothing on one of the lounge chairs that hadn't seen the light of day in years and handed it to her.

"Thanks," she said, bending over in front of me to run the towel through her hair.

A man only had so much self-control, and I'd just reached my limit.

I pulled the towel out of her hands and walked her backward until her back met the support column.

"Knox—"

I pressed a finger to her mouth, then pointed above us.

"Who wants medium rare?" Lou asked.

"Stef, this drink ain't gonna refill itself," Liza J said.

"What are you doing?" Naomi whispered.

Pinning her in place with my hips, she got the message pretty damn quick. When her mouth opened in an O, I yanked the triangles of her top apart.

Full, luscious, wet. My mouth watered, and it had nothing to do with the food being passed above us.

"Jesus, Daze. I see you like this, and I can't wait to get back in your bed."

I dipped my head and closed my mouth over one chilled peak. Her sexy little gasp, the way her hands clamped on my shoulders, the way she leaned into my mouth like she wanted it as bad as I did. It all went straight to my dick.

"I'd fuck you right here if I thought for a second I could get away with it."

She took one hand off my shoulder and shoved it between our bodies, cupping my erection through my jeans. I covered her hand with mine and squeezed. Hard. I thrust against our hands, greedy for the friction.

"Kids! Dinner," Amanda called from above us.

"Aunt Naomi, how many green beans do I hafta eat?"

The glassiness in Naomi's eyes cleared. "Oh. My. God," she mouthed at me.

I gave both nipples a not-so-gentle tweak before readjusting her top. I wanted to fuck her in that bikini. To untie one or two of those strings and guarantee all the right access. Then I wanted to take her every way possible until neither one of us could walk. Instead, I was going to have dinner with a hard-on and an audience.

Sometimes life just wasn't fucking fair.

She slugged me in the shoulder. "What is *wrong* with you?" she hissed. "Our families are right up there!"

"A whole lot of things," I said with a grin.

"You're the worst. We're coming!" she yelled.

"We will be later," I promised under my breath.

26

PMS and the Bully

Naomi

I arrived at Honky Tonk early for my shift in my Dad's pristine Ford Explorer, a bonus to having my parents in town. Another bonus was the fact that they were having a movie night sleepover with Waylay at Liza J's.

I was under orders to buy a car ASAP.

Between my poker winnings and the proceeds from the sale of my house, I found myself in a pretty solid financial position, even with the impending purchase of a decent car. Then there was the quickie Knox had coaxed me into that afternoon when he came over to help me put together Waylay's new desk.

I was feeling pretty damn good about life when I strolled into Honky Tonk. "Hello, ladies," I said to Fi and Silver. "You're looking gorgeous today."

"You're early and in a good mood," Fi noted, sliding the cash drawer into the register. "I hate that about you."

Silver glanced my way as she flipped the stools off the bar. She paused. "She's got orgasm face. She's not one of us."

Crap. The last thing Knox or I needed was

our coworkers gossiping about our incredibly satisfying sex life.

"Oh, come on," I scoffed, hiding my face behind a curtain of hair as I tied my apron. "A girl can be in a good mood without having orgasms. What's with the chocolate and heating pads?"

Next to the register was a plate of brownies wrapped with pink cellophane, a box of stick-on heating pads, and a bottle of Midol.

"Knox's monthly care package," Silver said. "Who gave you the O face?"

"Care package for what?" I asked, ignoring the question.

"All our cycles synced up. Stasia's too," Fi explained. "Every month, the boss puts together a period survival kit and is nice to us for a day or two."

"That's really nice of him," I said.

Fi slapped the bar. "Oh my god, you had sex with Knox!"

"What? Me? Knox?" I felt my face getting hot. "Why would you think that? Can I have a brownie?"

"She's definitely deflecting," Silver decided.

"Yeah, Naomi. Your poker face needs some serious work. This is so fucking exciting. You know he's never shagged an employee before. Man, I knew there were sparks! Didn't I tell you there were sparks?" Fi slapped Silver on the shoulder.

"Yeah, sparks," Silver agreed. "So are you

guys a thing? Or was it a heat-of-the-moment, my-brother's-just-been-shot kinda thing?"

"On a scale of 'meh' to 'my vagina is forever ruined,' how good was he?" Fi asked.

This was not going the way I'd planned. My gaze slid to the kitchen doors and back to the expectant faces before me. News traveled fast in this town, and I did not want to feed the gossip.

"You guys, I really don't want to talk about this."

They stood there staring at me. Then they looked at each other and nodded.

"Okay, here's how it's gonna go," Fi said. "You're going to tell us everything, and in exchange, we won't tell anyone anything."

"Or else what?" I hedged.

Silver's smile was wicked. "Or else we spend the whole shift wondering out loud who put that smile on your face in front of all the customers."

"You're evil."

"We're evil. But we can be bought," Fi reminded me.

"Your parents walked in on your one-night stand. Classic," Silver said ten minutes later when I'd finished verbally vomiting all over them.

"And your vagina is officially ruined," Fi added.

"And we aren't in a relationship. Unless you're my parents or a caseworker weighing my stability as a guardian, in which case we've been swept away by an unexpected romance."

"But you *are* having sex," Silver confirmed.

"Temporarily," I said with emphasis.

Silver raised a pierced eyebrow. Fi stopped gobbling down her brownie.

"Saying it out loud makes it sound stupid. Maybe we should finish getting ready to open?"

"Eh. I'm PMS-ing. I'd rather eat another brownie and talk about penis length and orgasm intensity," Fi said.

I was saved from responding by my phone signaling a text.

Sloane: My blabbermouth niece told me something I think you should know.
Me: What? Is my side part out of style?
Sloane: Yes. Also she said the teacher's been pretty rough on Way the last two days.
Me: What do you mean?
Sloane: Chloe said Mrs. Felch is being mean to Waylay. Yelling at her in front of the rest of the class. Making "weird" comments about her mom. Chloe and Nina got in trouble for defending her.
Me: Thanks for letting me know.
Sloane: You're going to go mama lion on an elementary school teacher, aren't you?

I pocketed my phone. "I hate to do this to you guys, but I need to go to Waylay's school."

"Is Way in trouble?" Fi asked.

"No, but Mrs. Felch is about to be. Mind covering for me until I get back?"

Silver looked up from the heating pad she was taping to her stomach. "I'll cover for you if you bring me back one of those pretzels with caramel dip from the place next to the school."

Fi's eyes lit up. "Ooh! Bring two!"

"Better make it three," Silver amended. "Max is coming in at four thirty, and she's on day two of the red tide."

"Three pretzels with caramel dip. Got it," I said, untying my apron and grabbing my purse. "You sure you don't mind covering for me?"

Fi waved away my concern. "It's always slow the first hour or two after opening. And Knox won't be here with all us gals in the middle of Shark Week."

"Shark Week?"

She pointed at the Midol and brownies.

"Oh, right. That Shark Week. Thank you for covering!" I blew them kisses and headed for the door.

The school was less than two blocks away, so I hoofed it. It gave me the time to work up a good head of steam. I was sick and tired of people thinking they could judge someone by their family's behavior. I'd lived in the shadow of Tina's misdeeds my entire life, and I hated that Waylay was facing the same kind of problem.

She was just a kid. She should be having sleep-overs, playing games, sneaking junk food. Not dealing with the fallout of her mother's reputation.

Worse yet, she hadn't trusted me enough to tell me she was having problems with her teacher. How could I fix a problem if I didn't know it existed?

Knockemout Elementary School was a squat brick building in the middle of town. There was the standard wood-chipped playground to the right and the long drive out front where buses loaded and unloaded every day.

The school day had already wrapped up, but I hoped I could catch Mrs. Felch in the building.

The front doors were all still propped open from the mass exodus of students, so I headed inside. It smelled like floor polish and disinfectant. It was only the first week of school, but the bulletin boards outside the sixth-grade classrooms were already full of artwork. Except for Room 303. The board was empty except for a calendar with a countdown on it and a piece of paper with the name Mrs. Felch.

I hadn't met her at Back-to-School Night. She'd been out sick, and I'd spent most of the hour gently reminding parents and school staff that I wasn't my sister. I kicked myself for not making more of an effort to meet her before leaving her in charge of my niece.

I spied a woman sitting behind the desk at the front of the classroom. Best guess put her in her early fifties. Her silver-streaked hair was pulled back in a bun so tight I bet she got headaches from it. She was dressed in head-to-toe shades of beige, and her lips were pursed in a thin line as she scrolled through something on her phone. She gave off the air of someone who was disappointed in just about everything life had to offer.

I gave a cursory knock and walked into the room. "Mrs. Felch, you don't know me, but—"

The woman looked up and bobbled her phone, eyes narrowing behind her glasses. "Don't play games with me. I know who you are."

Good lord. Hadn't the dang grapevine caught up to the teaching staff yet?

"I'm not Tina. I'm Naomi Witt. My niece, Waylay, is in your class, and I'd like to talk to you about how you've been treating her."

I'd never been good at confrontations. Hell, I'd squeezed my ass out of a church basement window to run away from a wedding rather than tell the groom I wasn't going to marry him.

But in that moment, I felt a fire burning in my belly. Backing down wasn't an option. Neither was retreat.

"How I've been treating her? I've been treating her the way she deserves to be treated," Mrs. Felch snarled. The lines on her face carved deeper. "I treat her the way the daughter of a whore deserves to be treated."

"*Excuse* me?"

"You heard me."

A movement out of the corner of my eye caught my attention, and I realized that I had a much bigger problem than a horrible sixth-grade teacher.

27

Field Mice Revenge

Knox

I walked into Honky Tonk through the kitchen, twirling my keys around my finger and whistling.

"Someone's in a good mood," Milford, the line cook, observed.

I wondered exactly how big of a dick I usually was that made my good mood breaking news, then decided I didn't really give a shit.

Making sure to school my expression into my normal scowl, I headed into the bar. There were about a half-dozen early birds scattered around the place. Max and Silver were eating brownies behind the bar and clutching their midsections.

Fi came out of the bathroom with her hands on her low back. "God. Why do I have to pee 147 times a day when I'm riding the cotton pony?" She groaned when she spotted me. "What the hell are you doing here? It's period night."

"I own the place," I reminded her, scanning the bar.

"Yeah. And you're also smart enough not to show up when you have three menstruating women on shift."

"Where's Naomi?" I asked.

"Don't you take that tone with me today, Knoxy. I will break your face."

I had taken no tone with her, but I knew better than to point that out. "I brought you brownies."

"You brought us brownies so we don't cry in the kitchen."

She had a point. Fi knew my secret. Tears were my kryptonite. I couldn't handle a woman crying. It made me feel desperate and helpless and pissed off.

"Where's Naomi?" I asked again, trying to modulate my tone.

"I'm fine, Knox. Thanks for asking. Even though I feel like my uterus is being crumpled up inside my body so it can be expelled through my lady canal, I'm *thrilled* to be working tonight."

I opened my mouth to retort, but she held up a finger. "Uh-uh. I wouldn't do that," she advised.

I shut my mouth and tagged Silver at the bar. "Where's Naomi?"

Her expression stayed carefully blank, but her eyes skated to Fi, who was making an exaggerated slashing motion across her throat.

"Seriously?" I asked.

My business manager rolled her eyes. "Fine. Naomi was here, but there was some trouble with Waylay's teacher. She went to take care of it and asked us to cover for her."

"She's bringing us pretzels afterward," Max said around the brownie she held between her teeth as she shuffled by with two fresh beers. I was pretty sure that was a health violation but was smart enough not to mention it.

I eyed the women before me. "You thought I'd be pissed that she went to take care of something at the school?"

Fi smirked. "No. But it's a slow day. Thought it would be more fun this way."

I closed my eyes and started to count to ten. "Why haven't I fired you yet?"

"Because I'm amazing!" she sang, spreading her arms wide. She flinched and clutched her stomach. "Fucking periods."

"Amen," Silver agreed.

"Strap on one of those damn heat pad things and take turns getting off your feet," I advised.

"Look who's Mr. Menstruation," Fi said.

"Working with the Synched Sisters has educated me in ways I never wanted to be. Who's the teacher?"

"What teacher?" Max asked as she blew past us again with a couple of empties. The brownie was now gone. I hoped it hadn't fallen into one of the beers.

"Waylay's teacher," I said in exasperation. "Did she say what the problem was?"

"Is there a reason you're so interested?" Fi asked, looking too damn smug for my liking.

"Yeah. I'm paying her to be here, and she's not here."

"Your tone is aggressive, and I don't react well to aggressive during my lady business," Silver warned.

This was why I didn't come near Honky Tonk during Code Red, which was how I labeled it in my calendar.

"Mrs. Felch," Max called from the corner two-top she'd commandeered. She was sitting on one chair with her feet propped on the second and a damp bar towel draped over her forehead and eyes.

"I'm personally not a fan of Mrs. Felch. One of my kids had her. She gave homework over Christmas," Fi recalled.

"Fuck."

Fi and Silver turned to look at me. Max peeked out from under her cold compress.

"Mrs. Felch is married," I said.

"That is usually what Mrs. means," Silver said, patronizing me.

"Mrs. Felch is married to Mr. Felch. *Nolan* Felch."

Fi got it first. "Ooh, shit. That's not good."

"Wait, didn't Tina—"

"Yeah. She did. I gotta go. Try not to scare off all the patrons."

Fi scoffed. "They're here for the free Bloody Mary shots we give out during crappy hour."

"Whatever. Later." Heading for the parking lot, I vowed never to come back to Honky Tonk during a Code Red.

I made it almost to my truck when Liza J's Buick rolled up. But it was Naomi's dad, worry lines carved into his forehead, behind the wheel instead of my grandmother. Amanda was in the passenger seat, looking agitated.

"Everything all right?" I asked, reading the mood.

"Waylay is missing," Amanda announced, a hand clutched to her heart. "She walked to the cottage to get her schoolwork together and was supposed to come straight back to Liza's. We were going to have dinner-and-a-movie night."

"She didn't come back, and her bike's gone," Lou said gruffly. "We're hoping Naomi has seen her."

I swore under my breath. "Naomi's not here. There was some trouble at the school with Way's teacher, and she went to handle it."

"Maybe that's where Waylay went," Amanda said, clutching her husband's arm.

"That's where I'm headed now," I said grimly.

"You're part of a parent-teacher conference?" Lou scoffed.

"No, but I'm sure as hell gonna have your daughter's back when she walks into an ambush."

I ignored the speed limit and stop signs on the short drive to the elementary school and noticed Lou did the same behind me. We pulled into adjacent parking spaces and stormed the front doors, a united front.

I hadn't stepped foot in the school since I was a student here. It looked as though not much had changed.

"How do we know where to go?" Amanda wondered when we walked in through the front doors.

I heard raised voices coming from one of the hallways.

"My money's on that way," I said.

"Your sister ruined my life!"

I didn't wait for the Witts. I headed toward the shouting at a dead run. I made it to the open door just in time to see a seething Mrs. Felch fisting her hands at her sides as she leaned into Naomi's personal space.

I stalked into the room, but neither woman paid me any attention.

"From what you've told me, your husband ruined your marriage. An innocent eleven-year-old certainly isn't to blame," Naomi said, hands on hips, not giving the woman an inch.

She was wearing another flirty denim skirt. This one had a distressed hem with threads that skimmed her thighs. I both loved the way it looked on her and hated the fact that she was wearing it to serve beer to men who weren't me.

"She's got her mother's blood, doesn't she? There's nothing innocent about any of you," Mrs. Felch hissed, pointing an accusing finger in Naomi's face.

My plans for Naomi and her tight little skirt would have to wait.

"Bullshit."

My announcement had both women whirling around to face me.

339

Mrs. Felch's eyes got big behind her glasses. I was a scary fucking guy when I wanted to be, and right now, I wanted to be downright terrifying. I took two steps forward, and she backed into her desk like a cornered rat in bifocals.

"Knox," Naomi said through clenched teeth. "I'm so glad you're here." She was tilting her head and subtly pointing toward the floating wall that created a coatroom just inside the doorway.

I glanced in the direction and caught a glimpse of blond and blue hair. Waylay, holding a jar of God knows what, gave me an embarrassed finger wiggle of a wave from her belly on the floor.

"For fuck's sake," I muttered.

"There's no need for language," Mrs. Felch barked.

"The fuck there isn't," I countered, angling myself to block part of the opening to the coatroom. "And I think Waylay's grandparents will agree."

I jerked my head toward Lou who, until that point, had been holding Amanda back with a good grip on her summer sweater.

"Seems we've got ourselves a family conference," I said, crossing my arms over my chest.

"Judging from how your daughter turned out, don't think for a second that I'm falling for this show of familial support," Mrs. Felch sniffed. "Waylay Witt is a juvenile delinquent, and her mother is a home-wrecking, pill-popping boil on the bottom of society."

"Thought you said there's no need for language."

"Crap on a cracker," Amanda whispered, and I guessed she'd just spotted her granddaughter's hiding place.

"Huh?" Lou was a little slower on the uptake until his wife pointed out the situation. "Ah, hell," he muttered under his breath. He stepped up to stand shoulder to shoulder with me. Amanda moved to his right. Together, we created a wall between Waylay and her shitty teacher.

Naomi looked relieved, then turned back to face the kraken. "Mrs. Felch," she snapped, bringing the woman's attention back to her.

I snapped my fingers at Waylay and pointed to the door. She started to belly-crawl her way toward the door.

Naomi waved her arms and paced toward the opposite side of the classroom like she was throwing a fit. "I have empathy for your situation. I really do. You certainly didn't deserve what your husband and my sister did to you. However, *you* are responsible for not just teaching these students but for making them feel safe in your classroom. And I have it on good authority that you are failing in spectacular fashion when it comes to that duty."

Waylay's sneakers disappeared into the hallway.

"Tina took my husband into her bed and—"

"Enough." I bit out the word, and the woman's lip trembled.

"Yeah. What he said," Amanda agreed, backing toward the door. "Oh, dear! I just remembered. I left my purse in the hallway." She hustled out the door . . . holding her purse.

Naomi returned to stand in front of me. "I'll give you the weekend to decide whether you're going to modify your behavior so that *all* your students, including my niece, feel safe in your classroom. If you refuse, then I'll not only have Waylay removed from your class, I'll go to the school board and I will raise hell."

I reached an arm around her chest and pulled her back to my front. Naomi the spitfire could be just a little terrifying when she wasn't screaming her frustrations into a pillow.

"She'll do it too," Lou cut in proudly. "She won't stop until you're out of the classroom. And the rest of us will be there to back her up every step of the way."

"It wasn't supposed to be like this," Mrs. Felch whispered. She sank wearily into the desk chair. "We were supposed to retire together. We were going to drive the RV cross-country. Now I can't even look at him. The only reason he stayed is because she dropped him as quick as she picked him up."

I guessed it couldn't be easy for Lou to hear this about one of his daughters, but the man hid it well.

I felt Naomi's anger drain out of her.

"You didn't deserve what happened to you," Naomi said again, her voice softer now. "But neither does Waylay. And I'm not going to let anyone make her feel like she's responsible for the decisions adults make. You and Waylay both deserve better than the hands you were dealt."

Mrs. Felch flinched, then sagged back in her chair.

I gave Naomi an approving squeeze.

"We'll leave you to your weekend," she said. "Feel free to email me your decision. Otherwise, I'll see you Monday morning."

"Waylay Regina Witt!"

Apparently Naomi wasn't done yelling when we returned to the parking lot, where Amanda and Waylay stood next to my grandmother's car.

"Now, Naomi," Amanda began.

"Don't you 'now, Naomi' me, Mom. Someone under five feet with blue streaks in her hair had better start explaining why I came down to discuss a situation with her teacher only to find my niece hiding in the coatroom with a jar of mice! You're supposed to be at Liza's with your grandparents."

Waylay looked at the toes of her sneakers. They were the pink ones I'd bought her. She'd added a heart charm to the laces. There were two mice nestled on a cushion of dried grass in the jar at her feet.

"Mrs. Felch was bein' a pain in the a—"

"Do *not* finish that sentence," Naomi said. "You're already in trouble."

Waylay's face went mutinous. "*I* didn't do anything wrong. I showed up to school on the first day, and she was mean to me. Like really

343

mean. She yelled at me in front of everyone in the cafeteria when I spilled my chocolate milk. She took recess time away from everyone and said it was my fault for not respecting what belonged to other people. Then, when she was handing out papers about some dumb bake sale to take home to our parents, she said I didn't need one since my mom was too busy in the bedroom to find the kitchen."

Naomi looked like she was about to have an aneurysm. "Get it together," I warned her, tucking her behind my back.

I put my hand on Waylay's shoulder and squeezed.

"Look, kid. I think we all get that you're not used to havin' an adult around who has your back. But you need to get used to it. Naomi's not goin' anywhere. You've got your grandparents too. And you've got me and Liza J and Nash. But you scared the shit out of all of us running off like that."

She scuffed her foot on the asphalt. "Sorry," she said sullenly.

"What I'm sayin' is you have a lot of people in your corner now. You don't need to go it alone. And your aunt Naomi can do a hell of a lot more than leave some mice in a teacher's desk drawer."

"I was also gonna give her computer a virus. One of those annoying ones that adds extra letters and numbers when you're typing," she said, her cheeks pink with indignation.

I hid my grin by biting the inside of my cheek.

"Okay. That's pretty good," I admitted. "But it's not a long-term solution. Your teacher is a problem that you can't solve on your own. You need to tell your aunt this shit so she can deal with it like she just did in there."

"Mrs. Felch looked scared," Waylay said, chancing a glance behind me at Naomi.

"Your aunt can be real scary when she stops taking her screaming into pillows."

"Am I in trouble?" Waylay asked.

"Yes," Naomi said firmly.

Just as Amanda insisted, "Of course not, sweetheart."

"Mom!"

"What?" Amanda asked, wide-eyed. "She's been through a traumatic few days at school, Naomi."

"Your mother is right," Lou said. "We should call an emergency appointment with the principal and the superintendent. Maybe they can convene a special school board meeting tonight."

"This is so embarrassing," Waylay groaned.

I didn't know what the hell I was doing wading into a family disagreement, but I did anyway. "Why don't we let Mrs. Felch stew for the weekend? Naomi already laid it out for her real clear. We'll deal with whatever needs dealt with Monday morning," I said.

"Why are you even here?" Lou demanded, turning his anger on me.

"Dad!" It looked like it was Naomi's turn to be embarrassed as she stepped to my side.

345

"Waylay, go let the mice out over there on the tree line," I ordered.

She shot me a wary look before scampering off toward the skinny strip of woods between the school and Knockemout Pretzels. I waited until she was out of earshot before turning back to Lou.

"I'm *here* because Naomi was walking into a situation she didn't know anything about. Felch has had a hard-on for Tina ever since her husband banged Tina this summer. The whole town was talking about it. Now, once again, Naomi's cleaning up a mess that Tina left behind. Something I get the feeling she's spent her whole life doing. So maybe you can cut her some slack or, better yet, help her out with the cleanup this time around."

Lou looked like he wanted to take a shot at me, but I saw my words had landed with Amanda. She put her hand on her husband's arm. "Knox is right, Lou. Us second-guessing Naomi isn't helping anyone."

Naomi took a breath and blew it out slowly. I ran my hand up her back, then down again.

"I need to get back to work," she said. "I've already missed an hour of my shift. Will you two please take Waylay home and try to keep her from running off again?"

"Of course, sweetheart. And now that we know that she's sneaky, we'll keep a closer watch on her."

"I'll take the front tire off her bike," Lou decided.

"I need to skip ahead to the chapter on discipline in my library book," Naomi decided. "Damn it! I hate reading out of chronological order."

"Judith's daughter changes the Wi-Fi password on her kids and doesn't change it back until they're ungrounded," Amanda suggested helpfully.

Waylay returned with a now empty jar, and I felt Naomi take another deep breath.

"Mrs. Felch is in way more trouble than you are, Waylay. But Knox is right. You have to come to me with this stuff. Don't tell me everything's fine when it's not fine. I'm here to help. You can't be sneaking out and exacting revenge on everyone who wrongs you. Especially not with innocent little field mice."

"I brought food and I was going to put water in the drawer with them," Waylay explained.

"We'll talk about this in the morning," Naomi said. "Your grandparents are going to take you home. It's up to them whether you have to scrub floors or if you still get to watch movies tonight."

"It'll definitely be movies," Lou whispered.

"But you have to do all the dinner dishes," Amanda added.

"I'm sorry for worrying you," Waylay said quietly. She lifted her eyes to look at Naomi. "And I'm sorry for not telling you."

"Apology accepted," Naomi said. She swooped down and gave the girl a quick hug. "Now, I have to get back to work."

"I'll drive you," I volunteered.

"Thank you. I'll see everyone in the morning," she said wearily.

There was a chorus of goodbyes, and Naomi headed for the truck.

I waited until she opened the passenger door, then interrupted Amanda, who was making plans to stop for ice cream on their way home. "Can you two do me a favor and swing by Honky Tonk to pick up your Explorer? I'll drive Naomi home tonight."

I had plans for her.

28

Third Base

Knox

"S he ran away from home," Naomi said, staring out the window and clutching the bag of warm pretzels in her lap.

"She didn't run away. She snuck out," I argued.

"Either way, how does that make me look as a guardian? I let an eleven-year-old walk into town with a jar of mice and a computer virus."

"Daze, you need to stop gettin' yourself so worked up over this custody thing. Do you really think any judge in their right mind is going to decide Way is better off with her mom?"

She turned flashing eyes on me. "How about when *your* life choices are under a microscope by the legal system, you can decide not to get worked up?"

I shook my head and turned onto a trail barely wide enough for my truck.

"This isn't work," she observed.

"Not goin' back to work yet," I told her as we bumped along the rutted track.

"I need to get back. I have a shift that I should have already been working," she insisted.

"Baby, you need to stop obsessing about the

things you should be doing and make some time for the shit you wanna do."

"I *want* to get back to work. I don't have time for you to murder me in the woods today."

The trees parted, and a field of tall grass opened up before us.

"Knox, what are you doing?"

"I just watched you stand up to that bully who was trying to take her shit out on a kid," I began.

"Some people don't know what to do with their pain," Naomi said, looking out the window again. "So they take it out on whoever is nearby."

"Yeah, well, I liked watching you in that excuse for a skirt standing up to a bully."

"So you kidnapped me?" she asked. "Where are we?"

I brought the truck to a stop along the tree line and shut off the engine. "Third Base. Least, that's what it was called when I was in high school. We used to sneak beers and hold bonfires out here. Half of my class lost their virginity in this field."

A hint of a smile played on her lips. "Did you?"

I slid my arm around the back of her seat. "Nah. Lost mine in Laura Beyler's barn."

"Knox Morgan, did you bring me out here to neck when I'm supposed to be at work?"

She sounded adorably appalled.

"Oh, I plan on doing more than necking," I said, leaning over to release her seat belt. Task accomplished, I plucked the pretzels off her lap and threw the bag into the back seat.

"You can't be serious. I have work."

"Baby, I don't joke about sex. Besides, you work for me."

"Yeah. In your *bar,* which is full of PMS-ing women waiting for their pretzels."

I shook my head. "Everyone in town knows it's a Code Red. It'll be a slow night."

"I am really uncomfortable with the idea of an entire town tracking its women's menstrual cycles."

"Hey, we're normalizing period shit," I argued. "Now, get your sexy ass over here."

Good Girl Naomi was warring with Bad Girl Naomi, but I could tell which one was going to win by the way she was biting her lip.

"Between that skirt and the way you stood up for Way, I barely managed to keep my hands off you in front of Way and your parents, and it almost killed me. We're lucky I got us here, driving with my dick so hard there's no blood left for my brain."

"Are you saying you're turned on by me yelling at people?"

"Daze, the sooner you stop talking, the sooner I can drag you across this console and make you forget all about work and shitty teachers."

She stared at me through heavy lids for a beat. "Okay."

I didn't give her a chance to reconsider. I hooked her under the arms and pulled her into my lap so she was straddling my thighs, her denim skirt bunched high around her waist.

"Did I mention how much I love these skirts?" I asked before crushing my mouth to hers.

She pulled away from me. "Actually, you said you hated them. Remember?"

I gritted my teeth as she grinned evilly and ground down on my cock through my jeans. "I lied."

"This is very irresponsible of us," she said.

I yanked the neckline of her Honky Tonk tank down, taking her bra with it so her bare tits were in my face. Her nipples were already begging for my mouth. If there had been an ounce of blood left in my brain, it headed south at that view.

"It's more irresponsible to make me watch you work your whole shift in that fucking skirt without getting you off first."

"I know I should be offended when you talk like that, but—"

I leaned in and took one perky, pink nipple between my lips. I didn't need her to finish the sentence. Through my jeans, I could already feel how wet she was for me. I knew what my words did to her, and it was nothing compared to what the rest of me was capable of.

She shuddered against me once as I began to suck, and then her fingers were at my belt.

I shifted my hips to give her better access, and the horn sounded.

She gasped. "Oops! Sorry. That was my butt. I mean, my butt hitting your horn. Not like my butt."

I found myself grinning against her breast. The woman was entertaining on more than just the most obvious levels.

Between the two of us, we managed to slide my jeans down to midthigh, freeing my throbbing cock and only setting off the horn once more. I didn't want to wait. I needed to be inside her, and judging from the breathy little moans that were clawing their way out of her throat, Naomi was with me. I lifted her with an arm around her hips and used my other hand to guide the head of my dick right where I needed it to be, nestled against that tight, wet wonderland.

My tight, wet wonderland.

Naomi belonged to me. For now at least. And that was enough.

With both hands at her hips, I yanked her down as I thrust up, sheathing myself inside her.

She screamed my name, and I had to run through my emergency mental gymnastics to keep from coming right then and there. Her quivering pussy had every inch of my cock in a stranglehold.

I held her there, impaled on me, as my mouth rediscovered her perfect breast. I swore I could feel the echo of each hard suck in the walls that held me captive.

It felt like heaven. It felt—

"Fuck, baby," I said, releasing her breast. "Fuck. Condom."

She let out a low moan. "Knox, if you move a muscle, I'm going to come. And if I come—"

"You're gonna milk mine right out of me," I surmised.

Her eyes were squeezed shut, lips parted. The picture of ecstasy in the late afternoon sun.

I wasn't some teenage kid. I didn't forget protection. Hell, not only did I have a condom in my wallet like any responsible man, I also had a handful in my glove box.

"You ever—"

She shook her head before I could get the rest of the question out. "Never."

"Me either." I ghosted my fingers over and around her breasts.

She opened her eyes then and bit her lip. "This feels too good."

"I don't want you doing anything you don't want to do," I warned.

But *I* wanted this. *I* wanted to finish bare. *I* wanted to let loose inside her and feel our releases mix. I wanted to be the first man to go there. To plant my flag in her memory as the first of something memorable.

"I–I'm on birth control," she said tentatively.

I let my tongue dart out to tease her other nipple. "I'm clean," I murmured. "I can show you."

Naomi was a data kind of girl. If she wanted a peek at my medical record, I had no problem. Especially if it meant I got to move in her, feel her ride me until she came with nothing between us.

"Okay," she said again.

It was better than winning the fucking lottery,

that feeling that lit up my chest. The knowledge that she trusted me to take care of her.

"You sure?" I pressed.

Her eyes were open and locked on mine. "Knox, it feels too good. I don't wanna play it safe. Not this time. I feel like being reckless and . . . whatever. Just move, please!"

I'd make it the best she ever had.

I slid my hands behind and under her, cupping the curves of her ass.

Testing us both, I held her up, pulling out just an inch.

We both groaned, and her forehead met mine. Moving inside her with nothing between us felt better than good. It felt *right*.

When she quivered around me, I had enough fucking rhapsodizing. It was time to take.

"You better hang on, baby," I warned. My heart was already pounding like I'd raced up a half-dozen flights of stairs. I waited until she gripped the back of my seat. "This is what's gonna happen, Naomi. I'm gonna start moving, and you're gonna come as fast and as hard as you can. Then I'm gonna take my time driving you up again, and when you go off that second time, I'll be right there with you."

"Good plan. Very organized. Measurable goals," she said, and then she was kissing the air right out of my lungs.

I withdrew another inch or two and captured her moan with my mouth. "Hold on," I reminded her, and then I was yanking her back down as I rammed my hips up. It took everything I had not to let go and drive into her again and again. "Jesus, Naomi," I breathed as her pussy fluttered around my shaft.

"I told you I'm close," she said, sounding annoyed and embarrassed.

"Everything you do makes me want more," I growled. Before she could react to my stupid-ass confession, I buried my face in her other breast and started to move. Slowly, purposefully. Even though it cost me.

On my third thrust, she came like a lightning strike, setting off the horn like a victory cry. As the rest of her body tensed, her walls rippled around my dick in the sweetest kind of torture. I almost went cross-eyed trying to keep my release in my balls where it churned.

I'd never had a woman like her. Never felt anything like this before. And if I stopped long enough to think about it, I'd recognize that as a red flag. But in the moment, I didn't fucking care. I could ignore it as long as Naomi Witt was riding my cock.

"That's my girl," I groaned as she gripped and released me to a rhythm more beautiful than music.

"Oh my God. Oh my God," she chanted until her body finally went limp on top of me.

I went still inside her and gathered her close. I could feel her heart pounding against my own. Then she poked me in the shoulder.

"You promised me another one," she said, the words muffled against my neck.

"Baby, I'm trying to hang on here to deliver."

She lifted her head to peer at me through strands of chestnut and caramel. I brushed it back, tucking her hair behind her ears, the gesture feeling oddly intimate. And I wished I hadn't done it. Because it felt like one more string knotting itself, tethering me to her.

"So it feels this good to you too? I mean, you're not just like 'this is fine'?" To illustrate her point, she added a half-hearted thrust with her hips, and I couldn't hold back the groan.

"Hell, Naomi, there's nothing 'fine' about what it feels like to have you come on my cock. Why the hell do you think I said I'd do this fake boyfriend crap?"

She smirked. "Because you saw how disappointed my parents were in me and you wanted to help me out like the grumpy, small-town hero you are."

"Smart-ass. I did it because I woke up, and you weren't next to me, and I wanted you there."

"You did?"

"I wanted you there so I could flip you over on your hands and knees and fuck you so hard you wouldn't be able to sit down for the next forty-eight hours without thinking about me."

She opened her mouth, and something between a moan and a whimper came out.

"I'm not done with you yet, Daisy," I said.

357

Inwardly, I cringed at the harshness of this statement. Midsex me was not usually so fucking chatty. But Naomi was doubting what I'd made her feel. And that wouldn't stand. Not even in the short term.

"Can I move again?" she asked.

"Jesus. God. Yes."

And then she was riding me, working my cock like it was a stallion in need of breaking. Every slick slide, every little moan, every time a fingernail bit into my skin, I felt the rest of the world recede a bit more until it was just Naomi and me.

Sweat beaded on our skin. Our breath mingled as we panted together.

There was nothing like being fully seated inside her. Nothing like claiming her and being claimed.

"Naomi." I gritted out her name as I felt her start to flutter around me again, tiny little pulses that drove me out of my fucking mind.

"Knox. Yes. Please," she whimpered.

I took her nipple on a long, deep pull. It was too much for both of us. As the first wave of her orgasm took her, I lost control, pumping into her hot, tight channel as if my life depended on it.

Maybe it did.

Because when that first hot spurt wrenched its way free, when she screamed my name for the world to hear, when she closed around me and milked a second and a third burst from me, I felt born again. Alive. Hollowed out and refilled to overflowing with something I didn't recognize. Something that scared the ever-living hell out of me.

But I just kept on coming, and so did she, our releases endless.

This. This was why once wasn't enough. This was why now I wasn't sure what was enough.

29

Knox's House

Knox

"Nice place," Naomi observed as I locked my front door behind us and flipped on the lights.

"Thanks. My grandfather built it," I said on a yawn. It had been a long day followed by a long night at Honky Tonk, and I needed sleep.

"Really?" she asked, her gaze lifting to the loft above the living room, the timber ceiling and the antler chandelier that hung there.

The cabin was small and leaned toward rustic. Two bedrooms, one bath. The floors were pine. The stone fireplace needed a good scrubbing but still did the job. The leather couch was finally broken in just the way I wanted it.

It was home.

"Are these your parents?" she asked, picking up a framed photo on one of the end tables.

I didn't know why I bothered keeping it. My parents were line dancing at a picnic in Liza J and Pop's yard. Smiles on their faces, feet in sync. Happier times that, in the moment, seemed like they'd go on forever.

It was, of course, a lie.

Happier times always came to an end.

"Listen, Daze. I'm beat."

Between my brother getting shot, the sudden onslaught of orgasms, and work, I needed a solid eight hours of sleep before I'd be worth anything.

"Oh. Yeah. Sure," she said, carefully putting the photo back on the table. Though I noticed she'd angled it toward the couch, not away from it like I'd done. "I'll head home. Thanks for the backup today with Way's teacher . . . and my parents. And then all the orgasms and stuff."

"Baby, you're not going home. I'm just telling you why I'm not makin' any moves when we go upstairs."

"I should just go home, Knox. I have to be up early to get Way at Liza's." She looked as exhausted as I felt.

I hadn't given it more than a passing thought in the past, but my girls at Honky Tonk dragged their asses home at two or three a.m. and on weekdays had to be up again by six or seven depending on the usefulness of their significant others.

I remembered a solid year stretch when Fi would fall asleep sitting up every day at her desk because her kids were shit sleepers. It got to the point where I had to do the thing I hated. I got involved.

I'd unleashed Liza J on her, and in less than a week, my grandmother had both kids on a schedule sleeping ten hours a night.

"You have off tomorrow, right?" I asked.

She nodded, then yawned.

"So we'll get up in"—I glanced down at my

361

watch, then swore—"three hours and go have breakfast at Liza J's."

It was the gentlemanly thing to do. Which usually wasn't a huge concern to me. But I felt the tiniest splinter of guilt thinking about staying in bed while Naomi dragged herself off to family fucking breakfast and then tried to keep Waylay from breaking the law for the rest of the day.

Besides, I could just come home after breakfast and sleep until whenever the fuck I wanted.

I liked the way her eyes went soft and dreamy for a second. Then practical, people-pleasing Naomi was back. "You don't have to get up with me. You need sleep. I'll go home tonight, and maybe we can . . ." Her gaze slid down my body, and her cheeks turned a delicate shade of pink. "Catch up some other time," she finished.

"Yeah. Nice try. Want some water?" I asked, towing her toward the kitchen.

It was bigger than the cottage's, but not by much. I could imagine some visitors would find it "charming" with its hickory cabinets, counter tops in a deep forest green, and a tiny island on wheels that I used to pile unopened mail on.

"Water?" she repeated.

"Yeah, baby. Do you want a drink of water before we go to bed?"

"Knox, I'm confused. This is just sex. We both agreed. Unless my parents are around, and then it's a relationship. But my parents aren't here, and I'm so tired I don't think even an orgasm could keep me awake. So what the hell are we doing?"

I filled a glass from the sink and then took her by the hand and led the way toward the stairs. "If you leave, I have to walk your ass home in the dark, then walk my ass back here. Which puts me hittin' the sack back by another fifteen minutes at least and, Daze, I'm really fucking tired."

"My stuff is at my house," she said, biting her lip in hesitation.

"What stuff do you need in the next three hours, Daisy?"

"A toothbrush."

"Got an extra upstairs."

"My face wash and lotion."

"Got water and soap," I said, tugging her up the stairs.

"I still don't—"

I stopped and faced her. "Baby, I don't want to think about it or wonder what it all means. I just want to put my head on a pillow and know that you're safe and asleep. I promise you, we can nitpick this mess to death tomorrow. But right now, I just need to close my eyes and not think about shit."

She rolled her eyes. "Fine. But we're definitely nitpicking this mess to death tomorrow and reconfirming the ground rules."

"Great. Can't wait." Before she could change her mind, I pulled her the rest of the way up the stairs and into my bedroom.

"Wow," she yawned, blinking at my bed.

A man's bed and his couch were the most important pieces of furniture in the house. I'd gone for a big-ass king-size sleigh bed stained dark.

It was unmade, as always. I never saw the point in making a bed if you were just going to have to unmake it to use it. It was a good thing Naomi was nearly dead on her feet, because if the rumpled sheets didn't send her packing, the short stack of underwear and T-shirts next to my nightstand would have.

I nudged her in the direction of the bathroom and rifled under the sink until I came up with a spare toothbrush still in its dusty, original package.

"I take it you don't have many overnight guests?" she asked, wiping the dust off the plastic.

I shrugged. I'd never spent the night with a woman in this house. I was already crossing the invisible boundaries of our agreement by having her spend the night. There was no fucking way I was going to hash out what it meant with her.

She was the one who was used to sharing a life, a sink, a bed with someone. She was the one coming out of a relationship.

Great. Now I was tired and annoyed.

We stood shoulder to shoulder, brushing our teeth. For some reason, the companionable routine reminded me of my childhood. Every evening when we were kids, Nash and I hung out on our parents' bed, waiting for them to finish brushing their teeth so they could read us the next chapter in whatever book we were in the middle of.

I shook off the memory and glanced at Naomi. She had a faraway look in her eyes. "What's wrong?" I asked.

"Everyone's talking about us," she said, rinsing her toothbrush.

"Who's everyone?"

"The entire town. Everyone is saying we're dating."

"I doubt that. Most of them are just saying we're fucking."

She flung a hand towel at me that I caught one-handed.

"Fine. My parents and Waylay's caseworker think we're in a relationship, and the rest of town thinks we're just having sex."

"So?"

She looked exasperated. "So? It makes me look like a . . . well, like my sister. I've only known you three weeks. Don't you care what people think about you? What they say about you?"

"Why would I do that? They can whisper all they want behind my back. As long as none of them are dumb enough to say it to my face, I don't give a shit what they say."

Naomi shook her head. "I wish I could be more like you."

"What? A selfish asshole?"

"No. Whatever the opposite of a people pleaser is."

"A people displeaser?" I supplied.

"You have no idea how exhausting it is worrying about everyone else all the time, feeling responsible for them, wanting them to be happy and like you."

She was right. I had no idea what it was like. "Then stop caring."

"Of course you would say that," she said, sounding disgruntled. She took the hand towel, wiped down her toothbrush and then the counter. "You make it sound so easy."

"It is that easy," I argued. "Don't like something? Stop doing it."

"The life philosophy of Knox Morgan, ladies and gentlemen," she said with an eye roll.

"Bed," I ordered. "It's too late for philosophy."

She glanced down at her outfit. Her feet were bare, but she was still wearing that denim skirt and shirt from her shift.

"I don't have any pajamas."

"I take it that means you don't sleep naked?" Just like making the bed, wearing pajamas was a waste in my opinion.

She stared at me.

"Of course you don't sleep naked."

"There could be a fire in the middle of the night," she insisted, crossing her arms.

"I don't have any turnout gear for you to sleep in."

"Har har."

"Fine." I left her in the bathroom and headed to my dresser, where I found a clean T-shirt. "Here," I said, returning to her.

She looked down at it, then up at me again. I

liked the way she looked. Sleepy and a little less than perfect, as if the shift and the late night had worn down her armor.

"Thanks," she said, staring at it and then me again until I got the hint.

"You do realize I've already seen you naked, right?"

"That's different. Go away."

Shaking my head, I left the bathroom, closing the door behind me.

Two minutes later, Naomi stood in the doorway in my T-shirt. She was tall, but the shirt still covered her to midthigh. Her face was scrubbed clean, and she'd pulled part of her hair up and back in a small knot on top of her head.

The girl next door was about to crawl into my bed. I knew it was a mistake, but it was one I wanted to make. Just this once.

We traded places, with Naomi slipping into my bedroom and me commandeering the bathroom to remove my contacts from my bleary eyes.

Running on fumes, I snapped off the bathroom light and crossed to my side of the bed. She was on her back, arms tucked under her head, staring up at the ceiling. I killed the bedside light and stripped in the dark, throwing my clothes in the direction of the dirty laundry pile.

I dragged back the blankets and finally fell into bed with a sigh. I waited a beat, staring up at the darkness. This didn't have to mean anything. This didn't have to be another string, another knot.

"You good?" I asked.

"My pillow smells weird," she said, sounding disgruntled.

"You're sleeping on Waylon's side." I pulled the pillow out from under her head, then threw mine at her.

"Hey!"

"Better?"

I heard her sniff the pillow. "Better," she agreed.

"Night, Naomi."

"Good night, Knox."

I woke to a thud, a yelp, and a curse.

"Naomi?" I rasped, ungluing my eyelids. She came into a soft focus at the foot of the bed, where she was performing some kind of gymnastics to get her skirt back on.

"Sorry," she whispered. "I need to shower before I go to Liza's for breakfast."

"There's a shower here," I pointed out, rising on an elbow to watch her drag her shirt on inside out.

"But I need fresh clothes and mascara. A hair dryer. Go back to sleep, Knox. There's no need for us both to be walking zombies."

Blearily I glared at the time on my phone. 7:05 a.m. Four hours didn't *really* count as spending the night with a woman, I decided.

The appeal of being a bachelor was the fact that my days were dictated by me. I didn't have to work around anyone else's plans or not do what I wanted to do just so they could do what they wanted.

But it seemed unfair even to me that Naomi should have to spend the day running on fumes while I slept in. Besides, breakfast did sound good.

My feet hit the floor with a thump.

"What are you doing?" she asked, trying to right her top. It was now right side out but backward.

"No reason for you to walk home, shower, and walk back to Liza J's. Not when there's a perfectly good shower here."

"I can't go to breakfast in my uniform," she said in exasperation. "Doing the walk of shame to family breakfast is *not* happening."

"Fine. Give me a list."

She looked as if I had just spoken to her in Swahili. "A list of what?"

"What you need to get through breakfast without shame. You shower. I'll get your stuff."

She stared at me. "You're working awfully hard for just a hookup."

I couldn't say why, but that statement pissed me off. Standing up, I picked a pair of jeans off the floor. "Gimme a list." I dragged on the jeans.

She put her hands on her hips and glared at me. "Has anyone told you you're a grump in the mornings?"

"Yeah. Every single person who's had the misfortune of seeing me before ten a.m. Tell me what you want from your place, then get your cute ass in the shower."

Four minutes later, I was headed out the door with an obscenely long list for a Saturday morning breakfast that my grandmother would preside over in her camo pajamas.

I jogged through my backyard to hers and came up on the cottage's back porch. The hide-a-key had been in the same place as long as I could remember, in a fake rock in one of the flower boxes on the railing. I snagged the key, fit it into the lock, and found the door was already unlocked.

Great, now I was going to have to lecture her on security.

The cottage smelled like fresh air, baked goods, and lemons.

The kitchen was sparkling clean except for the opened mail on the counter. Naomi kept it in a small upright organizer, probably alphabetized, but now all the envelopes were fanned out in a sloppy stack.

The rolltop desk in the nook off the living room was open, revealing a mostly tidy workspace with Naomi's laptop, a cup of colorful pens, and a stack of notebooks. The bottom drawer was open a few inches.

Though it was no mountain of underwear and T-shirts, I was glad to see a little disarray. I'd noticed the more stressed Naomi got, the cleaner she became. A little mess was a good sign.

I took the stairs two at a time and swung into the bathroom first to collect the toiletries and hair dryer. Then I hit Naomi's room and grabbed shorts and—because I was a man—a lacy, girly blouse with buttons.

Haul secured, I locked the back door and headed back to my place.

When I walked into the bedroom, I found Naomi standing in the steamy bathroom with wet hair, wearing nothing but a towel.

The view brought me to a sudden halt. I liked seeing her like this. Liked having an undressed, freshly showered Naomi in my space.

I liked it so much that I went on the offensive. "You gotta lock your doors, Daisy. I know this isn't the big city, but shit still happens out here. Like my brother getting shot."

She blinked at me, then snatched the bag of girl stuff from my hands. "I always lock the doors. I'm not an incompetent adult."

"Back door was unlocked," I reported.

She dug through the bag and laid the toiletries out in a neat line around my sink. I'd brought extra since I didn't give a shit about the difference between eyeliner and eyebrow pencil.

"I lock the doors every time I leave and every night," she argued, picking up the brush and running it through her damp hair.

I leaned casually against the doorframe and enjoyed the show as she methodically worked her way through her cosmetics. "What is all that shit, anyway?"

"Haven't you ever watched a woman get ready?" she asked, aiming a look of suspicion at me as she penciled an outline around her lips.

"It's just breakfast," I pointed out.

"But I don't want to look like I just rolled out of bed with you." The stare she gave me was pointed. I glanced in the mirror and noted that my hair was standing up in all directions. My beard was flat on one side. And I had a pillow crease under my left eye.

"Why not?" I asked.

"Because it's not polite."

I crossed my arms and grinned. "Baby, you lost me."

She turned her attention back to a palette of colors and started swiping some of them on her eyelids. "We're going to breakfast," she said, as if that explained anything.

"With family," I added.

"And I don't want to show up looking like I spent the last twenty-four hours having sex with you. Waylay needs a role model. Besides, my parents have enough to worry about without adding a second promiscuous daughter to their plates."

"Naomi, having sex doesn't make you promiscuous," I said, torn between amusement and annoyance.

"*I* know that. But every time I make a decision anywhere in the neighborhood of what Tina would do, I feel like it's my job to make it clear that I'm not her." She put down the eye shadow and picked up one of those eyelash curler things.

I was starting to get a clearer picture of the woman I couldn't stop thinking about naked.

"You're a piece of work, you know that?"

She managed to give me a scowl despite the fact that she was using that contraption on one of her eyes. "Not everyone can strut through town, not giving a shit about what other people think."

"Let's get one thing straight, Daisy. I don't strut."

She crossed her eyes at me in the mirror. "Fine. You sashay."

"Why do you feel like you have to keep proving to your parents that you're not Tina? Anyone with eyes and ears who spends thirty seconds with you can tell that."

"Parents have expectations for their kids. That's just the way it is. Some people want their kids to grow up to be doctors. Some people want their kids to grow up to be professional athletes. Some people just want to raise happy, healthy adults who contribute to their communities."

"Okay," I said, waiting for her to finish.

"My parents were in the latter group. But Tina didn't deliver. She never delivered. While I was bringing home A's and B's in school, she was bringing home Ds. In high school, when I joined the field hockey team and started a tutoring program, Tina played hooky and got busted with pot in the baseball dugout after school."

"Her choice," I pointed out.

"But imagine what it was like seeing the parents you love so much get hurt over and over again. I *had* to be the good one. I didn't have a choice. I couldn't afford any kind of teen rebellion or bounce between majors finding myself in college.

Not when they'd already struck out with one daughter."

"Is that why you decided to marry that Warner guy?" I asked.

Her face shuttered in the mirror. "Probably part of it," she said carefully. "He was a good choice. On paper."

"You can't spend your entire life trying to make everyone else happy, Naomi," I warned her.

"Why not?"

She looked genuinely baffled.

"Eventually you're going to give a little too much and you won't have enough left over for yourself."

"You sound like Stef," she said.

"Now who's being mean?" I teased. "Your parents don't want you to be perfect. They want you to be happy. Yet once again, you're jumping in and cleaning up your sister's mess. You stepped into the role of parent with no notice, no preparation."

"There was no other option."

"Just because one of the choices is shitty doesn't mean it's not an option. Did you even want kids?" I asked.

She met my gaze in the mirror. "Yeah. I did. A lot actually. I thought it would be through more traditional means. And that I'd at least get to enjoy the baby-making end of things. But I've always wanted a family. Now I'm making a mess of everything and can't even fill out an application correctly. And what if I don't want this guardianship to be temporary? What if I want Waylay to stay with me permanently? What if she doesn't want to stay with me? Or what if a judge decides I'm not good enough for her?" She wielded a lip gloss at me. "This is what it's like living in my brain."

"It's fucking exhausting."

"It is. And the *one time* I do something that's purely selfish and just for me, it blows up in my face."

"What did you do for you?" I asked.

"I had a one-night stand with a grumpy, tattooed barber."

30

The Breakfast of Shame

Naomi

"Y̶ou don't have to come along, you know," I pointed out. "You didn't get much sleep in the last forty-eight hours."

"Neither did you," Knox said, making a show of locking up the cabin before we left. I knew he was making a point.

I didn't like people who made points. At least not before I'd had my coffee.

We made the short walk to Liza J's in silence. The birds were singing, the sun was shining, and my mind was spinning like a dryer with a lopsided load.

We'd slept together. As in *fell asleep* in the same bed without having sex together. Not only that, but I'd woken up with Knox "Viking" Morgan spooning me.

I didn't know much about no strings. Hell, I had so many strings attached to so many things, I'd been tied up in knots for most of my adult life. But even *I* knew that sharing a bed and cuddling was way too intimate for what we'd both agreed to.

I mean, don't get me wrong. Waking up with Knox's hard—and I do mean *hard*—body at my back, his arm draped heavily over my waist, was one of the best ways in the world to wake up.

But it wasn't part of the agreement. There was a reason for rules. Rules would keep me from falling for the grumpy, cuddly Viking.

I chewed on my lower lip.

Men got tired and didn't want to walk women home or let women walk home alone only to be eaten by wildlife. The man had gone through a traumatic twenty-four hours. He probably wasn't making the most rational decisions, I decided. Maybe Knox was just a restless sleeper. Maybe he spooned his dog in bed every night.

Of course, that didn't explain why he'd volunteered to run next door and grab a bunch of my stuff while I showered. Why he'd put actual thought into an outfit for me. I glanced down at the high-waisted green-and-white shorts, the cute lacy top. He'd even grabbed underwear for me. Sure, it was a thong and didn't match my bra. But still.

" 'Bout done thinking everything to death?"

I shook myself from my reverie to find Knox shooting me one of those almost smiles.

"I was just running through my to-do list," I fibbed haughtily.

"Sure you were. Can we go in now?"

I realized we were standing in front of Liza J's house. The smell of Stef's world-famous maple bacon wafted through the screen door.

There was a single woof followed by a chorus of barks as four dogs barreled through the door and off the porch.

Waylon was last, ears flapping behind him, tongue lolling obscenely from his mouth.

"Hey, bud," Knox said, dropping to his knees to greet his dog and the other three as they jumped and yapped their enthusiasm.

I bent down and exchanged more dignified greetings with the pack before straightening.

"Okay, so what's the plan?" I asked him.

Knox gave Waylon's ears a last ruffle. "What plan?"

"Breakfast? With my family?" I prodded.

"Well, Daze, I don't know about you, but my plan is to guzzle half a pot of coffee, chow down on some bacon, and then go back to bed for another four or five hours."

"I mean, are we still . . . you know . . . pretending?"

Something passed over his face that I couldn't read.

"Yeah. We're still pretending," he said finally.

I didn't know if I was relieved or not.

Inside, we found Liza J and my dad standing sentry behind Stef as he peered into the oven at two baking sheets of bacon that smelled like heaven. Mom was setting the table in the sunroom. Waylay was making her way around the table, still in her new pink tie-dye pajamas, carefully pouring glasses of orange juice.

I felt a swift rush of affection for her and then remembered I had to come up with a suitable punishment for her today. I really needed to get to the discipline chapter in my library book.

"Mornin', lovebirds. Didn't expect to see you here, Knox," Liza J said, spotting us as she shuffled over to the coffee maker in a blue fuzzy robe over lightweight camouflage pajamas.

Knox draped an arm around my shoulders. "Mornin'," he returned. "I couldn't pass up the bacon."

"No one can," Stef said, pulling the trays out of the oven and setting them on the two cooling racks I'd discovered hidden behind the hutch in Liza J's dining room.

Waylay padded in on bare feet and sniffed with suspicion. "Why's it smell weird?"

"First of all, gorgeous, *you* smell weird," Stef said, giving her a wink. "Second, that's the cara-melized maple syrup."

Waylay perked up. "I like syrup." Her eyes slid to me. "Mornin', Aunt Naomi."

I ran my hand through her messy blond hair. "Morning, kiddo. Did you have fun with your grandparents last night, or did they make you scrub the floors?"

"Me and Grandma and Uncle Stef watched *The Princess Bride*. Grandpa fell asleep before the shrieking eels," she said. "Am I still grounded?"

Mom opened her mouth, looked at me, then shut it again.

"You are," I decided. "For the weekend."

"Can we still go to the library?"

I was new at this discipline thing, but I figured the library was safe enough. "Sure," I said and yawned.

"Someone needs her coffee," Mom sang. "Late night?" She looked pointedly at Knox and then winked at me.

"You know where else you two should go today?" Dad said. Now that the bacon was safely out of the oven, he was peering over Liza J's shoulder as she flipped an omelet.

"Where?" I asked warily.

He turned to look at me. "Car shopping. You need a car." Dad said it with authority, as if the idea of getting a car had somehow never occurred to me.

"I know, Dad. It's on the list."

It was on a literal list. A spreadsheet actually, comparing makes and models ranked by reliability, gas mileage, and cost.

"You and Waylay need something reliable," he continued. "You can't get around on bikes forever. It'll be winter before you know it."

"I know, Dad."

"If you need money, your mother and I can help out."

"Your father's right, dear," Mom said, handing Knox a cup of coffee and the second to me. She was wearing plaid pajama shorts and a matching button-down top.

"I don't need any money. I have money," I insisted.

"We'll go this afternoon," Dad decided.

I shook my head. "That's not necessary." I hadn't finished my spreadsheet yet, and I was *not* walking on a car lot without knowing exactly what I wanted and what it was worth.

"We've already got plans to look at cars today," Knox announced.

Crabby Viking says what? Car shopping plans were news to me. And unlike having a boyfriend, the purchase of a car wasn't nearly as easy to fake for my parents.

He drew me into his side. It was a possessive move that both confused me and turned me on. "Figured I'd take Naomi and Waylay to look for a ride," he said.

Dad harrumphed.

"I get to come too?" Waylay asked, climbing up on her knees on the barstool.

"Well, since it's our car, you have to help me decide," I told her.

"Let's get a motorcycle!"

"No," my mother and I answered together.

"Well, *I'm* getting one as soon as I'm old enough."

I closed my eyes, trying to ward off all the catastrophes that rolled through my mind like a high school driver's ed filmstrip. "I've changed my mind. You're grounded until you're thirty-five."

"I don't think you can legally do that," Waylay said.

"Sorry, Witty. I'm with the kid on this one," Stef said, leaning on his elbows next to her at the island. He broke a piece of bacon in half and handed one piece to my niece.

"Gotta vote with Way," Knox said, squeezing my

shoulder, one of those sort-of smiles dancing at the corners of his lips. "You can only ground her until she's eighteen."

Waylay punched a fist into the air victoriously and took a bite of bacon.

"Fine. You're grounded until you're eighteen. And no fair ganging up on me," I complained.

"Uncle Stef," Waylay said, her eyes going wide and solemn. "This is the best bacon I've ever had in my life."

"I *told* you," Stef said triumphantly. He slapped a hand onto the counter. The dogs, mistaking the noise for a knock, raced to the front door in a fit of barking.

"Got some news," Liza J announced. "Nash is coming home."

"That's awfully soon, isn't it?" I asked. The man had two bullet holes in him. It seemed like that deserved more than a few days in the hospital.

"He's going stir-crazy cooped up in there. He'll do better at home," Liza J predicted.

Knox nodded in agreement.

"Well, that means his place will need a good cleaning. Can't have germs getting in bullet wounds now, can we?" Mom said as if she knew people who got shot every day.

"Probably need some food too," Dad chimed in. "Bet everything in his fridge is rotten. I'll start a list."

Liza J and Knox exchanged confounded looks. I grinned.

382

"It's the Witt way," I explained. "It's best to just go with it."

"I slept with Knox twice in the last forty-eight hours and then I *slept with him* slept with him last night. And I don't know how much of it's a mistake. And it was just supposed to be one time and definitely no sleeping, but he keeps changing the rules on me," I blurted out to Stef.

We were on Liza J's front porch, waiting for Waylay to get her stuff so we could go back to the cottage and get ready for premature car shopping. It was the first time I'd gotten him alone since the sex and subsequent arrival of my parents.

We'd been trading texts for the last two days.

"You did it again? I *knew* it! I fuck—freaking *knew* it," he said, dancing from foot to foot.

"Great. Congratulations, Mr. Know It All. Now tell me what it all means?"

"How the hell should I know what it means? I'm the one who chickened out on asking that fine AF salon god for his phone number."

My jaw dropped. "Excuse me, but Stefan Liao has never chickened out on a hot guy before."

"Let's not make this about me and my temporary mental break. Go back to the sex part. Was it good?"

"Phenomenal. Best sex ever. Now I've trapped him in something resembling a relationship, and I have no idea what to say to Way about it. I don't want her thinking that it's okay to jump from

383

relationship to relationship. Or that it's not okay to be alone. Or that it's okay to have a one-night stand with a hot guy."

"Hate to break it to you, Little Miss Uptight, but all those things actually *are* okay."

"Thirty-six-year-old adult woman me knows that," I snapped. "But those things don't look okay in the eyes of family court, and is that really the example I want to set for an eleven-year-old?"

"I can see you've entered the overanalyzing everything part of your freak-out," Stef quipped.

"Stop being a jerk and start telling me what to do!"

He reached out and squished my cheeks between his hands. "Naomi. Did it ever occur to you that maybe this is your chance to start living a life *you* choose? Start doing things *you* want to do?"

"No," I said.

The screen door burst open, and Waylay jumped out with Waylon on her heels. "I can't find my math book."

"Where did you see it last?" I asked her.

"If I knew that, I'd know where it was."

The three of us headed in the direction of the cottage. Waylon darted out in front of us, pausing every few feet to sniff things and pee on them.

"Does Knox know you have his dog?" I asked.

"Dunno." Waylay shrugged. "So are you and Knox a thing?"

I stumbled over my own feet.

Stef snickered unsympathetically next to me.

I blew out a breath. "Honestly, Way, I have no idea. I don't know what we are or what I want from him or what he wants from me. So we probably won't be a thing forever. But we might be spending more time with him for a while. If it's okay with you."

She frowned thoughtfully at the ground as she kicked at a stone. "You mean you wouldn't hang out with him and stuff if I didn't want you to?"

"Well, yeah. You're kind of pretty important to me, so your opinion matters."

"Huh. Then I guess he can come over for dinner tonight if he wants to," she said.

Nash was home and resting in his freshly cleaned and restocked apartment. My parents were celebrating their weekly date night with dinner at a five-star Lebanese restaurant in Canton. Liza J had invited Stef to be her "hot date" for a dinner party at a local "fancy-ass horse farm."

As for me, I had a new (to me) SUV in my driveway, and my sort-of boyfriend and niece were in the backyard building a fire in the fire pit while I put away the leftovers.

Waylon was in the kitchen with me in case I dropped any of the aforementioned leftovers.

"Fine. But don't think you can look at me with that droopy face and get a treat every time," I warned the dog as I reached into the mason jar of dog treats I hadn't been able to resist at Nina's dad's pet shop.

Waylon wolfed down his biscuit with an appreciative full-butt wiggle.

"Ouch! Damn it!"

"Waylay! Language!" I yelled.

"Sorry!" she called back.

"Busted," Knox sang not quite quietly enough.

"Knox!"

"Sorry!"

I shook my head.

"What are we going to do with them?" I asked Waylon.

The dog belched and wagged his tail.

Outside, Waylay gave a triumphant whoop, and Knox punched both fists in the air as sparks became flames. They high-fived.

I snapped a picture of them celebrating and sent it to Stef.

Me: Spending the evening with two pyromaniacs. How's your night going?

He responded less than a minute later with a close-up of a dignified-looking horse.

Stef: I think I'm in love. How sexy would I be as a horse farmer?

Me: The sexiest.

"Aunt Naomi!" Waylay burst through the screen door as I wiped down the countertops. "We got the fire started. We're ready for s'mores!"

386

She had dirt on her face and grass stains on her T-shirt, but she looked like a happy eleven-year-old.

"Then I guess we'd better get them started." With a flourish, I pulled the dish towel off the s'mores platter I'd assembled.

"Whoa."

"Let's go, ladies," Knox called from outside.

"You heard the man," I said, nudging her toward the door.

"He makes you smile."

"What?"

"Knox. He makes you smile. A lot. And he looks at you like he likes you a lot."

I felt my cheeks flush. "Oh yeah?"

She nodded. "Yeah. It's cool."

We ate too many s'mores and sat around the campfire until dark. I expected Knox to make an excuse to head home, but he followed us inside and helped me clean up while Waylay—and Waylon—went upstairs to brush her teeth.

"I think my dog is in love with your niece," Knox observed. He pulled an open bottle of wine and a beer out of the fridge.

"There's definitely a crush happening," I agreed.

He pulled out a wineglass, filled it, and handed it to me.

Okay, maybe there were *two* crushes happening.

"Thanks for dinner," he said, opening his beer and leaning back against the counter.

"Thanks for haranguing the sales guy into submission," I said.

"It's a good vehicle," he said, hooking his fingers in the waist of my shorts and drawing me closer.

We'd spent the majority of the day together but without touching. It had been a special kind of torture to be so close to a man who made me feel so much I forgot to think yet not be able to reach out and touch him.

He smelled like smoke and chocolate. My new favorite scent. I couldn't help it. I wanted to taste him. So I did. Bringing my mouth to his, I sampled his flavor. Leisurely. Deliberately.

His free hand came around me, splaying over my lower back, holding me to him.

I breathed him in, letting his heat take the chill off my skin.

Suddenly, there was thunder on the stairs as both Waylay and the dog charged down.

"Damn it," Knox muttered.

I jumped back and picked up my wine.

"Can we watch TV before bed?" Waylay asked.

"Sure. I'll just say good night to Knox." I was giving him his out. The man had to be exhausted, and I was sure he had better things to do than watch YouTube episodes of teen girls doing makeup with us.

"I'm up for some TV," he said, sauntering into the living room with his beer. Waylay launched herself at the couch, curling into her favorite corner. The dog hopped up next to her. Knox took the opposite end and patted the cushion next to him.

So I sat down with my niece, my sort-of boyfriend, and his dog, and we watched a fifteen-year-old with two million subscribers tell us how to choose the right eyeliner for our eye color.

Knox's arm was warm and comforting behind me on the back of the couch.

Five minutes into the episode, I heard a soft snore. Knox had his feet propped up on the coffee table and his head pitched back against the cushion. His eyes were closed, and his mouth was open.

I looked at Waylay, and she grinned at me.

Knox snored again, and we both giggled quietly.

31

Shifty in the Stacks

Naomi

The first week of September steamed into town with summer humidity and the first hint of changing leaves. After a few days of smothering attention, Nash insisted he was well enough for desk duty and returned to work a few hours a day.

The dreadful Mrs. Felch had abruptly announced her retirement and moved to South Carolina to live with her sister. Waylay had a crush on her new teacher, Mr. Michaels, and she'd joined the soccer team. We'd survived our first official interview with the caseworker, and while my niece had made it known she wasn't a fan of the vegetables I was forcing on her, Mrs. Suarez had scheduled the home study, which I took as a hopeful sign.

When I wasn't cheering from the sidelines or sleeping with Knox or absorbing parenting books, I was working. I'd started my new job at the library and was loving it. Between Honky Tonk and the Community Outreach desk at the library, I felt like I was actually starting to find a groove that was all mine. Especially since most of the town had finally stopped calling me Not Tina.

• • •

Naomi,

God, I'm so sorry. I miss you. Things aren't right here without you. I had no right to take my stress out on you. I was just trying to provide the best life for you. If we would have waited like I'd wanted to, none of this would have happened.

Love,
Warner

I exited my email inbox with an efficient click and a quiet groan.

"Warner again?" Stef looked up from his laptop. The library was nearly empty today, and my best friend had commandeered the table next to the Community Outreach desk.

"Yes, Warner again," I said.

"Told you to stop opening them," Stef said.

"I know. I'm only opening every other one. Progress, right?"

"You're getting naked with the Viking. You don't need to be opening another man's whiny, passive-aggressive, why-aren't-you-here-to-do-my-laundry emails."

I winced and looked around to make sure there weren't any eavesdropping patrons. "Part of me likes seeing him grovel, even passive-aggressively."

"Fair," he mused.

"And another more logical part of me realizes

391

that none of this actually matters. The relationship I had with Warner was no more real than the one I'm pretending to have with Knox."

"Speaking of, you two sure are pretending a lot."

"I know the score," I assured him. "Which is more than I can say for when I was with Warner. I didn't get that Warner didn't really want to be with me. Knox has been nothing but transparent with his intentions."

Stef leaned back in his chair to study me.

"What?" I asked, checking to make sure I didn't have breakfast crumbs on my sweater.

"A woman as gorgeous, smart, and entertaining as you shouldn't have so many half-assed non-relationships. I'm starting to think the common denominator is you, Witty."

I stuck my tongue out at him. "Real nice, bestie."

"I'm serious. I pegged Knox and his baggage within thirty seconds of meeting him. But you carry yours closer. Like it's in an emotional fanny pack."

"You would never let me wear a fanny pack, emotional or not," I teased. "When are we going to talk about the fact that you still haven't asked Jeremiah for his number?"

"Never. Besides, he hasn't asked for mine either."

The elevator doors opened, and Sloane emerged, pushing a book cart. "How's it going up here?" Today's non-librarian-like outfit was slim jeans that ended above the ankles, suede peep-toe booties, and a black sweater with heart-shaped elbow patches. The frames of her glasses were red to match the hearts.

"Not bad. Stef here just accused me of carrying baggage in an emotional fanny pack, and I got Agatha and Blaze an appointment with the pro bono elder law attorney so they can talk about long-term care options for Agatha's dad," I said.

Sloane draped herself over the cart and rested her chin in her hands. "First of all, great work with our favorite biker babes. Second, Stef with the never-ending witticisms, please tell me you have a straight brother, first cousin, or old nephew. I'm not picky."

Stef grinned. "Ah, but you *are*."

She wrinkled her nose. "Never mind. It's only fun when you pick on Naomi."

"You know what they say," he said.

"Yeah, yeah. If you can't stand the heat, stay off the second floor of the library." With that, she disappeared into the stacks with the cart.

A few minutes later, Stef headed out to take a conference call regarding one of his mysterious business deals while I helped burly biker Wraith get an appointment with the closest Social Security office and sent out an email to library patrons about October's Book or Treat events.

I was just finishing up taking notes on the chapter on puberty in my latest parenting book when someone cleared their throat.

"Excuse me, I was wondering if you could help me."

He had hard green eyes and short, spiky red hair. Tattoos peeked out on the backs of his hands from the sleeves of his white button-down. He had a sheepish smile, an expensive-looking watch, and a gold chain around his neck.

There was something strange about the way he was looking at me.

Not that it was unusual. Anyone who had had the misfortune of meeting Tina generally needed a while to adjust to the whole twin thing.

"How can I help?" I asked with a smile.

He tapped the closed laptop under his arm. "I'm looking for someone who can do a little light tech support. This darn thing stopped recognizing my wireless mouse and reading flash drives. Know anyone who can help?"

His eye contact was intense, and it made me a little uncomfortable.

"Well, it definitely wouldn't be me," I joked with a forced laugh.

"Me either. My wife's usually my go-to for stuff like this, but she's on a business trip, and I can't wait until she gets back," he explained. "I just need someone to help me out. They don't have to be a professional or anything. I'd even be willing to pay a kid."

Something was off. Maybe I was just hungry. Or maybe my Code Red was coming up. Or maybe this guy stomped litters of kittens for a hobby, and my kinship guardian intuition was reacting.

The only person I knew who fit the bill was

Waylay. And I wasn't about to let someone who gave me the heebie-jeebies anywhere near her.

I flashed him a smile a few degrees warmer than perfunctory. "Gosh. You know what? I'm new in town and I'm just getting my bearings. I don't know anyone off the top of my head, but if you give me a phone number or email, I'll reach out as soon as I find a resource."

His index and middle fingers on his left hand drummed lightly on the lid of his laptop. *One two. One two. One two.*

For some reason, I found myself holding my breath.

"You know what? That would be great," he said with a warm grin. "Got a pen?"

Relieved, I pushed a Knockemout Public Library notepad across the desk to him and held out a pen. "Here you go." Our fingers brushed when he took it, and he held my gaze for a beat too long.

Then he smiled again and bent to scrawl a number on the pad. "Name's Flint," he said, tapping the pen over his name for emphasis. His eyes skimmed over my name tag. "Naomi."

I did not like the way he said my name as if he knew me, as if he were already intimately familiar with me.

"I'm sure I'll be able to find someone to help," I croaked.

He nodded. "Great. Sooner the better." Flint picked up the laptop and gave me a once-over. He tossed me a salute. "Later, Naomi."

"Goodbye."

I watched him stroll to the stairs. It took me an entire minute to figure out what was bothering me. It was his hands. Specifically, his left hand, which hadn't sported a wedding ring.

I was just being paranoid. Maybe it was a sign that I was getting better at this guardian thing. I brushed the encounter aside and headed into my tiny office to add *Local IT support* to the running list of questions I had for Sloane.

The woman might have been pixie-sized, but she certainly had big ideas about how to expand the library's services to the community. It was both exciting and interesting to be part of something that was so focused on helping people.

A shadow in the doorway caught my eye.

I jumped and slapped a hand to my chest. "Crap on a cracker, Knox. You scared the hell out of me!"

He leaned against the doorjamb and quirked an eyebrow. "Baby, I don't wanna tell you how to do your job or anything, but aren't you supposed to not yell in a library?"

32

Lunch and a Warning

Knox

I had things to do. Businesses to run. Employees to yell at. But I wasn't thinking about all that. I was thinking about her.

And here I was in the library, ignoring everything else because I woke up thinking about her and wanted to see her.

I'd spent a lot of time thinking about Naomi Witt since she blew into town. I was surprised that it only got worse the more time I spent with her.

She looked entirely too pretty today, standing there behind her desk, lost in some mental to-do list, wearing a curve-hugging sweater in a ridiculously female pink.

"What are you doing here?" she asked, her surprise turning to happiness. She closed the distance between us, stopping just shy of touching me. I liked how she was always leaning toward me, into me. Like her body wanted to be as close to mine as possible at all times. It didn't feel clingy like I'd always thought it would. It felt . . . not terrible.

"Thought I'd take you to lunch."

"Really?" She looked thrilled at the invitation, and I decided I didn't mind that either. Having a woman like Naomi look at me like I was the hero of her day felt damn good.

"No, Daisy. I just showed up here to mess with you. Yes, really."

"Well, I *am* hungry." Those plush lips painted a deep pink curved in an invitation I wasn't going to ignore.

I was hungry for something other than food. "Good. Let's go. How long's your break?"

"I get an hour."

Thank fucking God.

A minute later, we were walking out of the library and into the September sun. I steered her toward my pickup with a hand on her lower back.

"So what fine dining establishment will we be patronizing today?" she asked when I slid behind the wheel.

I reached into the back seat and dropped a paper bag in her lap. She opened it and peered inside.

"It's peanut butter and jelly," I explained.

"You made me a sandwich."

"There's chips in there too," I said defensively. "And that tea you like."

"Okay. I'm trying not to be charmed by the fact that you packed me a picnic lunch."

"It's not a picnic," I said, turning the key.

"Where are we going to eat our not picnic lunch?"

"Third Base, if you're up for it."

She squeezed her knees together and squirmed a little in her seat. Her lower lip snagged between her teeth. "What about the horn?" she asked.

"I brought a blanket."

"A blanket and a packed lunch. Definitely not a picnic," she teased.

She wouldn't be so smug when I had my hand down those tight little pants she was wearing. "We could just go back and eat in the break room at the library," I threatened.

She reached over and gripped my thigh. "Knox?"

The seriousness in her tone had my guard going up.

"What?"

"This doesn't feel like we're pretending."

I thumped my head against the back of the seat. I'd known this conversation would be coming, and I still didn't want to have it.

As far as I was concerned, we'd both stopped pretending almost as soon as we started. When I touched her, it was because I wanted to, not because I wanted someone to see me doing it.

"Do we have to do this, Daisy, when you've got a meter running on your lunch break?"

She looked down at her lap. "No. Of course not."

I gritted my teeth. "Yes, we do. If it's something you want to talk about, then talk about it. Stop worrying about pissing me off, because we both know it's bound to happen."

Her gaze lifted to mine. "I was just wondering . . . what we're doing."

"I don't know what we're doing. What I'm doing is enjoying spending time with you without worrying about what comes next or what happens in a month or a year. What are you doing?"

"Besides enjoying spending time with you?"

"Yeah."

Those pretty hazel eyes returned to her lap. "I'm worrying about what comes next," she confessed.

I nudged her chin up so she'd look at me. "Why does there have to be something that comes next? Why can't we both just enjoy this the way it is without worrying ourselves to death over something that hasn't happened yet?"

"That's just usually the way I operate," she said.

"How about we try this my way for the next while? My way gets you a non-picnic lunch and at least one orgasm before one p.m."

Her cheeks went pink, and while her smile wasn't as big as the one I'd gotten earlier for surprising her, it was good enough. "Let's go," she said.

I went instantly hard. All the thoughts I'd had of spreading her out on a blanket, naked and whimpering my name, rushed back. I wanted to taste her outside in the sun, the warm breeze. Wanted to feel her move under me while the rest of the world stood still.

I threw the truck in reverse and hit the gas.

We made it a block before Naomi's phone rang from the depths of her purse. She dug it out and frowned at the screen. "It's Nash."

I snatched the phone from her and answered the call.

"Knox!" she complained.

"What?" I snapped into the phone.

"Need to talk to Naomi," Nash said. He sounded grim.

"She's busy. Talk to me."

"I tried, asshole. I called you first, and you didn't pick up. Got some news about Tina."

There went my fucking picnic.

As I admired the view of Naomi's shapely ass in front of me, I wondered how my brother was dealing with the long flight of stairs with his injuries. Nash's place was on the second floor above Whiskey Clipper, and when I'd brought him home the previous weekend, he only made it to the top after I threatened to pick him up and carry him.

He opened the door just as I raised my fist to knock.

He looked pale, tired. And the asshole had his shirt off, revealing his wound dressing. He was holding fresh gauze and a roll of tape.

"You poor thing," Naomi crooned, grabbing the supplies out of his hands. "Let me help you."

Nash shot me a smirk when Florence Nightingale pushed her way inside. If he kept up the wounded hero routine with Naomi, I was going to raise his damn rent and push him down the stairs.

"This better be good," I warned him, following her inside.

The apartment had high ceilings, exposed brick, and tall, arched windows overlooking Main Street. There were two bedrooms, a bathroom I'd personally gutted, and an open concept living space with a small but kick-ass kitchen.

His dining room table was covered in paperwork and what looked like case files. He clearly had trouble following doctor's orders. Morgan men didn't care to be told what to do.

"Sit," Naomi said, pulling out a stool from the kitchen island. He eased himself down on it, his jaw tight as if just that movement hurt.

"You taking your pain meds?" I asked. I'd strong-armed him into filling the prescription. But the bottle was still sitting next to the sink where I'd left it.

My brother met my gaze. "Nope."

I knew why. Because one generation had the potential to poison the next. It was something we both lived with.

"It's not pretty, Naomi," Nash warned as she headed to the sink to wash her hands.

"Wounds never are. That's what first aid is for."

She dried her hands and gave me a sunny smile as she returned to his side.

"You're not going to faint, are you?" I asked her.

She stuck her tongue out at me. "I'll have you know, I have extensive first aid training."

Nash met my gaze as Naomi gently peeled the tape from his shoulder.

"A few years ago, I came across the scene of a car accident. It was late at night, raining. A deer had run out in front of the driver, and he swerved to miss it. He hit a tree head-on. There was blood everywhere. He was in so much pain, and all I could do was dial 911 and hold his hand. I'd never felt more helpless in my entire life," she explained.

She'd hate that, I realized. The woman who lived her entire life to make others safe and happy would have hated feeling helpless when someone was in pain.

"So you took a class?" Nash guessed as she eased the gauze away from the wound.

I saw the clench in his jaw, caught the tightness in his tone.

She hissed out a breath, and I looked up.

Nash's shoulder was bare. It wasn't a nice, neat hole. It was a chasm of angry tissue, black stitches, and the rust of dried blood.

"I took *three* classes," Naomi said.

A memory surfaced. Nash on his back on the playground, fresh blood flowing from his nose as Chris Turkowski sat on his chest and pummeled fists into my brother's face.

Chris had fared worse than Nash that day. I'd gotten suspended for two days, a consequence both my dad and I felt was worth it. "Family takes care of family," he'd said. At the time, he'd meant it.

I couldn't stop staring at my brother's wounds as blood pounded inside my head.

"Knox?" Naomi's voice was closer now.

I felt hands on my shoulders and realized Naomi was standing in front of me. "You wanna sit down for a minute, Viking? I don't think I can handle two patients at once."

Realizing she thought I was going to faint, I opened my mouth to clear up the misconception and explain that it was manly rage, not wobbly knees. But I changed my mind and went with it when I realized her concern for me had trumped Nash's bullet holes.

I let her push me down into one of the leather armchairs in the living room.

"You okay?" she asked, leaning down to look me in the eye.

"Better now," I said.

Over her shoulder, my brother flipped me the bird.

She brushed a kiss to my forehead. "Stay here. I'll get you a glass of water in a minute, okay?"

Nash coughed something that sounded suspiciously like "faker," but the cough ended in a groan of pain.

Served him right. I returned the one-fingered salute when Naomi rushed back to his side.

"Never saw you go weak in the knees at the sight of blood before," Nash observed.

"You wanna get to your point, or is this how you wrangle social calls since no one wants to be around your ass?"

Naomi shot me a "behave yourself" look as she opened a fresh strip of gauze. I saw my brother's jaw go tight when she pressed it to his wound. I looked away until Nash cleared his throat.

"Got some news on Tina," he said.

Naomi froze, holding a strip of tape. "Is she okay?"

Her twin sister had stolen from her, abandoned her child, and Naomi's first question was whether Tina was okay.

The woman needed to learn that some ties needed cutting.

"We don't know her whereabouts, but it seems like there's something in town that she didn't want to leave behind. We found her prints at the storage unit break-in."

I tensed, remembering the conversation in his hospital room.

"What storage unit break-in?" Naomi asked as she moved on to the wound lower on his torso.

"The trailer park landlord reported two separate break-ins. One at his office and one at his storage unit, where he keeps anything of value that tenants leave behind. The storage unit was a smash and grab. The lock was jimmied. Shit was broken. A bunch of stuff was missing. We found Tina's prints all over the place."

I forgot about my fake fainting spell and got out of the chair. "It's a small fucking town," I pointed out, crossing to the kitchen. "How the hell is she sneaking around without anyone spotting her?"

"Got a theory on that. We got some footage from a security camera at the entrance," Nash said, using his good arm to pull a file folder closer to him. He tipped it open, and a grainy photo showed a woman with long, dark hair dressed in a long dress.

Naomi leaned across my brother to peer at the

405

photo. I wasn't certain, but I thought Nash looked like he was sniffing her hair.

I dragged her into my side, away from my brother, and handed her the photo.

"What the fuck?" I mouthed at Nash.

He shrugged, then winced.

"Stubborn fucking idiot," I muttered. I guided Naomi to a stool out of Nash's reach, then stomped over to the sink. He still kept his over-the-counter shit and his excessive collection of supplements in the cabinet. I grabbed a bottle of Tylenol and poured a glass of tap water, then slid both across the counter to my dumbass brother.

I spotted a baking dish on the counter with some kind of dessert in it. Lifting the plastic wrap, I sniffed. Peach cobbler. Nice.

Since I was missing out on my own lunch and Nash was to blame, I grabbed a fork.

"That's my dress," Naomi said, handing the photo back to Nash. She'd gone pale. I snatched it out of his hand and stared at the image.

Fuck. It was her dress.

"Figured she was dressing like you in case she ran into anyone in town," Nash explained. "She must have grabbed it when she broke into your motel room."

Naomi was biting her lip again.

"What's wrong?" I demanded.

She shook her head. "Nothing."

My bullshit detector was activated.

"Daisy."

406

"It's just Tina used to do that when we were kids. I was home sick once our sophomore year of high school. She went to school dressed like me and told my history teacher—who I had a crush on— to go fuck himself. I got detention. All because my parents gave me the car the weekend before because she was grounded."

Christ.

"You better not have kept your mouth shut and sat through detention," I snapped, throwing the fork in the baking dish in disgust.

"Did she get whatever it was she wanted?" Naomi asked Nash.

"We don't know. I heard that Tina got herself hooked up with some new guy a few weeks back. Lucian did a little digging. Said the new guy was some badass out of DC and Tina bragged to a couple of friends that they had a big score coming up."

"Is that my mom's peach cobbler?" she asked, nodding at the dish I held.

"She stopped by this morning to drop it off. She also stole my laundry and watered my plants."

Naomi gave him a wobbly smile. "Welcome to the family. Prepare to be smothered."

Something was wrong, and she was trying to hide it. I put down the cobbler and picked up the picture again.

"Fuck."

"What?" Nash asked.

"I saw you in this dress. Outside the shop," I

407

said, remembering her standing in the window of Whiskey Clipper with Liza J and Waylay. She'd looked like a summer vision in the dress.

Her cheeks weren't pale now. They were flushed.

"Which means Tina didn't take this from the motel. She broke into the cottage."

Naomi busied herself by organizing the first aid supplies.

Nash swore and rubbed his good hand over his face. "I need to call Grave." He got up and snatched his phone off the dining table. "Yeah, Grave," he said. "We've got a new problem."

I waited until he headed into his bedroom before turning my attention back to Naomi. "She broke into your place, and you weren't gonna say a word." She looked up as I rounded the island. She held up her hands, but I kept coming until her palms were pressed against my chest. "You do not keep shit like that from me, Naomi. You owe her nothing. You can't live your whole life protecting people who don't fucking deserve it. Not when it puts *your* safety at risk."

She winced, and I realized I was yelling.

"What are you thinking? You have Way. If Tina and some low-life criminal fuck buddy are breaking into *your* fucking house, you don't cover that shit up. You don't protect the bad guy—you protect the kid."

She shoved me, but I didn't budge.

"You saw my motel room. You heard what Nash said—the storage unit was trashed. That's what

408

my sister does. She destroys," Naomi snapped. "If Tina broke into the cottage, she would have wrecked the place. She never could stand the idea of me having anything nicer than she did. So yeah. Maybe I noticed a few things out of place once or twice, and I chalked it up to Waylay or you or Liza. But Tina didn't break in."

"What are you sayin'?"

She wet her lips. "What if someone let her in?"

"Someone meaning Waylay?"

Naomi shot a nervous glance in Nash's direction. "What if Tina got word to her that she needed access, and Waylay left a door unlocked? You were the one who yelled at me for leaving the back door unlocked. Or what if Tina told her what she needed, and Waylay got it for her?"

"You think that kid would give Tina the time of day after she's had a few weeks with you? With your parents? Hell, even fucking Stef and Liza J. You made one big happy family for her. Why would she risk fucking that up?"

"Tina is her *mother*," Naomi insisted. "Family doesn't stop being family just because one of you does shitty things."

"That's exactly what happens to families, and you need to quit this loyalty to your fucking sister. She doesn't deserve it."

"It's not loyalty to Tina, you idiot," Naomi shouted back. She shoved against my chest again, but I was immovable.

"Educate me," I insisted.

409

"If Waylay had anything to do with letting Tina in, how is that going to look in the guardianship hearing? How am I fit to take custody when I can't even keep criminals out of my house? They'll take her away from me. I'll have let her down. I'll have let my parents down. Waylay will end up with strangers—" Her voice hitched.

I grabbed her and pulled her into me. "Baby. Stop."

"I tried," she said, fingers curling into my T-shirt.

"Tried what?"

"I tried not to hate Tina. My whole life, I tried so hard not to hate her."

I cupped the back of her head and buried her face in my neck.

"Don't fucking cry, Daze. Not over her. You've given her enough."

She sucked in a breath and blew it out.

"You can use me as a pillow if you wanna scream it out," I offered.

"Don't be sweet and funny right now."

"Baby, those are two things no one has ever accused me of being."

She pulled back and took another steadying breath. "This is not what I was expecting when you said you were taking me to lunch."

"I expected the yelling. Just thought we'd be doing it naked. We good?"

Her fingers were tracing little circles against my chest. "We're good. For now. I'm going to go collect myself in the bathroom."

"I'm gonna eat some more of your mom's cobbler."

She gave me another one of those wobbly smiles that made me feel things I didn't want to feel.

I reached out and tucked her hair behind her ear. "It's gonna be fine. No one's takin' Way. Nash and I'll take care of it."

She nuzzled her cheek against my hand. "You can't solve my problems for me."

"Oh, but you can solve everyone else's?" I pointed out. "You gotta stop worrying about making everything okay for everyone else and start thinkin' about making it okay for you."

She didn't say anything, but I felt like my words had landed.

I gave her a playful slap on the ass. "Go on. Go scream into some hand towels."

A minute later, Nash came out of the bedroom. "Grave is sending some boys out to see if we can lift any prints. Where's Naomi?"

"Bathroom. You find any prints in the landlord's office?" I asked Nash.

He shook his head. "It was a clean job."

"What are the odds they split up? Tina took the storage unit, and the boyfriend took the office."

Nash thought about it. "It plays."

"Naomi doesn't think Tina broke in. She's worried Way let Tina in. Worried how that'll play in the guardianship shit."

Nash blew out a breath. "Any judge that looks at those two sisters and decides Naomi isn't fit has their robe on too tight."

"She's a worrier. Which is why I don't want her worrying about some stranger sneakin' into her home and going through her things."

"Better the devil you know," he said.

I nodded.

"Speaking of, you going to see him this weekend?" Nash asked.

Deliberately, I took another forkful of cobbler even though my appetite was suddenly gone. "If he's there."

"Give him this from me." Nash limped over to the table and picked up a backpack. "And maybe think about not handing over cash."

"You're lucky I'm tired of fighting about this," I told him and took the bag.

"People keep telling me how lucky I am," he said.

"You're still here, aren't you?"

"You remember what she was wearing when she walked by your window," he said, nodding at the bathroom door.

"Yeah. So?"

"She means something to you."

"Does blood loss make you stupid?" I wondered.

"I'm just sayin', you care about her. Any other woman, you wouldn't have bothered calling her on her own bullshit. You wouldn't have known any other woman well enough to know she was bullshitting you, let alone care that she was."

"Getting to your point any time soon?"

"Yeah. Don't fuck it up like you usually do."

33

A Swift Kick

Naomi

"Why do kids' sports start at such ungodly hours? And why is the grass so wet? Look at these shoes. They'll never recover," Stef complained as we set up our folding chairs on the sideline of the soccer field.

"It's nine in the morning, not four a.m.," I said dryly. "Maybe if you and Liza hadn't made and then drank an entire pitcher of margaritas last night, you wouldn't be cringing like a vampire at the light of day."

He collapsed into his chair, looking impossibly stylish in Ray-Bans and a thick knit sweater. "It was my last night in town before my trip to Paris. I couldn't say no to margaritas. Besides, it's easy to be Suzy Sunshine when you're getting laid regularly."

"Zip it, Betty Big Mouth," I said, shooting a look at the rest of Waylay's cheering section. My parents were sitting with Liza J, who didn't seem any the worse for wear for her half of the margaritas. Mom was doing her mom thing and introducing herself to everyone in a twenty-foot radius, asking them the names of their players, and proudly pointing out Waylay in her number six jersey.

Wraith, badass biker and silver fox, strode down the sideline. He was wearing a Metallica T-shirt, black jeans, and a scowl perfectly framed by his gray Fu Manchu mustache. "Looking lovely as always, Liza J," he said with a wolfish smile.

"Peddle that charm someplace else, biker boy," she shot back. But I noticed two dots of color on her cheeks.

"Bring it in, Knock 'Em Outs," Wraith bellowed. Fifteen girls in all shapes, sizes, and colors jogged and skipped their way over to the unlikely head coach.

"That guy looks like a probation violation, not a girls' soccer coach," Stef observed.

"That's Wraith. His granddaughter Delilah is the one with the pigtails. She plays forward. She's unbelievably fast," I told him.

Waylay looked up from her team huddle and waved at me. I grinned and waved back.

The ref blew two short blasts on the whistle, and two girls from each team jogged to the center circle. "What's happening? Did the game start?" Stef asked.

"They're doing the coin toss. You're lucky you're so pretty. What if your future husband is into sports?"

Stef shuddered. "Perish the thought."

"The coin toss determines which team gets the ball for kickoff and which direction they're trying to score."

"Look at you, soccer mom," he teased.

Self-consciously, I straightened my Knock 'Em Out hoodie. Thanks to a school fundraiser, I now owned a capsule wardrobe of school cheer gear. The mascot was an oversize boxing glove named Punchy that I found both charming and inappropriate.

"I may have done a little reading up on the sport," I said. I'd done a lot of research. I'd reread *Rock Bottom Girl* and watched *Ted Lasso*, *Bend It Like Beckham*, and *She's the Man* for good measure.

The whistle on the field signaled the start of the game, and I cheered along with the rest of the crowd as the action got underway.

Two minutes into play, I was holding my breath and Stef's hand in a death grip as Waylay got the ball and started dribbling for the goal.

"Go, Waylay! Go!" Dad shouted as he came out of his chair.

When we were ten years old, Tina had played softball for one season. Dad had been her biggest fan. It was nice to see he hadn't lost his enthusiasm.

Waylay faked a move to the right before heading in the opposite direction around the defender and firing off a pass to Chloe, Sloane's niece.

"That was good, right?" Stef asked. "It looked good. Sneaky and full of deception."

"The coach says she's a natural," I said proudly before yelling, "Go, Chloe!"

Chloe lost the ball out of bounds, and play was paused so three players could tie their shoelaces.

"A natural. That's impressive."

"She's quick, she's sneaky, and she's a team player. There's just one or two little kinks that need working out."

"What kind of kinks?" Stef asked.

"What did I miss?" Sloane appeared next to me in jeans and a Nirvana tank top under a soft gray cardigan. She had her pink-and-blond hair piled high in a knot on top of her head and stylish sunglasses. Her lips were painted ruby red. She waved to Chloe and plopped down in her own camp chair.

"Just the first two minutes. No score. And Wraith hasn't screamed 'Come on, ladies!' yet," I reported.

On cue, the burly biker cupped his hands to his mouth and shouted, "Come on, ladies!"

"And all was right with the world," Sloane said with a satisfied smile. "Any yellow cards for Way yet?"

I shook my head. "Not yet." Though if the past two games were accurate predictors, it was only a matter of time.

"Is that like an award?" Stef asked.

"Not exactly," she said, winking at me before turning back to my best friend. "You're looking annoyingly gorgeous today."

He preened, fluffing the collar of his sweater. "Why, thank you, Sexy Librarian. Love those boots."

She kicked up her feet to admire the knee-high waterproof footwear. "Thanks. I discovered early on in Chloe's soccer career that I wasn't a fan of wet shoes and squishy socks."

"Now she tells me," he complained.

"By the way, loving this whole curly vibe," Sloane said, waving her hand in front of my face.

I tossed my hair dramatically. "Thanks. Waylay showed me a tutorial."

"We're the new generation of hot soccer moms," Stef decided.

"I'll drink to that," Sloane agreed, hoisting her tumbler that said *This Is Definitely Not Wine*.

"So where's your hot soccer daddy?" Stef asked me.

"Thank God someone asked," Sloane said, shifting in her chair. "Here are all the questions I've stored up. How good is the sex? Is he as grumpy immediately after orgasm as he is the rest of the time, or are there cracks in the stony facade that reveal the soft, teddy-bear heart beating beneath?"

"Has he torn any clothing off your body?" Stef asked. "If so, I know a guy who makes entire wardrobes with Velcro closures."

"Of course you do," I said dryly.

Sloane leaned forward. "Is he a flowers and a cook-you-dinner kind of guy? Or is he more of a growl-at-any-man-who-dares-to-look-at-your-boobs dude?"

"Definitely a growler," Stef decided.

"You guys! My parents and his grandmother are right there," I hissed. "Besides, we're at a children's soccer game."

"She's going to tell us how inappropriate we're

being but what she doesn't realize is how every conversation happening around this field is about sex," he complained.

"They are not," I insisted.

"Oh, believe me. They are. Chloe's been playing since she was six. Those dads over there might look like they're talking about power tools and lawn mowers, but they're actually talking about vasectomies," Sloane said, pointing at a group of dads huddled together next to the bleachers.

"I forget. Did you tell us why Knox isn't here?" Stef said, feigning innocence.

I sighed. "He's not here because I didn't invite him." What I didn't tell them was I didn't invite him because I didn't think he'd come. Knox Morgan didn't seem like the type of man who would willingly show up at a kid's sporting event and make small talk for an hour.

He was the kind of man who pinned you down and made you come in positions that shouldn't have been possible. Like last night when he'd pressed me flat on my stomach and entered me from behind—

My inner walls clenched involuntarily at the decadent memory.

"Why didn't you invite him?" Sloane pressed, ignoring the game in favor of the sideline inquisition.

I rolled my eyes. "I don't know. Probably because he wouldn't have come. And I don't want Waylay to get too used to him being around."

"Naomi, I say this with love. This is the first time since high school Knox has dated anyone in town. That's huge. It means he sees something special about you that he hasn't seen in anyone else."

I felt like a fraud.

I wasn't special. I hadn't landed a never-falling-in-love bachelor. I'd gotten swept up in an admittedly scorching-hot one-night stand, and he'd gotten caught in the consequences of banging a good girl.

"Is that Nash?" Stef asked, mercifully changing the subject.

I looked up and spotted him ambling slowly in my direction.

Sloane hummed. "Those Morgan brothers sure were built to catch the eye."

She wasn't wrong.

Nash Morgan looked every bit the wounded hero. I noticed quite a few of the moms and even one or two of the dads thinking the same thing. He was wearing worn jeans and a long-sleeved Henley. He had a baseball cap pulled down low, and I noticed he'd ditched the sling for his arm. He walked slowly, carefully. It looked casual, but I guessed the pace was dictated more by pain and exhaustion than by a desire to look cool.

"Mornin'," he said when he arrived.

"Hey," I said. "Want a seat?"

He shook his head, eyes on the field as the Knock 'Em Outs played defense.

419

Waylay glanced up and spotted him and waved.

He waved with his good arm, but I saw the grimace under the smile.

The man should be sitting at home resting and healing, not strolling around town without his sling. I realized my annoyance with his brother was spilling over onto Nash.

"Sit," I insisted, rising. I all but manhandled him into my chair.

"I don't need to sit, Naomi. I don't need to be at home resting. I need to be out here doing what I'm good at."

"And what's that?" I asked. "Looking like you got hit by a fleet of school buses?"

"Ouch," Stef said. "Better listen to her, Chief. She's mean when she's riled."

"I don't get riled," I scoffed.

"You should be riled given the bomb that got dropped on you," Nash said.

Uh-oh.

"I changed my mind. You can stand up and walk away," I decided.

He looked smug then. "You didn't tell them?"

"Tell us what?" Sloane and Stef said at the same time.

"I didn't get a chance," I fibbed.

"Did you get a chance to tell your parents? Or Liza J, seein' as how she owns the property in question?"

"What's happening right now?" Sloane wondered.

Stef's eyes narrowed. "I think our close-mouthed

little friend here is keeping more from us than just her exploits in bed."

"Oh, for Pete's sake," I huffed.

"Naomi didn't mention to you that Tina was connected to a break-in in town?" Nash asked, knowing full well I hadn't.

"She most definitely didn't mention that."

"How about that in order to commit the robbery, Tina broke into Naomi's cottage and stole one of her dresses?"

Sloane tilted her sunglasses down her nose to look at me. "Not cool, babe. Not cool at all."

"She pulled the ol' wrong twin thing again, didn't she?" Stef asked, not looking at me. It wasn't a good sign.

"Look, I just found out about this—"

"I told you three days ago, Naomi," Nash reminded me.

"I'm not real clear on the law in Virginia. Is it okay to put duct tape over a police officer's mouth?"

"Not when he's on the clock," Nash said with a grin.

"Why wouldn't you tell us? Why wouldn't you say something? If we need to be on the lookout for your sister, it's better if we know about it," Sloane pointed out.

"Let me explain something about our little Witty here," Stef said to Sloane.

"And here we go," I muttered.

"See, Naomi doesn't like to inconvenience anyone by doing anything annoying like talking about what's wrong, asking for help, or standing up for what she needs and wants. She prefers to scurry around like a mouse, making sure everyone else's needs are met."

"Well, that's just fucked up," Sloane decided.

I winced. "Look, guys. I understand that you're concerned. I get it. I am too. But right now, my priority is to get custody of my niece. I don't have the time or the energy to worry about anything else."

"Your evil twin has been in your house that you share with her daughter," Sloane interjected.

"She stole from you. She committed a crime disguised as you so once again you'd be the one to pay the consequences. And you didn't think it was worth mentioning?"

"Thanks a lot, Nash," I said.

Sloane crossed her arms over her chest. "Don't blame a man who just took two bullets," she said.

"Guys, don't you think you're overreacting?"

"No. We're reacting appropriately. You're the one who is underreacting. Your safety, Waylay's safety, is on the line. That deserves a reaction," Stef said.

I looked down at my hands. "So it would make you all feel better that I am terrified, frozen in the core of my soul, fearful that something is going to happen and Waylay is going to be taken away from me. That some stranger is going to end up raising my niece, or worse, that my sister, the person

I'm supposed to be closest to in this world, could come waltzing back into town and take her from me without me knowing. That between trying to prove to a caseworker who keeps seeing me at my worst that I'm the most responsible option she has, holding down two jobs, and reminding a little girl that not everything has to be the way it was for the first eleven years of her life, you want me to pencil in a conversation about how I have to exhaust myself just so I can sleep at night and not stare at the ceiling thinking of all the ways this could go horribly wrong."

"Uh, yeah. That would make me feel better than being intentionally cut out," Sloane said.

"*Thank* you," Stef said. "Nash, you wanna bring this home for us?"

"Naomi, you've got a lot of people who care about you. Maybe it's time you let them take care instead of you doing all the caretaking for once."

I stuck out my chin. "I'll take that under advisement," I said.

"That's her snooty tone," Stef said. "There's no getting through until she calms down."

"I'm going for a walk," I said huffily.

I hadn't made it very far when I heard, "Naomi, hold up."

I wanted to keep walking, to flip him the middle finger, but because I was me, I stopped in my tracks and waited for Nash to catch up.

"I'm not doing this to piss you off," he said. His eyes were bluer than Knox's, but they burned with that same Morgan intensity that had my stomach flipping upside down and inside out. "You need to be on the lookout. Your family needs to too. Keeping shit like this from them is irresponsible, and that's the kind of thing that doesn't look good in guardianship cases."

"You said I had nothing to worry about!"

"I'm speaking to you in a language you understand. Being a guardian, being a parent, it isn't about getting gold stars from some authority figure. It's about doing what's right even when it's hard. *Especially* when it's hard."

Easy for him to say. A caseworker hadn't caught him mostly naked after a one-night stand.

He reached out and gripped my shoulder with one hand. "Do you hear me?" he asked.

"I'd think real hard about removing that hand if I were you."

My head swiveled, and that was when I saw him. Knox sauntering our way. But there was nothing casual about the look in his eyes. He looked pissed.

Nash kept his hand where it was even as Knox stepped into our little twosome.

A second later, I found myself hauled up against Knox's side, his arm draped over my shoulder. Our audience was dividing its attention between the play on the field and the drama off it.

I smiled like we were chitchatting about butterflies and the weather.

The brothers glared at each other.

"I was just reminding your girl here that family takes care of family," Nash said.

"Now you're done reminding her. Why don't you get your ass back home and rest the fuck up so you're in shape to take care of family?"

"I'm enjoying the game. Think I'll stick around," Nash said. "Good to see you, Naomi."

I said nothing and watched him wander over to Liza J and my parents. Neither of the Morgan brothers appeared to be in good moods in the mornings.

"What are you doing here?" I asked, tilting my head back to look at Knox.

His gaze was on the field where Nina missed the ball entirely and instead connected with the shins of the opposing player.

"Heard there was a game. Thought I'd swing by."

His thumb was rubbing lazy circles against my upper arm. I felt a tingling that originated at the site of his touch and traveled through the rest of my body. My grumpy, tattooed sort-of boyfriend had dragged himself out of bed on an early Saturday morning after a closing shift at the bar just to show up for me and Waylay. I wasn't sure what to do with that information.

"It's early," I pointed out.

"Yep."

"Nash is just worried," I said, trying to move the conversation along.

"He does that."

The crowd noise picked up, and the game drew my attention. I felt Knox tense beside me as Waylay intercepted a pass and dribbled down the field.

"Go all the way, Way," Wraith yelled.

"Keep going, Waylay," Dad shouted.

"Come on, kid," Knox said under his breath, his attention riveted on the number six jersey.

My fingers curled into Knox's shirt as she closed in on the goal.

Just as she reared her leg back to let the ball fly, another player ran into her, and they both dropped to the ground.

There was a collective groan from the fans.

Nina and Chloe pulled Waylay to her feet, and I saw how red her face was.

"Uh-oh."

"Uh-oh, what?" Knox asked.

"What the shit, Ref?" Waylay bellowed.

"Ah, crap," I whispered.

"Did she just say 'shit' to the ref?" Knox asked.

The referee blew the whistle and strode up to Waylay, digging in his front pocket.

I groaned as the yellow card was produced and held up in front of my niece's mutinous little face.

"She does this every game. It's like she can't control her mouth," I groaned.

"Come on, Ref," Wraith yelled. "That was a foul."

"Sorry, Coach. Can't use that language on the field," the referee said.

Waylay opened her mouth again. Thankfully

Chloe had the foresight to slap a hand over the gaping chasm of four-letter words. Waylay fought against her.

"This is her third yellow card in three games. I can't get her to stop."

Knox stuck his fingers in his mouth and whistled. Everyone looked in our direction, including Waylay.

"Way," he said, crooking his finger. "Get over here."

Chloe released her, and Waylay, gaze on her feet, cheeks red, marched over to the line.

Knox released me and hooked Waylay by the back of the neck.

"I get it, kid. I do. But you can't say that shit on the field or in school."

"Why not? You say it. My mom says it."

"We're adults and we don't have a bunch of other adults breathin' down our necks, telling us what not to do."

"So what am I supposed to do? I got tripped! I could have scored."

"You say it as loud as you want to in your head. You let it come out of your eyes, your pores, every exhale, but you do *not* say it on the field again. You're fuckin' better than that, Way. You've got a temper, but there's a hell of a lot more power in controlling it than letting it fly. Use it, or it'll use you. You get me?"

She nodded solemnly. "I think so. When can I swear?"

"When you and me are watching football."

Waylay's gaze slid to my face, gauging my reaction.

"Don't you worry about your aunt. She's proud as hell of you. But you're only holding yourself back when you blow up like that. So let's give her something else to be proud about. Yeah?"

She sighed. Then nodded again. "Yeah. Okay. But I get to swear when we watch football?"

"Damn right you do," Knox said, ruffling her hair.

"And when I'm not in school anymore?"

"You can swear as much as you fucking want after you're out of college. Maybe grad school too, if you want a PhD or some shit."

The corner of her mouth lifted.

"That's better," he said. "Now, get your ass out there and put the ball in the back of the net so we can get ice cream after."

"But it's morning," she said, again looking at me as if I were some anti-swearing, anti-ice cream monster.

"No better time for ice cream than after a big win," he assured her.

She grinned up at him. "Okay. Thanks, Knox. Sorry, Aunt Naomi."

"You're forgiven," I assured her. "I'm already proud of you. Now, go be awesome."

So it wasn't my best advice to impart. But I was feeling rather swoony as Knox stood shoulder to shoulder with Wraith. My father, then Nash, joined him. Together they created a wall of testosterone, ready to protect and guide their girls.

"Just when you think he can't get any hotter," my mom said, sidling up next to me.

"Are you talking about Knox or Dad?" I asked.

"Both. All of them really. Coach Wraith certainly has a charm about him. And Nash is just as sexy as his brother."

"Mom!"

"It's just an observation. We Witt women have excellent taste in men. Well, most of us."

I covered my mouth with my hand and tried to stifle the laugh.

Time was ticking down, and the score was still tied 1–1.

"Let's go, ladies!" Wraith shouted.

I saw Waylay glance our way, caught the tiny smile on her face, and I felt the tingles again. She had a cheering section waiting to celebrate with her, and it meant something to her.

"You're doing an amazing job with her," Mom said.

"Really?"

"Look at that smile. Look at how she keeps glancing over here, reassuring herself that we're all still here. Say what you will about Tina, but giving you her daughter was the best choice she's ever made."

My eyes clouded with tears. "Thanks, Mom," I whispered.

She looped her arm through mine, then tensed. "She has the ball again!"

Wraith's granddaughter had gotten tangled up with two defenders and sent the ball sailing to Waylay's feet.

"Go!" we shouted as one, the crowd coming to its feet.

Mom and I clung to each other as Waylay dribbled around the last defender between her and the goal.

"Oh my God, I'm going to be sick."

"Let 'er rip, Waylay," Mom shrieked.

So she did. I held my breath as we watched the ball sail in slow motion toward the goal.

The crowd was screaming. I could hear Stef over everyone yelling, "Get it in the net thing!"

The goalie dove for it.

But the ball spiraled just past her fingertips into the back of the net.

I screamed along with Mom as we jumped up and down together.

"That's my granddaughter!" Mom screeched.

"Fuck yeah!" Wraith bellowed.

"You're damn right," Liza J shouted.

Sloane and Stef were hugging each other.

The ref blew the final whistle. "That's game!"

Waylay stood stock-still, staring at the ball in the back of the net as if she couldn't believe what she'd just done. And then she turned. Her teammates raced to her, shrieking and giggling. But she was looking beyond them. She was looking at me. And then she was running.

And so was I. I caught her when she jumped into my arms and swung her around.

"You did it!"

"Did you see? Did you see what I did, Aunt Naomi?"

"I saw, honey. I'm so proud of you!"

"Can we get ice cream, and can I swear when I watch football with Knox?"

"Yes and I guess so."

She hugged me tight around the neck and whispered, "This is the best day of my life."

I was trying to blink back tears when someone pulled her from my arms. It was Knox, and he was settling Waylay on his shoulders as the rest of the players and parents gathered around to congratulate her. Knox shot me one of his rare, full-on grins that made me dizzy.

"Sloane and I have talked, and you're forgiven," Stef said, slinging his arm around me.

"As long as we're invited for ice cream," Sloane added.

"And included in your life," Stef insisted.

I pulled them both in for a hard hug, and over their shoulders, I saw Dad clap Knox on the back.

34

The Groom

Naomi

I threaded the stem of the earring through my lobe and leaned back to admire the effect.

"What do you think?" I asked Waylay, who was sprawled across my bed on her stomach, chin pillowed in her hands.

She studied the earrings. "Better," she decided. "They sparkle like Honky Tonk on your shirt, and they stand out more when you toss your hair."

"I don't toss my hair," I said, ruffling hers. My niece was more and more willing to tolerate affection from me these days.

"Oh yes, you do. Whenever you catch Knox looking at you, you're all . . ." She paused to shake out her blond hair and bat her eyes.

"I do not!"

"Do so."

"I'm the adult and I'm in charge and I say I don't," I insisted, flopping down on the bed next to her.

"You also get this mushy face whenever he walks into a room or you get a text from him."

"Oh, is it like the mushy face you make whenever someone says Mr. Michaels's name?" I teased.

Waylay's face transformed into what could aptly be described as mushy.

432

"Ha! See! *That* is a mushy face," I said, pointing accusingly at her.

"You wish," she scoffed, still smiling. "Can I use some of your hair spray since you messed up my hair?"

"Sure," I said.

She slipped off the bed and picked up the can I left on the dresser.

"Are you sure you packed everything you need?" I asked, eying the pink duffel bag in the doorway. Waylay was invited to Nina's birthday sleepover. It was the first time she'd be spending the night with a nonfamily member, and I was feeling the nerves.

"I'm sure," she said. Her tongue poked out between her teeth as she carefully brushed her hair over her forehead just so before hitting it with a shot of spray.

"I'm working the closing shift tonight, so if you decide you don't want to spend the night, you can just call Grandma and Grandpa or Liza or Knox, and one of them will come pick you up."

She crossed her eyes at me in the mirror. "Why wouldn't I want to spend the night? It's a sleepover." She was already dressed in pajamas, a request on the invitation. But she was wearing the pink sneakers Knox had given her with the ever-present heart charm.

"I just want you to know that no matter what, you can always call, and someone will be there," I said. "Even when you're older."

I cleared my throat, and Waylay put down the hair spray.

"What?" she asked, turning around to face me.

"What what?" I hedged.

"You always clear your throat before you say something you think someone isn't going to like."

Damn astute kid. "Have you heard from your mom?"

She looked down at her feet. "No. Why?"

"Someone said she was in town not too long ago," I said.

"She was?" Waylay frowned like the news was disturbing.

I nodded. "I didn't talk to her."

"Does this mean she's going to take me back?" she asked.

I started to clear my throat, then stopped. I didn't know how to answer that. "Is that something you'd like?" I asked instead.

Waylay was staring hard at her shoes now. "I'm okay here with you," she said finally.

I felt the tension release from my shoulders. "I like having you with me."

"You do?"

"I do. Even if your hair-tossing impression of me is terrible."

She grinned, then stopped. "She always comes back."

It sounded different when she said it this time. It sounded more like a warning.

"We'll figure that out when we have to," I told

her. "Let's get you to your sleepover. Are you sure you packed your toothbrush?"

"Geez, Aunt Naomi! This isn't my first sleep-over!"

"Okay. Okay! What about underwear?"

Me: How's Paris?
Stef: I drank too much champagne and danced with a man named Gaston. So pretty fucking great. But I still miss you and the fam.
Me: We miss you too.
Stef: Any drama happening that you "forgot" to tell me about?
Me: It's so nice that you don't hold a grudge. And no. No drama to report except Waylay is going to a sleepover.
Stef: Does that mean you'll be having your own sleepover? If so, wear the teddy I sent you! It'll melt Knox's mind! Oops. Gotta go. Gaston is beckoning!

Honky Tonk on a Friday night was a rowdy time. The crowds were big, the music loud, and no one cared if they were hungover in the morning, so the drink orders were plentiful.

I swept my hair up off the back of my neck as I waited for Max to finish keying in an order.

"Where's Knox tonight?" Silver called from behind the bar.

"Out with Lucian," I yelled back over "Sweet

435

Home Alabama." The band was decent, but they were drowned out by the crowd singing over them. "He said he'd come by later."

Max moved away from the POS and started throwing drinks on trays. "Tips are good tonight," she said.

"Sounds like it could be a shots night," I said with an eyebrow wiggle.

"There's a new guy in your section," Max said, pointing to the wall on the far side of the dance floor. "How's the sleepover going?"

"Way messaged me to tell me to stop messaging her, and Gael sent me a picture of the girls doing mani-pedis and face masks," I told her. "She looks like she's having the time of her life."

I dropped off two fresh beers at a table of equestrians and gave a quick hello to Hinkel McCord and Bud Nickelbee on my way across the bar.

I caught a glimpse of the new patron. He'd angled his chair against the wall, half in shadow. But I could still make out his red hair. The guy from the library. The one who had asked about tech support.

I felt a nervous tickle at the back of my neck. Maybe he lived in Knockemout. Maybe I was overthinking it, and he was just a regular person with a broken laptop who liked a cold beer on a Friday night.

And maybe he wasn't.

"Here you go, guys," I said, doling out drinks to a four-top that had turned into a six-top.

"Thanks, Naomi. And thank you for hooking my aunt up with that home health organization," said Neecey, the gossipy waitress from Dino's.

"My pleasure. Hey, does anyone know that guy along the back wall?" I asked.

Four heads swiveled in unison. Knockemout wasn't much for subtlety.

"Can't say he looks familiar," Neecey said. "That red hair sure stands out. I feel like I'd remember him if I met him."

"Is he giving you trouble, Nay?" Wraith demanded, looking deadly serious.

I forced a laugh. "No. I just recognized him from the library. I didn't know if he was a local."

I suddenly wished Knox was here.

Two seconds later, I was really glad he wasn't. Because this time when the front door opened, I prayed for the floor to open up and swallow me.

"Now who the hell is that dandy?" Wraith wondered out loud.

"Oh, no. No, no, no, no, no," I whispered.

Warner Dennison the Third was scanning the bar, an expression of derision on his handsome face.

I thought about turning around and hightailing it for the kitchen. But it was too late. He locked eyes with me, not bothering to hide his surprise.

"Naomi," he called just as the band cut off their song.

Heads turned to look at me and then back at Warner.

I stayed rooted to the spot, but he was on the move, weaving his way through tables to get to me.

"What are you doing here?" I demanded.

"Me? What the hell are you doing in a place like this? And what are you wearing?" he said, reaching for me. His hands gripped my biceps like he was going to pull me in for an embrace, but I resisted.

"I work here," I said, planting a hand firmly on his chest.

A motorcycle revved its engine outside, and he flinched. "Not anymore," Warner said. "This is ridiculous. You made your point. You're coming home."

"Home?" I managed a dry laugh. "Warner, I sold my house. I live here now."

"Don't be ridiculous," he said. "You're coming home with me."

Not wanting to cause a scene, I gave up trying to extricate myself from his grasp. "What are you talking about? We're not together anymore."

"You ran out on our wedding, then ignored my calls and emails for weeks. You wanted to make a point, and you made it."

"What point exactly do you think I was making?"

His nostrils flared, and I noticed the clench of his jaw. He was getting upset, and it turned my stomach.

"You wanted me to see what life would be like without you. I get it."

We had the rapt attention of the bar. "Warner, let's talk somewhere else," I suggested. I pulled him past the bar and into the hallway by the restrooms.

"I miss you, Naomi. I miss our dinners together. I miss coming home and finding out you did all my laundry for me. I miss taking you out and showing you off."

I shook my head, hoping to rattle some sense into my brain. I couldn't believe he was here.

"Look," he said, "I apologize for what happened. I was stressed. I had too much to drink. It won't happen again."

"How did you find me?" I asked, finally extricating myself from his grasp.

"My mom is Facebook friends with yours. She saw some of the pictures your mom has been posting."

For once, I regretted not telling my mom exactly why I'd run out on my wedding. If she'd known why I left Warner, she sure as hell wouldn't have pointed the way here.

Warner took my wrists in his hands.

"Everything all right here," Max asked, appearing at the mouth of the hall.

"Everything's fine," I lied.

"Mind your own damn business," Warner muttered without taking his eyes off me.

"Warner!" I remembered all the little insults he'd say under his breath directed at me and countless others.

"Let's go somewhere where we can talk," he said, squeezing my wrists tighter.

"No. You need to listen to me. I'm not going anywhere with you, and I'm certainly not getting back together with you. It's over. We're over. There's nothing more to talk about. Now go home, Warner."

He stepped forward into my space. "I'm not going anywhere unless you're with me," he insisted.

I could smell alcohol on his breath and winced. "How much have you had to drink?"

"For fuck's sake, Naomi. Stop trying to blame everything on a drink or two. Now, I let you have your space, and look what you did with it." He swept an arm out. "This isn't you. You don't belong in a place like this with people like them."

"Let go of me, Warner," I said calmly.

Instead of letting me go, he pushed me back against the wall and held me there by my biceps.

I didn't like it. It wasn't like when Knox boxed me in and my senses were full of him, when I wanted to do anything to be closer to him. This was different.

"You need to go, Warner," I said.

"You want me to go, you're going with me."

I shook my head. "I can't leave. I'm working."

"Fuck this place, Naomi. Fuck your little temper tantrum. I'm willing to forgive you."

"Take your fucking hands off her. Now."

My knees went weak at Knox's voice.

"Move along, asshole. This is between me and my fiancée," Warner said.

440

"Not the brightest answer," Lucian said mildly.

Knox and Lucian were standing at the mouth of the hallway. Lucian had his hand on Knox's shoulder. I couldn't tell if he was restraining him or telling him he had his back.

Then suddenly Knox wasn't standing at the mouth of the hall, and Warner didn't have his hands on me anymore.

"Give him the first shot," Lucian called.

Warner swung, and I watched in horror as he landed a punch that snapped Knox's head back.

"Good enough," Lucian said, his hands in the pockets of his slacks, the picture of relaxation.

Knox let his fists do the talking. The first punch connected with Warner's nose, and I heard the crunch. Blindly, Warner struck out. The blow glanced off Knox's shoulder. As blood poured from Warner's nose, Knox threw another punch and then another before Warner crumpled to the floor. Before Knox could follow him down, Lucian was pulling him back.

"Enough," he said calmly as Knox fought to free himself. "Take care of Naomi."

When Lucian said my name, Knox's gaze abandoned my bloodied ex-fiancé and found me.

"What the fuck?" Warner snarled as Lucian hauled him to his feet. "I'm calling my lawyer! Your ass will be in jail by morning!"

"Good luck with that. His brother's the chief of police, and my lawyer is ten times more expensive than yours. Watch the door," Lucian warned. And then he used Warner's face to open the kitchen door. A cheer went up in the bar as the two men disappeared.

And then I wasn't thinking about who was going to clean up the bloody smear on the glass because Knox was in front of me, looking a thousand shades of pissed off.

35

The Whole Story
and a Happy Ending

Knox

"I have to go to the restroom," Naomi announced and bolted into the ladies' room.

"Goddammit," I muttered, clenching my hands into fists. Adrenaline and rage raced through my veins, heating my blood to boiling.

I debated going into no-man's-land after her, but Max, Silver, and Fi beat me to it.

"You can't all leave the floor at the same fucking time," I called through the door.

"Fuck off, Knoxy. We got this," Fi yelled back.

"And we got this, Knox," Wraith said, throwing a bar towel over his shoulder and stepping behind the bar. "You're all gettin' beers or shots, 'cause I don't know how the fuck to pour anything else."

A raucous cheer rose up from the customers.

The kitchen door swung open, and Milford the cook walked out with two baskets of brisket nachos in one hand and an ice pack wrapped in a towel in the other. He tossed me the ice, then let out an earsplitting whistle.

Sloane jumped up and grabbed the baskets. "Yo! Who got the brisket nachos?"

Hands went up all over the bar.

"If I find out any of you are lying, I'll personally ruin your life for an entire year."

Sloane was no mild-mannered librarian. She had a legendary temper that, when roused, was a Category 5 shitstorm.

All but two hands wisely went down.

"That's better," she said.

"We got this, boss. See to your lady," Milford insisted.

"Did Lucian—"

"Mr. Rollins is taking out the trash," he said with a grin before ducking back into the kitchen.

I wanted to, but I was afraid her posse wouldn't let me near her. I could punch an asshole out without a second thought, but I was smart enough to be a little terrified of the Honky Tonk women.

"Naomi," I said, pounding a fist on the bathroom door. "If you don't get your ass out here, I'm either comin' in there or I'm gonna go knock more sense into that son of a bitch."

The door opened, and Naomi, with smudged eye makeup, glared at me. "You will do no such thing."

Relief coursed through me, and I leaned into her.

"I'm gonna touch you now because I need to. And I'm warning you in advance, because if I touch you and you flinch, I'm gonna go out in the parking lot and start kicking ass until he's too broken to ever touch another woman again."

Her eyes widened, but she nodded.

I tried to be gentle as I took her by the hand.

"We good?" I asked.

She nodded again.

It was good enough for me. I pulled her past the restrooms and Fi's office into the next hallway that led to my office.

"I can't believe this happened," she groaned. "I'm so embarrassed."

She hadn't been embarrassed. She'd been fucking terrified. The look in her eyes when I stepped into the hall was one I'd never forget as long as I lived.

"The nerve of him showing up here, saying he wants me back because he misses how I cleaned up after him."

I squeezed her hand. "Pay attention, Daisy."

"To what? The way you turned his face into ground beef? Do you think you broke his nose?"

I knew I had. That was the point.

"Pay attention to this," I said, pointing at the keypad next to the door. "The code is 0522."

She stared at the keypad, then back at me. "Why are you giving me the code?"

"If that guy or anyone else you don't want to see shows up, you come back here, and you plug in 0522."

"I'm trying to have a nervous breakdown, and you want me to memorize numbers."

"Enter the code, Naomi."

She did as she was told while muttering about what pains in the ass all men were. She wasn't wrong.

"Good girl. See the green light?"

She nodded.

"Open the door."

"Knox, I should get back out there. People are going to be talking. I've got six tables," she said, her hand hovering over the handle.

"You should open the damn door and take a breath."

Those gorgeous fucking hazel eyes of hers widened, and I felt the world slow to a stop. When she did that, when she looked at me with hope, trust, and just a little bit of lust, it did things to me. Things I didn't want to dissect because it felt good, and I didn't want to waste time wondering how it was going to go bad.

"Okay," she said finally, pushing the door open.

I hustled her across the threshold and closed the door behind us.

"Wow. The Fortress of Solitude," she said with reverence.

"It's my office," I said dryly.

"It's your safe space. Your lair. No one but Waylon is allowed in here. And you just gave me the code."

"Don't make me regret it," I said, moving in to back her against the door, fighting against the need to grab her and hold her tight.

"I'll try not to," she promised on a breathy sigh.

"What happened out there was a shit show," I began, putting my hands on either side of her head.

She winced. "I know. I'm so sorry. I had no idea he was coming. I haven't talked to him since the rehearsal dinner. I tried to get him away from the crowd and handle it privately, but—"

"Baby, a man ever gets you in that position again, I want you to knee him in the balls as hard as you can, and when he doubles over, you knee him in the fucking face. Then you run like hell. I don't give a shit about causing scenes. I give a shit that I walked into my bar and found a man with his hands on my girl."

Her lower lip trembled, and I wanted to hunt down Warner Whatever the Fuck His Name Was and put his head through a plate glass window.

"I'm sorry," she whispered.

"Baby, I don't want you to be sorry. I don't want you to be scared. I want you to be as pissed off as I am that some asshole thought he could put his hands on you. I want you to know your worth so no one in their right mind ever thinks they can treat you like that. You get me?"

She nodded tentatively.

"Good. Think it's time you tell me the whole story, Daze."

"We don't really need to talk—"

"You're not getting out of this room until you tell me everything. And I mean every fucking thing."

"But we're not really togeth—"

I pinched her lips closed. "Uh-uh, Naomi. It doesn't matter what the fucking label says. I care about you, and if you don't start talkin', I can't do what I need to do to make sure it never happens again."

She was still for a long beat.

"If I tell you, will you let me go back to work?" she asked through my fingers.

"Yes. I'll let you go back to work."

"If I tell you, will you promise not to hunt Warner down?"

I was not going to like this one bit and I knew it.

"Yes," I lied.

"Fine."

I took my hand away, and she ducked under my arm to stand in the middle of the room between my desk and the couch.

"It's my fault," she began.

"Bullshit."

She whirled around and fixed me with a look. "I'm not telling you anything if you're going to interject like one of those old man Muppets in the balcony. We'll both just die of starvation in here, and eventually someone will smell our decaying bodies and break down the door."

I leaned against the front of my desk and stretched my legs out. "Fine. Continue with your asinine assessment."

"Excellent alliteration," she said.

"Talk, Daze."

She blew out a breath. "Fine. Okay. We were together for a while."

"History. You've got it. You moved on, and he hasn't."

She nodded.

"We'd been together long enough that I had my

eye on the next step." She glanced at me. "I don't know if you know this about me, but I really like checking things off my list."

"No shit."

"Anyway, on paper, we were compatible. It made sense. We made sense. And it wasn't like he was making plans for next year's vacations. But he wasn't moving as quickly as I thought he should."

"You told him to shit or get off the pot," I guessed.

"Much more eloquently, of course. I told him I saw a future for us. I was working for his family's company, and we'd been dating for three years. It just made sense. I told him if he didn't want to be with me, he needed to cut me loose. When he slid a jeweler's box over the table at his favorite Italian place a few weeks later, part of me was so relieved."

"The other part?"

"I think I knew it was a mistake right there."

I shook my head and crossed my arms. "Baby, you knew it was a mistake long before then."

"Well, you know what they say about hindsight."

"It makes you feel like an idiot?"

Her lips quirked. "Something like that. You don't really want to hear all this."

"Finish it," I growled. "I spilled my guts to you the night Nash was shot. This'll even us out."

She sighed, and I knew I'd won.

"So we started planning the wedding. And by *we,* I mean his mother and me because he was busy with work and didn't want to deal with the details. Things were happening with the company. He was under a lot of stress. He started drinking more. Snapping at me for little things. I tried to be better, do more, expect less."

My hands itched to close around that fuckface's throat.

"About a month before the wedding, we were out to dinner with another couple, and he had too much to drink. I was driving us home, and he accused me of flirting with the other guy. I laughed. It was so absurd. He didn't think it was funny. He . . ."

She paused and winced.

"Say it," I said gruffly.

"H-he grabbed me by the hair and yanked my head back. I was so surprised I swerved and almost hit a parked car."

It took everything I had not to jump up from the desk and run into the parking lot to kick this fucking guy's ass.

"He said he didn't mean it," she continued as if her words hadn't just set off a ticking time bomb inside me. "He apologized profusely. He sent me flowers every day for a week. 'It was the stress,' he said. He was trying for a promotion to set us up for our future."

I was choking on suppressed rage and wasn't sure how long I could pretend to be calm.

"We were so close to the wedding day, and he really did seem like he was sorry. I was stupid enough, eager enough to move on to the next step that I believed him. Things were fine. Better than fine. Until the night of the rehearsal."

My fingers dug into my biceps.

She was pacing now in front of me. "He showed up to the rehearsal smelling like a distillery, and he had several more drinks during dinner. I overheard his mother making snide comments about how she wished she could have invited more people but that she couldn't because my parents couldn't afford it."

Fuckface's mom sounded like she needed her own kind of ass kicking.

"I was so mad I confronted him when we left the restaurant." She shuddered, and I was afraid I was going to grind my fillings into dust. "Thank God we were alone in the parking lot. My parents had already gone home. Stef and the rest of the wedding party were still inside.

"He was so angry. Just like a switch had flipped. I never saw it coming."

She closed her eyes, and I knew she was reliving the moment all over again.

"He slapped me right across the face. Hard. Not hard enough to knock me down, but enough to humiliate me. I just stood there in shock, holding my cheek. I couldn't believe he'd do something like that."

I doubted that Naomi was aware she'd lifted a hand to her cheek as if she could still feel the hit.

I couldn't hold it in anymore. I turned for the door and was ready to rip the knob off when I felt her hands on my back.

"Knox, where are you going?"

I flipped the lock and wrenched the door open. "To dig a shallow grave so I have a place to put him after I get tired of throwing punches."

Her fingernails dug into my skin under my shirt, giving me something else to feel besides fury.

"Don't leave me alone," she said, then pressed herself against my back.

Fuck.

"He started pacing and yelling. It was my fault, he told me. He wasn't ready to get married. He had goals he wanted to accomplish before focusing on his personal life. It was my fault for pushing him. All he was trying to do was give me everything I wanted, and there I was complaining to him the night before the wedding he didn't want to have."

"That's fucking bullshit, Naomi, and you know it."

"Yeah," she squeaked, resting her forehead between my shoulder blades. I felt something damp leak through the shirt.

Damn it.

I turned and took her in my arms, holding her face against my chest. Her breath hitched. "Baby, you're killin' me."

"I'm so embarrassed," she whispered. "It was a slap. He didn't put me in the hospital. Didn't threaten my life."

"Doesn't make it anywhere near right. A man doesn't put hands on a woman like that. Ever."

"But I wasn't exactly innocent. I tried to force a

452

man to marry me. I almost said 'I do' even after he hit me. How pathetic is that? I was in that church basement in my dress, worrying about what other people would think if I didn't go through with it. Worrying about letting them down."

I thumbed away the tears that tracked down her cheeks. Each one felt like a knife to my heart.

"I still don't know if I would have made the right choice if Tina hadn't called me and said she was in trouble. That was when I knew I wasn't going to go through with it."

After everything Tina had done, at least she'd provided the excuse Naomi needed when she needed it.

"Daisy, you gave him a choice. It doesn't matter how shitty the options are. It's still his choice to make. He could spend the rest of his life with you or without you. He *didn't* give you a choice when he hurt you."

"But I should have listened to what he was trying to tell me. He didn't want to commit, and I forced him to."

"He had a choice," I repeated. "Look. A man doesn't go all in with a woman, it's for a reason. Maybe he's looking for something better. Maybe he's just comfortable with his place in your world and doesn't want to make a place for you in his. Either way, he makes no forward progress unless he's forced into it.

"After that, even if he pops the question, even if he shows up at the altar, he'll hold on to the fact

453

that it wasn't his idea. He washes his hands of responsibility for the entire relationship. But the bottom fucking line is, he had a choice every step of the way. You didn't force him into anything."

She looked down. "He never thought I was good enough for him."

"Baby, truth is, on his best day, he was never gonna be good enough for *you,* and he fucking knew it."

So he'd manipulated her and he'd tried to prove he was better by showing he was stronger, more powerful. By using force. And it would only have gotten worse.

"Damn it, Knox. You cannot be sweet to me right now!"

"Do *not* cry. Do not shed one more tear over some asshole who never deserved you in the first place. Or I'm going to go break both his arms and legs."

She cast her eyes down, then looked back up at me. "Thank you."

"For what?"

"For being here. For . . . taking care of me and cleaning up my mess. It really means a lot."

I thumbed away another stray tear. "What did I say about crying?"

"That one was for you, not him."

Instead of hunting Warner down and kicking him in the gut until my boot wore through, I did something more important. I lowered my mouth to take hers.

She instantly went soft and pliable against me,

surrendering. I spun us around so she had her back to the door.

"Knox?" she whispered.

Then I pressed my knee between her thighs and pinned her against the door with my hips as I plundered her mouth. She melted against me, eager and needy.

I was instantly hard.

The sexy little moan she made in the back of her throat when I ground my erection against her made me lose my fucking mind. I licked and kissed and tasted her until the air around us was electrified, until the pulse in my blood matched the beat of her heart.

I pumped my cock against her once, twice, three times, before shoving my hand between our bodies and under that skirt that I loved to hate.

When I found the silk edge of her underwear, I growled. I knew just by the touch it was one of the pairs I'd bought her. And I loved knowing she wore something I gave her close to her skin in a place I'd be the only one to see.

"He doesn't deserve one second of your energy. Never did," I said, yanking the underwear to the side with more haste than finesse.

"What are you doing?" she asked, her eyes glazed with desire.

"Reminding you what you deserve."

I thrust two fingers into her wet heat and swallowed her cry with my mouth. She was already rippling around me, begging to come.

"Do you want me to stop?" My voice was harsher than I intended, but I couldn't be soft, gentle, when she was making me harder than concrete.

"If you stop, I'll murder you," she groaned.

"That's my girl," I said, nipping at the sensitive skin of her neck.

I fucked her with my fingers, starting slow and building speed. I held her gaze with an obsessive desire to watch the orgasm I gave her ruin her. But I needed something more. I needed to taste her.

She whimpered when I dropped to my knees. The whimper became a low moan when I pressed my mouth between her legs.

"Ride my hand, Naomi. Ride it while I make you come. Remember who you are. What you deserve."

It was the last order I gave, because my tongue was busy teasing circles over her sensitive clit. She tasted like heaven as she bucked against my face.

My dick throbbed behind my zipper with a need so intense I didn't recognize it. *Mine.* I wanted to claim her, to make her mine so assholes knew they didn't have a chance.

"Knox," she whimpered, and I felt the clutch and pull of her around my fingers. It was fucking beautiful.

"That's right, baby," I murmured. "Feel me in you."

I sucked gently while working the swollen bud with my tongue.

She let out a wrenching moan, and I felt her come apart around my fingers. She was a miracle.

A work of art. And no one deserved her. Not Warner. Not even me.

But not deserving something wasn't going to stop me from taking.

The waves broke. The clenching became a languid flutter, and still my cock ached. I wanted to thrust into her and feel the echoes of her orgasm on my shaft.

Then she was pulling me to my feet, and her fingers were at my belt. My palms went to the door as she reverently released my erection, and she sank to her knees.

"You don't have to do this, Naomi." My whisper was harsh with need.

"I want to."

Her lips were parted. I felt her hot breath on my thigh, and my cock jerked. She made an approving noise, and before I could say or do anything, those perfect pink lips were parting, and my tip disappeared between them.

It was like a lightning strike.

My last coherent thought was that the only thing that saved Warner Fuckface from the beating of his life was Naomi's perfect mouth on my cock.

36

The Break-In

Knox

N ash yawned and scraped a hand over his face. He was sitting at his dining table in sweat pants. His usually clean-shaven mug had the beginnings of a beard.

"Look, I told you. I don't remember jack shit from the shooting. I don't even remember pulling the car over."

It was after two a.m., and Lucian had insisted we put our heads together on the situations.

I flipped my phone over to see if Naomi had texted me yet. She was supposed to text as soon as she got home. After the night she'd had, I felt unsettled letting her drive home by herself. But Lucian was insistent that we needed to talk to Nash.

"Is that normal? Not remembering?" I asked.

Nash shrugged with his good shoulder. "How the fuck should I know? This is the first time I got shot."

He was being flippant, but there were shadows under his eyes that had nothing to do with the time of night.

Lucian, on the other hand, looked as if he was

just hitting his stride. He was in what was left of another expensive suit. His tie and jacket hung over the back of Nash's couch. Even as a kid, he'd slept short and light. Every sleepover we'd ever had, he'd been the last to fall asleep and the first to wake. We never talked about what demons kept him up at night. We didn't have to.

"We need the dashcam footage," Lucian said. He leaned forward, elbows on knees, a glass of bourbon in his hand.

My brother was already shaking his head. "Fuck you, Lucy. You know I can't do that. It's evidence in an ongoing investigation. I know law and order don't mean much to you two—"

"We've got the same goal. Finding out who the fuck decided to put two bullets in you and leave you for dead," I interjected. "If I were you, I wouldn't be pissed off about the extra eyes and ears." I flipped my phone over again.

No messages.

"What's your problem?" Nash asked, nodding at my phone. "Liza J kicking your ass in Words with Friends again?"

"Naomi isn't home yet."

"It's a five-minute drive," Nash pointed out.

Lucian looked at me. "You didn't tell him?"

"Tell me what?"

"Naomi's ex showed up at Honky Tonk tonight. Put his hands on her. Scared her."

"Jesus. Where did you put the body?"

Lucian smiled slyly. "You don't want to know."

459

Nash pinched the bridge of his nose. "I really don't want this paperwork."

"Relax," I said. "He's not dead. But if he ever shows his goddamn face in this town again, I make no promises."

"Knox gave him the first shot in front of witnesses," Lucian explained.

"What else did he do in front of witnesses? Break his fucking neck?"

"Just the idiot's nose. I escorted him out into the parking lot and helped him understand if he ever came within a hundred miles of Naomi again, my lawyer was going to make it his personal mission to bankrupt him, his family, and his family's business."

"Lucy also smashed his face against the kitchen door," I added cheerfully, wanting to give credit where credit was due.

My brother picked up the untouched bourbon Lucian had put in front of him and downed it. "Goddammit. I hate being left out of shit."

"You didn't miss much," I told him.

"What the hell are you doing here?" Nash demanded, looking at me.

"I'm staring at you two pains in my ass."

"What the hell are you doing here staring at us when you should be home with her? She's probably messed up over the whole thing. Scared. Embarrassed. Worried about how it's gonna look in a guardianship hearing. This on top of the Tina shit is the last thing she needs."

460

I didn't like how well my brother knew Naomi.

"She's fine. We talked it out. I'm heading to her place as soon as you get your head out of your ass and hand over the dashcam footage."

"What Tina shit?" Lucian asked.

Nash was filling him in on the details of Tina's break-ins when my phone rang. I all but vaulted out of my seat to answer it.

"About damn time, Daisy."

"Knox?" The way she said my name had my hackles rising.

"What's wrong?" I said, already grabbing my car keys.

Nash and Lucian were on their feet too.

"Someone was here. Someone broke in. It's a mess. It's going to take me forever to clean this up."

"Get out of the house," I snarled.

Lucian was shrugging into his jacket, and Nash was doing his best to pull a shirt on over his sweats. I tossed him his sneakers.

"They're not here. I checked," Naomi said in my ear.

"We're gonna have words about that," I assured her grimly. "Now get back in your fucking car, lock the fucking doors, and drive to Liza J's. Do not get out of your fucking car until your dad comes out to get you."

"Knox, it's the middle of the night—"

"I don't give a shit if it's the middle of his colonoscopy. Get in the car now. I'm hanging up,

461

and I want you to call Nash. Stay on the line with him while I call your dad."

"Knox—"

"Don't argue with me, Naomi. Get in the damn car." I heard her grumbling under her breath and then the telltale sounds of an ignition starting. "Good girl. Call Nash."

I hung up before she could say anything else and scrolled through my contacts to Lou's number.

"Cottage?" Nash asked. His phone lit up. Naomi's name was on it.

"Yeah."

"I'll drive Nash," Lucian said, snatching the keys off the hook by the door.

"You can't drive a department vehicle, Lucy," Nash argued.

"Watch me."

"Yeah, Lou?" I said when Naomi's dad answered. "We got a problem."

We came in hot, looking like a high-speed car chase with me in the lead, followed by Lucian and Nash, lights blazing in a Knockemout PD SUV.

My hands tightened on the wheel when I saw everyone, dogs included, out on Liza J's porch. What part of "stay the fuck inside" didn't they understand?

I slammed on my brakes in front of Naomi's cottage. Lucian slid in next to me.

I turned to him. "Do me a favor and get everyone

inside so they're not standing around waiting for someone to start picking them off."

Wordlessly, Lucian nodded and melted into the night.

"Backup's on the way," Nash said as we jogged up the porch steps. The screen door was hanging by one hinge, the door beyond it wide open.

"Naomi said no one's inside."

"And she knows that how?" Nash said, sounding almost as pissed as I felt.

"Because before she called me, she walked through the house holding a bread knife."

"And you're gonna have words with her about that, right?"

"What do you think?"

"I think you're gonna have words."

I had to admit, it was kind of nice to have my brother back.

"Fuck," I said when we entered.

"Mess" was an understatement. Couch cushions were thrown on the floor. The desk drawers had all been pulled out, their contents dumped. The coat closet was open, its inventory scattered throughout the living room.

The kitchen cabinets and drawers had all been gutted. The refrigerator door hung open with half the food dumped on the linoleum.

"Someone was pissed off and in a hurry," Nash observed.

I started up the steps, trying to keep a lid on my rage. Twice in one night, she'd been violated, and

I'd been a step behind each time. I felt . . . helpless, useless. What good was I if I couldn't keep her safe?

I heard my brother on the stairs behind me, his ascent slower than my own.

Spotting Waylay's pink comforter in the hallway, I headed into her room. It had fared worse than the first floor. Her new clothes had been ripped from the closet and dresser. The bedding was torn off, the mattress flipped and leaning against the wall. The picture frames that had hung on the walls most of my life were on the floor. Some of them broken.

"The ex or the sister?" Nash wondered out loud.

Naomi's bedroom had been hastily tossed, the bed stripped, the closet open and emptied. The same with the dresser.

There was a mess of cosmetics on top of the dresser that I doubted Naomi had made. BITCH was scrawled across the mirror in lipstick.

I was seeing red that had nothing to do with the shade of lipstick.

"Keep your cool," Nash advised. "You snapping and going off the rails on a temper tantrum isn't going to help."

We poked into every nook and cranny upstairs, making sure the place was empty. By the time we hit the first floor again, Nash was pale and sweaty, and two more cruisers had pulled in.

The surrounding woods were painted blue and red from the emergency lights.

I went out on the front porch to force fresh air

into my lungs so I could choke down the rising anger.

I spotted her, standing in the dirt lane still dressed in her work uniform with one of my grandfather's old flannel shirts layered on top. Waylon was leaning against her shins, as protective as a basset hound got.

I wasn't even conscious of jogging down the porch steps. I just knew I was being pulled to her.

"Are you okay?" she asked, looking worried.

I shook my head and wrapped my arms around her.

She was asking *me* if I was okay.

"I'm fine," I lied.

37

Shave and a Haircut

Naomi

W here are we going?" I asked Knox as we left
Knockemout in the rearview mirror.

"Are we going shopping?" Waylay asked hopefully from the back seat.

She'd taken the news that we were temporarily moving into Liza J's well. Of course, I'd flat out lied to her, telling her there was a bug problem at the cottage and that we'd be staying with everyone at Liza J's for a few days.

Waylay was thrilled for the extended sleepover.

My parents, on the other hand, were struggling. Not with having us all under one roof. That part had them in near ecstasy. But Knox had insisted I spill the truth. The whole truth, beginning with why I'd run out on Warner.

While my mother wrote a strongly worded message to Warner's mother on Facebook at four a.m., Knox had to physically restrain my father from leaving to go after Warner.

Dad calmed down considerably after Lucian assured him that Knox had not only mopped the floor with Warner, he'd also broken the man's nose.

The truth hurt, as I'd expected it to, which was why I hadn't shared in the first place. But my parents had stood up under its weight.

Over Mom's anxiety pancakes, we'd talked until nearly five a.m. before I'd fallen into bed with Knox in his childhood bedroom. I was certain I'd never be able to sleep, but with his heavy arm anchoring me to his side, I'd fallen into a dreamless oblivion and stayed there until ten.

When I woke up, I was alone because Knox had driven into town to pick up Waylay from her sleepover.

I'd taken my gigantic vat of coffee on the front porch and waited for them, thinking about how the man just kept blurring the lines of our agreement. And when they returned, when Knox put his hand on top of Waylay's blond head, ruffled her hair, and gave her an affectionate shove, I realized just how blurry those lines in my heart were getting. I was in trouble. And it had nothing to do with a break-in or a criminal sister or an ex-fiancé.

I was falling for the man I'd sworn I wouldn't. But Knox made it impossible not to. He made it inevitable.

Unfortunately, at that moment, the caseworker had shown up ready to do the home study that I'd completely forgotten about. I was not imagining the look of surprise on Mrs. Suarez's face when I tried to herd Waylay into Liza J's house while issuing a vague excuse as to why we were unprepared for her visit.

Thankfully, Knox had stepped in once again, ordering Waylay into the kitchen to get us coffees for the road. When she was out of earshot, he was the one who explained the situation to Mrs. Suarez.

I did *not* have a good feeling about what this meant for the custody hearing.

"We're not going shopping," Knox told Waylay as he took the on-ramp for the highway.

"What's all the stuff in the back for?" Waylay asked.

Between freaking out over what our caseworker thought of me allowing multiple break-ins to happen, I was curious too. Before he'd closed the cover over the truck bed, we'd spotted more than a dozen shopping bags.

"Supplies," he said mysteriously.

His phone rang, and I saw Jeremiah's name on the screen.

"Yeah," Knox said by way of a greeting.

The man was not one for small talk.

"We'll be there in about forty-five," he said into the phone. "Yeah. See you there."

"There" turned out to be Hannah's Place, a homeless shelter on the outskirts of Washington, DC.

It was a newer brick building on a large fenced lot. Knox pulled the truck through the gate and swung it around toward the entrance, where I saw Jeremiah standing under an awning.

"The second string has arrived," Jeremiah said with a grin as we piled out. "Great 'do, Way."

Waylay proudly patted a hand to the little French braid she'd worked around her head like a crown. "Thanks."

The woman beside Jeremiah was short, stocky, and very, very brave, because she charged right on up to Knox and wrapped him in a hard hug. "There's my second favorite barber," she said.

Knox hugged her back. "How did I lose the top spot this time?"

She leaned back and grinned wickedly. "Jer brought me two hundred rolls of toilet paper."

"We'll see how you feel about me after you see what I brought," he said.

"I see you brought me two new volunteers," she said.

"Shirley, meet Naomi and Waylay," Knox said. "Shirley left a seven-figure corporate gig to run this shelter."

"Who needs boardrooms and corner offices when you can spend your days doing good?" Shirley said, shaking my hand and then Waylay's.

"It's so nice to meet you," I said.

"Likewise. Especially if you've got two working hands and don't mind stocking shelves and packing boxes."

"Ready and able," I said, elbowing Waylay, who was looking a little morose.

"Put 'em where you want 'em," Knox said. "I'll set up shop, and we can get started."

Waylay and I followed Shirley as she led the way inside.

"I'd rather be shopping," Waylay whispered to me.

"Maybe we can find a mall afterward," I said, giving her shoulders a squeeze.

One thing was for sure—Knox Morgan was full of surprises.

"I guess it's kinda cool they do this," Waylay said as we watched Knox and Jeremiah run their makeshift outdoor salon through the tall windows.

While we had spent two hours sorting food and clothing donations with other volunteers, Knox and Jeremiah had entertained an endless stream of shelter residents in their chairs under the awning on the sidewalk.

It was a beautiful day edging toward fall, and the mood was festive.

The staff, volunteers, and residents had formed a kind of large, unruly family making something as bleak as homelessness feel like a challenge to be conquered, not a stigma to be reinforced.

Together, Knox and Jeremiah transformed ignored, unruly, disheveled hair into sleek, stylish looks, and in doing so, I realized they were also changing the way each client saw themselves.

Currently, Jeremiah was working a hand razor over a little boy's dark hair, keeping him in an almost constant state of giggles. The man in Knox's chair had sat down with a long, scraggly beard and wispy gray hair. His tan face was deeply lined, his thin shoulders stooped. He wore clean sweatpants and a long-sleeved T-shirt, both a few sizes too big.

His eyes were closed in what looked like a moment of unguarded bliss as Knox draped a hot towel over his face and readied his shaving supplies.

"Yeah. Kinda cool," I agreed, stroking a hand over Waylay's hair.

"Those two have been doing this once a month for years," Shirley said, appearing next to me. "Our residents get a kick out of having $200 haircuts, and it sure changes the way other people see them. We consider ourselves pretty dang lucky to have caught Knox Morgan's attention with our work here."

I wondered if he had his name on this building too. And if he did, did it bother him less than the police station?

I watched him remove the towel with a flourish, making the man in his chair grin.

"Grabbed you a coffee."

A huge to-go cup materialized before my eyes as I straightened from the table where I was folding T-shirts.

Knox stood there, holding a second, smaller cup with the kind of look in his eyes that made my heart somersault in my chest.

The man had played hero to two dozen people today—not counting me—and then he'd run out to grab me a cauldron of coffee.

471

It hit me like a warm, glowing wave that swept my feet out from under me.

"Thanks," I said, going misty-eyed.

"The fuck, Daze?"

Of course he noticed I was about to cry over caffeine. Because he noticed everything.

"Baby, what's wrong? Someone say something to you?" He was glaring through the window as if looking for someone to blame.

"No!" I assured him. "I'm just . . . This is . . . amazing, Knox. You know that, right?"

"It's a haircut, Naomi," he said dryly.

I shook my head. As a woman, I inherently understood that a haircut was rarely just a haircut. "No. It's more than that. You're changing the way the world sees each one of these people. And you're changing the way they feel about themselves."

"Shut up," he said gruffly. But the corner of his mouth lifted, and then he was plucking the coffee out of my hands, putting it on the table next to the stack of shirts, and pulling me into his chest.

"You shut up," I said, planting my hands on his shoulders.

"Where's Way?" he asked, those blue eyes searching for her.

Damn it.

That stupid golden glow was back and threatening to burst out of my chest. The man had spent the day giving homeless men and women haircuts. Then he'd brought me coffee and was now on alert, making sure Waylay was safe. He was as protective of her as he was me.

I was a goner.

"She's over there with Shirley," I said, pointing in the direction of the playground, where Waylay was pushing a little girl on the swings while Shirley led some kind of game.

Waylay spotted us watching her and waved.

I waved back, that glow in my chest refusing to budge now.

I needed to get out of here. Away from those strong arms so I could remind myself why we wouldn't work. Why we weren't really together.

Because Knox doesn't want to be. Because when it comes down to it, no one ever really chooses me.

That mean little voice did the trick, popping my pretty balloon of hope like a dart.

Knox tensed against me, his hold tightening.

"Are you okay?" I asked.

"Got yourself a girl, Knox?" a thin, reedy voice asked.

I turned in his arms to see the man who'd been in Knox's chair earlier. Now rather than looking like a lost soul, he looked years younger. A silver fox with his hair cut short and swept back from his face. His beard lay neat and gray along his strong jawline.

Knox's arms tightened around me, holding my back to his front.

"Two actually," I said with a smile, pointing over to where Waylay was giggling at something a boy her age said.

"Pretty," the man said. "Just like her mama."

Technically, I could have corrected him, but since Waylay's mom was my identical twin, I decided to just pocket it as the compliment it was intended. "Thank you," I said.

"Aren't ya gonna introduce us?" the man asked Knox as he scratched at his forearm. There was a subtle unsteadiness to his movements.

There were a few beats of awkward silence, which I was compelled to interrupt.

"I'm Naomi," I said, holding a hand out to the man.

"Naomi," he repeated. "I'm—"

"This is Duke," Knox interrupted.

Duke nodded, looking down at his feet for a second.

"It's nice to meet you, Duke," I said, my hand still extended.

"Then the pleasure is mine," he said finally. He accepted my hand, his palm rough and warm against mine. He had striking eyes the color of sterling silver. "Take good care of 'em, Knox," he said finally.

Knox grunted in response and pulled me back a step, my hand sliding out of Duke's. The man shuffled off in the direction of the big commercial kitchen.

"We're leavin'," Knox announced. "Go get Way."

Something had crawled up Knox's ass. Good. It would keep me from falling head over heels for the man.

Wordlessly, I picked up the coffee he'd brought me and headed outside to collect Waylay.

I coaxed her off the playground, telling her that it was time to go home. As we were saying our goodbyes, I spotted Knox by the truck with Duke.

He was handing over a backpack that looked as though it was stuffed full. They were having some kind of discussion that looked intense. Duke kept nodding while looking at his feet and scratching absently at his arms.

He didn't look up until Knox held out a white envelope and said something.

"Who's Knox talking to?" Waylay asked.

"A man named Duke. He cut his hair earlier."

"Is he okay?"

I didn't know if she meant Knox or Duke. "I don't know, honey."

38

F.I.N.E.

Knox

I'd fucked up in so many ways already, I couldn't stop myself from making it worse. Even knowing what I had to do next.

"Knox," Naomi moaned, her voice muffled by a pillow. This time, she wasn't screaming in frustration. She was doing her best to stay quiet while I fucked her in my grandmother's house. In the bedroom I'd grown up in.

She was on her hands and knees in front of me.

I thought it would be easier if I couldn't see those eyes. If I didn't get to watch the way they went glassy under heavy lids when I made her come one last time.

I was fucking wrong.

I tightened my grip on the back of her neck and hit the brakes on my thrusts. It cost me. But holding there, sheathed to the hilt inside her, was worth it.

She shuddered against me, around me, when I pressed an open-mouthed kiss to her shoulder blade. My tongue darted out to taste her skin. I wanted to breathe her in. To commit every second of this feeling to my memory.

I was in too deep. I was drowning. She'd pulled

me in over my head, and I was the dumb bastard who'd gone willingly. Forgetting everything I'd learned, every promise I'd ever made, every reason why I couldn't do this.

The possibility that it was already too late loomed large.

"Knox." Her sob was broken, and I felt her walls flutter around my throbbing dick. My blood pulsed in response.

I stroked my hand down her back, worshiping the silky warmth under my palm.

Naomi pulled her head out of the pillow and looked over her shoulder at me. Her hair was a mess, her lips swollen, lids heavy. She was seconds from coming. From giving me that miracle. My balls tightened, and I dug my teeth into my lip.

I needed this. I needed to give her this. One last time.

I dragged her up so we were both on our knees, her back flush to my front.

She lifted her arms overhead, reaching back to grip my neck, my shoulder.

"Please, Knox. Please," she begged.

I didn't need any further encouragement. I gripped her breast with one hand and sent the other sliding lower, between her legs where we were still joined.

One testing thrust, and her head fell back against my shoulder.

I pulled out almost all the way before driving back in.

She was coming. Her muscles undulated around me, gripping my cock, as I worked her clit, mindlessly driving her over the edge.

And then I was following her. Diving off the cliff behind her, letting her orgasm milk mine. I came hard, deep. Giving up that first hot spurt to her felt so fucking right.

She bowed back, accepting what I had to give her. Relishing it even.

I fucking loved it.

I fucking loved *her*.

It wasn't until I was empty, still moving in her, still chasing that high, that I remembered how fucking wrong it was. How fucked up I was doing this to her when I knew what came next.

But I couldn't stop myself.

Just like I couldn't stop myself from pushing us both to the mattress, my arms wrapped tight around her chest, holding her to me.

I was still inside her as I plotted how I was going to end it all.

An hour later, Naomi was sound asleep as I slipped out of bed.

I wanted a drink. A double of something strong enough to make me forget, to make me stop caring. And because I craved the numbness, I ignored it and filled a glass of water instead.

"Someone's dehydrated."

I was rattled enough to let my own grandmother startle me.

"Jesus, Liza J. What're you sneakin' around for?"

She flipped on the light switch, studying me behind her bifocals.

"Been a long time since you snuck a girl into your bed here," she observed. She was wearing plaid pajama shorts and a matching short-sleeved top. She looked like a lumberjack on summer vacation.

"I never snuck a girl into my bed under your roof," I lied.

"Bullshit. So Callie Edwards just happened to be checking the porch roof at one o'clock in the morning summer of your senior year?"

I'd forgotten about Callie. And all the other ones. It was like my brain only had room for one woman now. And that was the problem.

"Don't mind seein' you with them," she said, bumping me out of the way so she could get her own glass of water.

"Seein' me with who?"

Liza J shot me a "cut the bullshit" look. "Naomi. Waylay too. You seem happy."

I wasn't. I was anything but happy. I was one step away from a downward spiral I'd never recover from. A spiral that would destroy everything I'd built.

"It's nothing serious," I said, feeling defensive.

"I saw the look on your face when you came here last night. When you saw how close trouble got to your girl."

479

"She's not my girl," I insisted, deliberately ignoring her point.

"She's not yours, she's bound to end up as someone else's. Pretty girl like that? Thoughtful. Sweet. Funny. Sooner or later, someone with an IQ higher than yours will be along."

"Good."

She'd find someone else. She deserved someone else. Someone far from here, where I wouldn't have to run into her in the produce aisle or see her across the bar or down the street. Naomi Witt would just fade away into a ghost of a memory.

Except I knew it wasn't true. She wouldn't fade away. The hook was set. I'd taken the bait. There wouldn't be a day in the rest of my life that I didn't think about her. That I wouldn't say her name in my head a dozen times just to remind myself that I had her once.

I chugged the water, trying to fight off the tightness in my throat.

"Your brother looks at her like she's a home-cooked Sunday dinner," Liza J observed shrewdly. "Maybe he'd be smart enough to know how lucky he was."

Some of the water missed my throat and hit my lungs. I choked, then coughed.

As I gasped for air, it played out in my head. Naomi and Waylay sitting across the Thanksgiving table. Nash's hand on the back of her neck. Smiling at her, knowin' what was in store once everyone else went home for the night.

I could see her moving over him in the dark, those sweet lips parting. Hair tumbling over her eyes as she breathed out the name. *Nash.*

Someone else would get to hear their name from her mouth. Someone else would get to feel like the luckiest man alive. Someone else would bring her midafternoon coffees and watch those hazel eyes light up.

Someone else would take her and Waylay back-to-school shopping.

And that someone very well could be my own brother.

"You okay?" Liza J asked, dragging me out of my vision.

"I'm fine." Another lie.

"You know what they say about 'fine'—fucked up, insecure, neurotic, and emotional," Liza J muttered. "Turn the lights off when you're done. Electricity don't grow on trees."

I turned the lights out and stood there in the dark kitchen hating myself.

I had shards of glass in the lining of my gut.

That was how it felt to hold the door to Dino's open for Naomi. She was wearing another dress, but instead of the long, flowing silhouette of her summer sundresses, this one was fitted with long sleeves. I knew from getting dressed next to her this morning that she was also wearing one of the pairs of underwear I'd bought her.

The fact that it was the last time that I'd have the

right to watch her get dressed had nearly brought me to my knees that morning.

So had breakfast with her entire fucking family.

One big happy family gathered around the table. Even desk-duty Nash had joined the fun. Hell, Stef had FaceTimed in from Paris just to judge the bacon Naomi made.

Amanda was thrilled to have everyone under the same roof and had whipped up a fancy-ass breakfast. Lou, who'd spent most of their time in town hating my guts, now acted like I was a Stef-level addition to the family.

He'd change his tune soon enough, I guessed.

This *one big happy family* deal wasn't real, and the sooner everyone stopped pretending it was, the better.

I'd walked Waylay to the bus stop while Naomi got ready for work. I didn't feel comfortable letting either one of them out of my sight while there was the possibility that whoever had broken in was still in town. Still looking to do more damage.

Which made what I was about to do even more of a problem.

When Naomi started for a table near the window, I steered her to a booth in the back. Public, but not too public.

"So I made a list for Nash," she said, pulling a piece of paper out of her purse and smoothing it out on the table. Blissfully unaware of what I was about to do.

My brother's name caught me off guard. "A list of what?" I demanded.

"Of the dates that I think Tina could have broken into the cottage and of any suspicious people I could remember. There's not much there, and I don't know how it's going to help. But he said it would help if I could at least narrow down the timing of the earlier break-in," she said, picking up a menu.

"I'll pass it on to him," I said, wishing for a stiff drink.

"Is everything okay?" she asked, cocking her head to study me. "You look tired."

"Daze, we gotta talk." The words were choking me. My skin felt too tight. Everything felt wrong.

"Since when do you feel like stringing words together?" she teased.

She trusted me. The thought made me feel like dog shit. Here she was, thinking her boyfriend was treating her to lunch in the middle of the day. But I'd warned her, hadn't I? I'd told her not to let herself get too close to me.

"Things have gotten . . . complicated," I said.

"Look, I know you're worried about the break-in," Naomi said. "But I think when the new security system goes in, it will be a load off our minds. Warner is back home, so if it was him throwing some destructive temper tantrum, he's too far away to do it again. And if it was Tina, the odds are she either found what she was looking for or realized I don't have it. You don't need to worry about me and Way."

I didn't respond. I couldn't. I just needed to get the words out.

She reached across the table and squeezed my wrist. "By the way, I just want you to know how grateful I am that you're here. And you're helping. It makes me feel like I'm not alone. Like maybe for the first time ever, I don't have to be completely responsible for every single thing. Thank you for that, Knox."

I closed my eyes and tried not to throw up.

"Look, like I said." I had to grit my teeth to get through it. "Things are complicated, and part of that's on me."

She looked up and frowned. "Are you okay? You look tired."

I was fucking exhausted. And full of self-loathing.

"I'm fine," I insisted. "But I think it's time to move on."

Got yourself a girl? The words echoed in my mind.

Her hand stilled on my arm. "Move on?"

"I've had a good time. I hope you have too. But we need to stop this thing before one of us gets too attached."

She stared at me, those hazel eyes stunned and unblinking.

Fuck.

"You mean me," she said, her voice barely above a whisper.

"I mean what we're doing is . . ." *Scaring the*

shit out of me. "This thing between us has run its course." *Because I can't trust myself with you,* I thought.

"You brought me here to a public place to break up with me? Unbelievable."

Her hand was gone now, and I knew I'd never feel it again. I didn't know what had the power to break me faster, knowing that or knowing what would happen if I didn't end this now.

"Look, Naomi, we both knew the score when we started this. I just think before one of us gets in over their head, we need to pull back."

"I'm such an idiot," she whispered, bringing her fingertips to her temples.

"I know you've got the custody hearing coming up next month, and I'm willing to still keep up the appearance that we're together if you think it'll help you in court. And I'm still gonna be keeping an eye on you and Way until we know for sure who busted into your place."

"How magnanimous of you," she said, her tone icy.

I could handle angry. Hell, I could eat angry for breakfast every day. It was the tears, the hurt, the *pain* I couldn't deal with.

"I said from the beginning I don't do strings." I'd warned her. I'd tried to do the right thing. Yet here she was looking at me like I'd deliberately wounded her.

And then suddenly the look was gone. The softness vanished from her face, the fire from her eyes.

"I understand," she said. "I'm a lot. Waylay's a lot. This whole thing is a lot. Even on my best day, I'm too much and yet not enough." Her laugh was humorless.

"Don't, Daisy," I ordered before I could help myself.

She took a slow, deep breath, then gave me a perfunctory smile that felt like a fucking cleaver to the heart. "I believe that's the last time you get to tell me what to do and call me Daisy."

I felt something rising inside me that had nothing to do with the relief I'd expected. No. This thing growing inside me felt like the white-hot edges of panic. "Don't be like that."

She slid out of the booth and stood up. "You didn't have to do it this way. Out in public so I wouldn't make some kind of scene. I'm a big girl, Knox. And someday, I'm going to find the kind of man who wants an uppity, needy pain in the ass. One who wants to wade into my mess and stay for the duration. Obviously, you're not him. At least you told me that from the start."

I stood too, feeling like I'd somehow lost control of the situation. "I didn't say that."

"Those are your words, and you're right. I should have listened the first time you said them."

She grabbed her purse and snatched the paper off the table in front of me.

"Thank you for your offer of pretending to be interested in me, but I think I'll pass." She wouldn't look me in the eye.

"Nothing needs to change, Naomi. You can still work at the bar. You and Liza J still have an arrangement. Everything else can stay the same."

"I have to go," she said, starting for the door.

I grabbed her arm and pulled her into me. It had felt so natural, and it had the other benefit of forcing her to look at me. The knot in my gut loosened temporarily when her gaze met mine.

"Here," I said, yanking the envelope out of my back pocket and handing it over.

"What's this? A list of reasons I wasn't good enough?"

"It's cash," I said.

She recoiled like I'd told her it was an envelope of spiders.

"Take it. It'll help you and Way out."

She slapped the envelope against my chest. "I don't want your money. I don't want anything from you now. But especially not your money."

With that, she tried to yank free. It was a reflex that had me tightening my grip.

"Take. Your. Hands. Off. Me, Knox," Naomi said softly.

It wasn't fire in her eyes now. It was ice.

"Naomi, it doesn't have to be this way."

"Goodbye, Knox."

She slipped out of my grip, leaving me staring after her like an idiot.

39

Breaking Up, Down, and Through

Naomi

Too complicated. Too much. Too needy. Not worth it.

The thoughts swirled in my head on a vicious merry-go-round as I marched down the sidewalk, Knockemout blurring around me through unshed tears.

I'd made a life here. I'd built up a fantasy in my mind. Taken afternoon coffees and whispered dirty talk to mean something else entirely. He didn't want me. He never had.

Worse, he hadn't wanted Waylay either. I'd taken my young, impressionable charge and dragged her into my relationship with a man who was never going to be there for her in the long term.

I'd seen it in his eyes. The pity. He felt sorry for me. *Poor, stupid Naomi falling for the bad boy who'd made no promises.*

And the money. The *gall* of the man thinking he could break my heart and then fork over cash like I was a prostitute and like it would somehow make everything all right. It added a new layer to the humiliation.

I was going to go to Liza J's, fake a migraine,

488

and spend the rest of the day in bed. Then I was going to have an overdue chat with myself about picking the wrong fucking guy. Again.

And when I was done lecturing myself, I was going to make sure that Waylay never let herself get stuck in positions like this.

Oh God. I lived in the small town of freaking small towns. I'd see him around. Everywhere. At the coffee shop. At work. This was *his* town. Not mine.

Did I even belong here?

"Hey, Naomi!" Bud Nickelbee called as he ducked out of the hardware store. "Just wanted to let you know I popped out this morning and fixed your front door."

I stopped in my tracks. "You did?"

He bobbed his head. "Heard about the trouble and didn't want you to have to worry about getting the repairs done."

I hugged him hard. "You have no idea how much that means to me. Thank you, Bud."

He shrugged against me, then awkwardly patted my back. "Just figured you had enough crap to deal with and thought you could use a break."

"You're a good man, Bud."

"Okaaaaaay," he said. "You all right? You need me to call someone? I can have Knox come get you."

I shook my head rapidly from side to side until the hardware store and its owner blurred before me. "No!" I barked. "I mean, thanks but no."

The door to Dino's opened, and my stomach dropped into my toes when Knox stepped outside onto the sidewalk.

I turned away, praying for invisibility.

"Naomi," he called.

I started walking in the opposite direction.

"Naomi, come on. Stop," Knox said.

But with just a few words, he'd permanently lost the privilege of me listening to him when he told me what to do.

"Now, Knox. I don't think the lady wants to talk to you right now," I heard Bud advise.

"Step aside, Bud," I heard Knox growl.

I was an idiot. But at least I was a fast-moving idiot.

I walked briskly down the block, determined to leave Knox in my rearview mirror just like my ex-fiancé.

A man doesn't go all in with a woman, it's for a reason.

Maybe he's looking for something better.

My chest physically ached as Knox's words about Warner echoed in my head.

Was there someone out there who would find me to be enough? Not too much or too little, but the person they'd been waiting for their whole life.

Tears burned my eyes as I turned the corner at a jog.

I blamed them for not seeing the woman who stepped out of the storefront.

"I'm so sorry," I said a split second after barreling into her.

"Ms. Witt."

Oh dear God, no.

Yolanda Suarez, stern caseworker who had never once seen me at my best, looked nonplussed at the full-body contact.

I opened my mouth, but no sound came out.

"Are you all right?" she asked.

The lie was on the tip of my tongue. So familiar it almost felt true. But it wasn't. Sometimes the truth was bigger than any intention.

"No, I'm not."

Ten minutes later, I stared down at a heart drawn in the foam of the latte in front of me.

"So that's everything. I pretended to be in a relationship with a man who told me not to fall in love with him, and then I did. My ex-fiancé showed up at my job and caused a scene. Someone broke into our house, and no one is sure if it was him, Tina, or a random criminal. Oh, and Waylay tried to get revenge on a mean teacher with field mice."

Across from me, Mrs. Suarez picked up her green tea and sipped. She set the mug down. "Well then."

"Brought you some cookies," Justice said, looking mournful. He slid a plate onto the table near my elbow.

"Were these hearts?" I asked, holding up what was clearly one half of a pink frosted heart.

He winced. "I broke 'em in half. Was hoping you wouldn't notice."

"Thank you, Justice. That's so sweet of you," I said. Before leaving, he squeezed my shoulder, and I had to bite the inside of my cheek to keep from crying.

"Basically what I'm saying is I'm a big enough mess that I can't hide it, and you deserve to know the truth. But I promise you—even though my life doesn't look like it—I am extremely organized and resourceful, and I will do whatever it takes to keep Waylay safe."

"Naomi," she said, "Waylay is lucky to have you as a guardian, and any court in the state is going to come to the same conclusion. Her attendance at school is improved. Her grades are up. She has real friends. You're making a positive impact on that little girl's life."

For once in my life, I didn't want a gold star. I wanted someone to see me. Really see me for the hot mess I was. "What about all the things I'm doing wrong?"

I thought I detected a hint of pity in Mrs. Suarez's smile. "That's parenting. We're all doing our best. We're exhausted, confused, and feeling like we're constantly being judged by everyone else who looks like they've got it all figured out. But no one does. We're all just making it up as we go."

"Really?" I whispered.

She leaned forward. "Last night, I grounded my twelve-year-old for three days because he was on my last nerve before he told me that he liked his friend Evan's mom's meatballs better than mine." She took another sip of tea. "And today I'll apologize and unground him if he cleaned his room. Even though Evan's mom gets her meatballs from the freezer section of Grover's Groceries."

I managed a tremulous smile. "It's just life is so much harder than I thought it would be," I confessed. "I thought if I had a plan and followed the rules, it would be easy."

"Can I give you some advice?" she asked.

"Please do."

"At some point, you have got to stop worrying so much about what everyone else needs and start thinking about what you need."

I blinked. "I would think selflessness was a good quality in a guardian," I said with a defensive sniff.

"So is setting an example for your niece about how she doesn't need to turn herself inside out to be loved. How she doesn't need to set herself on fire to keep someone else warm. Demanding to have your own needs met isn't problematic—it's heroic, and kids are watching. They're always watching. If you set an example that tells her the only way she's worthy of love is by giving everyone everything, she'll internalize that message."

I dropped my forehead to the table with a groan.

"There's a difference between taking care of someone because you love them and taking care of someone because you want them to love you," she continued.

There was a *big* difference. One of them was genuine and giving, and the other was manipulative and controlling.

"You're going to be fine, Naomi," Mrs. Suarez assured me. "You've got a big heart, and sooner or later, once all this drama is over, someone is going to look at you and recognize it. And they're going to want to take care of you for a change."

Yeah, right.

I was realizing that the only person I could count on in this life was me. And Stef, of course. But him being gay definitely put a damper on our romance.

"About Knox," she said.

I picked my head up off the table. Just hearing his name was a jagged splinter in my heart.

"What about him?"

"I don't know another woman in town who wouldn't have fallen under Knox Morgan's spell given the time and attention he gave you. I'll also say this—I've never seen him look at anyone the way he looks at you. If he was faking those feelings, someone needs to get that man an Academy Award. I've known him for a good, long time, and I've never known him to do anything he didn't want to do, especially when it comes to women. If he willingly agreed to the guise of a relationship, he wanted it."

"It was his idea," I whispered. A spark of hope lit inside me. One I immediately extinguished.

A man doesn't go all in with a woman, it's for a reason.

"He had a shit time with his mom's death and everything that came after," she continued. "He didn't have the happily-ever-after example you grew up with. Sometimes when you don't know what's possible, you can't hope for it yourself."

"Mrs. Suarez."

"I think at this point you can call me Yolanda."

"Yolanda, we're practically the same age. How do you have all this wisdom?"

"I've been married twice and have four kids. My parents have been married for fifty years. My husband's parents have been divorced and remarried so many times neither of us can keep count. If there's one thing I understand, it's love and how damn messy it can be."

"Hi, sweetie. How was lunch?" My mom was dressed in a dirt-streaked T-shirt and sun hat. She had a glass of iced tea in one hand and a gardening glove on the other.

"Hi, Mom," I said, trying to keep my eyes averted as I headed for the front porch. Amanda Witt had a keen sense of when something was wrong with someone, and this was not a conversation I felt like having. "Where's Way?"

"Your father took her to the mall. What's wrong? What happened? Did someone choke on a breadstick at lunch?"

I shook my head, not trusting my voice.

"Did something happen with Knox?" she asked, softer now.

I tried to swallow around the lump in my throat, but I was choking on unshed tears.

"Okay. Let's go sit down," she said, guiding me down the hall to the bedroom she was sharing with my father.

It was a bright, pretty room done in creams and grays. There was a large four-poster bed and windows that overlooked the backyard and creek. A vase of fresh flowers sat on a table tucked between two armchairs that occupied the space in front of the windows.

"I'll just spread this out," Mom said, draping my father's ratty bathrobe over one of the armchairs. She hated the robe and had tried six ways to Sunday over the years to get rid of it. But Dad always found a way to resurrect it. She plopped down on the robe-covered chair and patted the one next to her. "Sit. Talk."

I shook my head even as I sat. "Mom, I'm really not in the mood to talk right now."

"Well, tough shit, sweetie."

"Mom!"

She shrugged. "I've let you get away with this 'don't be a burden' routine for far too long. It was easier for me to rely on you to always behave. To always be the easy daughter. And that's not fair to you."

"What are you saying?"

"I'm saying, dear, sweet, heart-of-gold daughter of mine, stop trying to be so damn perfect."

I wasn't sure if I was prepared to have this

conversation any more than the Knox conversation.

"You've lived your whole life trying to make up for your sister. Trying to never burden anyone, never ask for anything you needed, never disappoint."

"I feel like that's something a parent wouldn't want to complain about," I said defensively.

"Naomi, I never wanted you to be perfect. I just wanted you to be happy."

"I'm . . . happy," I lied.

"Your father and I did everything we could to help Tina be happy and healthy. But it wasn't her path. And it took years, but we finally understood that it wasn't our path to turn her into someone she's not. We did our best with your sister. But Tina's choices are not a measure of our worth. It's a tough lesson, but we got it. Now it's your turn. You can't live your entire life trying to make up for your sister's mistakes."

"I wouldn't say that's how I've lived my *entire* life," I hedged.

Mom reached over and brushed her hand over my cheek. I felt the grit of dirt transfer to my skin. "Whoops! Sorry about that." She licked her thumb and leaned in for the Mom polish.

"I'm too old for this," I complained, backing away.

"Listen, sweetie. You're allowed to have needs. You're allowed to make mistakes. You're allowed to make decisions your father or I might not agree with. It's your life. You're a beautiful, big-hearted, intelligent woman who needs to start figuring out what she wants."

What did I want?

Right now, I just wanted to crawl in bed and pull the covers over my head for a week. But I couldn't. I had responsibilities. And one of those responsibilities had conned my father into taking her to the mall.

"Do you even want to be a guardian?" Mom asked.

I stilled at the question.

"I can't imagine that taking in a soon-to-be twelve-year-old fit neatly into your life plan."

"Mom, I couldn't just let her end up with strangers."

"What about your father and me? You didn't think we'd be thrilled to make room in our lives for a granddaughter?"

"You shouldn't have to raise your daughter's daughter. It's not fair. Dad's retired. You'll be there soon. That cruise was the first big trip you two have ever taken together."

"Do you want to be her guardian?" Mom repeated, ignoring my excellent points.

Did I want this? Did I want to be a surrogate mother to Waylay?

I felt an echo of that warm glow in my chest. It pushed back against the cold that had settled there.

"Yeah," I said, feeling my mouth do the impossible and curve into a small smile. It was the truth. I wanted this more than I'd ever wanted anything on my to-do list. More than any goal I was single-mindedly marching toward. "I really do. I love her. I love being around her. I love when she comes home from school bursting with news to tell me. I love watching her grow into this smart, strong, confident kid who, every once in a while, lets her guard down and lets me in."

"I know how that feels," Mom said gently. "I wish it would happen more often."

Ouch. Direct hit.

"Knox and I broke up," I said in a rush. "We were never really together. We were just having really, really great sex. But I accidentally fell in love with him, which he warned me not to do. And now he thinks I'm too complicated and not worth the effort."

Mom looked at her iced tea, then back at me. "I think we're gonna need a stronger drink."

Hours later, I tiptoed out onto the deck with my phone in hand. The phone *he'd* bought me. Which meant it needed to be smashed into a million pieces at my earliest convenience.

The rest of the family was cleaning up from dinner. A dinner that Knox was conspicuously absent from. My mom had distracted Waylay from his absence by demanding an after-dinner fashion show of the new winter coat and sweaters my pushover father had bought her.

I had a headache from fake smiling.

I dialed the number before I could chicken out.

"Witty! What's up? Did they find the bastard who broke in?"

I'd texted him and Sloane about the break-in. But this deserved a phone call.

"Stef." My voice broke on his name.

"Shit. What happened? Are you okay? Is Waylay okay?"

I shook my head, trying to dislodge the lump in my throat. Then I remembered what Knox had said.

"Do not shed one more tear over some asshole who never deserved you in the first place."

I cleared my throat. "Knox ended things."

"That gorgeous piece of garbage. Fake ended things or for real ended things?"

"Real ended things. I'm too complicated."

"What the hell does he want? A simpleton? Simpletons are terrible in bed, and they're worse at blow jobs."

I managed a pathetic chuckle.

"Listen to me, Naomi. If that man isn't smart enough to recognize how amazingly intelligent and beautiful and kind and caring and wickedly awesome at board games you are, it's his loss. Which makes him the simpleton. I forbid you to spend one second of your time overthinking this and coming to the false conclusion you're the one with the problem."

Well, there went my evening plans.

"I can't believe I fell for him, Stef. What was I thinking?"

"You were thinking, 'here's a gorgeous man who's great in bed who walks my niece to the bus stop, breaks my ex's nose, and brings me midafternoon coffee so I don't get cranky.' All the signs were there because he put them there. If you ask me—which I know you didn't—I'm betting he wasn't faking it. He was feeling it, and it scared the shit out of him. The beautiful, tattooed piece of chickenshit."

"I really need to stop texting you about everything that happens in my day," I decided. "It's codependent."

"I'll bring it up with our couples therapist," Stef quipped. "Listen. I'll be back in Knockemout in a few days. What do you want to do until then? Get out of Dodge? Buy a new 'fuck you' wardrobe?"

He meant it. If I said I felt like flying to Rome and spending a ridiculous amount of money on shoes, he would book the plane tickets. If I told him I wanted to get revenge on Knox by filling his house with Styrofoam peanuts and cat litter, Stef would show up at my house with a U-Haul packed with retribution supplies.

Maybe I didn't need a life partner. Maybe I already had one.

"I think I want to pretend he doesn't exist long enough that I forget he does," I decided.

I wanted to make him not matter. I wanted to not feel a damn thing when he walked into a room. I wanted to forget I'd ever fallen for him in the first place.

"That's annoyingly mature of you," Stef observed.

"But I want him to suffer while I forget," I added.

"That's my girl," he said. "So it's a straight-forward ice queen with a side of swan."

I managed a watery smile despite the gaping hole in my chest cavity. "That sounds about right."

"Keep an eye on your mailbox for an order from Sephora," Stef said.

No amount of expensive cosmetics would make me feel better. But I also knew that this was Stef showing me how much he loved me, and I could let him.

"Thanks, Stef," I whispered.

"Hey. Keep your chin up, Witty. You've got a kid to set an example for. Resilience isn't a bad trait to pass on. Get out there and have some fun. Even if it doesn't feel fun right away, just fake it till you make it."

I had a feeling I'd be faking it for a very long time.

Knox Morgan wasn't the kind of man you got over. Ever.

40

The Consequences of Being an Idiot

Knox

S top looking at me like that," I ordered.

Waylon huffed out a sigh that ruffled his jowls. He looked more mournful than usual, which was saying something for a basset hound. He was also sitting in my lap, with his paws on my chest, creepily staring at me.

Apparently my dog wasn't a fan of the fact that we were back at the cabin full-time.

He didn't see it as sparing Naomi from seeing me at the dinner table.

He didn't care that it was the right fucking thing to do.

It *was* the right thing to do, I reminded myself.

No matter how hurt she'd looked.

"Fuck," I muttered to myself, swiping a hand over my beard.

Dragging it out would have only made things more complicated, hurt more feelings.

She'd been so relaxed and happy, sitting across from me at Dino's. So damn gorgeous I couldn't look directly at her or look away. Then the light had gone right out of her.

I'd done that. I'd extinguished it.

But it was the right fucking thing.

I'd feel better soon. I always did. The relief from ending a complication would come, and I wouldn't feel so . . . unsettled.

With nothing better to do, I popped the top on my third beer.

It was Monday. I'd put in a full afternoon at Whiskey Clipper, moving into my office when clients and staff started shooting dirty looks at me. Word spread fast in Knockemout. I'd planned on working tonight at the bar, but when I'd walked in the door at Honky Tonk, Max and Silver had booed me. Then Fi flipped me the bird and told me to come back when I learned how to be less of an asshole.

This was why I didn't mess around with Knockemout women. They were rattlesnake mean when riled.

So here I was. Home for the night. Enjoying my solitude.

It would all blow over soon. I'd stop feeling like shit. Naomi would get over it. And everyone would move the fuck on.

Waylon let out another grumble and shot a pointed, droopy look at his empty food dish.

"Fine."

He jumped down, and I fed him, then returned to the living room, where I flopped down on the couch and reached for the remote.

Instead, my fingers found the picture frame. Since I had nothing better to do, I picked it up and studied it. My parents had been happy. They'd built a life for me and Nash. A good one.

Until it had all crumbled because the foundation was unstable.

I ran a finger over my mom's smiling face in the photo and wondered for just a moment what she'd think of Naomi and Waylay.

What she'd think of me.

After a long pull from the bottle, I shifted my attention to my father's face. He wasn't looking at the camera, at whoever had taken the picture. His attention was on my mom. She'd been the light and the glue. Everything that had made our family strong and happy. And when she'd gone, we'd collapsed in on ourselves.

I put the photo down, angling it away so I wouldn't have to look into the past anymore.

The past and the future were two places I had no business being. The only thing that mattered was right now. And right now . . . well, I still felt like shit.

Ready to numb out for a night, I reached for the remote again when a loud knock sent Waylon galloping to the front door, ears flapping.

I followed at a more dignified pace.

Crisp, September evening air wafted in when I opened the door.

Nash stood on the doorstep, jaw clenched, hands fisted at his side.

"You're lucky I gotta do this right-handed."

"Do wha—"

I didn't get a chance to finish the question before my brother's fist connected with my face. Like any good sucker punch, it rang my bell and knocked me back a full step.

"Ow! Fuck! What the hell, Nash?"

He pushed past me and stomped inside. "What did I tell you?" he snarled over his shoulder. He opened my fridge and helped himself to a beer.

"Jesus. Tell me about what?" I asked, working my jaw back and forth.

"Naomi," Lucian said.

"Christ, Lucy. Where did you come from?"

"I drove." He clapped me on the shoulder and followed Nash into the kitchen. "Feel better?" he asked my brother.

Nash handed him a beer and shrugged. "Not really. He's got a hard face to go with that thick head."

"What are you two assholes doing here?" I demanded, swiping Lucian's beer and holding it to my jaw.

Nash handed him a fresh one.

"Naomi, of course," Lucian said, accepting the beer and squatting down to pet Waylon.

"For fuck's sake. That shit is none of your business."

"Maybe not. But you are," Lucian said.

"I told you not to fuck it up," Nash said.

"This is bullshit. You can't just come into my house, punch me in the face, play with my dog, and drink my beer."

"We can when you're being a stupid, stubborn son of a bitch," my brother snapped.

"No. Do not sit. Don't make yourselves comfortable. I finally have a night to myself and I'm not wasting it with you two."

Lucian took his beer and wandered into the living room. He sank into one of the armchairs and put his feet up on the coffee table, looking content enough to stay there for the rest of the night.

"Sometimes I really hate you assholes," I complained.

"Feeling's mutual," Nash growled. But his hand was gentle when he leaned over to give Waylon the loving he demanded. The dog's tail blurred into happiness.

"You don't hate us," Lucian declared mildly. "You hate yourself."

"Fuck off. Why would I hate myself?" I needed to move. I needed to buy a thousand acres and build a damn cabin in the damn middle and never tell a damn soul where I lived.

"Because you just told the best thing that ever happened to you to take a damn hike," Nash said.

"A woman is never going to be the best thing that happens to me," I insisted. The words tasted suspiciously like a lie.

"You are the stupidest son of a bitch in the state," my brother said wearily.

"He's not wrong," Lucian agreed.

"Why in the hell do you two have your panties

507

in a twist over who I do or don't date? It was never real anyway."

"You're making a huge fucking mistake," Nash insisted.

"What do you care? Now you get your shot at her." The thought of it, just the split second imagining him with Naomi, nearly brought me to my knees.

My brother set down his beer. "Yeah, I'm definitely hitting him again."

Lucian dropped his head back against the cushion. "I said I'd give you one. You've had it. Find a new way to get through his thick skull."

"Fine. Let's try something new. The truth."

"How novel," Lucian said.

I wasn't going to get rid of either of them until they'd said their piece. "Say what you need to say, then get the hell out."

"This happens every time he sees him," Nash complained to Lucian.

Lucian nodded. "I am aware."

I didn't like that my brother and my best friend seemed to have a history of making up and discussing my issues.

"Sees who?"

Nash leveled me with a look.

I rolled my eyes. "Oh, come the fuck on. I broke it off with Naomi because she was gonna get herself hurt. I did the right thing, and it had nothing to do with anyone else. So stop trying to fucking analyze me."

"So it's just a coincidence that you see him, and the very next day, you decide things are getting too serious?"

"He has nothing to do with anything I do," I insisted.

"How much did you give him?" Nash asked.

"What are you talking about?"

"How much cash did you give him? That's what you do. You try to solve problems with money. Try to buy your way out of feeling pain. But you can't. You can't buy Dad into sobriety. You couldn't buy me into a life you were comfortable with. And you sure as fuck can't make yourself feel better about breaking Naomi's heart by handing her a wad of cash."

Lucian's gaze cut to me. "Tell me you didn't."

I slammed my bottle down on the counter, sending a geyser of beer everywhere. "I *warned* her. I *told* her not to get attached. She knew there was no chance. It's not my fault she's this romantic who thought I could change. I *can't* change. I don't *want* to change. And why the fuck am I even having this conversation with you? I didn't do anything wrong. I told her not to fall."

"Actions speak louder than words, dipshit." Nash threw up his good hand. "Lucy, you take this."

Lucian leaned forward in his chair, elbows resting on his knees.

"I believe what your brother is trying to tell you is that while you said you couldn't and wouldn't care, your actions told her something else."

"We had sex," I said flatly. *Great sex. Mind-blowing sex.*

Lucian shook his head. "You showed up for her time and time again. You gave her a place to live, a job. You went to her niece's school. You bashed in her ex's face."

"Bought her a cell phone. Helped her get a car," Nash added.

"You looked at her like she was the only woman you saw. You made her believe," Lucian continued. Waylon trotted over to him and hefted his bulk into my friend's lap.

"And then you tried to buy her off," Nash said.

I closed my eyes. "I didn't try to buy her off. I wanted to make sure she was taken care of."

And she'd thrown it back in my face.

"And what part of that sentiment says 'I don't care about you'?" Lucian asked.

"You can't use cash as a replacement for actually showing up for someone."

Nash's voice was miserable enough that I opened my eyes and looked at him. Really looked at him.

Is that what he thought I'd done when I'd offered him the lottery money? When I'd all but shoved it down his throat?

His career in law enforcement had been a sticking point for us. But rather than sit down and talk to him about it, I'd tried to pull his strings with the promise of a pile of cash. Enough that he'd never have to worry or work again. I saw it as taking care.

"You should have kept the money. Maybe then you wouldn't have ended up bleeding in a fucking ditch," I said evenly.

Nash shook his head. "You still don't get it, do you, Knox?"

"Get what? That you're more stubborn than I am? That if you'd listened to me, that carjacking coward wouldn't have almost ended your life? By the way, Lucy, you dig up anything yet?"

"Working on it," Lucian said.

Nash ignored the sidebar. "You don't get that I'd still put on that uniform. Even if I knew I was going to take another hit tomorrow. I'd still walk into that building your money paid for even if I knew it was my last day on earth. Because that's what you fucking do when you love something. You show up. Even if you're pissing your pants scared. And if you two don't stay the fuck out of police business, or if you even think about going vigilante, I will throw both your asses in a cell."

"Agree to disagree," Lucian said. Waylon's tail thumped on the arm of the chair.

"You about done?" I asked, suddenly too tired to fight.

"About. You wanna do the right thing, you need to tell Naomi the real reason you let her go."

"Oh? And what's the real reason?" I asked wearily.

"That you're scared down to your fucking bones that you'll fall hard and end up like Dad. Like Liza J. That you won't be able to hold up under the bad."

His words landed like arrows zeroing in on a bull's-eye I didn't know I was wearing.

"It's funny. I used to think my big brother was the smartest guy on the planet. Now, I realize he's just a delusional fool." He started for the door, pausing when he got to it. "You could have been happy, man. Not just safe. Happy. Like we used to be."

Lucian scooped Waylon onto the floor and followed him out the door.

When they'd gone, taking my beer and their righteous frustrations with them, I sat in the dark and stared at the blank TV, doing my best not to think about what they'd said.

I went so far as to start looking for large parcels of land far the fuck away from Knockemout.

My phone signaled a text.

Stef: Seriously? I warned you, man. You couldn't have just not been a selfish dick?

I tossed my phone aside and closed my eyes. Could it possibly be true that my best efforts to take care of the people I cared about amounted to me pushing a mountain of money between us? Money gave them security, and it protected me.

The pounding on my door jolted Waylon awake.

He gave a short, sharp bark, then decided the chair was more comfortable and immediately went back to sleep.

"Go the fuck away," I called.

"Open the damn door, Morgan."

It wasn't Nash or Lucian back for round two. It was worse.

I opened the door to find Naomi's dad standing there in pajama pants and a sweatshirt. Lou looked pissed. But the bourbon I'd switched to after my last uninvited guests drank all my beer numbed me.

"If you came here to punch me in the face, someone already beat you to it."

"Good. I hope it was Naomi," Lou said, pushing his way inside.

I really needed that thousand acres.

"She's too classy for that."

Lou stopped in the foyer and turned to face me. "She is. She's also too hurt to see the truth."

"Why is everyone so obsessed with 'the truth'?" I asked, using air quotes. "Why can't people just mind their own damn business and stick to their own truths?"

"Because it's easier to see someone else's. And more fun to kick someone else's ass when they've got their head shoved up it."

"I thought you, of all people, would be doing a victory dance over this. You never liked me with her."

"I never *trusted* you with her. There's a difference."

"And I suppose you came here to educate me."

"I suppose I did. Someone's got to."

I'd add a moat around my bunker as a last line of defense.

"I'm forty-fucking-three years old, Lou. I don't need a father-son moment."

"Tough shit. Because that's what you're gonna get. I'm sorry that you suffered so much loss so early in life. I'm sorry that your mom died and your dad abandoned you. Liza's told us bits and pieces. I'm sorry you lost your grandfather just a few years later. It's not fair. And I can't blame you for wanting to hide from all that pain."

"I'm not hiding. I'm a goddamn open book. I told your daughter what she could expect from me. It's not my fault she got her hopes up."

"That would be true if it weren't for one thing."

I scrubbed my hand over my face. "If I let you tell me the one thing, will you leave?"

"You didn't do it because you didn't care. You did it because you cared too damn much, and it scared you."

I snorted into my glass, trying my best to ignore the tightening in my chest.

"Son, you fucked up big-time," he continued. "I may be Naomi's father, and that might bias me, but I know my daughter is one of a kind. A once-in-a-lifetime woman. Just like her mom. And I don't like what it says about how you feel about yourself that you don't think you deserve her."

I put my glass down. He hadn't said that I didn't deserve her. He'd said I thought I didn't deserve her.

"Do you deserve Amanda?" I asked.

"Hell no! Still don't. But I've spent every day of my life since I met her trying to be the kind of man who does. She made me a better man. She gave me the kind of life I never dreamed I'd have. And yeah, we've had our rough times. Most of them revolving around Tina. But fact is, I've never once regretted sticking."

I remained stalwartly silent, wishing I could be anywhere else but here.

"Sooner or later, you have to accept that you're not responsible for other people's choices. Worse, sometimes you can't fix what's wrong with them."

He looked me dead in the eye when he said it.

"I'm not responsible for my daughter's choices or the outcomes of those choices. You're not responsible for your father's. But you are responsible for the choices you make. And that includes walking away from the best thing that will ever happen to you."

"Look, Lou, this has been a nice chat and all—"

He clapped me on the shoulder. His grip was solid, firm. "You couldn't save your mom from an accident any more than you could save your dad from addiction. Now you worry you won't be able to save anyone else. Or stand losing someone else."

My throat was tight, and it burned.

Lou's grip tightened. "Somewhere deep down is a man stronger than your father ever was. I see it. Your grandmother sees it. My daughter sees it. Maybe it's time you take a look in the mirror."

41

The New Naomi

Naomi

Knox: Look. I know I could have handled things differently. But trust me. It's better this way. If you or Waylay need anything, I want to know.

Knox: Liza J probably already told you, but the security company is installing the alarm at the cottage Saturday. What time is Waylay's soccer game?

Knox: Are you okay?

Knox: Just because we're not together doesn't mean I don't still want you and Waylay to be safe.

Knox: You can't avoid me forever.

Knox: Can't we be fucking adults about this? It's a small fucking town. We're gonna run into each other sooner or later.

I pried open one bleary eye and peered at my phone screen.

Satisfied it wasn't a certain dead-to-me Morgan brother, I swiped to answer. "What?" I croaked.

"Wakey wakey, Witty," came Stef's cheery voice from half a world away.

I gave a muffled groan in response and rolled over.

I had the covers pulled over my head in a juvenile attempt to block out the entire world. Unfortunately, it had the unintended consequence of also surrounding me with the scent of *him*. Sleeping in a bed we'd shared while I'd fallen for the farce was not conducive to anything but a downward spiral.

If I was going to survive this, I needed to burn these sheets and buy Liza J a new set.

"Judging from your effusive greeting, I'm guessing you haven't yet dragged your definitely-getting-over-him-today ass out of bed yet," Stef surmised.

I grunted.

"You're lucky I'm not on the same continent as you right now because your time is up," he chirped.

"What time?"

"Your 'woe is me, I miss my stupid hot fake boyfriend' time. It's been five days. The acceptable mourning period is over. You are officially being reborn as New Naomi."

Being reborn sounded like a lot of work.

"Can't I just wither away as Old Naomi?" Old Naomi had spent the last few days putting on a fake smile for Waylay and library patrons, then spending a few hours a day half-heartedly trying to clean up the wreckage in the cottage. All while avoiding thinking about Knox.

I was exhausted.

"Not an option. It is six thirty a.m. your time. Your day starts now."

"Why are you so mean?" I groaned.

"I'm your mean fairy godfather. You have a transformation to begin, my little caterpillar."

"I don't want to be a butterfly. I want to smother in my cocoon."

"Tough shit. If you don't get out of bed in the next ten seconds, I'm bringing in the big guns."

"I'm out," I lied.

He said something derisive in French. "In case you need a translator, that was French for bullshit. Now, I want you to get your lying ass out of bed and go take a shower because Liza reports that your hair is greasier than the deep fryer at a sports bar on wing night. Then I want you to open that Sephora order I sent you and snap the fuck out of this funk."

"I like funks."

"You do not. You like game plans and to-do lists. I'm giving you both."

"Having friends who know you really well is overrated," I complained to my pillow.

"Okay. Fine. But I want it on record that you made me do this."

"Do what?"

"You have an eleven-year-old girl looking up to you. Do you really want to teach her that when a boy hurts your feelings, you give up on life?"

I sat up. "I hate you."

"No, you don't."

"Why can't I wallow?"

It was more than hurt feelings, and he knew it.

Knox had warned me. He'd told me not to fall for him, not to mistake his actions for real feelings. And I'd *still* fallen for him. That made me an idiot. At least with Warner, he'd tried to hide his true self from me.

It was an excuse, not a great one, but an excuse all the same.

But there was no such excuse with Knox.

I loved him. For real loved him. Loved him enough that I wasn't sure I could survive the anguish of being tossed aside.

"Because all that 'I'm such an idiot' and 'how could I fall for him' negative self-talk is a waste of time and energy. It's also setting a shitty example for Waylay, who's had enough shitty examples to last a lifetime. Get your ass out of bed, take a shower, and get ready to show Waylay how to burn an asshole's life to the ground."

My feet hit the floor. "You're really good at this pep talk thing."

"You deserve better, Witty. I know somewhere deep down you don't think so. But you deserve a man who's going to put you first."

"I love you."

"Love you too, babe. I gotta go. But I want a post-shower, makeover selfie. And I'm emailing you your game plan for the day."

From: Stef
To: Naomi
Subject: New Naomi Day One

1. Get your ass out of bed.
2. Shower.
3. Makeup.
4. Hair.
5. Wardrobe. (I know how much you like checking things off your list.)
6. Breakfast of champions.
7. Waylay's soccer practice. Smile. Light up the damn field with your gracious beauty.
8. Host a spontaneous social gathering. Invite friends, family, and Nash (that part is very important). Look amazing (also very important). Have an actual good time (most important), or fake it till you make it.
9. Go to bed smug.
10. Rinse. Repeat.

With the satisfaction of four items already crossed off my to-do list, I ventured downstairs. The rest of the house was still silent.

Stef knew me too well. And it really was easier to fake a positive attitude when I looked good on the outside.

There was a fresh pot of coffee waiting for me. I poured generously into a cheery red mug and studied the kitchen while I sipped.

The room had taken on a new life since the first time I'd been invited inside. It felt like most of the house had. The curtains had not only been opened but washed, ironed, and rehung. Morning sun streamed through clean glass.

Years of dust and grime had been scraped away, cabinets and drawers of junk purged. Bedrooms closed up for nearly two decades were now full of life. The kitchen, dining room, and sunroom had become the heart of a home full of people.

Together, we'd breathed life back into the space that had gone far too long without.

I took my coffee into the sunroom and stood at the windows, watching the creek catch fallen leaves and usher them downstream.

The loss was still there.

The holes left behind by Liza J's daughter and husband hadn't magically been filled. But it felt to me like there was more surrounding those holes now. Saturday soccer games. Family dinners. Movie nights when everyone talked too much to hear what was happening on-screen. Lazy evenings spent grilling dinner and playing in the creek.

Dogs. Kids. Wine. Dessert. Game nights.

We'd built something special here around Liza J and her loneliness. Around me and my mistakes. This wasn't the end. Mistakes were meant to be learned from, overcome. They weren't meant to destroy.

Resilience.

In my opinion, Waylay was already the epitome of resilience. She'd dealt with a childhood of instability and insecurity and was learning to trust the adults in her life. Maybe it was a little easier because she'd never let herself down the way I had. I admired her for that.

I supposed I could learn from her example on that.

I heard the shuffle of slippered feet punctuated by the excited *tip-tapping* of dog nails on tile.

"Morning, Aunt Naomi. What's for breakfast?" Waylay yawned from the kitchen.

I left my morning moping and returned to the kitchen. "Morning. What are you hungry for?"

She shrugged and settled on a stool at the island. Her blond hair was standing up on one side of her head and squished down on the other. She was wearing pink camouflage pajamas and fluffy slippers that Randy and Kitty tried to steal and hide in their dog beds at least once a day.

"Um. How about cheesy eggs?" she said. "Wow. You look nice."

"Thanks," I said, reaching for a pan.

"Where's Knox?"

Waylay's question felt like a blade to the heart.

"He moved back to his cabin," I said carefully.

Waylay rolled her eyes. "I know *that*. Why? I thought things were good with you guys? You were kissing all the time and laughing a lot."

My instinct was to lie. To protect her. After all, she was just a kid. But I'd done so much protecting already, and it just kept blowing up in my face.

"There's a couple of things we need to talk about," I told her as I gathered the butter and eggs from the fridge.

"I only told Donnie Pacer that he was a dick waffle because he pushed Chloe and told her she was a shithead loser," Waylay said defensively. "And I didn't use the f-word because I'm not allowed to."

I stood up with a carton of eggs in my hand and blinked. "You know what? We'll get back to that in a minute."

But my niece wasn't ready to give up her defense. "Knox said it's good to stand up for people. That it's up to the strong ones to take care of the ones who need protecting. He said I'm one of the strong ones."

Crap.

I swallowed around the lump in my throat and blinked back the tears that burned my eyes, threatening to ruin my mascara.

This time, the grief wasn't just for me. It was for a little girl with a hero who didn't want either one of us.

"That's true," I said. "And it's a good thing you're one of the strong ones, because I have to tell you some hard stuff."

"Is my mom coming back?" Waylay whispered.

I didn't know how to answer that. So I started somewhere else instead. "The cottage isn't infested with bugs," I blurted out. Randy the beagle jumped at my legs and peered up at me with soulful brown eyes. I leaned down to ruffle his ears.

"It isn't?"

"No, honey. I told you that because I didn't want you to worry. But it turns out it's better for you to know what's going on. Someone broke in. They made a huge mess and took some things. Chief Nash thinks they were looking for something. We don't know what they were looking for or if they found it."

Waylay was staring down at the counter.

"That's why we moved in here with Liza and your grandparents."

"What about Knox?"

I swallowed hard. "We broke up."

The finger she was using to trace the grain in the counter stilled.

"Why'd you break up?"

Damn kids and their unanswerable questions.

"I'm not sure, honey. Sometimes people just want different things."

"Well, what did he want? Weren't we good enough for him?"

I covered her hand with mine and squeezed. "I think we're more than good enough for him, and maybe that's what scared him."

"You should have told me."

"I should have," I agreed.

"I'm not some baby who's going to freak out, you know," she said.

"I know. Out of the two of us, I'm a much bigger baby."

That earned me the smallest of smiles.

"Was it Mom?"

"Was what your mom?"

"Did Mom break in? She does that kind of stuff."

This was why I didn't have honest conversations with people. They asked questions that required even more honesty.

I blew out a breath. "I'm honestly not sure. It's possible. Is there anything you can think of that she'd be looking for?"

She shrugged those little girl shoulders that had already carried more weight than was fair. "Dunno. Maybe something worth a lot of money."

"Well, whether it was your mom or not, you don't have anything to worry about. Liza's having a security system installed today."

She nodded, fingers back to tracing patterns on the counter.

"You wanna tell me how you're feeling about all this?" I asked.

She leaned down to scratch Kitty on her head. "Dunno. Bad, I guess. And mad."

"Me too," I agreed.

"Knox left us. I thought he liked us. Really liked us."

My heart broke all over again, and I vowed that I would make Knox Morgan pay. I went to her and wrapped an arm around her. "He did, honey. But sometimes people get scared when they start to care too much."

She grunted. "I guess. But I can still be mad at him, right?"

I brushed her hair out of her eyes. "Yes. You can. Your feelings are real and valid. Don't let anyone tell you you shouldn't feel the way you feel. Okay?"

"Yeah. Okay."

"So how do you feel about having a party tonight if Liza says it's okay?" I asked, giving her another squeeze.

Waylay perked up. "What kind of party?"

"I was thinking about a bonfire with apple cider and s'mores," I said, cracking an egg into a glass mixing bowl.

"That sounds cool. Can I invite Chloe and Nina?"

I loved that she had friends and a home that she wanted to share with them.

"Of course. I'll check in with their parents today."

"Maybe we can have Liza pick some of the country music Knox and Nash's mom liked," she suggested.

"That's a great idea, Way. Speaking of parties . . ."

Waylay heaved a sigh and looked up at the ceiling.

"Your birthday is coming up," I reminded her. Between Liza J, my parents, and me, we already had a closet full of wrapped gifts. We'd been badgering her about her big day for weeks, but she'd remained annoyingly noncommittal. "Have you figured out how you want to celebrate?"

She rolled her eyes. "Oh my gosh, Aunt Naomi! I told you nine million times I don't like birthdays. They're dumb and disappointing and lame."

Despite everything, I smiled.

"Not to guilt-trip you, but your grandma will go into hysterics if you don't at least let her bake you a cake."

I saw the calculating look on her face. "What kind of cake?"

I booped her nose with a spatula. "That's the best part about birthdays. You get to pick."

"Huh. I'll think about it."

"That's all I ask."

I had just poured the eggs into the skillet when I felt arms around my waist and a face press into my back.

"I'm sorry Knox was a douche waffle, Aunt Naomi," Waylay said, her voice muffled.

My throat tightened as I squeezed her hands with my own. It was such a new, fragile thing, this affection she showed me in moments when I least expected it. I was afraid I'd do or say the wrong thing and scare her off. "I am too. But we'll be okay. We'll be better than okay," I promised.

She released me. "Hey. Those jerks didn't steal my new jeans with the pink flowers when they broke in, did they?"

Fi: I don't know what's going on between you two. But Knox just offered me $1,000 to put you on the schedule tonight since you called in sick your last two shifts. I can either split it with you or tell him to fuck off. Your call!

Me: Sorry. I can't. I'm hosting a bonfire tonight and you're invited.

Fi: Fuck yeah! Can I bring my annoying family?

Me: I'd be disappointed if you didn't.

42

The Old Knox

Knox

I wasn't going to admit it, but the ice princess routine was killing me. It had been five days since I'd told Naomi the truth. Since I'd ended things to spare her feelings. And I was fucking miserable.

The relief I'd expected from ending things never came. Instead, I felt sick and uneasy. Almost guilty. It felt worse than my first over-thirty hangover.

I wanted things to go back to the way they'd been before Naomi showed up with fucking daisies in her hair. But they couldn't. Not with her in town avoiding me.

It was no small feat, given that she lived with my grandmother. She'd called off from her shifts at Honky Tonk. I'd expected relief that I didn't have to face her, but the longer she went without answering my texts or calls, the more uneasy I felt.

She should have gotten over this by now. Hell, I should have gotten over this by now.

"Your five o'clock canceled," Stasia said when I returned to Whiskey Clipper from my late lunch break spent at Dino's, getting glares and cold pizza that I didn't even feel like eating.

She and Jeremiah were cleaning up for closing.

"Seriously?" It was the third client to cancel on me this week. Two of them had rescheduled with Jeremiah and sat in his chair tossing me judgmental looks. None of them had the balls to say anything. But they didn't need to. I took enough of a beating from the Honky Tonk girls.

"Guess you must have pissed them off somehow," Stasia mused.

"It's no one's goddamn business who I see or don't see," I said, dunking the comb back in the alcohol and stowing my scissors.

"That's the thing about a small town," Jeremiah said. "Everyone's business is everyone's business."

"Yeah? Well, everyone can kiss my ass."

"He definitely seems much happier since he got out of that terrible relationship," Stasia said. She pretended to scratch her nose with her middle finger.

"Who signs your paychecks?" I reminded her.

"Some things are worth more than money."

I didn't need this abuse. I had shit to do. A life to live. And these assholes could just get on with forgetting all about me and Naomi.

"I'm goin' to Honky Tonk," I said.

"Have a great night," Jeremiah called after me. I threw a middle finger in his direction.

Instead of the bar, I ducked into my office. It didn't feel like a sanctuary. It felt like a prison. I'd spent more time locked in here this week than I had the previous month. I'd never been this caught up on paperwork or this disconnected from what was going on with my businesses.

"Why the hell does anyone in this town give a damn who I date or don't date?" I muttered to myself.

I picked up the rent check for one of the apartments upstairs. The tenant had also included a "You fucked up" note scrawled on a sticky note.

I was starting to worry that everyone else was right. That I'd done the wrong thing. And that sat about as well with me as the idea of wearing a suit and tie every day for the rest of my life.

I liked freedom. That was why I owned my own businesses. That lottery ticket had bought me stability and freedom. Although I supposed running my own businesses also sometimes felt like a thousand fucking zip ties lashing me to responsibility. But it was a responsibility I chose.

I could run my businesses without worrying about other people . . . Well, except for the ones I employed. And served.

Fuck.

I needed to get out of my head.

I headed down the hall and let myself into Honky Tonk. It was early still for a Friday, but the music was loud, and I could smell wings cooking in the kitchen. It felt like home. Even though my eyes did a quick scan of the bar, looking for Naomi. She wasn't there and the disappointment I felt cut like a goddamn knife.

Silver and Max were both behind the bar. Fi was

shooting the shit with Wraith. All three of them looked at me.

"Evening," I said, testing the waters.

"Boo!" they chorused. Silver and Max were giving me the thumbs-down. Fi was giving me one thumbs-down and one middle finger. The other server, Brad, a new hire brought on to even out the estrogen, refused to make eye contact with me.

"Seriously?"

The handful of patrons snickered.

"I could fire every last one of you," I reminded them.

They crossed their arms in unison. "I'd like to see you try," Max said.

"Yeah. I'm sure you'd bartend and serve and manage just fine all by yourself on a Saturday night," Silver said. Her nose ring moved with the flare of her nostrils.

Fuck.

I knew when I wasn't wanted.

Fine. I could go home and enjoy the peace and quiet of single life. Again. Maybe tonight it wouldn't feel so fucking empty. I'd get used to it.

"Fine. I'm leaving," I said.

"Good," said Max.

"Bye," said Silver.

"Fuck off," Fi said. "I'm leaving too."

"Fine. Whatever." I'd go home and work out a new schedule where these three never shared the bar again, I decided. Even if it meant hiring five more people. I'd hire guys who didn't get periods and didn't give me shit.

I fantasized about that life on the leisurely ride I took on my bike, winding around Knockemout and beyond before finally heading home. After all, I didn't have someone waiting for me. Someone to answer to. I could do what I wanted. Which was exactly what I wanted out of life.

I was so distracted by reminding myself how great my life was without Naomi that I almost missed the vehicles at Liza J's.

For a second, I panicked, wondering if something had happened. If there'd been another break-in or worse.

Then I heard the music, the laughter.

I drove by slowly, hoping for a glimpse of her. No such luck. I parked my bike in my driveway and was headed for the front door when the tang of bonfire hit my nostrils.

If Liza J wanted to have a party and not tell me, that was her business, I decided, letting myself inside.

Waylon attacked, his paws scrabbling at my jeans as he barked and moaned about how hungry he was since his afternoon snack.

"Yeah, yeah. Come on. Pee break first, then dinner."

I went straight to the kitchen and opened the back door. The dog bulleted out between my legs.

He didn't stop in his usual pee stop. His stumpy legs were too busy galloping toward Liza J's house.

I could see the fire from my vantage point. Someone had built a bonfire next to the creek. There were tables with food, camp chairs, and over a dozen people milling around, looking like they were having a great time.

Liza J's dogs, Randy and Kitty, broke away from the food tables to greet Waylon. I spotted Waylay, her blond hair under a bright pink hat that I bet Amanda had knit for her. Her friends Nina and Chloe were horsing around in the side yard. The pang in my chest took me by surprise. Waylay dropped to her knees in the grass and gave Waylon a good scruffing. He rolled onto his back in ecstasy.

I rubbed my hand absently over my chest, wondering if it was indigestion from the shitty cold pizza.

Headlights slashed across the yard as another car pulled in. A minivan that I recognized. Fi, her husband, and their kids piled out carrying camp chairs, covered dishes, and a six-pack.

Great. My own family and now my employees were taking her side in all this. This was why I needed a thousand acres far away from here.

Then I saw her.

Naomi by firelight.

She wore those tight leggings that showed off every inch of her mile-long legs. Boots with the girlie fur trim. A thick, cropped sweater under an insulated vest. Her hair was a mass of curls that glowed amber in the firelight. She was wearing a knit hat just like Waylay's, only in a deep red.

She was smiling. Laughing. Glowing.

The pang in my chest became a physical ache, and I wondered if I should call a cardiologist. This wasn't normal. This wasn't how it was supposed to go.

I ended things before they got too sticky and felt nothing but relief immediately after. If I ever ran into one of my conquests again, which was rare, it was easy. Pleasant. I never promised anything, and they never expected anything.

But this time, despite my best efforts, there had been expectations. Though she didn't look like she was suffering. She was next to the creek, standing close to my asshole brother, having what looked like an intimate chat.

Her gloved hand reached out and clutched his arm.

My fists clenched at my sides. Red filtered into the corners of my vision.

My brother hadn't wasted a goddamn second, had he?

It wasn't a conscious decision to go to her, but my feet had a mind of their own. I strode across the grass toward the happy little group with destruction in mind.

I didn't want her with him. I didn't want her with anyone.

I couldn't stand the idea of seeing her stand next to him, let alone whatever else they were doing. Fuck.

Liza J called to me, and Amanda flashed me a pitying smile as I marched through the festivities.

"You two didn't waste any goddamn time, did you?" I snapped when I caught them on the other side of the fire.

Nash had the audacity to laugh right in my face.

But Naomi was something else. The easy smile on her face disappeared, and when she looked at me, it wasn't an ice princess I saw, ready to freeze me out. It was a woman on fire ready to burn me alive.

The relief was swift and overwhelming. The tightness in my chest loosened by millimeters. Freezing me out meant she didn't care. But that fire I saw in those gorgeous hazel eyes told me she hated my guts.

That was better than cold disinterest any day.

Nash took a step forward, effectively putting himself between me and Naomi, which only served to piss me off even more.

"You got a problem?" he asked me.

I had a six-foot-three problem with a few bullet holes in it.

"Problem? With you helping yourself to my leftovers? Nah. Better she doesn't go to waste."

I was such a fucking asshole, and I'd gone way too far. I deserved the beating Nash was about to throw me. Part of me wanted it. Wanted the physical punishment to take the place of the emotional shitstorm that was ripping me apart inside.

I couldn't think straight with her this close. This close, and I couldn't touch her. Couldn't reach out and lay claim to what I'd thrown away.

Nash's fist pulled back, but before he could let it fly, another body stepped between us.

"You're a child throwing a temper tantrum," Naomi snapped, inches from me. "And you're not invited. So go home."

"Daisy," I said, reaching for her on autopilot.

Yet another body wedged itself between us.

"If you don't want to go down in history as the dumbest asshole in this town, I suggest you step the hell back," Sloane said.

She was glaring up at me like I'd just decked Santa Claus at a library luncheon.

"Get out of my way, Sloane," I snarled in her face.

Then there was a hand on my chest, and I was being shoved back *hard*.

"Wrong target, friend." Lucian, looking more casual in jeans and a fleece than I'd seen him in a decade, fisted his hands in my coat.

The rage in his eyes clued me in that I was skating on thin ice. I could take my brother, especially when he was one-armed. But I wasn't stupid enough to think I could take on Nash and Lucian and live to tell the tale.

"I don't need your protection, you big, rich idiot," Sloane snapped at Lucian.

He ignored her in favor of backing me away from the fire. Away from my family. From my stupid dog, who had his snout in what looked like a casserole dish of hot dogs.

"Let me go, Lucy," I warned him.

"I will when you're not determined to go down and take innocent bystanders with you."

Interesting. He was pissed not because I'd come at Nash and Naomi but because I'd gotten in Sloane's face.

"Thought you couldn't stand her," I taunted.

Lucian gave me another shove, and I stumbled backward.

"Christ, Knox. You don't have to be such an asshole all the time."

"Born that way," I shot back.

"Bullshit. What you show to the world is a choice. And right now, you're making the stupid choice."

"I did the right thing, man."

Lucian produced a cigarette and a lighter. "Keep telling yourself that if it helps you sleep at night."

"I told her not to get attached. I warned her." I looked over Lucian's shoulder and saw Naomi standing next to the fire, her back to me, Nash's arm around her.

My chest tightened again, and that pang was a goddamn knife wound now.

Maybe I'd told her not to get attached, but I hadn't done myself the same courtesy. I never thought it was something I had to worry about.

But Naomi Witt, runaway bride and compulsive cleaner, had her hooks in me.

"I did the right thing," I said again as if repeating it would make it true.

With his eyes on me, Lucian lit his cigarette. "It never occurred to you that the right thing would have been to be the man your father couldn't be?"

Fuck. That one landed like a bell ringer.

"Go fuck yourself, Lucy."

"Try to unfuck yourself, Knox." And with that, he wandered back to the fire, leaving me alone in the dark.

I saw a flash of pink out of the corner of my eye and found Waylay standing a few feet away from me. Waylon sat at her feet.

"Hey, Way," I said, suddenly feeling like the biggest, stupidest asshole on the planet.

"Hey, Knox."

"How's it going?"

She shrugged, those blue eyes fixed on me, her face blank.

"How did soccer practice go? I meant to swing by but—"

"It's okay. You don't have to pretend. Aunt Naomi 'n me are used to people not wanting us."

"Way, that's *not* fucking fair. That's not why things didn't work out between your aunt and me."

"Whatever. You probably shouldn't swear in front of kids. They might learn something from you."

Ouch.

"I'm serious, kid. You two are too good for me. Sooner or later, you both would have figured it out. You deserve better."

She looked down at the toes of her boots. Her little heart charm glimmered against her laces, and I realized she wasn't wearing the sneakers I gave her. That hurt too. "If you really thought that, you'd be working hard to be good enough. Not dumping us like we're trash."

"I never said you were trash."

"You never said much of anything, did you?" she said. "Now, leave Aunt Naomi alone. You're right. She deserves better than some guy who isn't smart enough to see how awesome she is."

"I know how awesome she is. I know how awesome you are," I argued.

"Not awesome enough to stay though," she said. The glare she sent me was years beyond eleven in maturity. I hated myself for giving her one more reason to doubt that she was anything but the smart, beautiful badass she was.

"Waylay! Come on," Nina called, holding a giant bag of marshmallows aloft.

"You should go," Waylay told me. "You make Aunt Naomi sad, and I don't like that."

"You gonna put field mice in my house?" I asked, hoping a joke would repair some of the damage.

"Why bother? There's no point in getting revenge on someone too dumb to care." She turned and started toward the fire, then stopped again. "I'm keeping your dog," she said. "Come on, Waylon."

I watched a kid that I not only liked but respected wander off toward the party with my own damn dog. Naomi greeted Waylay with a one-armed hug, and the two of them turned their backs on me.

To be contrary, I snagged one of the hot dogs off the table and a beer. I gave my grandmother a half-assed salute and then headed back to my place alone.

When I got there, I threw both in the trash.

43

Day Drinking

Naomi

Knox: I owe you an apology about last night at Liza's. I was out of line.

I took a deep breath, turned off my car, and stared at the side door to Honky Tonk. It was my first shift back since the breakup, and I was tied up in knots. It was a weekend lunch shift. The odds of Knox actually being inside were negative.

But I still needed a pep talk before getting out of the car.

I'd been okay at my other job all week. The library felt like a fresh start and didn't have memories of Knox around every corner. But Honky Tonk was different.

"You can do this. Get out of the car. Rake in the tip money, and smile until your face hurts."

Knox had thrown his little hissy fit at the bonfire and had to be escorted out by Lucian. I'd done a half-assed job pumping Sloane for information about Lucian's chivalry. But inside I was reeling from being that close to Knox again.

He'd looked angry and almost hurt. As if me standing next to his brother had been some sort of betrayal. It was laughable. The man had discarded me like an unwanted receipt and had the nerve to tell me I was moving on too fast when all I'd done was give Nash the list I'd been working on about people or incidents that felt off to me.

I looked in the rearview mirror. "You are an ice queen swan," I told my reflection. Then I got out of the car and marched inside.

Relief coursed through me when I didn't see him inside. Milford and another line cook were already firing up the kitchen, prepping for the day. I said my hellos and headed into the bar. It was still dark. The stools were stacked, so I turned on the music and the lights and set about getting the place ready.

I'd flipped all the stools, reassembled the soda machine, and was turning on the soup warmer when the side door opened.

Knox stepped inside, his eyes cutting directly to me.

The breath left my chest, and I suddenly couldn't remember how to inhale.

Damn it. How could a man who'd hurt me so badly look so good? It wasn't fair. He was wearing jeans and another long-sleeved Henley, this one in a forest green. There was a fading bruise on his chin that made him look like trouble. The sexy, delicious kind of trouble.

But the new Naomi was smarter than that. I wasn't going back there.

He nodded at me, but I returned my attention to the soup and tried to pretend he didn't exist. At least until he came too close to ignore.

"Hey," he said.

"Hey," I repeated, putting the metal lid over the warmer and throwing the plastic wrap away.

"I'm on the bar today," he said after a moment's hesitation.

"Okay." I brushed past him to get to the dish-washing station where two divided trays of clean glasses waited. I hefted one, then found it being snatched from my hands. "I've got it," I insisted.

"Now I've got it," Knox said, carting it up to the soda machine and dropping it on the stainless steel counter.

I rolled my eyes and grabbed the second tray. It too was promptly removed from my possession. Ignoring him, I flicked on the heat lamps on the expo line and moved to the POS to check the receipt tape.

I could feel him watching me. His gaze had a weight and temperature to it. I hated being so aware of him.

I could practically feel him skimming me from head to toe. I'd worn jeans today instead of one of my denim skirts, feeling like every layer of protection was necessary.

"Naomi." His voice was a rough rasp around my name, and it made me shiver.

I glanced at him and gave him my best fake smile. "Yeah?"

He shoved his hand through his hair, then crossed his arms.

"I owe you an apology. Last night—"

544

"Don't worry about it. It's forgotten," I said, making a show of checking my apron for my bank and notebook.

"This doesn't have to be . . . you know. Weird."

"Oh, it's not weird for me," I lied. "It's all in the past. Water under the bridge. We're both moving on."

His eyes looked like molten silver as he stared me down. The air between us was charged with what felt like an impending lightning strike. But I forced myself to hold his gaze.

"Right," he said with a clench in his jaw. "Fine."

I didn't know exactly how much Knox had moved on until an hour into the slowest shift ever. Normally a Saturday lunch shift could be counted on for some kind of business, but the whole seven patrons seemed to be content to sip their beers and chew their food 137 times. Even with the new server, Brad, to train, I had too much time to think.

Rather than hang around the bar and deal with Knox's moody stare, I cleaned.

I was scrubbing down the wall next to the service bar, working on a particularly tricky stain, when the front door opened, and a woman walked in. Or strutted. She wore black suede boots with stiletto heels, the kind of jeans that looked as though they'd been painted on, and a cropped leather jacket.

She had a trio of bracelets wrapped around her right wrist. Her nails were painted a gorgeous, murderous red. I made a mental note to ask her what the color was.

Her dark hair was cut short and worn tousled on top. She had cheekbones that could cut glass, an expertly applied smoky eye, and a wry grin.

I wanted to be her friend. To go shopping with her. To find out everything about her so I too could retrace her steps and discover that kind of confidence for myself.

That grin widened when she spotted Knox behind the bar, and I suddenly wasn't sure I wanted to be friends anymore. I snuck a glance at Knox and knew I definitely didn't want to be friends. Not with the way he was looking at her with affectionate familiarity.

She didn't say a word, just strolled across the bar, eyes on him. When she got there, she didn't slide onto a stool and order what I guessed would be the world's coolest drink. No. She reached across, grabbed him by the shirt, and laid a kiss right on his mouth.

My stomach dropped out of my body and continued to plummet toward the earth's core.

"Oh, shit," Wraith groaned from his table.

"Uh, is that the boss's girlfriend?" Brad, the server I was supposed to be training, asked.

"I guess so," I said, sounding as if I was being strangled. "I'll be back. Hold this." I handed Brad the dirty rag and gave the bar wide berth.

"Naomi!" Knox sounded pissed. But his moods were no longer my concern.

My heart was pounding so hard I could hear it in my ears as I headed toward the restroom with every eye in the place on me.

I pretended I didn't hear him calling my name or her greeting him.

"Knox? Seriously? It's about damn time," a throaty voice said.

"Fucking A, Lina. You couldn't have called first? This is the worst goddamn timing."

I didn't hear anything else because I pushed through the restroom door and went straight to the sink. I wasn't sure if I wanted to cry, throw up, or pick up the trash can and throw it at Knox's head. I was trying to get myself under control and considering a plan that would involve all three of my options when the door swung open.

My ex-imaginary friend strolled inside, hands in her back pockets, gaze on me.

I could only imagine what she saw. A pathetic, lovesick, midthirties loser with horrible taste in men. That was what I saw in the mirror every morning before I covered it up with mascara and lipstick.

"Naomi," she said.

I cleared my throat, hoping to dissolve the lump that had taken up residence there. "That's me," I said brightly. It sounded like I was choking on thumbtacks, but at least I'd rearranged my face into a carefully blank expression.

"Wow. Game face. I like it. Good for you," she said. "No wonder you've got his balls tied up in knots."

I didn't know what to say, so I pulled a paper towel free and ran it around the perfectly dry, clean counter.

"I'm Lina," she said, closing the distance between us, her hand outstretched. "Angelina, but I don't like the mouthful."

I took the offered hand automatically and shook. "Nice to meet you," I lied.

She laughed. "No, it isn't. Not with that first impression. But I'm going to make up for that and buy you a drink."

"No offense, Lina, but the last thing I want to do is sit down at my ex-boyfriend's bar to have drinks with his new girlfriend."

"None taken. But I'm not his new girlfriend. Matter of fact, I'm an ex-ier ex than you are. And we're definitely not drinking here. We need to go someplace without Knox's big, dumb ears."

I really hoped she wasn't messing with me.

"What do you say?" Lina asked, cocking her head. "Knox is having heart palpitations out there, and every other person is on their phone reporting to the grapevine what just happened. I say we give them all something to freak out over."

"I can't just walk out on a shift," I said.

"Sure you can. We have stories to share. Com-miserations to commiserate. Drinks to drink. He's got that cute little helper out there. He'll be fine. And you deserve a break after that shit show."

I took a deep breath and debated. The idea of staying on shift here with Knox was one step below having my toenails ripped out one at a time during a gynecological exam.

"What color is your nail polish?" I asked.

"Burgundy Bloodbath."

Sloane: Just heard that Knox's new girlfriend showed up at the bar and they started having sex on the pool table. Are you okay????? Do you need shovels and tarps?

Me: I've been kidnapped by new girlfriend who is actual old ex-girlfriend. We're day drinking at Hellhound.

Sloane: Let me find some pants! Be there in fifteen!

Hellhound was a biker bar fifteen minutes out of town heading in the direction of DC. Outside, the parking lot was half full of motorcycles. The crap brown clapboard siding didn't do anything to make the place look more welcoming.

Inside, the lights were dim, the pool tables were plentiful, and Rob Zombie music thudded from a jukebox in the corner. The bar was sticky, and I had to quash the urge to ask for a sponge and some Pine-Sol.

"What'll it be?" the bartender asked. He wasn't smiling, but he also wasn't overly intimidating. He was the tall, burly type with gray hair and a beard. He wore a leather vest over a white long-sleeved tee. The sleeves were pushed up to his elbows to reveal tattoos down both arms.

They made me think of Knox. Which made me want alcohol.

"What's your name, handsome?" Lina asked, settling on a stool.

"Joel."

"Joel, I'll have your best scotch. Make it a double," she decided.

Damn it. I knew she'd order a cool drink.

"You got it. For you, darlin'?" He looked at me.

"Oh. Uh, I'll have a white wine," I said, feeling like the least interesting person in the bar.

He winked at me. "Comin' right up."

"He's no Knox, but I dig the silver fox thing," Lina mused.

My hum was noncommittal.

"Oh, come on. Even if Knox is a shithead—which he is—you can still appreciate the very fine exterior," Lina insisted.

I wasn't in the mood to appreciate anything about the Viking who'd trampled my heart.

Silver Fox Joel plopped our drinks in front of us and left again.

"What are we doing here?" I asked.

Lina lifted her glass. "Having drinks. Getting to know each other."

"Why?"

"Because you didn't see the look on Knox's face right after I laid that closed-mouth kiss on him."

Close-mouthed was good.

Wait.

No. It didn't matter.

Even if Lina wasn't with Knox, he'd dumped me. I didn't need to concern myself with competition.

I ran my finger around the rim of my glass. "What happened to his face?"

She pointed an index finger at me. "Fear. I've known that man since he was barely a man, and I've *never* seen him scared. But I saw fear when he watched you walk away."

I sighed. I didn't want to hear that. I didn't want to pretend that there was hope where there was none. "I don't know why he'd be afraid of me walking away. He's the one who already did the walking."

"Let me guess. It wasn't you. It was him. He doesn't do relationships or complications or responsibilities. There's no future, and he's letting you go so you can get on with yours."

I blinked. "You *do* know him."

"I'll have you know I hold the impressive title of first official non-girlfriend, thank you very much. It was my junior year in college. He was twenty-four. We met at a party, and it lasted four glorious, hormone- and hangover-filled weeks before the idiot got cold feet and handed me my walking papers."

"Judging by your greeting, I'm guessing things ended better for you than they did for me."

Lina smiled and took a sip of scotch. "He underestimated my stubbornness. See, I could do without him as a boyfriend. But I wanted to keep him around as a friend. So I forced him into a friendship. We talk every couple of months. Before he hit that lottery, we'd meet up every couple of years. Always someplace neutral. We'd play wingman for each other."

I downed the wine in three big gulps. Before I even put the glass down on the bar, another one arrived.

"Thanks, Joel." I traded the empty glass for the full one. "What's his problem anyway?"

Lina snorted and sipped again. "What's anyone's problem? Baggage. People meet, sparks fly, then they spend all their time trying to hide who they really are so they can stay attractive. Then we're surprised when it doesn't work out."

She had a point.

"If everyone just introduced themselves with their baggage, imagine how much time we'd save. Hi, I'm Lina. I have daddy issues and a jealous streak combined with a temper that means you should never cross me. Also, I've been known to eat an entire tray of brownies in one sitting, and I never fold laundry."

I couldn't help but laugh.

"Your turn," she said.

"Hi, Lina. I'm Naomi, and I keep falling for guys who don't see a future with me. But I keep hoping the future I'm envisioning for the both of us will be good enough to keep them around. Also, I hate my twin sister, and it makes me feel like a bad person. Oh, and Knox Morgan ruined orgasms for me for the rest of my life."

It was Lina's turn to laugh. Another scotch appeared in front of her. "This guy knows what's up," she said, pointing to our bartender friend.

"Two ladies come into this place talking about the same man, and Imma keep the drinks coming," he assured us.

"Joel, you're a true gentleman," Lina said.

The front door burst open, and Sloane appeared. She was makeup-free and wearing knockoff Uggs, leggings, and an oversize Virginia Tech football jersey. Her hair hung in a thick braid over her shoulder.

"You must be the new trollop," Sloane said.

"And you must be the cavalry coming to save Princess Naomi from the she beast," Lina guessed.

I snorted into my wine. "Sloane, this is Lina. Lina is the original Knox ex-girlfriend. Sloane is an overprotective librarian with great hair." I pointed down the bar. "And that's Joel, our silver fox bartender."

Sloane took the stool next to me, and before her butt had gotten comfortable, Joel appeared. "You date the same guy too?" he asked.

She rested her chin in her hand. "No, Joel, I did not. I'm just here for moral support."

"You wanna drink while you morally support?"

"Sure do. How's your Bloody Mary?"

"Spicy as fuck."

"I'll take a Bloody Mary and a round of Fireball."

Joel saluted and wandered off to make the drinks. One of the men at the pool table closest to us ambled over. He had impressive spikes on the shoulders of his vest and a Fu Manchu to write home about. "Buy you bitches a drink?"

We swiveled on our stools as one.

"No, thank you," I said.

"Fuck off," Lina replied with a mean smile.

"If you think referring to us as 'bitches' is going to get you invited into the conversation, let alone one of our beds, you're about to be deeply disappointed," Sloane said.

"Move along, Reaper," Joel told him without looking up from the quart of vodka he was pouring into Sloane's glass.

My phone buzzed on the bar, and I glanced down.

Knox: That wasn't what it looked like. I'm not seeing Lina.
Knox: Not that it's any of your business.
Knox: Fuck. At least text me back and tell me where you are.

For someone who was done with me, he sure texted a whole heck of a lot.

Me: It's this awesome place called None of Your Business. Stop. Texting. Me.

I slid my phone over to Sloane. "Here. You're in charge of this."

Lina held up her phone to show us a text.

554

Knox: Where the fuck did you take her?

"See?" she said. "Fear."

"I don't think I'm going back to work today," I said.

"Hey, Waylay's hanging out at the museum in DC with Nina and her dads. There's no better way to spend a fall Saturday than getting blitzed."

"What's a Waylay?" Lina asked.

"My niece."

"The niece Naomi didn't know about because her estranged twin sister sucks," Sloane added. She twirled the tip of her braid around her fingers and stared blankly at the football game on the screen.

"Are you okay?" I asked her.

"I'm fine. I'm just sick of men."

"Amen, sister," I said, raising my glass at her.

"My sister, Chloe's mom? She's bi. Every time she dates a man who pisses her off, she ends up dating nothing but women for, like, twelve months. She's my hero. Makes me wish I didn't like penis so much."

Joel set a Bloody Mary with a floating stick of bacon in front of Sloane and didn't bat an eye at the word *penis*.

I winced. "Please don't say penis."

"My experience with Knox's equipment is almost twenty years old, so I can only imagine how much better he's gotten with age," Lina said with sympathy.

"You know, with this whole guardianship, maybe

555

it's just better to focus on being a parent figure and forget about being a woman with . . ."

"Sexual needs?" Sloane filled in.

I picked up my wine. "How many glasses would it take to forget about sex?"

"Usually around one and a half bottles. But that comes with a hangover that cuts you off at the knees for three days, so I wouldn't recommend," Lina said.

"He really made me believe," I whispered.

Joel lined up the shots in front of us, and I stared at mine.

"I know he said things wouldn't go anywhere. But he made me believe. He kept showing up. Not just for me but for Waylay too."

"Back the truck up. Knox Morgan? Spent time with your kid? Willingly?"

"He took her shopping. He showed up at her soccer game and got her to stop swearing. He told her that strong people stand up for the ones who can't stand up for themselves. He picked her up at a sleepover. Watched football with her."

Lina shook her head. "He's so fucked up."

"All men are," Sloane said.

Joel stopped and gave her the eye.

"Except you, Joel. You're a hero among villains," she amended.

With a nod, he handed over a fresh glass of wine for me and vanished again.

Sloane attached herself to the straw of her drink like it was a protein shake after a bodybuilding competition.

"Okay, seriously. What's going on with you?" I asked. "Does this have something to do with Lucian last night?"

"Lucian? Now, that's a sexy name," Lina said.

Sloane snorted.

"A sexy name to go with a sexy man," I agreed.

"There is nothing sexy about Lucian Rollins," Sloane said when she came up for air.

"Okay. You're definitely lying. Either that or an entire section of the Dewey decimal system fell on your head."

She shook her head and picked up her shot. "I'm not talking about Lucian. None of us are talking about Lucian. We're talking about Knox."

"Can we stop talking about him?" I asked. It felt like an X-ACTO knife to the heart every time I heard his name.

"Of course," Lina said.

"Cheers," Sloane said, lifting her shot glass.

We clinked glasses and knocked back the whiskey.

A man with a toothpick dangling precariously from his mouth wandered up and leaned an elbow on the bar, crowding Lina. His T-shirt didn't quite cover the belly that peeked out over the top of his black jeans.

"Which one of you ladies wants to come check out the back of my bike?"

Joel lined up another round of shots in front of us.

Lina picked up her shot. Sloane and I followed

suit, and we all knocked them back. Lina put the glass down on the bar, and before Toothpick knew what was happening, she had the stiletto of her boot digging into his chest.

"Go away before I make you bleed in front of your friends," she said.

"I like her *and* her shoes," Sloane whispered next to me.

"Christ, Python, leave 'em alone before your old lady shows up and cuts off your balls."

"Listen to the nice man, Python," Lina said, giving him a shove with her foot. He slid down the bar a foot, then put his hands up.

"Just askin'. Didn't know you were lesbos."

"Because that's the only reason we wouldn't want to fuck you, right?" Sloane said.

Sloane was a lightweight, and she'd already had two shots and a very strong Bloody Mary.

"Can we maybe get some water?" I asked Joel.

He nodded, then cupped his hands. "Listen up, assholes. The ladies aren't lookin' for a ride or a good time. Next idiot who bothers them is gettin' thrown out."

There was a general muttering around us, and then everyone went back to what they were doing.

"Joel, are you married?" I asked.

He held up his left hand to show me a gold band.

"All the good ones are taken," I complained.

The front door opened again.

"You have got to be kidding me," Sloane groaned.

Joel handed over a fresh Bloody Mary, and she dove for it.

I swiveled around on my stool, wobbling a bit as the alcohol fought my equilibrium.

"Oh, my," Lina purred next to me. "Who are they?"

"More cavalry," Sloane muttered.

Lucian and Nash wandered up to the bar looking six shades of gorgeous.

44

The Babysitters

Naomi

T his can't be a coincidence," I observed.

"Knox called the cops," Lucian said, nodding at Nash. "And the cops called me."

Nash skimmed me with a look. "You all right?"

"I'm fine. Why are you here?"

Nash blew out a breath, his gaze moving on to Lina. She arched an eyebrow at him.

"We're babysitting," he said finally.

My mouth dropped open. "We don't need baby-sitters. Especially not babysitters who are just going to report everything we say back to Knox."

"I hate to point out the obvious, but given everything that's happened, I don't think you should be out unprotected like this," Nash said.

"Who said I'm unprotected? Lina just nearly pierced a man's sternum with her stiletto," I complained. "How did you find us?"

"I wouldn't worry about that," Lucian said without looking away from Sloane, who was glaring at him like he was Satan incarnate.

"You've got to be a Morgan," Lina said, resting her elbows on the bar and giving Nash a head-to-toe sweep.

"Lina, this is Nash. Knox's brother," I said.

"On that note, I think I'll be heading home," Sloane said, sliding off her stool. She didn't get far. Lucian stepped in on her, trapping her between the bar and his body without touching her.

She tilted her head all the way back to look up at him.

She was a foot shorter than the man, but that didn't stop Sloane from shooting ninja throwing stars out of her eyeballs.

"You'll stay," he insisted darkly.

"I'm going," she argued.

"I count three empty glasses on the bar in front of you. You'll stay."

"I'll call a rideshare. Now get out of my way before I make you sing soprano."

Lina gave up ogling Nash and leaned over my shoulder. "Okay. What's their story?"

"I don't know. They won't tell anyone."

"Ooh. I love a torrid secret past," she said.

"We can hear you," Sloane said dryly without breaking her sexy staring contest with Lucian.

"We're all friends here," I began.

"No, we're not," Lucian insisted.

Sloane's eyes blazed, making her look like a fiery pixie about to commit a homicide. "Finally. Something we agree on."

My phone vibrated at Sloane's elbow. Seconds later, Lina's phone signaled a text. Nash and Lucian both reached for their pockets at the same time.

"For someone who doesn't care about you, Knox

sure seems concerned about how you're doing," Lina said, holding up her phone again.

"And what you're saying about him," Lucian said with a smirk.

I shook my head. "I think I'm gonna share that ride with Sloane."

"No!" Lina grabbed my hand and squeezed. "Don't give him the satisfaction of ruining your day. Stay. We'll get more drinks. Talk more shit. And everyone who stays has to swear a blood oath they won't report back to Knox."

"I'm not staying if he's staying," Sloane said, shooting a murderous look at Lucian.

"And the only way you're leaving is in my car, so sit down and order some goddamn food," Lucian ordered.

Sloane opened her mouth, and for a second, I was worried she was going to bite him.

I clapped a hand over her mouth. "Let's get some nachos and another round of drinks."

Missed Calls: Knox 4.

"No fair! You said they were off-limits, Joel," a drunkard with a skullcap and tattoos under his eyes complained from one of the pool tables when we sat down at a table with Lucian and Nash.

Joel flipped him the middle finger while our babysitters shared a look.

"See? I told you we didn't need babysitters. We have Silver Fox Joel," I said.

"Maybe we just want to spend some quality time with you," Nash said, giving me the patented Morgan grin of sexiness.

I sighed hard enough to blow a napkin across the table.

"What's wrong, Nay?" Sloane asked.

I thought about it for a beat. "Everything," I answered finally. "Everything is wrong or broken or a mess. I used to have a plan. I used to have it all together. I know you guys might not believe this, but people didn't use to break into my house. I didn't have to fend off ex-fiancés or worry about the example I was setting for an eleven-year-old going on thirty."

I looked around the table at their concerned faces.

"I'm sorry. I shouldn't have said that. Forget the words came out of my face."

Sloane pointed a finger in my face. "Stop that."

I picked up my glass of water and blew bubbles in it. "Stop what?"

"Stop acting like you don't have the right to express your own feelings."

Lina, looking stone sober despite the fact that she was on her fourth scotch, knocked her knuckles on the table. "Hear, hear. What's up with that?"

"She's the good twin," Sloane explained. "Her sister sucks and put the family through the wringer. So Naomi made it her life mission to be the good kid and not inconvenience anyone with things like her feelings or her wants and needs."

"Hey! Mean!" I complained.

She squeezed my hand. "I speak the truth with love."

"I'm new here," Lina said, "but wouldn't it be a good idea to show your niece what a strong, independent woman looks like when she lives her life?"

"Why does everyone keep saying that to me?" I groaned. "You know what I did for me? Just me?"

"What did you do?" Lucian asked kindly. I noticed that his chair was angled toward Sloane, crowding her almost protectively.

"Knox. I did Knox just for me. I wanted to feel good and forget about the hurricane of crap for just one night. And look what happened! He warned me. He told me not to get attached. That there was no chance at a future. And I still fell for him. What is wrong with me?"

"Care to chime in here, gentlemen?" Lina suggested.

The men exchanged another look full of manly meaning.

"I can hear them mentally going through the man code appendix," I whispered.

Nash wearily scraped his hand through his hair. It was a gesture that reminded me of his brother. "Are you okay? Do you need to rest?" I asked.

He rolled his eyes. "I'm fine, Naomi."

"Nash got shot," Sloane explained to Lina.

Her assessing gaze slid over him as if she could

see through his clothing down to his skin. "That sucks," she said, lifting her glass to take a sip.

"Not one of my favorite experiences," he admitted. "Naomi, you've gotta stop wondering what's wrong with you or what you did wrong and understand the problem is with Knox."

"Agreed," Lucian said.

"Look, we lost a lot when we were kids. That can fuck with some people's heads," Nash said.

Lina studied him with interest. "What did it do to yours?"

His grin was a flash of humor. "I'm a lot smarter than my brother."

She looked at me. "See? No one wants to be real and put their baggage on the table."

"When you trust someone to see you for who you really are, the betrayal is a thousand times worse than if you hadn't handed them the weapons in the first place," Lucian said quietly.

I heard Sloane's sharp intake of breath.

Nash must have picked up on it too, because he changed the subject.

"So, Lina. What brings you to town?" he asked, crossing his arms and leaning back in his chair.

"What are you, a cop?" she joked.

I found that very amusing. Sloane found me spraying a fine mist of water over the table just as amusing, and we both dissolved into giggles.

A ghost of a smile played on Lucian's lips.

"Nash is a cop," I told Lina. "He's *the* cop. The big, important one."

She eyed him over the rim of her glass. "Interesting."

"What did bring you to town?" I asked her.

"Found myself with some time off and I was in the area. Thought I'd pay my old friend a visit," she said.

"What do you do?" Sloane asked.

Lina ran her finger through a water ring on the table. "I'm in insurance. I'd tell you more, but it's incredibly boring. Not nearly as exciting as getting shot. How did it happen?" she asked Nash.

He shrugged his good shoulder. "Traffic stop gone bad."

"They catch who did it?" she asked.

"Not yet," Lucian answered.

The chill in his tone had a shiver running down my spine.

"I'm going to hit the restroom," I said.

"I'll come," Sloane volunteered, jumping out of her chair like it was electrocuting her.

I followed her into the gloomy hallway, but when she held the door open for me, Nash stopped me. "You got a second?" he asked.

My bladder was nearing the red zone, but this sounded important.

"Sure," I said, signaling to Sloane to commence peeing without me.

"I just wanted you to know that I'm looking into the list you gave me," he said. "I'm not officially back on duty, but that just means this is getting my undivided attention."

"I appreciate that, Nash," I said, giving his arm a squeeze. It wasn't a crime to appreciate the muscle, right?

"If you remember any other details about this red-haired guy, you'll let me know?"

"Sure," I said, my head bobbing. "I only talked to him that one time. But he stands out in a crowd. Muscular, tattooed, bright red hair."

Nash's eyes got a funny faraway look to them.

"Are you okay?" I asked again.

He gave an almost imperceptible head shake. "Yeah. Fine."

"Do you think he could have something to do with the break-in?"

Nash did the Morgan nervous tic of running his hand through his hair. "He's a wild card, and I don't like wild cards. This guy just happens to show up at the library to talk to you?"

"He said he needed help with a computer problem."

He nodded, and I could see him rearranging puzzle pieces in his head, trying to find the pattern. "Then you see him in the bar the night someone breaks into your place. That's not a coincidence."

I shivered.

"I just keep hoping, whoever they were, they found whatever they were looking for. If they found it, there's no reason to come back."

"I hope so too," he said. "Did you talk to Waylay about it?"

"I did finally. She took it pretty well. She was

567

more concerned about whether any of her new clothes were stolen than the break-in itself. She didn't seem to know what Tina or anyone else would have been looking for. I mean, it's not like we had a pallet of stolen TVs sitting around in the living room."

"Been thinking," Nash said, rubbing a hand over his jaw. "It doesn't have to be stolen goods. If Tina was bragging about a big payday, it could have been a different kind of job."

"Like what?"

"People get paid to do a lot of shit. Maybe she gave up on moving stolen property and got mixed up in something else. Maybe they got their hands on information that someone else wanted. Or that someone didn't want anyone else to know."

"How does someone lose or hide information?"

He smiled sweetly at me. "Not everyone's as organized as you are, honey."

"If this whole thing is about something Tina was irresponsible enough to lose, I am going to be pissed," I told him. "She went through nine house keys. Nine. And don't even get me started on the car keys."

His smile stayed fixed in place. "It's gonna be all right, Naomi. I promise you."

I nodded. But I couldn't stop thinking of all the ways Tina had managed to hurt me despite my parents' best efforts. How were a small-town police department and a wounded chief supposed to protect us?

And then it hit me. Maybe it was time for me to start standing up for myself.

Nash leaned against the wall. His expression gave nothing away, but I was willing to bet money that he was in pain.

"There is something I wanted to ask you," he said, looking serious.

"There is?" I croaked. Sure, Nash was as unfairly gorgeous as his jerk of a brother. He certainly had a more amiable personality. And he was great with kids. Great with Waylay. But if he asked me out just days after his brother, I was going to have to let him down easy.

I had zero headspace for another Morgan brother, and I needed to focus on my niece and the guardianship.

"You mind if I have a word with Waylay?" he asked.

I jolted, rewinding his words to see if I'd somehow missed the dinner invitation. Nope. "Waylay? Why?"

"I might ask the right question and help her remember something important from before her mom left. She knows Tina better than any of us."

I bristled. "Do you think she has something to do with this?"

"No, honey, I don't. But I know what it's like to be a kid who keeps quiet, plays things close to the vest."

I could see that about him. Knox was the stand-up-and-pitch-a-fit-about-a-problem kind of guy. On the outside, Nash was Mr. Nice Guy, but there was a quiet depth there, and I wondered what secrets lurked beneath that surface.

"Okay," I agreed. "But I'd like to be with you when you do talk to her. She's finally starting to trust me. To open up to me. So I want to be there."

"Absolutely." He tucked a strand of hair behind my ear, and I thought about what a good guy he was. Then I wished it was Knox's fingers in my hair. And then I got mad all over again.

The restroom door opened, and Sloane walked out. More accurately, she stumbled. I caught her, and she smiled up at me and squished my cheeks between her hands. "You are sooooo pretty!"

"I'll escort this one back to the table," Nash volunteered.

"You're really pretty too, Nash," Sloane said.

"I know. It's a curse, Sloaney Baloney."

"Aww. You remember," she crooned as he led her back to the bar.

I stepped into the ladies' room and decided it was not a room I wanted to linger in. So I made quick work of taking care of business and then ducked back into the hall. There were no babysitters lurking, so I pulled out my phone and opened my email.

Glancing over my shoulder to make sure Lucian or Nash hadn't materialized, I started a new message.

To: Tina
From: Naomi
Subject: What you're looking for

Tina,
I don't know what you're looking for. But if it gets you out of my life, I'll help you find it. Tell me what I'm looking for and how I can get it to you.

N

If I could find whatever it was Tina wanted first, I'd have the leverage I needed to get her out of my life. If it wasn't something like nuclear codes, I could let her have it or I could at least use it as bait to lure her out of hiding.

I waited for the tiny pinprick of guilt, but it never came. I was still waiting when my phone rang in my hand.

Knox Morgan.

I didn't know if it was the Fireball or all the pitying pep talks, but I felt more than ready to take charge. Squaring my shoulders, I answered the call. "What?"

"Naomi? Thank God." He sounded relieved.

"What do you want, Knox?"

"Look, I don't know what Lina told you, but this wasn't what you think."

"What I think," I said, cutting him off, "is that your love life is none of my business."

"Oh, come on. Don't be like that."

"I'll be any damn way I want to be, and you have no say in it. You need to stop texting and calling. We're over. You walked."

"Naomi, just because we're not together doesn't mean I don't want you safe."

His voice, the rawness in it, went straight to my chest. I felt like I couldn't breathe.

"That's very chivalrous of you, but I don't need you to keep me safe. There's a whole other line of defense in place. You're officially free. Enjoy it."

"Daze, I don't know how to make you understand."

"That's just it, Knox. I *do* understand. I understand that you cared, and it scared you. I understand that Waylay and I weren't reward enough to get you to face that fear. I get it. I'm dealing. You made the call, now you have to deal with the consequences. But I'm not like Lina. I'm not going to insist on being friends. In fact, consider this my notice. Tomorrow night is my last shift at Honky Tonk. Just because we live in the same damn small town doesn't mean we have to see each other all the damn time."

"Naomi, this isn't what I wanted."

"Honestly, I don't care what you want. For once, I'm thinking about what *I* want. Now stop calling. Stop texting. Call off your babysitters, and let me live my life. Because you're no longer a part of it."

"Look. If this is about what I said about you and Nash, I apologize. He told me—"

"I'm going to stop you right there before you call me *your leftovers* again. I don't care what you say or think about me and any man I might choose to see. I don't need your opinions or your half-assed apologies. Who apologizes by saying 'I apologize'?" I demanded, making sure my imitation of him was far from flattering.

There was silence on the other end, and for a second, I hoped he'd hung up on me.

"How much have you had to drink?" he asked.

I held the phone up to my face and screamed into it.

I heard the scrape of chairs, and moments later, Lucian and Nash were standing in the mouth of the hallway. I held up a finger to keep them at bay. "I suggest you lose this number, because if you call me again, I won't make Waylay give your dog back."

"Naomi—"

I hung up and stuffed the phone into my pocket. "Can one of you give me a ride home? I have a headache."

But it was nothing compared to the ache in my chest.

45

The Bar Fight

Knox

I blew into Honky Tonk under a full head of steam. I hadn't slept last night. Not after that phone call with Naomi. The woman was a stubborn nightmare. She didn't care that I was trying to do what was best for her. She didn't want to see it from my perspective. Quitting a good job just because she got her feelings hurt was a stupid fucking reason to turn her back on cash.

And I was going to tell her that.

Instead of the usual greetings from the kitchen staff, I got a couple of furtive glances, and suddenly everyone was too busy with what they were doing to even acknowledge me.

Everyone needed to get their heads out of their asses and get over it.

I pushed through the doors into the bar and found Naomi leaning over a table in the corner, laughing at something her mom was saying. Lou and Amanda were there for the drinks portion of their weekly date night.

I knew it had nothing to do with supporting my business and everything to do with showing their support for their daughter.

The rest of her section was already full. Because she drew people to her.

Knockemout had welcomed her just as it had me and my brother all those years ago. If she thought she was going to leave me behind, she was about to be disappointed.

A long, denim-clad leg kicked out in front of me, blocking my path. "Whoa, cowboy. You look like you're about to murder someone."

"I don't have time for games, Lina," I told her.

"Then stop playing them."

"I'm not the one playing. I fucking told her just like I told you how it was going to go. It went the way I said. She's got no right to be pissed at me."

"You ever think about telling her the real reason why you are the way you are?" she asked, lifting a glass of what I had a feeling was my private stock of bourbon.

"What are you talking about?" I asked evenly.

She rolled her neck like she was warming up for a fight. "Listen, Knox. Women have this sixth sense when we're being served up half-truths."

"You got a point?"

Naomi left her table with a little wave and was headed to the next one, a four-top full of bikers.

"She knows there's more to it than what you're sharing. I knew it. And I'd be willing to bet every woman in between knew it too. We're suckers for a wounded man. We think we can be the one you'll let in. The one who'll magically fix you with our love."

"Come on, Lina."

"I'm serious. But you just keep pushing all of us away. And I think that's because you don't want to acknowledge your truth."

"You sound like a fucking TV therapist."

"Bottom line, my friend. Naomi deserves your truth. Even if it's ugly. She's not going to forgive you and 'get over it,' as you so eloquently put it, unless you're straight with her. I think you owe it to her."

"I really don't like you right now," I told her.

She grinned. "And I really don't care." She polished off her drink and set the empty on the bar. "I'll see you later. Try not to fuck it up even more."

It was with those words ringing in my ears that I rounded the bar and caught Naomi at the POS.

She hadn't seen me yet, so I stood there looking my fill, my body tense with the need to touch her. Her face was flushed. Her hair was styled in sexy waves. She was back in one of those damn jean skirts. This one looked new and even shorter than the others. She wore cowboy boots and a long-sleeved Honky Tonk V-neck. She looked like every man's fantasy.

She looked like *my* fantasy.

"Need to talk to you," I said.

She jolted when I spoke, then looked me up and down before turning away.

I grabbed her arm. "That's not a request."

"In case you haven't noticed, I have seven tables,

576

boss. I'm busy. It's my last night. There's nothing that needs to be said."

"You're wrong, Daisy. It's not your last night, and there's a lot I need you to hear."

We were close. Too close. My senses were full of her. Her scent, the velvet softness of her skin, the sound of her voice. It all went straight to my gut.

She felt it too. The attraction hadn't simply vanished because I'd called it quits. If anything, the last week spent without her made me want her even more.

I fucking missed waking up next to her. Missed seeing her at Liza J's table. Missed walking Waylay to the bus stop. Missed the way I felt when Naomi kissed me like she couldn't help herself.

The music from the speakers kicked over to a lively country anthem, and the bar cheered.

"I'm busy, Viking. If you drag me out of here, you're only hurting your own profit margins."

I clenched my jaw. "Get your tables sorted. You're on break in fifteen. My office."

"Yeah, okay," she said, her tone dripping with sarcasm.

"If you're not in my office in fifteen, I will come out here, throw you over my shoulder, and carry your ass back there." I leaned in closer, almost close enough to kiss her. "And there is no way that skirt of yours is up for that."

I felt her shiver against me when my lips brushed her ear.

"Fifteen minutes, Naomi," I said and left her standing there.

Sixteen minutes later, I was alone in my office and royally pissed. I yanked the door open so hard the hinges rattled. When I hit the bar, Naomi's head came up at the service bar like a doe sensing danger.

I went straight for her.

Those eyes went wide when she read my intention.

"Warned you," I told her as she took a step back and then another.

"Don't you dare, Knox!"

But I fucking dared.

I caught her by the arm and bent at the waist. She was up over my shoulder in less than a second. It was like a record scratch. The bar went completely silent except for Darius Rucker on the speakers.

"Max, run those drinks," I said, nodding at Naomi's tray.

Naomi squirmed, trying to right herself, but I wasn't having any of it. I gave her a hard slap on the ass, catching denim, cotton, and bare skin.

The bar erupted into pandemonium.

Naomi squeaked and reached for the hem of her skirt.

She was wearing the underwear I bought her, and I knew that as frosty as she'd been, she fucking missed me.

"Everyone can see my underwear!" she yelped.

I laid my palm over her ass. "Better?"

"I am going to slap you so hard your head spins around," she threatened as I marched us out of the bar and toward my office.

By the time I hit the code on the door, she'd stopped fighting me and hung upside down with her arms crossed in what I could only assume was a pout.

I hated to take my hands off her. I wished there was a way to get through this without letting her go. But I wasn't a great conversationalist under normal circumstances, and when I had an aching dick, I was even worse.

I grabbed her by the hips and let her slide down my body until her toes hit the floor. For a moment, we stood there, pressed against each other like we were one. And for just a second, as she looked into my eyes with her palms pressed flat on my chest, everything felt right.

Then she was pushing away from me and stepping back.

"What the hell do you want from me, Knox? You said you didn't want to be together. We're not together. I'm not following you around, begging for another chance. I respected your wishes."

I was worried she'd get the wrong answer if she looked below my belt, so I steered her to the chair behind my desk.

"Sit."

She glared at me for a full thirty seconds with her arms crossed before giving in. "Fine," she said, flopping down in my chair.

But the distance didn't make me feel better. I was starting to realize the only thing that did was being close to her.

"You keep saying you want one thing and then acting like you want something completely different," she said.

"I know."

That shut her up.

I needed to move, so I paced in front of the desk, needing to keep something between us.

"There's something you don't know."

Her fingers drummed on her arms. "You gonna enlighten me anytime soon, or do I have to kiss all those tips out there goodbye?"

I shoved my hands through my hair, scraped one down over my beard. I felt sweaty and twitchy. "Don't rush me, okay?"

"I am not going to miss working for you," she said.

"Fuck. Naomi. Just give me a second. I don't talk about this shit to anyone. Okay?"

"Why start now?" She stood up.

"You met my father." I blurted out the words.

Slowly, she sank back into the chair.

I started pacing again. "At the shelter," I said.

"Oh my God. Duke," she said. The realization hit her. "You cut his hair. You introduced us."

I hadn't introduced them. Naomi had introduced herself.

"When my mom died, he didn't deal. He started drinking. Stopped going to work. Got busted for a

DUI. That's when Liza J and Pop took us in. They were grieving too. For them, being around me and Nash wasn't some painful reminder of what they lost. But for my father . . . He couldn't even look at us. The drinking continued here. Right here at the bar before it was Honky Tonk."

Maybe that was why I bought it. Why I'd felt compelled to turn it into something better.

"When the alcohol stopped numbing him, he went looking for something harder."

So many memories I'd thought I'd buried came rushing back.

Dad with bloodshot eyes, scratches and scabs all on his arms. Bruises and cuts he didn't remember on his face.

Dad curled on the floor of the kitchen, screaming about bugs.

Dad unresponsive on Nash's bed, an empty bottle of pills next to him.

I chanced a glance up at her. Naomi was sitting stock-still, eyes wide and sad. It was better than the frosty indifference.

"He was in and out of rehab half a dozen times before my grandparents kicked him out." I shoved my hand through my hair and gripped the back of my neck.

Naomi didn't say anything.

"He never got his shit together. Never tried. Nash and I weren't enough of a reason for him to hang on. We lost my mom, but she didn't choose to leave us." I swallowed hard. "Dad? He chose. He

581

abandoned us. He wakes up every day and makes the same choice."

She blew out a shaky breath, and I saw tears in her eyes.

"Don't," I warned her.

She gave a little nod and blinked them back. I turned away from her, determined to get it all said.

"Liza J and Pop did their best to make it okay for us. We had Lucian. We had school. We had dogs and the creek. It took a few years, but it was good. We were okay. We were living our lives. And then Pop had a heart attack. Keeled over fixing the downspout on the back of the house. Dead before he hit the ground."

I heard the chair move, and a second later, Naomi's arms came around my waist. She didn't say anything, just pressed herself against my back and held on. I let her. It was selfish, but I wanted the comfort of her body against mine.

I took a breath to fight off the tightness in my chest. "It was like losing them all over again. So much useless fucking loss. It was too much for Liza J. She broke down and cried in front of the casket. This silent, never-ending well of tears as she stood over the man she'd loved for her entire life. I've never felt more helpless in my entire goddamn existence. She shuttered the lodge. Drew the curtains to keep the light out. She stopped living."

Once again, I hadn't been enough to make someone I loved want to go on.

582

"Those curtains stayed closed until you," I whispered.

I felt her hitch against me, heard a ragged breath.

"Fuck, Naomi. I told you not to cry."

"I'm not crying," she sniffled.

I dragged her around to my front. Tears streaked her beautiful face. Her lower lip trembled.

"That's in my blood. My dad. Liza J. They couldn't deal. They lost themselves, and everything around them spiraled out of control. I come from that. I can't afford to give up like that. I already have people who depend on me. Hell, some days it feels like this whole damn town needs something from me. I can't put myself in a position where I'll let them all down."

She let out a slow, shaky breath. "I can see how you'd feel that way," she said finally.

"Don't feel sorry for me." I squeezed her arms.

She swiped a hand under her eyes. "I'm not feeling sorry for you. I'm wondering how you're not a larger teeming mess of trauma and insecurities. You and your brother should be very proud of yourselves."

I snorted, then gave in to the urge to pull her into me. I rested my chin on the top of her head.

"I'm sorry, Naomi. But I don't know how to be different."

She stilled against me, then tilted her head back to look at me. "Wow. Knox Morgan just said he was sorry."

"Yeah, well, don't get used to it."

Her face crumpled, and I realized what a stupid fucking thing it was to say.

"Shit. I'm sorry, baby. I'm an asshole."

"Yeah," she agreed, sniffing heroically.

I looked around my office. But I was a man. I didn't keep a box of tissues handy. "Here," I said, maneuvering us toward the couch where my gym bag sat. I yanked a T-shirt out of it and used it to mop up the tears that were ripping me to shreds inside. The fact that she let me made them a little easier to handle.

"Knox?"

"Yeah, Daze?"

"I hope someday you meet the woman who makes it all worth it."

I nudged her chin up. "Baby, I don't think you get it. If it wasn't you and Way, it's never gonna be anybody."

"That's really sweet and really messed up at the same time," she whispered.

"I know."

"Thank you for telling me."

"Thanks for listening."

I felt . . . different. Lighter somehow, as if I'd managed to throw open my own curtains or some shit like that.

"We good?" I asked, threading my fingers through her hair and tucking it behind her ears. "Or do you still hate me?"

"Well, I hate you a whole lot less than when I started my shift."

My lips quirked. "Does this mean you'd be willing to stay on? Customers love you. Staff loves you. And the boss is pretty damn fond of you."

I was more than fond of her. Holding her like this. Talking to her like this. Something was happening in my chest, and it felt like fireworks.

She pressed her lips together and brought her hands to my chest. "Knox," she said.

I shook my head. "I know. It's not fair to ask you to hang around when I can't be what you deserve."

"I don't think my heart is safe around you."

"Naomi, the last thing I want to do is hurt you."

She closed her eyes. "I know that. I get it. But I don't know how to protect myself from the hope."

I nudged her chin up. "Look at me."

She did as I told her.

"Talk."

She rolled her eyes. "I mean, look at us, Knox. We both know this is going nowhere, yet we're still literally entwined."

God, I loved that fancy vocabulary of hers.

"I'll be able to remind myself for a while that you can't be with me. But sooner or later, I'm going to start forgetting. Because you're you. And you want to take care of everybody and everything. You'll buy Waylay a dress that she loves. Or my mom will talk you into golfing with her on the weekends. Or you'll bring me coffee when I most need it again. Or you'll punch my ex in the face again. And I'll forget. And I'll fall all over again."

"What do you want me to do?" I asked, gathering

her against me again. "I can't be who you want me to be. But I can't let you go."

She cupped a hand to my cheek and stared up at me with something that looked a hell of a lot like love. "Unfortunately, Viking, those are your only two choices. Someone once told me in this very room that it doesn't matter how shitty the options are. It's still a choice."

"I think that guy also told you that there's a man out there who knew on his best day he was never gonna be good enough for *you*."

She gave me a squeeze and then started to slide out of my grip. "I need to get back out there."

It went against every instinct I had to let her go, but I did it anyway.

I felt strange. Open, exposed, raw. But also better. She'd forgiven me. I'd shown her who I really was, what I came from, and she'd accepted it all.

"Any chance I could get my dog back?" I asked.

She gave me a sad smile. "That's between you and Waylay. I think maybe she could use an apology from you too. She's with Liza tonight."

I nodded. "Yeah. Okay. Naomi?"

She stopped at the door and looked back.

"Do you think if we would have carried on . . . I mean, if we hadn't called it off, is it possible that you would have . . ." I couldn't get the words out. They clogged my throat and closed it up.

"Yeah," she said with a sad smile that had my insides churning.

"Yeah, what?" I pressed.

"I would have loved you."

"How do you know?" I demanded, my voice a rasp.

"Because I already do, dummy."

And with that, she walked out of my office.

46

Tina Sucks

Naomi

I went straight to the restroom to repair my face. Knox Morgan sure did a number on a woman's makeup. After I cleaned up the sad clown face and reapplied my lipstick, I gave my reflection a long, hard look.

The tiny shards of my broken heart were now ground into a fine dust thanks to Knox's confession.

"No wonder," I whispered to my reflection.

There were things a person never got over. We both just wanted someone to love us enough to make up for all the times we hadn't been enough. It felt like such a waste that we could feel the way we did, but neither of us could be that person for the other.

I couldn't make Knox love me enough, and the sooner I got over that, the better. Maybe someday we could be friends. If I won the custody hearing, and if Waylay and I decided to make Knockemout our permanent home.

Thinking of Waylay, I dug my phone out of my apron to check my messages. Earlier this week, I'd approved a messaging app for her laptop so she could text me if she needed to. In return, she'd downloaded a GIF keyboard on my phone so we could exchange GIFs throughout the day.

"Oh, great," I groaned when I saw the dozen new texts.

Silver: Nice undies.

Max: This better mean you guys are making up!!!!

Mom: Six flame emojis.

Fi: We're covering your tables so feel free to have as many orgasms in Knoxy's office as you need.

Sloane: Lina just texted (along with nine other people at the bar). Did that son of a bitch really carry you off like he was a caveman? I hope you rearranged his face and his balls.

Waylay: Aunt Naomi, I'm in trouble.

The breath in my lungs froze when I read the last text. She'd sent it fifteen minutes ago. With shaking hands, I fired off a response as I rushed out of the restroom.

Me: Are you okay? What's wrong?

There were a lot of reasons an eleven-year-old could think they were in trouble, I rationalized. It didn't mean there was an actual emergency. Maybe she forgot her math homework. Maybe she accidentally broke Liza J's favorite garden cherub. Maybe she'd gotten her period.

I also had three missed calls in the last five minutes from an unknown number. Something was wrong.

I headed for the kitchen and scrolled through my contacts for Liza J's number.

"Everything okay, Naomi?" Milford asked as I hustled for the parking lot.

"Yeah. I think so. Just have to make a quick call," I said before pushing through the exterior door into the cold night air.

I was getting ready to hit Call when headlights from a car blinded me. I held up my hand to block the light and stepped back.

"Naomi."

My arms dropped limply to my side. I knew that voice.

"Tina?"

My twin sister leaned out the driver's side window. I felt like I was looking in the mirror again. A fun house mirror. Her formerly bleached hair was now a dark brown and cut short in a style similar to mine. Our eyes were the same hazel. The differences were subtle. She was wearing a cheap fake leather jacket. She had multiple earrings in both ears. Her eyeliner was thick and blue.

But she looked as worried as I felt.

"He's got Waylay! He took her," she said.

My stomach dropped, and a wave of nausea crested as every muscle in my body tightened. "What? Who took her? Where is she?"

"It's all my fault," Tina wailed. "We need to go.

You have to help me. I know where he took her."

"We should call the police," I said, remembering I had a phone in my hand.

"Call 'em on the way. We gotta move fast," she said. "Come on."

Operating on autopilot, I opened the passenger door and climbed in. I was reaching for my seat belt when something furry clamped over my wrist.

"What are you doing?" I shrieked.

Tina grabbed my other arm, her fingernails digging into my wrist. I tried to pull away but wasn't quick enough. She snapped the other cuff in place.

"For the smart one, you sure are stupid," she said, lighting a cigarette.

My evil twin had just handcuffed me to the dashboard with furry sex cuffs.

"Where's Waylay?"

"Relax." She blew a stream of smoke in my direction. "The kid's fine. You will be too if you cooperate."

"Cooperate how? With who?" I yanked against the cuffs.

She let out a cackle as she pulled out of the parking lot. "Pretty funny, right? Found those in a box of sex toys in my old asshole landlord's storage unit."

"Gross!" I was going to need to scrub myself with bleach when this was over.

My phone was facedown on the floor. If I could get to it, I could call someone. I yanked on the cuffs again, yelping when they bit into my skin.

"Got your email," my sister said conversationally. "Figured between you and that kid of mine, we'd find what I'm lookin' for real quick."

"Find what?" I nudged my phone with the toe of my boot in an effort to flip it over. The angle wasn't quite right, and instead of flipping it over, it slid farther under the dash.

"Doesn't surprise me that you don't know. One thing that doesn't suck about my kid is she sure knows how to keep her damn mouth shut. My man and I got our hands on some pretty important information that a lot of people would pay a lot of money to get. Kept it on a flash drive. Flash drive went missing."

"What does this have to do with Waylay?" This time, the nudge was just enough to flip the phone over . . . and unfortunately turn the screen on. The glow was not subtle.

"Oh-ho! Nice try, Goody." My sister leaned down and reached for the phone. The car swerved off the road onto the berm, headlights shining on a long run of pasture fence.

"Watch out!" I ducked as we smashed right through the fence and came to a stop in the grassy horse pasture. My head smacked against the dashboard, and I saw stars.

"Whoops!" Tina said, sitting up holding my phone.

"Ouch! God, you haven't gotten any better at driving, have you?"

"Orgasms and undies," she mused, scrolling through my texts. "Huh. Maybe you got more interesting since high school."

I leaned down so I could use a shackled hand to prod my aching forehead.

"You better not have hurt Waylay, you irresponsible ignoramus."

"Vocabulary's still workin' just fine. What the hell do you take me for? I wouldn't hurt my own daughter."

She sounded insulted.

"Look," I said wearily. "Just take me to Waylay."

"That's the plan, Goody."

Goody was short for Goody Two-Shoes, the nickname Tina had saddled me with when we were all of nine years old and she wanted to see how high we could shoot arrows into the air with our uncle's crossbow that she found.

I wished I had that crossbow now.

"I cannot believe we're related."

"Makes two of us," she said, tossing her cigarette followed by my phone out the window.

She cranked the radio and stomped on the accelerator. The car fishtailed wildly on the damp grass before careening through the gaping hole in the fence.

Thirty minutes later, Tina turned off the pothole-ridden road that cut through a run-down industrial section of a DC suburb. She pulled up to a chain-link fence and laid on the horn.

Subtlety was not my sister's specialty.

I'd spent the entire drive thinking about Waylay. And Knox. About my parents. Liza J. Nash. Sloane. The Honky Tonk girls. About how I'd finally somehow managed to make a home for myself only to have Tina show up and ruin it all. Again.

Two shadowy figures dressed in denim and leather appeared and wrestled the gate open with an earsplitting screech.

I needed to stick to my strengths and play it smart. I'd get to Waylay and then find a way out. I could do this.

We pulled through the gate, and Tina brought the car to a stop in front of a loading dock. She lit another cigarette. Her fourth of the trip.

"You shouldn't smoke so much."

"What are you? The lung police?"

"It gives you wrinkles."

"That's what plastic surgeons are for," Tina said, hefting her significantly larger fake breasts. "That's the problem with you. Always too worried about the consequences to have any fun."

"And you never gave the consequences a thought," I pointed out. "Look at where that got you. You abandoned and then kidnapped Waylay. Abducted me. Not to mention stole from me on multiple occasions. Now you're moving stolen products."

"Yeah? And which one of us is having more fun?"

"Actually, I've been sleeping with Knox Morgan."

She eyed me through the smoke. "You're shitting me."

I shook my head. "I am not shitting you."

She thumped the steering wheel and cackled. "Well, well. Look at little Goody Two-Shoes finally loosening up. Next thing you'll be jumpin' on the pole at amateur night and shoplifting scratch-offs."

I seriously doubted that.

"What? Who knows? Maybe you loosen up enough, we might find that sisterly bond you were always whining about," Tina said, slapping my thigh with what might have been affection. "But first, we gotta get this business taken care of."

I held up my handcuffed hands. "What kind of business can I take care of with sex cuffs on?"

She reached into the pocket of her door and produced a set of keys. "Here's the thing. Need you to do me a favor."

"Anything for you, Tina," I said dryly.

"I bet my man a hundred dollars I could get you here without knocking you out or forcing you. Told him you were a natural-born sucker. He said there was no way I could get you to march on in there all free will and shit. So here's how this is gonna go. I'm gonna uncuff you and take you upstairs to my man and kid. You're not gonna tell him about these." She ruffled the purple leopard fur on the cuff closest to her.

My sister was an idiot.

"If I uncuff you and you try to run or if you open your tattletale mouth up there, I'll make sure you never see Waylay again."

An idiot with a surprising grasp of what motivated people.

She grinned. "Yeah. I knew you'd like her. Figured she'd like you too, seein' as how you're into all that girlie shit. Knew you'd be the best place to park my kid till I was ready to hit the road."

"Waylay's a great girl," I said.

"She ain't some whiny tattletale like *some* people," she said, shooting me a pointed look. "Anyway, I win my bet, you get to spend some quality time with the kid before we head off to our payday."

She wanted to take Waylay with her. I felt an icy sickness settle in my gut but said nothing.

"We got a deal?"

I nodded. "Yeah. Yes. We have a deal."

"Let's get me my hundred bucks," Tina said cheerfully.

I counted three more swarthy degenerates, all with guns, inside the warehouse. The first floor had nearly a dozen flashy vehicles parked inside. Some were under tarps, some sat with their hoods up and doors open. On the other side of the loading dock were boxes of TVs and what looked like other stolen goods.

It was cold, and I wasn't dressed for it.

"Let's go, Goody. Got shit to do," Tina said, leading the way up the metal stairs to the second floor, an area that looked like it had once housed offices. My sister threw open the door and strutted inside. "Mama's home," she announced.

I hesitated outside the door and sent up a silent prayer to the good twin gods. I was scared. I would have given anything to have Knox or Nash or the entire Knockemout Police Department with me. But that wasn't going to happen.

I needed to be my own hero tonight or I was going to lose everything.

I straightened my shoulders and crossed the threshold to do what I did best, triage the mess. There was heat inside, thank God. Not much, but enough that at least my lady parts wouldn't freeze. There was also a distinct odor of old takeout food, most likely coming from the stack of pizza boxes and to-go containers on a long folding table.

Dingy glass windows overlooked the warehouse floor and the exterior. Against a third wall was a futon topped with what looked like very expensive sheets and no fewer than six pillows.

There were two rolling racks of designer clothing that created a makeshift closet. A dozen pairs of high-end men's sneakers and loafers were organized on another folding table.

The floor was sticky. The ceiling had holes in it. And there was a thick layer of grime on the windows.

I itched to find the Lysol and start scrubbing until I spotted the table stacked nearly a foot high with bundles of cash.

"Told ya," Tina said triumphantly, hooking her thumb in my direction. "Walked right in, didn't she?"

I stopped short when I recognized the man in the large, leather office chair in front of the flat-screen TV.

It was the red-haired guy from the library and Honky Tonk. Only this time, he wasn't dressed to blend in. He was wearing a flashy pair of jeans and a bright orange Balenciaga hoodie.

He was rubbing a cloth over an already gleaming handgun.

I gulped.

"Well, well. If it isn't my old lady's doppelganger. Remember me?" he said with a villainous smirk.

"Mr. Flint," I said.

Tina snorted. "His name's Duncan. Duncan Hugo. As in the Hugo crime syndicate."

She was bragging, making him sound as if she'd just told me she was dating a sexy humanitarian lawyer or an orthodontist with a beach house.

"What did I tell you, T? You don't say my fucking name to any fucking one," Duncan barked.

"Pfft. She's my sister," she said, flipping open a pizza box and pulling out a slice. "If I can't tell her, who can I tell?"

Duncan pinched the bridge of his nose. A move I'd seen my father and Knox make. I wondered if all Witt women had this effect on men.

"This ain't ladies' night out, woman," Duncan reminded her. "This is business."

"It's business after you pay up. You lost. I won. Cough up the cash."

I didn't think it was the best idea to taunt the man holding the gun, but Tina did what Tina always did—whatever she wanted to do regardless of the consequences.

"Put it on my tab," the man said, continuing to study me. He brought the barrel of the gun up to scratch his temple.

"I don't think that's a safe way to handle a firearm," I interjected.

He studied me for several seconds, then his face broke into a mean grin. "That's funny. You're funny."

Great. Now he was pointing the gun at me like it was a finger.

"Fuck your tab, Dunc. Gimme the cash," Tina insisted.

"Where's Waylay?" I demanded.

"Oh, yeah. Where's the kid?" Tina asked, glancing around.

Duncan's grin got wider and meaner. With his boot, he gave the chair next to him a kick. It rolled across the floor, the seat slowly spinning to face us.

"Mmph mmm!"

Waylay, wearing pajamas and sneakers, was gagged and tied to the chair. She looked mutinous, her expression mirroring her mother's. Waylon was sitting in her lap. His tail thumped when he spotted me.

I forgot all about being scared and almost felt

599

sorry for the redheaded moron. If Tina or I didn't kill him for tying up Waylay, Knox would for stealing his dog.

"Why is she tied up?" Tina demanded.

Duncan shrugged and used the barrel of the gun to scratch an itch between his shoulder blades. "Little bitch called me a dickweasel and tried to kick me in the balls. Fuckin' bit me too," he said, holding up his forearm to show off the bandage.

"Well, were you bein' a dickweasel?" my sister asked, crossing her arms.

Waylay, eyes narrowed, nodded vehemently.

"Me?" He pointed the gun at his chest, all innocence. "I just told her not to eat another piece of pizza, else she'd get fat, and no one likes fat chicks."

Tina stomped over and drilled a finger into his chest. "You don't tell *my* kid about getting fat. That shit goes to a girl's head. Body dysmorphia and shit like that."

I was impressed.

"Bitches are so sensitive," Duncan said to me as if he could expect my agreement.

"Give me my money and untie her," Tina demanded.

I couldn't help but notice the order of her priorities and tabled my newfound respect for my sister.

Exasperated, I started toward Waylay. Waylon scrambled off her lap and tried to approach but was stopped by his leash.

600

"Uh-uh. One more step, and we're gonna have a problem, Not Tina." The warning was accompanied by the racking of a gun as Duncan came to his feet.

I glared at him. "My name is Naomi."

"Don't care if your name is Queen Latifah. I need you to stand right where you are." He gestured with the gun. "Now, Waylay—whatever the fuck kind of name that is—where's the fucking flash drive? You got ten seconds to tell me, or I'm gonna shoot your aunt right between the eyes."

The cigarette in Tina's mouth fell to the floor as she gaped at him. "The fuck? That wasn't part of the plan, you asshole!"

"You shut your mouth, or I'll drop you next to your sister. Hey! What's sadder than a dead twin? *Two* dead twins!" Duncan howled at his own feeble humor.

"You dirty double-crosser," Tina snarled.

He stopped laughing. "Now hold on there, T. I ain't double-crossed you yet. I meant what I said. We can take the drive, sell it, and start building something real. Something that's got nothing to do with my fuckin' dad or the fuckin' family business!" His arms flailed, the barrel of the gun pointing everywhere at once.

"Could you please gesticulate without the gun?" I suggested.

"Christ. Again with the daddy issues," Tina scoffed at Duncan. "My daddy is a big-time crime lord. It's so hard to live up to his example. Boo-friggin'-hoo."

Again I began to inch my way toward Waylay.

"You know I don't like it when you talk to me like my mom," Duncan howled.

"You're actin' like you're large and in charge. But who's the one who tricked the kid into the car by pretending to be my sister? Who's the one who got Naomi here?"

"Hey! I'm doin' this for you, T. We could finally get the equipment to make those fake IDs you're always runnin' your mouth about. Or set up a black market organ donor farm."

I wrinkled my nose. "Gross! Is that a real thing?"

"Don't you yuck my yum, Hot Tina," he said to me.

Oh boy.

Tina backhanded him in the shoulder. "What did you just call her?"

I used the distraction to sneak closer to Waylay.

"Ow! I meant *Not* Tina," Duncan insisted.

My niece chose that moment to heave herself forward, trying to tip the chair over, only succeeding in knocking into the table with the fat stacks of cash.

I raced forward, untangling dog leash and rope.

"One more move, and both of them get it," Duncan warned, the gun trained on me as he stared at Waylay. "You got five seconds, kid, to start talking. Where's the drive?"

Waylay's eyes were wide and scared and pinned to me.

"Five . . . four . . . three . . . two . . ."

47

Missing

Knox

"W hat the hell did you do with Naomi?" Fi demanded, waving her lollipop in my face when I hit the bar floor.

I noticed Naomi's parents were gone, and their table had been turned over.

"I talked to her. *Nicely,*" I said when her eyes narrowed. "Why?"

"Couldn't have been that nice since all her tables are getting restless with empty drinks."

I peered over Fi's shoulder, doing what I always did, looking for Naomi. But Fi was right. She wasn't there.

"If you chased her off in the middle of a shift—"

"I didn't chase her off. We talked. It was good. We're good. Did you check the bathroom?"

"Now, gee, why didn't I think of that?" Fi said, her voice dripping with sarcasm.

"Did you ask him what the hell he did with Naomi?" Max asked as she buzzed by.

Something cold settled in my gut. Ignoring my employees, I pushed through the doors into the kitchen. "Naomi in here?"

Milford looked up from the chicken he was

grilling and tilted his head toward the door to the parking lot. "Went out a couple minutes ago to make a call. She looked upset. You say something mean to her again?"

I didn't bother answering. Instead I went straight for the door and shoved it open. Fi was on my heels. The night air had a crisp bite to it that did nothing to thaw the icy fear inside me. There was no sign of Naomi.

"Fuck." I did not have a good feeling about this.

"She's probably just getting some fresh air since you broke her heart and then embarrassed her in front of half the town," Fi guessed, scanning the lot with me. But she didn't sound sure either.

"I don't like this," I muttered. "Naomi!" But there was no response.

"Naomi, Knox is sorry for being an ass!" Fi shouted into the night next to me.

Nothing.

My phone vibrated in my pocket, and I yanked it out.

Nash.

"What?"

"Just a heads-up. I'm on my way to Liza J's. She said Waylay's gone. Took your dog out for a pee break, and neither one of them came back."

The ice in my gut turned into an iceberg.

"How long ago?"

"About forty minutes. Liza J went out looking for them. Thinks she saw taillights heading for the road. Said she tried to call Naomi, but she's not

604

picking up her phone. I tried too and got voicemail. I'm sure it's nothing, but I need you to tell Naomi."

Fuck. Fuck. Fuck.

My heart was hitting like a damn bass drum.

"Naomi stepped out to make a call, and no one's seen her since. I'm standing in the fucking parking lot, and she's not here."

"Goddammit."

"I don't like this," I said, dragging a hand through my hair. "I'm gonna go look for them."

"Do me a favor first and call Naomi's parents. I'm gonna get Liza J and have some of my guys do a sweep of the woods."

"She's not gonna be there," I told him.

"Gotta start somewhere. Call you back," Nash said.

I immediately dialed Naomi's number and headed back inside. Fi followed me with wide, worried eyes.

I snapped my fingers at her. "Get on the security feed for the parking lot."

She didn't give me an ounce of shit, just bobbed her head and hurried off in the direction of the office.

"Naomi okay, boss?" Milford asked.

"She's not out there."

"Hey! I could use a hand out here. The natives are gettin' restless and thirsty," Max said, swinging through the kitchen door. She took one look at us and stopped in her tracks. "What?"

"Can't find Naomi," I told her as the phone rang and rang in my ear.

"What the hell did you say to her this time?" Max demanded.

"Hi, you've reached Naomi Witt. Thanks for calling! Leave a message."

I hit redial as worry crept over me like an icy black cloud.

"Come on, Daze. Pick up," I muttered.

"Let me try," Max said, pulling out her phone.

"Tell me the second you talk to her. I need to know where she is."

"What's happening?" Silver asked, sticking her head in the door.

"Waylay and Naomi are missing," I snapped.

All eyes landed on me.

"What are the odds that they'd both go missing at the same time?" Max asked.

I shook my head and scrolled through my contacts. My hands were shaking. I dialed Lou's number.

"I know it's date night, and I know I'm not your favorite person right now, but I think we've got trouble," I told him when he answered.

"What's wrong?"

"Liza J said Waylay went missing again. She and Nash are out looking for her now, but Naomi walked out of the bar to make a call, and I can't find her either."

"I'll meet you at Honky Tonk in two minutes," he said.

"If something happened to them, Lou . . ." I couldn't even finish the thought.

"We're gonna find them. Keep it together, son."

"Knox." The worry in Fi's tone had me turning fast.

"I gotta go," I said and hung up. "What did you find?"

"Her coat and bag are still behind the bar. And the camera has her getting into a car in the parking lot about ten minutes ago."

Ten minutes felt like a lifetime. "What kind of car? Who was driving?"

"I couldn't tell. On either count. Some dark, crappy sedan. But it looks like she got in willingly."

"What the hell's going on?" Wraith demanded, poking his head into the kitchen. "There's gonna be a revolt out here soon if someone doesn't start pouring beers."

"Naomi's missing," Fi told him.

"Fuck me."

"Waylay too," Max added with a tearful sniffle.

"Double fuck," Wraith said, then disappeared back into the bar.

"Her phone," Fi said.

"She's not answering."

"But she's on your family plan, isn't she?"

My mind was going a million miles a minute. I needed to get out there and start looking for her. Every second I wasted was one second that she got farther away. "Yeah."

Max slapped me in the arm. "You can track her!"

Technology for the fucking win. I shoved my phone at her. "Find her."

As she moved deft fingers over the screen, I headed for my office. I grabbed my coat and keys and returned to the bar.

It wasn't the pandemonium I'd expected from pissed-off drinkers on a Saturday night. It was organized chaos. Wraith stood on the bar, boots planted between beer glasses. Everyone was gathered around, shrugging into coats.

"Last seen getting into a dark gray four-door shitmobile wearing a denim skirt and long-sleeved shirt that says Honky Tonk."

"What the hell is this?" I demanded.

"Search party," Silver said as she shoved her arms into a gray tweed coat.

The front door opened, and everyone turned expectantly.

It was Lou and Amanda.

"Let 'em through," Wraith ordered. The crowd parted for them, and they hurried forward.

"I got her!" Max said, holding my phone up triumphantly. "Looks like she's just off Route 7 near the Lucky Horseshoe Farm."

I snatched it out of her hand. "Call Nash," I said, pointing to Lou.

Lou turned to Amanda. "Call Nash. I'm going with him."

I didn't waste time arguing. We hit the parking lot, and I had the truck started before either of us closed the doors. I floored it out of the lot, fishtailing onto the road.

"Who took her?"

"I don't know for sure," I said, gripping the wheel tighter. "But if Waylay's missing too, my money's on Tina."

Lou swore under his breath.

My phone rang. It was Nash. I hit the speaker button.

"You find Way?" I asked.

"No. I'm bringing Liza J into town. Got some footage off the Morrison's doorbell cam. Dark, shitty sedan pulled out of Liza's about an hour ago. A big, black SUV was parked on the shoulder, waiting for it. Headlights set off the motion sensor. Timeline fits for Liza J seein' the brake lights. Also got a call about a hit and run. Someone smashed through the Loys' fence along the road over at Lucky Horseshoe."

Lou and I glanced at each other. "We're on our way there now, tracking Naomi's phone."

"Don't do anything stupid," Nash ordered.

Lucky Horseshoe was a short drive, made shorter by the fact that I hit ninety miles per hour.

"Should be right up here," Lou said, peering at my phone.

I let off the gas, then hit the brakes hard when I saw the fence. "Shit."

Tire marks swerved off the road and smashed right through the rail fence. I turned the wheel so my lights could follow the path and put the truck in park.

Mr. and Mrs. Loy were standing in the pasture surveying the damage. Mrs. Loy was huddled up in an oversize flannel jacket and smoking a small cigar. Mr. Loy came right at us.

"Can you believe this? Some son of a bitch smashed through the fence and then drove back out again!"

"Grab the flashlight in the glove box," I told Lou.

"Naomi!" I called the second my feet hit the ground. The frosty grass crunched under my boots.

There was no answer.

Lou flashed the light into the pasture, and we followed the tracks. "Looks like they stopped here before driving back out," he said.

"Must have been one drunk idiot."

Something caught my eye in the grass, and I bent to pick it up. It was a cellphone with sparkly daisies on the case.

A chill stopped my heart and had me fighting for breath.

"Is that hers?" Lou asked.

"Yeah."

"Goddammit."

"What's that? Is that evidence?" Mr. Loy demanded.

I drove back to Honky Tonk in a fog. Lou was talking, but I wasn't listening. I was too busy replaying my last conversation with Naomi. I hadn't wanted to lose her, so I'd pushed her away and lost her anyway.

She was right. This was worse. So much fucking worse.

Someone had coordinated this. Someone had conspired to take them both away from me. And I was going to make them fucking pay.

I pulled up to the front door of the bar, and half the damn town poured out.

"Where is she?"

"You find her?"

"Does he look like he found her, Elmer, you idiot?"

"He looks pretty pissed off."

Ignoring the crowd and the questions, I pushed inside and found half the Knockemout PD surrounded by the other half of town. The specials board had been erased, replaced with a hand-drawn map of Knockemout cut into quadrants.

Fi, Max, and Silver charged me, and Nash looked up.

"You didn't find them," Fi said.

I shook my head.

A shrill whistle cut through the noise, and everyone shut up.

"Thanks, Lucy," Nash said to Lucian, who immediately returned to whatever phone call he was making. "As I was saying, we've got an APB out on Naomi Witt, Waylay Witt, a gray sedan, and a black, newer model Chevy Tahoe. We're starting the search in town and expanding outward."

Amanda, dragging Liza J with her, hurried over to Lou, who pulled her into his side. "We'll find 'em," he promised. Then he wrapped his free arm around my grandmother.

611

I couldn't breathe. Couldn't swallow. Couldn't move from the spot. I thought I'd been afraid before. Afraid of turning into my father. Of crumbling after a loss. But this fear was worse. I hadn't told her I fucking loved her. I hadn't told either one of them. And someone had taken them from me. I hadn't crumbled. It was worse. I hadn't had the goddamn guts to love someone enough to crumble.

I shoved my hands through my hair and kept them there as the reality of what I'd walked away from set in.

I felt a hand clamp down on my shoulder. "Keep it together," Lucian said. "We'll find them."

"How? How the fuck will we find them? We know jack shit."

"We've got a plate number on a 2002 gray Ford Taurus that was reported stolen from Lawlerville an hour ago," Lucian said.

"We don't have plate numbers yet," Nash said, pausing to glance down at his phone. "Scratch that. 2002 gray Ford Taurus with a primer gray trunk lid." He read off a license plate number.

"Lawlerville is half an hour from here," I said, running the calculations in my head. It was the edge of a suburb of DC.

"You'd have to be pretty stupid to steal a car and then drive it back to the scene of the crime," Lucian pointed out.

"If Tina is involved with this, stupid is a factor."

The front door opened, and Sloane and Lina

612

rushed in. Sloane looked breathless and scared. Lina looked scary.

"What can I do?" Sloane asked.

"Whose ass do you want me to kick?" Lina demanded.

I needed to move. I needed to get out of here and find my girls, rip apart every single person who played a role in taking them, and then spend the rest of my life begging for Naomi's forgiveness.

"Give us a moment, ladies," Lucian said and steered me back outside. "There's more."

"What more?"

"I have a name."

I grabbed him by the lapels of his wool coat. "Give me the name," I growled.

Lucian's hands closed over mine. "It's not going to help like you think it will."

"Start talking before I start punching."

"Duncan Hugo."

I released him. "Hugo as in the Hugo crime family?"

Anthony Hugo was a crime lord who operated out of both DC and Baltimore. Drugs. Prostitution. Weapons. Enforcement. Political blackmail. You name it, it had his filthy fingerprints on it.

"Duncan is the son. And a bit of a fuckup. It was his chop shop where the car used in Nash's shooting was found. I didn't think it was a coincidence, but I wanted more information to corroborate before I brought it to you and Nash."

"How long have you known?" I demanded, my hands balling into fists.

"Not long enough for you to waste time and energy on me tonight."

"Goddammit, Lucy."

"Rumor has it he had a nasty and recent split from his father. Seems Duncan wants to strike out on his own. Rumors also mention a woman he's been working with as well as fucking for the past few months."

It clicked into place as neatly as the last piece of a puzzle. Tina Fucking Witt.

"Where is he?"

Lucian tucked his hands into his pockets, his expression giving nothing away. "That's the problem. Since he had his falling-out with his father, no one seems to know his whereabouts."

"Or they're not telling you."

"Sooner or later, everyone tells me everything," he said.

I didn't have time to worry about how dark that sounded. "You tell Nash any of this?" I asked, digging my keys out of my pocket.

"Just the plate number. Could be a coincidence."

"It's not."

The door opened behind me, and Sloane stepped out.

"Are you going to look for them?" she asked.

I nodded, then turned to Lucian. "I'll start in Lawlerville and work my way toward DC."

"Hold on," he said.

"I'm coming with you," Sloane announced.

Lucian stepped in front of her. "You're staying here."

"She's my friend, and Waylay is practically a second niece."

"You're staying here."

I didn't have time to listen to Lucian use his scary-ass intimidation voice.

"I think you're making the incredibly ignorant assumption that you have any say over what I do or don't do."

"If I find out you leave town limits tonight, I will see that your beloved library never gets another dime of funding. Then I'll buy every piece of land around your house and build apartment complexes so tall you never see the sun again."

"You rich son of a . . ."

I left them to it. I opened the door to my truck and climbed behind the wheel. A second later, the passenger door opened, and Lucian got in. "Where are we going?"

"I'm starting at the top. I'm going to beat the hell out of Anthony Hugo until he tells us where his asshole son is. Then I'm going to find him and beat the hell out of him until I break every bone in his face. Then I'm going to marry Naomi Witt."

"This should be fun," my best friend said, pulling out his phone.

"You can give Nash a heads-up on the way and then tap that creepy source network of yours to find me Anthony Hugo."

615

We were ten minutes out of town with two credible locations for the biggest crime lord in Washington, DC. One of the sources even coughed up the gate code for the property. Lucian Rollins was a scary motherfucker.

His phone rang again.

"This is Lucian." He listened for a few seconds, then handed me the phone. "For you."

It was probably my brother bitching me out for taking the law into my own hands. "What?" I said.

"Knox. Grim here."

Grim was the high-stakes-poker-playing, mostly almost-legal motorcycle club president.

"This is not a good time to plan another poker game, man."

"Not poker-related. Club business. Got some info I thought you might be interested in."

"Unless it's the whereabouts of Anthony or Duncan Hugo, I'm not interested."

"Then you're about to be real interested. That pretty little waitress of yours just marched her fine ass right on into Duncan Hugo's new chop shop."

My heart was hammering away against my rib cage. "What did you just say?"

"My guys have been sitting on the building for reasons."

"I'm not the cops," I reminded him.

"Let's just say some local businesses aren't real happy about the competition."

Translation: Grim's club was planning to hit the chop shop.

"Been keeping tabs on all the comings and goings. Just got photo confirmation. She's a twin, right?"

"Yeah, why?"

"I remember her talking about her twin sister at the last game. Looks like she wasn't bullshitting about the twin. Bitch had Naomi handcuffed to the dashboard."

I dropped my foot on the accelerator. "Address," I demanded.

48

The Ol' Switcheroo

Naomi

F ive . . . four . . . three . . . two . . ."

"Wait! What makes you think Waylay knows where whatever the hell you're looking for is?" I asked, desperate to keep Duncan distracted from his deadly countdown. "She's just a child."

"Mmph mmm," Waylay grumbled, clearly offended.

Tina didn't say anything. Her eyes were glued to Duncan, and I was surprised he hadn't caught fire from the flames shooting out of them. The man had no idea the fuse he'd just lit. I only hoped my sister's impending explosion wouldn't get us all killed.

"Simple addition. Tina took the flash drive, and it disappeared. Only one other person in that house. The little brat who likes technology and stealin' stuff."

"Tina told you it disappeared?"

"No, Santy Claus did," Duncan said, rolling his eyes.

"Did it ever occur to you that Tina is hiding the flash drive? Maybe she took it to cut you out of the deal."

Both Tina and Duncan were now looking at me. I didn't know if I'd made things better or worse, but at least the gun was pointing at the floor. I dropped to my knees and attacked the knot on Waylay's wrist.

"Don't listen to her," Tina said, seeming to come back to life. "She's just doing what she used to do with our parents. Trying to manipulate you."

"I hate that shit," he said, raising the gun once again. "Now where was I? Five?"

"Nine?" I suggested weakly.

"You have to go to the bathroom," Tina announced to me.

"What?"

She gave me a hard look. "You have to go to the bathroom," she said again before turning back to Duncan. "She got her period. You don't want to shoot her *and* get period all over the place, do you, Dunc?"

"Gross. Don't tell me that woman shit," he complained, looking like he was about to vomit.

"I'll take her to the bathroom, and we'll get the kid to talk about where she stashed the drive," she said with a pointed look in Waylay's direction. "Then I'll run out and get you some of that fried chicken that you like."

Tina was definitely up to something. She had that crafty look on her face. And I definitely hadn't gotten my period. The Honky Tonk Code Red was two weeks out.

"That's more like it," Duncan said, satisfied that

his woman was back in line. "Wasn't really gonna shoot you, T."

"I know you're under a lot of stress, baby," Tina said as she dragged me across the room toward a door marked RES OOM. "Take a break. Drink a beer. We'll be right back," she called over her shoulder.

She shoved me through the door into a bathroom that needed to be hosed down with a truckload of bleach.

"Take your clothes off," she said when the door swung shut.

"What? Tina, we can't leave Waylay alone with him. He's insane."

"I'm gettin' that. Now take off your goddamn clothes," she said, dropping her pants.

"You've lost your mind. This isn't just another bad decision with horrible consequences. You've gone off the deep end, haven't you?"

"For fuck's sake. I'm not trying to have incestual relations with you. This ain't a porno. We're trading places. He's not gonna let *you* walk out of here and get help. But he'll let me leave." She stripped her shirt off over her head and threw it in my direction. It hit me in the face.

"Then leave and call the police," I hissed.

"I'm not leavin' Way with that stupid mother-fucker."

"You already abandoned her once!"

"I left her with *you,* smarty-pants. Knew you'd take care of her until I got my score."

I knew I shouldn't really take that as a compliment, but it was about as close as Tina got to giving them.

"He's fondling that Beretta like it's his dick, and he's got a loaded PPK under the pizza box," she continued. "You know how to work one? Are you willing to shoot a man in the fucking balls and risk prison?"

"No and yes. If it gets Waylay out of here alive."

"Well, I'm yes and yes. Pretty damn good shot too. So gimme your damn skirt. And you go call the cops."

"Can't you just send Knox or Nash a text and tell them where we are?"

"Phone's in the car," she said, dragging my skirt up her hips. "Dunc's paranoid about being tracked by the government. Won't let a cell phone near him here."

I pulled her shirt over my head. "Fine. Okay. So what's the plan then?"

"We go out there. I'm you, but I give Waylay the code."

"What's the code?"

"I say 'I read this article on the devastation of the rain forest,' and she knows it's code for get ready to run."

I supposed it was Tina's version of having a family fire drill. "Okay. Then what?"

"She'll make up the location of wherever she hid the thing. Dunc'll send his guys to get it. You'll

621

leave to get celebratory chicken, but really you'll go down to the car and call 911."

This didn't sound like a great plan. And I trusted my sister about as far as I could spit, which was not far at all. But I didn't have any other options. "What will you do?" I stalled. "Even if you get past Duncan, there are men with guns outside."

"I'll do whatever it takes to get Waylay out of here."

I zipped her jeans and then stepped into her boots.

We looked at each other.

"Your boobs are exploding out of my shirt," I observed.

She reached for the roll of toilet paper. "Stuff."

"Seriously?" I squeaked.

"As long as you and me have big tits, he won't notice the difference. He's seven beers into his night."

"You have *got* to get better taste in men," I complained as I shoved wads of toilet paper into my bra.

She shrugged. "He's not so bad when he's not drunk."

"Yo! Ladies! Get your asses out here. I'm ready to shoot someone."

"He sounds like a dreamboat," I grumbled.

"Try not to walk like you got a stick up your ass," Tina hissed, shoving me toward the door.

"Try to talk like you didn't have to cheat your way through the eighth grade."

We returned to Bachelor Central, and I was

relieved to see that Waylay was still alive and looking mutinous. Waylon was sitting next to her chair like a guard. His tail thumped when he saw me, and I worried that Duncan would notice.

Fortunately, he was too engrossed in a video game that apparently involved shooting scantily dressed women.

"Ha! Suck my barrel, bitch!"

Tina cleared her throat and looked at Waylay. "I read this article on the devastation of the rain forest."

Waylay's eyes widened above the duct tape. I nodded at her, and then at her mother. She blinked twice. Tina elbowed me.

"Ouch. I mean, quit blabbering about reading shit and go sit down over there . . . by my kid," I said, tossing my hair over my shoulder and gesturing in Waylay's direction.

"Waylay, honey sweetie pie, are you okay? I'm so sorry this is all happening. It's all my fault probably because I'm so snobby and act like I'm better than everyone," Tina said, flopping down on the torn ottoman next to her daughter. Her knees spread wide, and I could see straight up my—er, her—skirt.

Waylay rolled her eyes.

Behind me, I heard Duncan get to his feet. I was startled by a stinging slap on my butt. "That ass is lookin' mighty fine in those jeans tonight, Teen," he said before shotgunning the rest of his beer. He threw the can over his shoulder and belched.

"I have the *best* taste in men," I said, glaring at Tina.

"Heh. Your sister has the same thong as you," Duncan said, pointing at Tina's exposed crotch. "You guys really are twins."

The man was an idiot. Unfortunately, he was an idiot with a gun. And I had no better options than Tina's plan.

"Ti—I mean, Naomi and I were talking," I began.

"She didn't get period all over the place in there, did she?"

I gritted my teeth. "No. It's just the usual bodily fluids all over the floor and walls."

Tina cleared her throat pointedly. Poor Waylon was looking back and forth between her and me like he was trying to puzzle out what was going on.

"Anyway, your aunt who loves you very much and I talked, Waylay. We agreed that it's safe for you to tell Duncan where you hid the flash drive," I said.

"Yeah. You can tell me, kid. I'm trustworthy as shit," Duncan said, apparently forgetting that he'd just threatened the lives of her mother and aunt only minutes ago.

"Just tell him where you absconded it, and he'll send his men to go get it," Tina said, enunciating slowly.

That was definitely *not* the right use of the word *absconded*.

Duncan nudged me with his elbow. "Go take the tape off her mouth."

I approached Waylay and leaned in. "It's me, Naomi," I whispered.

She crossed her eyes as if to say "Duh." Waylon stood up and licked my shin.

"Oh, now he likes you," Duncan said. "Dogs are as fickle as bitches. An hour ago, he couldn't stop growlin' at you, and now he wants to hump your leg."

I peeled back the corner of the tape.

"Sorry, kiddo," I whispered and yanked the tape free.

"Son of a goddamn bitch, ow!" Waylay yelled.

I suddenly missed Knox from the depths of my soul.

"Tell me where the drive is, kid," Duncan said. The gun appeared in my peripheral vision as he advanced on us.

Waylay took what looked like a heroic breath. "I hid it at the library in Knockemout. I taped it under a shelf in the historical fiction section."

Smart, smart girl. If Duncan sent his men to break into the library, they'd essentially be breaking into a police station.

"Thank you for telling us. I'm very proud of you for your honesty and integrity," Tina said in what I assumed was her impression of me. She sounded British.

"You'll probably want to go get that now while the library's closed," I said to Duncan.

"Yeah, maybe," he said, but his eyes were on Tina, and he looked thoughtful.

"I guess I'll go get that chicken," I said, edging toward the door.

"Not so fast."

I felt cold metal at the base of my neck and froze. Tina's plan officially sucked.

Waylon growled low. And that too made me miss Knox. Even if the man didn't love me, I knew he wouldn't hesitate to turn Duncan's face into an abstract painting.

"My whole life, everyone's underestimated me," Duncan said conversationally. "Called me an idiot. Said I was stupid and dumb. So I went with it. Played the moron. People don't watch what they're saying around a moron. And they don't try as hard to hide what they're doing, *Naomi*."

Crap.

"You two are the morons here. You actually think I'd fall for the ol' switcheroo?" he scoffed.

"How did you know?" I asked, stalling for time.

"Your tits aren't crooked."

"You mean Tina's aren't."

"No, dumbass. Tina's are crooked. Yours aren't. Who's the idiot now?" He said this while gesturing with the gun.

Since it wasn't trained on me, I turned to face him.

Tina was frantically trying to work Waylay's bonds free.

Knee. Balls. Nose.

626

Knox's instructions came back to me almost as if he were standing next to me.

"I liked you, Tina. Really fucking liked you, and now I hafta kill you. How do you think that makes me feel?" He raised his gun, and I knew somewhere deep inside that this time, he intended to use it.

Tina was looking at me hard. And for once in my life, I could read her mind.

"Hey, Duncan?" I said.

The second his eyes were on me, everything moved in slow motion. Tina gave Waylay's chair a shove out of the line of fire and dove in the opposite direction, reaching for the pizza box.

"This!" I grabbed his shoulders and rammed my knee up into his crotch. The gun went off as he doubled over.

My ears rang. But I could still hear Knox in my head.

Nose.

Clinging to his shoulders, I brought my knee up again and this time connected with his face.

I couldn't hear if there was a crunch, but judging by the way the man crumpled to the ground, I'd done it correctly.

Over the ringing in my ears, I thought I heard more shots. But they sounded like they were farther away. A siren too.

I left Duncan where he lay and sprinted to Waylay. Spinning her chair around, I was beyond relieved to see she was unharmed.

"Are you okay?" I asked as my shaking fingers started to untie her.

"That was awesome, Aunt Naomi!" she said.

"You stupid piece of shit!" Tina had the pizza gun trained on Duncan as he got to his hands and knees. "You were gonna shoot my daughter, my sister, and *me?*"

"Mom, the cops are here," Waylay called as I finally freed her wrists.

Tina gave Duncan a kick to his midsection. "You're lucky I don't have time to shoot you." Then she turned away from him. "Here," she said, handing me the gun.

I held it at arm's length and prayed it wouldn't go off.

"You're not seriously running, are you?" I asked.

It was an admittedly stupid question.

Of course my sister was running. It was what she did after making a mess.

Tina grabbed a grungy black duffel bag off the floor and shoved several stacks of cash into it. Then she dumped the rest of the pizza on top, leaving the piece with the bullet hole.

"I'm allergic to cops," she said, hitching the strap over her shoulder, and looked at her daughter. "See ya around, kid."

"Bye, Mom," Waylay said, waving with her freed hand.

Behind me, Duncan groaned on the floor. Waylon growled.

"Been fun. Thanks for the skirt, Goody. Take

care of my kid," she said with a little salute, and then she disappeared out the window onto the fire escape.

The rope finally loosened and I threw it to the floor.

"She'll be back," Waylay predicted, standing up and shaking out her hands.

I didn't doubt it.

"Come on. Let's get out of here," I said, putting the gun down and untying Waylon's leash from the leg of the desk. It wasn't just my hands that were shaking. Now it was my entire body. I wasn't going to feel safe until we were home at Liza J's. Maybe not even then.

The image of the gun pointing at my niece was permanently engraved in my brain. I doubted I'd ever sleep again.

"Aunt Naomi!"

The panic in Waylay's voice had me spinning around. Instinctively, I put myself between her and danger and right into Duncan's bruising grip.

His hand closed around my neck, cutting off my breath.

Blood poured from his nose. For the briefest moment, I felt a flicker of satisfaction that I'd done that. I'd stood up to him. But the moment was fleeting as blackness crept in along the edges of my vision.

"You ruined everything!" he howled.

Time froze and solidified into a picture of the end as he brought the gun to my head.

This couldn't be how it ended. Not with Waylay watching. Not with help in the building.

Not without Knox.

I felt Waylay's arms come around me from behind. One last hug. I couldn't move or speak. I couldn't tell her to run. My world was going dark.

The door burst open, startling me and Duncan. He turned his head in time to see one of his men fall backward into the room. Scratch that. He didn't fall. The man was thrown like a rag doll.

With the last of my energy, I landed a kick to Duncan's shin.

"Waylay, run!" someone ordered. The voice sounded so beautifully familiar, yet so far away.

Help was in the room.

Waylay would be okay.

I slipped into the darkness.

49

The Cavalry

Knox

I hit him low and hard, driving his body into the floor. Some part of me was aware of Naomi crumpling to the ground.

I needed to go to her, but I couldn't stop hitting the man beneath me.

My fist plowed into his face again and again until someone hooked me from behind and pulled me back.

"Enough," Lucian said.

Duncan Hugo ceased to exist to me.

There was only Naomi and Waylay. Waylay knelt next to her, holding her hand to her chest. The tears welling in her blue eyes knifed into my gut.

"Wake up, Aunt Naomi," she whispered.

I closed the distance and grabbed Waylay, hugging her to me.

"Make her wake up, Knox," she begged.

My idiot dog crawled his way between them and started to howl.

Lucian was on his phone, holding his fingers to Naomi's bruised neck. "We need an ambulance," he said tersely.

Still clutching Waylay to me, I leaned over

Naomi and cupped the face of the woman I loved. The woman I'd lost. The woman I couldn't live without.

"Wake the fuck up, Daze," I growled. My eyes and throat burned. My vision blurred as hot tears clouded everything.

I almost missed it. The flicker of those long lashes. Then I was sure it was a hallucination when those beautiful fucking hazel eyes opened.

"Coffee," she croaked.

Christ, I loved this woman.

Waylay tensed against me, her arm nearly choking me around the neck. "You didn't leave me!"

"Thank fucking God," Lucian whispered, swiping the back of his hand over his brow and collapsing back on his elbows on the floor.

"Of course I didn't leave you," Naomi rasped. The bruises on her throat made me want to end the life of the man who'd put them there. But I had a more important priority.

"Welcome back, Daze," I whispered. I leaned down and pressed my mouth to her cheek, breathing her in.

"Knox," she sighed. "You came."

Before I could answer, the side door I'd used to sneak in while Lucian created the distraction burst open. I saw the gun and the gleam in the man's eyes and knew what was about to happen. Operating on instinct, I pulled Waylay to my front and used my body to pin her and Naomi to the ground.

Two shots rang out in rapid succession, but I felt nothing. No pain. Just my girls, warm and alive beneath me.

I chanced a glance up and saw the gunman on the floor.

"You fucking idiots," Nash said, leaning against the wall. He had a cut on his face and blood on his T-shirt, and he was sweating profusely.

"You did that right-handed?" Lucian asked, impressed.

My brother flipped him off as he slid down the wall. "I told you idiots I'm fucking good at my job."

"Are we alive?" Waylay asked under me.

"We're alive, honey," Naomi assured her.

Carefully, I eased my weight off them. They both stared up at me with identical grins. I pointed at Waylay. "You're gettin' a damn birthday party. And after that, we're gettin' married," I told Naomi.

Naomi's eyes went wide, and she reached for me, hands frantically prodding my torso.

"What's wrong, baby?"

"Are you shot? Did you hit your head?"

"No, Daze. I'm fine."

"Did I hit my head?"

"No, baby."

"I must have. I thought I heard you just say we were getting married."

"You think I'm dumb enough to let you two go?"

"Uh, yeah," Waylay, Lucian, and Nash said together.

"Can I have a dress for the party *and* a dress for the wedding?" Waylay asked.

"You can have ten dresses," I promised her.

"You're going to spoil her," Naomi said, running her hand over Waylay's hair.

"Fucking right I am. I'm gonna spoil you too."

Her smile put pieces back together inside me that I hadn't even noticed were broken.

"Where's Duncan?" Waylay asked.

Lucian got to his feet and scanned the space. "He's gone."

"You've got to be fucking kidding me," Nash muttered. "This is why amateurs shouldn't get involved in police business."

"I can't wait till I'm a grown-up and I can swear all the time," Waylay announced.

We all heard footsteps on the stairs at the same time. Nash shifted to point his gun at the door. I pulled mine from the waistband of my jeans and aimed.

Lina and Sloane burst into the room together.

"Christ, I could have shot you," Nash complained, lowering his gun. "What the hell are you doing here? How'd you find us?"

Sloane looked a little green around the gills. "We followed Nash."

"You left a trail of bodies from the parking lot. Didn't leave any fun for the rest of us," Lina said, kneeling next to my brother. Gently, she pushed the sleeve of his shirt up. "Popped your stitches, hotshot."

"Can barely feel it," Nash lied through his teeth.

Sloane spotted Naomi and started toward us. But Lucian was already in motion crossing the room like a god about to crush a mortal.

They met in the middle of the room, stopping inches apart.

"I told you to stay in town," he snarled.

"Get out of my way, you big . . ." Her voice trailed off, and I saw she was staring at the body Nash had dropped. Her face went white.

"Sloane." When the librarian didn't look at him, Lucian grasped her chin and firmly turned it toward him.

"Knee. Balls. Nose," Naomi whispered to me.

"That's my girl." I gave her a squeeze.

"Naomi, you okay?" Lina called from where she was tending my brother.

"I'm pretty great," Naomi said, looking up at me with the kind of smile that could light up a man's life.

"I fucking love you," I whispered to her. She opened her mouth, but I shook my head. "Nope. You don't get to say it back yet. Figure I have at least a week of telling you before I'll deserve to hear it back. Got it?"

Her smile got impossibly brighter, and her eyes filled with tears.

"Sorry," she sniffled, bringing her hands to her face. "I know you don't like tears."

"Think I'm okay with these," I told her and lowered my mouth to hers.

"Barf," Waylay complained.

Naomi shook with laughter against me. Blindly, I reached over and found Waylay's face with my hand and gave the girl a gentle shove. She tipped over, laughing.

There was another flurry of activity on the stairs, and then the doorway filled with cops. "Drop your weapons!"

"About damn time," Nash muttered, dropping his Glock and holding up his badge.

I sat on the back of the ambulance in the middle of the night next to Naomi while a detective asked us yet another round of questions. I couldn't stand to be more than a foot or two away from her. I'd almost lost her and Waylay.

If Grim hadn't come through . . . If I'd been one minute later . . . If Nash hadn't been that accurate with his right hand . . .

All of those ifs, and yet I was still here, holding on for dear life to the best thing that ever happened to me.

"What the hell is this? A parade?" asked one of the uniformed officers. A motorcycle rolled in. Followed by another and another. A dozen total. They were followed by four vehicles.

Engines cut. Doors opened. And Knockemout showed the fuck up.

I blinked a few times when I saw Wraith helping my grandmother off the back of his bike. Lou and Amanda climbed out of their SUV and started running. Jeremiah, Stasia, and Stef were right behind them. Silver and Max jumped out of Fi's minivan along with Milford and four of Honky Tonk's regulars.

Justice and Tallulah got off their respective bikes and hurried forward.

"Can we wrap this up?" I asked the detective.

"Just one more question, Ms. Witt," she said. "A patrol car picked up a woman claiming to be Naomi Witt. Caught her trying to steal a Mustang two blocks from here. Do you have any idea who she might be?"

"You've got to be kidding me," Naomi groaned.

I spotted Nash and Lucian leaving a huddle of officers. My brother nodded for me to join them.

I gestured for Lou to take my place. "I'll be right back, Daze," I told her.

Naomi smiled up at me as her dad hustled over, Amanda on his heels. She paused long enough to give me a loud kiss on the cheek and a hard smack on the ass.

"Thank you for saving my girls," she whispered to me before turning her attention to her daughter. "We brought you coffee, sweetheart!"

"You about done fucking things up?" Stef asked me.

"I just told our girl that we're getting married. So yeah. I'm about done."

"Good. Then I don't have to destroy your life," he said. "I leave you alone for less than two weeks, and look what happens, Witty."

637

"Oh my God, Stef! When did you get home?"

I felt a hand in mine as I crossed the asphalt and looked down. Waylay had linked her fingers through mine. She had Waylon's leash in her other hand. My dog looked like he just wanted to lie down and sleep for a month.

"Did you mean it about the dresses?" she asked as we walked toward my brother.

I released her hand and pulled her into my side with an arm around her shoulders. "Sure did, kid."

"Did you mean it about what you said to Aunt Naomi? About loving her and stuff?"

I stopped us and turned her to face me. "I've never been more serious about anything in my life," I assured her.

"So you're not going to leave us again?"

I gave her shoulders a squeeze. "Never. I was miserable without you two."

"Me too?" she asked.

I saw the spark of hope that she just as quickly pushed aside.

"Way, you're smart. You're brave. You're gorgeous. And I'm gonna hate it when you start dating. I fucking love you. And not just because you're part of a package deal."

She looked so solemn it almost crushed my heart.

"Will you still maybe love me if I tell you something? Something bad?"

If Duncan Hugo put his hands on Waylay, I was going to hunt him down, chop them off, and feed them to him.

"Kid, there is nothing you can tell me that's going to make me not love you."

"Promise?"

"I swear to you on your kick-ass sneakers."

She looked down at them, then back at me, the corner of her mouth turned up. "Maybe I kind of fucking love you too."

I hauled her in for a hug, holding her face against my sternum. When she wrapped her arms around my waist, I felt like my heart was suddenly too big for my fucking chest.

"But don't tell Aunt Naomi I said it that way."

"Deal."

She pulled back. "Okay. So here's the thing . . ."

Two minutes later, I escorted Waylay over to Nash and Lucian. An EMT had closed Nash's stitches. Both men had butterfly bandages over various visible cuts and scrapes. The three of us were going to be hurting tomorrow. And the next day. And probably the next.

"Naomi said Tina and Duncan were looking for a flash drive with some kind of information on it," Nash explained. "No one seems to know what information was on it or what happened to the drive."

"Waylay, why don't you go see if your aunt needs anything," Lucian suggested.

I tracked the direction of his gaze and saw it was pinned on Sloane, who was hovering near Naomi, her parents, and Stef.

"Actually, Way has some information she wants

to share," I said. I gave her shoulder a squeeze. "Go ahead, kid."

She took a breath and then bent down to untie her shoe.

"They were looking for this," she said, straightening with the heart charm now in her hand.

Nash took it from her. He held the charm between his fingers, then frowned. Carefully, he pulled it apart at the middle. "Well, I'll be damned."

"It's a flash drive," Waylay explained. "Mom was all worked up about this drive that she brought home. Kept saying she was finally gettin' her payday and that soon she'd be driving a big-ass SUV and eatin' steak for every meal. I got curious and I peeked. It was just a list of names and addresses. I thought maybe it was important. So I copied the file onto my drive just in case. She's always losing sh—I mean things."

I nodded at her to go on.

"Mom got mad at me for something stupid and cut my hair as punishment. So I decided to punish her back. I took the drive so she'd think she lost it, and then I hid it in the library but not in the historical fiction section like I told Duncan. It's actually taped to the bottom of one of the archive drawers. I didn't know they were going to break into Aunt Naomi's and kidnap us and stuff. I swear," she said.

Nash put his hand on her shoulder. "You're not in trouble here, Waylay. You did the right thing telling me about this."

"He said he was gonna shoot Aunt Naomi if I

didn't tell him where it was. I was trying to tell him, but he taped my mouth shut," she said.

I growled at this new information.

"None of this is your fault," Nash assured her again.

But it was her mother's, and I wasn't sorry that she was in custody. I did, however, decide it wasn't a great time to tell Waylay about it.

"There's one more thing," she said.

"What's that?" Nash asked.

"Your name was on the list."

Lucian and I exchanged a look.

"We need to see the list," Lucian announced.

Nash reached out and covered Waylay's ears. "The fuck you do, assholes. Police business. Come on, Way. Let's clear it with your aunt, and then we can get Sloane to let us in the library."

"Okay," she said. "Knox?"

"Yeah, kid?"

She crooked her finger at me, and I leaned down. I tried not to smile when she got done whispering in my ear.

"Got it. I'll see you at home," I said, giving her hair a ruffle.

We watched Nash guide her over to the ambulance.

"We need that damn list," Lucian said.

I felt my lips curve.

"What?" he asked.

"That's not the only copy. She also uploaded it to the library's server."

He stood stock-still for a beat, then let out a bark of laughter. Sloane's gaze flew to him, and I realized that Lucian rarely laughed. Not like he used to, when we were kids and everything was a punchline waiting to happen.

"You are going to hate your life when she starts dating," he said.

I couldn't fucking wait.

We started back toward Naomi, who was on her feet under a blanket and holding a coffee. Despite everything I'd seen tonight, despite everything I'd done wrong, the smile she directed at me lit me up from the inside out.

I slapped Lucian on the shoulder. "Hey. How do you feel about being co-best man?"

Epilogue
Party Time

Naomi

"Mmph. Knox. We have to get back to the party," I murmured against his mouth.

He had me pinned against the wall in Liza J's den as the most epic twelfth birthday party happened in the backyard. And the front yard. And in the kitchen, dining room, and sunroom.

There were kids, parents, and bikers everywhere.

The man who was currently kissing the ever-living breath out of me had sat down with Waylay and asked her for a list of every single thing she could possibly want. And then he'd delivered on each and every one.

Which was why there was an inflatable obstacle course in the backyard, a petting zoo in the front yard, and not a vegetable in sight on the food table that was buckling under the weight of pizza, nachos, popcorn, and *two* birthday cakes.

His tongue teased its way into my mouth again, and my knees went weak. The erection he had pressed against my stomach was driving my lady parts wild.

"You have your parents, Liza J, Stef, and Sloane out there playing host. Give me five minutes," he growled over my lips.

"Five minutes?"

He wedged a hand between our bodies and slid it up my dress. When his fingers found me, my hips bucked involuntarily against him.

"Might only need four to get you there," he decided.

He could have had me there in about fifteen seconds, but I was feeling greedy.

"Deal," I whispered.

He dragged me with him to lock the glass doors, then guided us to the credenza against the wall and placed me on it.

"What are all these boxes in here for?" I asked, noticing a stack of them in the corner.

"Don't worry about it," he said.

I decided to follow his advice when he yanked my underwear down my legs until I could step out of them.

"Five minutes," he reminded me as he hooked my heels on the edge of the wood and spread my knees wide. Before I could say something smart, he was freeing his thick, hard cock from his jeans and feeding it into my body inch by glorious inch.

We moaned together as he thrust hard to fill me completely.

"I can't. Believe. You talked me. Into this," I said, my teeth chattering as he began to thrust mercilessly.

"You're already gripping me, baby." He gritted the words out.

Knox had been insatiable since the "incident," as

I'd dubbed it. He'd barely let me out of his sight. And I was okay with it. Especially since so much of the time we spent together was naked. Well, between talking to the police. Both the Knockemout PD and the other departments involved.

It turned out that the infamous list included the names of several cops and their criminal informants spread out across five counties in NOVA.

Duncan's father had gotten his hands on the information and intended to work his way down the list, eliminating all the cops and their informants. Duncan, wanting to impress his father, had decided to take a shot at one of those names on the list: Nash.

But after the botched job brought his father's wrath down on him, Duncan decided it was more lucrative to steal the information and sell it to the highest bidder.

All this information came from my sister. Tina had sung like a canary in an orange jumpsuit and was looking at a pretty lenient deal if her information brought down any part of the Hugo crime family.

With Tina behind bars, the path toward guardianship was about as clear as it could be. It would still be a long one, but at least we'd cleared it of the major obstacles.

And while Duncan Hugo was still out there somewhere, police all over the state were looking for him, and I had a feeling his freedom was coming to an end soon.

"More kids," Knox rasped.

"What?" I asked, pulling back from his mouth.

He pistoned his hips forward and buried himself to the hilt. "I want more kids."

I felt the clutch and pull of my muscles around him and knew I was going to come any second.

"What?" I repeated dumbly.

"Way would make a great big sister," he said. With a wolfish grin, he hooked his fingers in the neck of my dress and yanked it and my bra down, exposing my breasts. He dipped his head, his mouth hovering an inch above my straining nipple. "You up for it?"

He wanted kids. He wanted a family with me and Waylay. My heart was close to exploding. And so was my vagina.

"Y-yes," I managed.

"Good." He looked smug, victorious, and so damn sexy as he lowered his mouth to my breast.

I bowed back and let him plunder me right over the edge.

I was still in the midst of an earth-shattering orgasm when he stilled at the end of me and held. A guttural groan wrenched free as I felt the first hot pulse of his release deep inside me.

"Love you, Naomi," he murmured, his lips worshiping my bare skin.

"I l—" But he was clamping a hand over my mouth even as he continued to glide in and out of me like he was trying to savor every second of our closeness.

"Not yet, baby."

It had been a week since the incident, since his first "I love you," and he still wouldn't let me say it back. "Soon?" I asked.

"Soon," he promised.

I was the luckiest woman in the world.

Knox left the den first, claiming he had something he needed to see to. I was still trying to fix my hair and dress and hoping it wasn't a rock-climbing wall or a hot-air balloon when I walked out of the room and ran right into Liza J, who was perched on a floral upholstered chair I'd unearthed in the basement and moved into the foyer.

"You scared me!"

"I've been thinking," she said without preamble. "This house is too big for one old woman."

My fingers gave up on my hair. "You're not thinking of selling, are you?" I couldn't imagine this house without her. I couldn't imagine her without this house.

"Nah. Too many memories. Too much history. Thinkin' about moving back into the cottage."

"Oh?" I felt my eyebrows wing up. I didn't know what to say to that. I'd always assumed that Waylay and I would move back into the cottage at some point. Now I wondered if this was Liza J's way of evicting us.

"This place needs a family in it. A big messy one. Bonfires and babies. Smart-assed teenagers. Dogs."

"Well, it's already got dogs," I pointed out.

She nodded briskly. "Yep. So it's settled then."

"What's settled?"

"I take the cottage. You and Knox and Waylay live here."

My mouth dropped open while my brain began to run through a dozen new furniture placement ideas.

"Um, I . . . I don't know what to say, Liza."

"Ain't nothing to say. Already talked to Knox about it this week."

"What did he say?"

She looked at me as if I'd just asked her to give up red meat. "What the hell do you think he said?" she asked, sounding disgruntled. "He's out there throwing your girl the best damn party this town's ever seen, ain't he? He's already planning the wedding, ain't he?"

I nodded, unable to speak. First Waylay's party. Then the discussion on kids. Now, the house of my dreams. I felt like Knox had asked *me* to write down a list of everything I'd wanted and set about making it all happen.

Liza J reached out and gave my hand a squeeze. "Good talk. Imma go see if we can cut into those cakes yet."

I was still staring at the chair she vacated when Stef appeared in the hallway.

"Waylay needs you, Witty," he said.

I snapped out of my daze. "Okay. Where is she?"

He hooked his thumb in the direction of the

backyard. "Out back. You okay?" he asked with a knowing grin.

I shook my head. "Knox just snuck me away for a quickie, told me he wants to have more kids with me, and then Liza gave us this house."

Stef let out a low whistle. "Sounds like you could use a drink."

"Or seven."

He escorted me through the dining room, where there just happened to be two flutes of champagne waiting. He handed one to me, and we exited through the sunroom doors onto the deck.

"SURPRISE!"

I took a step back and clutched a hand to my heart as a large portion of the citizens of Knockemout cheered from the yard below.

"It's not a surprise party, you guys," I told them.

There was a ripple of laughter, and I wondered why they were all looking so happy, like they were anticipating something.

My parents stood off to the side of the deck with Liza J and Waylay, all grinning at me.

"What's going on?" I turned to Stef, but he was backing away and blowing me kisses.

"Naomi."

I turned and found Knox standing behind me, his face so serious my stomach dropped.

"What's wrong?" I asked, twisting around and looking to see if someone was hurt or missing. But all our people were here. Everyone we cared about was right here in this yard, smiling.

He had a box in his hand. A small, black velvet box.

Oh my God.

I peered over my shoulder at Waylay, worried I was ruining her party. The day was about her, not me. But she was holding my mom's hand and bouncing on her toes, the biggest smile I'd ever seen on her face.

"Naomi," Knox said again.

I turned back to him and pressed my fingers to my mouth.

"Yes?" It came out as a muffled squeak.

"Told you I wanted a wedding."

I nodded, not trusting my voice anymore.

"But I didn't tell you why."

He took a step forward, then another one until we were standing toe-to-toe.

I felt like I couldn't quite catch my breath.

"I don't deserve you," he said, sending a glance over my shoulder. "But a smart man once told me that what matters most is that I spend the rest of my life trying to be the kind of man who deserves you. So that's what I'm gonna do. I'm gonna remember how fucking lucky I am, every single day. And I'm gonna do my best to be the best for you.

"Because you, Naomi Witt, are incredible. You're beautiful. You're sweet. You've got a fancy-ass vocabulary. You make people feel seen and heard. You make broken things whole again. Me. You made *me* whole. And every time you smile at me, I feel like I hit the lottery again."

The tears were threatening to spill over, and there was nothing I could do to stop them. He opened the box, but I couldn't see anything through the waterworks. Knowing Knox, the ring was over-the-top and somehow still exactly perfect.

"So I told you once. And now I'm gonna ask you. Marry me, Daze."

I didn't point out that he hadn't exactly asked—it was more like he ordered. I was too busy nodding my head.

"Need you to say it, baby," he coaxed.

"Yes." I managed to get the word out and found myself against the very solid, very warm chest of my fiancé. Everyone I loved was cheering for us, and Knox was kissing me—in a very inappropriate way for having an audience.

He pulled back just an inch. "I love you so fucking much, Daisy."

I gave a hitching sigh and tried not to start wailing. I managed a not very dignified nod.

"Now you can say it," he prompted me, cupping my face in his hands, those gray-blue eyes telling me exactly what he needed to hear.

"I love you, Knox."

"Damn right you do, baby."

He held me tightly, then released one arm and opened it. Waylay appeared and slid under it, grinning up at me through tears of her own. I wrapped my free arm around her, binding the three of us together. Waylon wedged his head between us and barked.

"You did good, Knox," Waylay said. "I'm proud of you."

"You about ready for some cake?" he asked her.

"Don't forget to make a wish, honey," I told her.

She grinned up at me. "Don't gotta. I already got everything I wanted."

And just like that, the tears were back.

"Me too, honey. Me too."

"Okay. New family rule. Neither of you is allowed to cry ever again," Knox said, his voice hoarse.

He sounded pretty serious about it. That just made us cry harder.

Later that night, after the party was over, the guests had gone home, and Knox had gotten me naked again, we lay in the dark in our room. His fingers traced lazy lines up and down my back as I cuddled against his chest.

Down the hall, half a dozen girls giggled in Waylay's room.

Liza J had wasted no time making good on her promise. She'd packed a suitcase and the dog dishes and was spending her first night in the cottage.

"Today was the best day," I whispered, admiring how the ring on my finger caught the light from the bathroom and twinkled. I was right. It was over-the-top. A massive solitaire diamond flanked by three smaller stones on each side. I was going to need to start lifting weights with my other hand just to keep my muscles even.

Knox pressed a kiss to the top of my head. "Every day since I met you has been the best day."

"Don't be sweet, or I'll break your new family rule," I warned him.

He shifted under me. "I got a couple of other things for you."

"Knox, no offense, but after the best birthday party this town's ever seen, Liza giving us the house, and you demanding I marry you in front of all our friends and family, I don't think I can take anything else."

"Suit yourself," he said.

I lasted all of ten seconds. "Okay. Gimme."

He sat up and snapped on the bedside lamp. He was grinning, and it made my heart turn to liquid gold.

"First, tomorrow you gotta help me pack."

"Pack?"

"I'm moving in here officially, and I don't know what shit your parents will want and what they won't."

"My parents?"

"Liza J gave us the house. I'm giving your parents the cabin."

I sat up and pulled the sheet up to my chest. "You're giving my parents the cabin," I repeated.

He gave me a wolfish look. "Your ears still ringin', Daze?"

"Maybe. Or maybe it's all the orgasms you keep

giving me that are slowing down my auditory processing."

He hooked me behind the neck and tugged me closer. "Your mom just got a job at Waylay's school. Part-time counselor. She starts in January."

I brought the heels of my hands to my eyes. "My parents are . . ."

"Movin' to Knockemout."

"How did you do this? How did you . . . Waylay gets to grow up with her grandparents right next door!" Every damn dream I'd ever had was coming true, and he was making it happen.

"One thing you gotta understand, Naomi. If there's anything in this world you want, I'm gonna get it for you. No questions asked. You want it, it's yours. So here." He thrust a stack of papers at me.

Blindly, I held them up. They looked like some kind of legal contract. "What are these?"

"Flip to the signature page," he instructed.

I followed the handy yellow tab and found my sister's signature scrawled across the line.

The words *guardianship* and *parental rights* popped off the page.

"Oh my God," I whispered.

"She signed over parental rights to you. It's official. No more hearings or home visits. Way is ours."

I couldn't speak. Couldn't breathe. I could only cry silently.

"Damn it, baby. I hate when you do this," Knox

grumbled, gathering me up and dropping me in his lap.

I nodded, still crying as I wrapped my arms around him and held on tight.

"Now, it's time for something I want."

The man could have anything as far as I was concerned. Both my kidneys. My favorite purse. Anything at all.

"If you're trying to have sex with me for the fourth time today, I'm gonna need some Advil, an ice pack, and a gallon of water first," I teased through sobs and sniffles.

His laugh was a rumble in his chest as he threaded his fingers through my hair and stroked.

"I want the wedding sooner rather than later. I'm not wasting another minute without making you my wife. You can have anything you want. A big church wedding. A backyard barbecue. A five-figure wedding dress. But I have one demand."

Of course it was a demand and not a request. "What's that?"

"I want daisies in your hair."

Bonus Epilogue

Five Years Later

Knox

With an abundance of caution, I handed the bundle over to Waylay on the porch and dug out the keys from my front pocket.

She grinned down at the tiny face and long lashes, then back up at me.

"You guys did good," she said.

She was seventeen now, and I had heart palpitations every time I thought about her leaving us for college in a year. I wasn't ready. But I knew from the look on her face that she'd be making more trips home than she'd originally planned to be with her sisters.

Sisters.

I watched my wife sway from side to side in one of those long, flowing sundresses that still managed to drive me crazy. I made sure she had a closet full of them.

The toddler on her hip had her thumb in her mouth, eyelids growing heavy.

Naomi's smile was soft, content, and it was focused on me.

In that moment, I felt it all. Love for the woman who brought me back to life. Who gave me a reason to wake up every morning with a smile. Who loved me enough to smooth out my rough edges.

We'd been through the wringer in the beginning, and then again when building that big family didn't work out the way we'd planned. But we faced it the way we did everything. Together.

Now, here we stood with our three daughters, two of whom were the biggest secret we'd ever kept. After years of preparing, the adoption dropped into our laps.

We hadn't even had time to get their rooms ready when the call came. Three-year-old Bridget and her brand-new baby sister, Gillian.

Sliding my palm over my wife's cheek, I cupped the back of her neck and pulled her closer. I kissed her forehead, then brushed my lips over our daughter's hair.

"Mom and Dad and Liza are going to be beside themselves," Naomi predicted as I fit the key into the lock. "I wish there was a way we could tell them all at once."

For a second, I wished fiercely that my own mother could have met her grandkids. That she could see how her sons had grown up and the women we'd chosen. But loss was part of love.

"How many seconds are you going to wait before you get on the phone?" I teased.

"As many seconds as it takes for me to pee, get Bridget a snack, and make Gilly a bottle."

"Snack!" My daughter was suddenly wide awake.

"Listen. About that," Waylay said, her grin a little sheepish.

"What did you do, Way?" I demanded.

"I didn't tell anyone anything specific," she said. "But I *did* tell them we had big news to share today."

On cue, the front door was wrenched open from the inside.

"Your father and I have been climbing the walls *all day,*" Amanda announced, hands on hips. I spotted Lou in the living room, watching TV with Nash and Lucian.

"Just your mother. I've been very calm," Lou yelled.

"What's this big news?" Stef asked, coming up behind my mother-in-law.

"Yeah? Why all the secrecy?" my brother's wife wanted to know.

"Did you bring dinner?" my grandmother demanded, appearing next to them.

"Is this about Waylay's soccer scholarship?" Wraith asked. No matter how long it went on, I still couldn't get used to the biker dating my grandmother. Even though they seemed to make each other deliriously happy.

"Uh, guys," Jeremiah said, squeezing Stef's shoulder.

Sloane peeked over Amanda's shoulder as I stepped aside. "Look," she breathed.

Amanda noticed first. Her scream of joy brought Lou, Nash, and Lucian tearing out of the den, looking for a threat. It also woke the baby, who was not pleased about being screamed awake.

Fi came trundling out of the kitchen.

"What the hell is all the screaming—" She cut herself off with a bloodcurdling scream of her own.

"Babies!" Amanda sobbed as Waylay handed over the crying Gillian to her. "We have babies!"

"Come to Grandpa," Lou said, holding his hands out to Bridget. "I promise I'll always have candy for you." She balked shyly for a moment, but the word *candy* worked its magic, and she reached for him.

If I wasn't mistaken, my father-in-law had to choke back a sob of his own.

"Look how perfect she is," Amanda said to Sloane as she tickled the baby's tiny fingers.

"Now, I get why you were texting me with all those girl hair questions," Jeremiah said with a grin.

I'd been pumping him for the best products and styling techniques, because my daughters were going to have the best hair in Knockemout.

Waylay's boyfriend, Theo, stepped forward and pulled her into his side. I glared at him, but it didn't have the heat it usually did. "Theo," I said.

"Mr. Morgan," he said.

I was definitely losing my touch, because he didn't drop his arm from my daughter's shoulders.

Naomi elbowed me in the ribs.

"Dad, behave," Waylay said, rolling her eyes.

Liza J was holding Gillian now, and Nash was juggling Bridget, making her belly laugh.

"Well, I think this calls for pizza," Amanda decided. "Lucian, you order it. Lou, go get Knox's measuring tape."

"What for?" Lou asked.

"You and the menfolk are going to go measure the girls' bedrooms so we can get started on the nurseries. Ladies, to the wine cabinet. We have colors and themes to pick, day cares to research, and shopping lists to make," Amanda ordered.

"I'm going with the womenfolk," Stef decided. He paused and gave Jeremiah a kiss on the mouth.

"Save me a glass," his husband called after him.

Naomi gave me a squeeze around the waist. "I love you, Knox Morgan," she whispered.

I never got tired of hearing it.

"Love you, baby." She slipped out of my grasp, and I watched her follow the women into the dining room, her dress flowing around her ankles.

"You did good, Knoxy," Lina said, lingering in the foyer.

I hugged her hard. "You're the one with twins," I reminded her.

"Who are napping in Way's room right now. Don't let me forget them."

A new generation under this roof and our family finally felt complete.

There was a knock on the open door behind me. "Dad."

"Am I intruding?" He looked good. Healthy.

Steady. All of which still managed to surprise me every time I saw him.

John Wayne Morgan was now three years sober. He lived in DC with his girlfriend and their two rescue cats. He worked as a very effective fundraiser for Hannah's Place, which had expanded with locations in downtown DC and Maryland.

"Waylay texted. Told me you had some big news. I can come back when you're not busy," he offered.

"Dad." Nash put down the ladder he was hauling for God knows what reasons and greeted him with a back-slapping hug. I wasn't quite there yet with our father. But every visit, every call, every unbroken promise brought us a millimeter closer.

"You're just in time to meet your new grand-daughters," I told him.

Dad's face brightened. "Granddaughters."

"The agency called three days ago and said we had two little girls ready to join the family," I explained. "We didn't want to tell anyone until we got them home."

"Granddaughters," he said again in wonder, like he felt like the luckiest man in the world. I felt another millimeter between us disappear.

"Come on in," I said, laying my hand on his shoulder and guiding him into the estrogen-filled war room where Amanda and Liza J had paint samples and every available laptop and tablet spread out on the table.

Sloane was feeding the baby a bottle while

Bridget sat in the center of the table, eating a bowl of cut-up grapes. My daughters were surrounded with love and strong, smart women.

"Duke! I'm so glad you could make it," Amanda said, getting up to press a kiss to Dad's cheek. "Come meet your new girls!"

My father was absorbed into the circle of women and Stef.

I felt hands on my belt, and then Naomi was towing me out of the room backward.

"Where are you taking me?" I asked, amused.

She released my belt and took me by the hand, leading me into the living room, where our wedding portrait hung above the fireplace. It still hit me in the chest every time I looked at it. Naomi—breathtaking and blushing in her gown, the daisies woven into her hair like a crown. She had her arm around Waylay, who had insisted on a floor-length lemon-yellow gown and daisies of her own. They were both laughing. As for me? I looked pretty damn good in my suit. And pretty damn happy as I looked after my wife and daughter.

"I know life is going to be absolutely insane for the next few years," Naomi said, cupping my face in her hands. "I know we're going to be exhausted and overworked and scared to death most if not all of the time. But I also know that none of this would be happening if it weren't for you."

"Baby, I'm not gonna be able to handle it if you lose it right here," I warned her.

One upside of infertility issues was that I didn't

have to watch my wife suffer through pregnancy hormones. I'd have handled her tears, but probably not well.

"I'm not going to cry," she said.

My wife was a dirty liar, because I could already see the sheen gathering in those hazel eyes I loved so damn much.

"But I am going to tell you that you make every day the best one of my life. That I'll never stop being grateful that you—"

"Got my head out of my ass?" I suggested.

She shook her head. "That you decided Way and I were worth it. Thank you for this life, Knox Morgan. There's no one else who would make such an adventure out of giving me everything I ever wanted."

Somehow, she'd done it again. It always surprised me when Naomi found another broken piece in me and made it whole again.

"I love you, Knox. And I'm never going to stop being grateful for everything you are and all that you've done."

My throat was feeling awfully tight. And there was a burning sensation at the back of my eyes that I didn't much care for.

I grabbed Naomi and pulled her into me, burying my face in her hair.

"I love you," I rasped.

The words weren't enough. They didn't come close to the feeling I had in my chest when I woke up to her cuddled up next to me, safe and sleeping.

They didn't do justice to what I felt when she walked into a room and brought the sunshine with her. And they sure as hell didn't hold a candle to the way I felt when she looked me in the eye and told me I'd given her everything she wanted.

I decided I'd spend the rest of my life making sure I showed her how I felt since I couldn't tell her.

Author's Note

Dear Reader,

I finished this book at 11:03 p.m. on November 4, 2021, and promptly burst into tears.

I started it five months earlier, just a few days before David, Claire Kingsley's beloved husband and my sweet friend, passed away suddenly. Not only was I leveled by his death, but he was the third friend's husband to leave this world far too soon in two months.

I was crushed. It never occurred to me that there would be a world without David, let alone a world in which three of my closest friends would be widowed tragically in their forties.

I didn't know what this book was about when I started it. Even when I was halfway through it, I still wasn't sure. But now that I've finished it, I finally get it. This book is about the bravery it takes for us to love someone when we all know how every love story ends. It's about choosing love over fear again and again. It's about showing up and being brave even when we know it's going to hurt like hell.

Knox's fear of losing someone he loved and falling apart was so real for me. I ended up working through a lot of my own grief and fear while I wrote this story. At times, I couldn't get past the loss my friends were suffering. Other times, I had the presence of mind to remember how lucky we all are to love someone so much their loss is devastating.

My wish for all of us is that we love whole-heartedly and are present enough in our relationships that when we part, our only regret is quantity, not quality. That we all understand that the pain of loss is what gives the rest of our lives color and flavor and texture.

Thank you for reading and being brave, my friends.

xoxo,
Lucy

Acknowledgments

Kari March Designs for the perfect cover design.

Jessica, Dawn, and Heather for your editorial fabulosity.

Joyce and Tammy for beta reading TWNGO and assuring me that it wasn't an emotional dumpster fire.

Josie, Jen, and Claire for being strong enough to comfort others even in the face of your worst loss.

Mr. Lucy for telling me to quit worrying about deadlines and pub dates and just focus on writing the best story I could.

Sparkling water for pretending to be soda.

My readers for supporting me even when it took so damn long to write this book. You're the greatest.

Christa, Dawn, and the rest of the Sourcebooks team for believing in the magic of TWNGO and being so enthusiastic about bringing this book to a wider audience.

About the Author

Lucy Score is a *USA Today* and *Wall Street Journal* and #1 Amazon bestselling author. She grew up in a literary family who insisted that the dinner table was for reading and earned a degree in journalism. She writes full-time from the Pennsylvania home she and Mr. Lucy share with their obnoxious cat, Cleo. When not spending hours crafting heart-breaker heroes and kick-ass heroines, Lucy can be found on the couch, in the kitchen, or at the gym. She hopes to someday write from a sailboat, oceanfront condo, or tropical island with reliable Wi-Fi.

Sign up for her newsletter and stay up on all the latest Lucy book news.

You can also follow her here:

Website: lucyscore.com
Facebook: lucyscorewrites
Instagram: scorelucy
BookBub: bookbub.com/authors/lucy-score
Binge Books: bingebooks.com/author
   /lucy-score
Readers Group: facebook.com/groups
   /BingeReaders Anonymous

Center Point Large Print
600 Brooks Road / PO Box 1
Thorndike, ME 04986-0001 USA

(207) 568-3717

US & Canada:
1 800 929-9108
www.centerpointlargeprint.com